KOOKABURRA'S LAST LAUGH

KOOKABURRA'S LAST LAUGH

Leonard Szymczak

ISBN-10: 0-9969566-3-8
ISBN-13: 978-0-9969566-3-5
Library of Congress Control Number: 2016902676
Published by GPS Books
Dana Point, CA

Cover Design: Fiona Jayde
Interior Design: Tamara Cribley
Author photograph: Lifetouch Portraits
Published in the United States of America

Psychological—Fiction. 2. Australia—Fiction. 3. Coming of Age—Fiction. 4. Humor.

Praise for *Kookabura's Last Laugh*

"*Kookaburra's Last Laugh* is a fast-paced, insightful, laugh-out-loud funny and poignant novel. Don't miss it!"

~ Laura Taylor, award-winning author of 22 novels.

"That master weaver of psychological thrillers, Leonard Szymczak, gave us another exciting page turner. What's more fun than reaching inward to meet ourselves and battle our own demons?"

~ Danna Beal, author of *The Extraordinary Workplace: Replacing Fear with Trust and Compassion*

"*Kookaburra's Last Laugh* is suspenseful, enthralling, and funny. I felt as if I was there in Australia. I couldn't put the book down!"

~ Jennifer Savino, author of *Your Breath Heals*

"This story's premise is exciting, fresh, and original. The narrative is skillfully written in a bold first person point-of-view...This is a fine piece written with the touch of a seasoned writer."

~ Amazon Breakthrough Novel Award Editorial Review

"My patient (or not so patient) wait for a sequel to *Cuckoo Forevermore* has finally been rewarded in this gripping page-turner. *Kookaburra's Last Laugh* is Szymczak's best work yet. His background as a psychotherapist shines in the main character of psychologist Peter Pinowski, who takes us on a wild and humorous journey through trials, victories, and defeats. What a ride!"

~ Harry Tucker, author in *97 Things Every Project Manager Should Know: Collective Wisdom form the Experts*

"I love the sense of humor of the author, and how he allows us to see the world through Peter Pinowski. *Kookaburra's Last Laugh* is not only funny, but as Peter confronts his own fears, he helps us ask the same question: Who am I? This creative journey serves as a blueprint for our own journey back home to our True Self."

~ Maria Mar, author of *Angelina and the Law of Attraction*

"This book is serious and funny at the same time. These characters are all nut cases but really likeable despite (or because) of how flawed they are. The main character's struggle to make sense of it all through a series of "cliff-hanger" experiences is vicariously healing and freeing."

~ Kathy Juline, author of *It Is About You: Living Fully, Living Free Through the Creative Power of Your Thought*

"After thoroughly enjoying Leonard's first novel, I was even more excited by his sequel, *Kookaburra's Last Laugh*. In fact, I found the humor funnier (which I love!) and the emotional level deeper. Good on you, Leonard!"

~ Mary Harris, Executive Editor of Hidden Thoughts Press

"I know Leonard as a fun loving storyteller and therapist. He makes me laugh while I explore my inner feelings. Thumbs up for *Kookaburra's Last Laugh*!"

~ Mari J. Frank, author of *From Victim to Victor*

"I was immediately sucked into the story and the main character. I would highly recommend this book to anyone who enjoys a great story, travel, adventure, and personal transformation. It's fresh, interesting, exciting, and has an edge to it."

~ Marguerite Bonnett, author of *Let It Go:
12 New steps for Tapping the Power of Your Mind to
Overcome Addiction with FasterEFT*

"Reading *Kookaburra's Last Laugh*, I felt as though I was watching a beautiful movie."

~ Kirk Moore, author of *Tara's Angels*

Leonard's writing is compelling. Loved the Australian setting, quirky characters, and heartfelt message. *Kookaburra's Last Laugh* is fabulous!"

~ Arthur J. Tassinello, author of *Quantum Shift into Greatness*

Other Great Books by Leonard Szymczak

Cuckoo Forevermore

The Roadmap Home: Your GPS to Inner Peace

This book is dedicated to courageous souls who hear the call, dare to dream, step off the beaten path, and find their way home.

BLUE MOUNTAINS,
NEW SOUTH WALES, AUSTRALIA

A trickle of blood oozed down the side of my head as I lay dazed against the trunk of a Blue Mountain ash. I reached for the gash on my forehead and recoiled at the sight of bloodstained fingers. Hungry flies buzzed around my hand. I flailed at the bastards. Where the hell was I?

Everything looked blurry, out of focus. I scrabbled among the wet leaves and came up empty. My fingers frantically scoured the ground. Please God, give me back my sight. Then, like a bloody miracle, I found my glasses in a pile of fallen bark. One of the plastic arms was missing, but, thankfully, the lenses weren't cracked. Being lost *and* blind would've crushed any hope of survival.

I wiped mud off the glasses, then balanced the broken frame on the bridge of my nose. I gazed up at the towering tree and saw strips of bark hanging perilously off the high branches. A gust of wind sent slivers hurtling down like arrows. I covered my head as the bark tumbled on and around me, collecting into a heap at the base of the polished white trunk.

Feeling under attack, I staggered to my feet. Dark, ominous clouds cast moving shadows through the canopy of tall eucalyptus trees. Climbers, like elongated snakes, stretched up the side of a nearby coachwood tree covered with white splotches of lichen. Hairy

tree ferns and emerald mosses joined the mushrooms sprouting in the dense rainforest. They seemed ready to pounce.

Crack...pop, pop!

I froze. "Steady, mate," I calmed myself. "It's only a bloody whipbird."

The sound of a whip cracked in the distance, followed by *pop, pop*. The mating call of the whipbird resonated among the trees. I tried to humor myself by imagining a bird with a long tail, dressed in black leather, cracking a whip.

My nervous smile quickly vanished. The metallic taste of blood in my mouth brought a sense of urgency. Like a fog lifting, I realized I was lost in a fern-filled gully somewhere in the Blue Mountain's Jamison Valley. I clumsily brushed the leaves off my muddied jeans and surveyed the damage. No broken bones. But my fall down the ravine left my hip badly bruised, and my head pounding like a drum. I wasn't sure how long I had been unconscious. The gash on my forehead oozed sticky blood and attracted a horde of flies. Not the best place to have a concussion.

Nauseated, I leaned against the smooth, creamy trunk and winced in pain. My right elbow and lower arm had been scraped raw when I had tumbled over rocks and fallen timber. I brushed away the flies and reached for my head to quell the pain. Blood dribbled down my nose. All this, because I had to take a crap!

Then I remembered the leeches. The hideous black leeches! I frantically checked my shoes and clothes and found a few mangy suckers crawling up my leg. Too weary to run from them again, I grabbed a sharp rock and frantically scraped off the mongrels. They wouldn't surrender. The pencil-thin creatures stood erect, like blades of grass, sniffing for blood. When they inch-wormed their elongated bodies, I showed no mercy. I crushed them with my shoe, again and again, killing all, sparing none. I was at war. They were responsible for starting my stampede through the woods. There would be no survivors.

I felt one under my blue T-shirt and screamed. An engorged ugly beast was attached to my belly. I ripped off its suction-cupped mouth and crushed the black flesh between my fingers. My eyes were transfixed by the blood oozing from my hand. Then I gazed at red dripping from my stomach where the leech had released its anticoagulant. The sight of it all, as well as the gash in my head, made me woozy. I pressed the shirt against my body to stem the bleeding and slouched against the tree. I watched a dark red blotch seep through the fabric, staining the Aboriginal print of a black ghostlike figure encircled by white dots.

I desperately needed my companions. The four of us were returning from the waterfall when I left my friends and departed the road frequently traveled onto a path no one traveled, just to relieve myself. The plunge into the ravine and the concussion from crashing against the tree left me totally disoriented. I had no idea how to find my way back to Federal Pass, the path that meandered along the base of the sandstone cliffs. The dense rainforest offered no vantage point where I could spot the ridge. And the black clouds overhead obscured the sun.

My weary body and throbbing head told me to rest and wait for help. Sam Woodland once worked with Aborigines in Alice Springs. The bush expert wouldn't let me die here all alone. But then again, I couldn't just wait. I had to keep moving and find shelter. There were poisonous tiger snakes and red-bellied black snakes slithering around this leech-infested forest.

The wind blew across the treetops. I listened intently for human voices. Nothing but the whipbird and the metallic, high-pitched *tink-tink* of the bellbirds. And the ominous sounds of strange creatures lurking in the distance.

My decision to sign up for a weekend of personal growth and inner peace had turned into a goddamn safari through a rainforest. It was all Sam's fault. She insisted we bushwalk the Jamison

Valley, instead of viewing it from above in the scenic cable car, like I suggested.

I smelled trouble the first time I laid eyes on her, two days ago in the conference room at the Rosella Lodge.

⪻⪻⪻⪻

"Who are you?"

"Peter Pinowski."

The social worker with spiky gray hair pounced. "Who are you?"

"A psychologist."

The hawk circled her prey. "Who are you?"

I surveyed the craters on her pitted face. "I'm 35...and single."

Her lips pursed into the shape of a beak. "Who are you?"

I glared at Sam's chestnut wool sweater and mumbled, "This is a silly exercise. I'm five-foot-eleven, with blue eyes and brown hair."

She moved her cushion closer and tapped my knee. "Who are you?"

Feeling like a stalked quarry, I wiped the sweat from my brow and nervously scanned the room where four others were paired off with their inquisitors. Some volunteered information. Others sat meekly with blank expressions.

Sam tapped my knee again and repeated the question.

I stared into her brown eyes and smirked, "My father calls me P.P."

"Who are you?"

"Unemployed. Pittwater School downsized and gave me the boot because I had the least seniority. Mind you, dealing with kids with Attention Deficit Disorder made me hyperactive."

"Who ARE you?"

"Stressed out," I bellowed. "Hell, without a job, unpaid bills, few friends, and zero love life, I've been spending my days watching the surf or surfing the net. I was blindsided by a panic attack while sipping chicken soup. No way was I going back on benzos. I traveled that road five years ago and wasn't about to replace anxiety with addiction. So I signed up for this stupid weekend."

"Let's stop," interrupted Gretchen Mahler. The portly, seventy-five-year-old psychologist reminded me of a female wizard with snow white, wispy hair. Dressed in a lavender tracksuit, our wizened leader faced five pairs of participants who sat on cushions opposite one another.

Her eyes rested on me. "You had difficulty with the question."

"I...wasn't sure what to say."

With the help of a carved, wooden cane, she slowly sauntered toward me. She rested her hand on my shoulder and cooed like a mother dove. "You're safe here, my dear. Let go and be free. That takes great courage."

There was a fine line between courage and stupidity. I clearly had erred on side of the latter when I signed up for this weekend: *The Roadmap Home: Finding Inner Peace.*

"My dear, this workshop will release your fears," she announced all too enthusiastically.

Despite her seventy-five years, she showed the vigor of a younger woman and seemed proud of her body despite her wrinkled face, excess weight, and limp. She pointed her cane in a circular motion at the rest of the participants. "Move your cushions and form a circle."

As we reorganized ourselves, I surveyed six wide-eyed women who outweighed and outnumbered the four of us blokes. Some looked excited, while others joined me in a state of frozen anticipation, like possums caught in headlights.

Gretchen circled the carpeted room and touched everyone's shoulder in a reassuring manner. "My experimental laboratory will wake you from a dreamlike existence so you can find your home. Home is about belonging to a place, a group of people, a wellspring of love. We'll create a place where you feel safe and protected, nurtured and loved. You'll discover inner peace, even in the face of conflict."

Using her cane, she eased herself into a chair. "I found strength in adversity."

Actually, it was more like a compost pile of dysfunction. According to Gretchen, her mother was sixteen when she gave her up for adoption to a childless, Bible-bashing couple determined to save a lost soul with a rod. As soon as she could, Gretchen married the first man who showed interest. Two years later, he left her for another woman. Abandonment became her bedfellow—with friends and lovers.

Gretchen peered at the group's riveted eyes. "I felt deeply flawed and decided to take my life late one night. At the railing of the Harbour Bridge, I stood ready to jump, when I heard a sickening crash. A truck collided with a motorcyclist who skidded right in front of me. The injured man screamed, 'Help me!' That cry woke me up."

Gretchen lifted her cane and tapped the shoulder of a wimpy-looking bloke who had fallen asleep. She spoke to the startled man. "Whenever I fall asleep, I face setbacks. When I remain awake, others come forward and help me return home."

She stroked her snowy white hair and sighed. "Finding the way home can be long and tortuous. It demands a willingness to awaken from a numbed existence. Stories must be shared, tears must be released, forgiveness must be found, and unconditional love must be embraced."

Gretchen ceremoniously banged the tip of the cane against the floor. "Like Dorothy in *The Wizard of Oz*, you need courage, heart, and a brain. The comforting arms of the Divine will welcome you home. It's time to step onto the Yellow Brick Road."

She eased herself out of the chair and limped to the middle of the circle. "Our first task is to create a safe, nurturing place. That's why I chose this comfy lodge, away from the hustle and bustle of Sydney."

The setting was, indeed, spectacular. The Rosella Lodge faced the Blue Mountains National Park, renowned as a scenic wonderland. With deep lush valleys, plunging waterfalls and abundant wildlife, it was a popular holiday spot with Sydney less than two hours away.

Evening had enveloped the mountains. Hundreds of flying insects banged against the picture window, clamoring to enter the well-lit room. A gray possum startled us when it jumped on the veranda. The marsupial's large eyes sparkled pink, off the reflecting outdoor lights, as it sniffed for food.

Gretchen observed the outdoor antics and rubbed her growling tummy. "I'm getting a bit peckish," she said. "Before we finish the evening, let's have a final sharing exercise. Pair up with your partner and describe your family. How did you feel growing up?"

Before Sam Woodland could open her mouth, I pounced. "You go first."

She squinted her hawkish brown eyes. "You'll have to share eventually, Peter."

She brushed her chestnut sweater. "My parents named me Samantha, but I prefer 'Sam.' Dad wanted a son and expected me to act like one. When sober, he was great. When drunk, he was awful. Gambled on the ponies and played long odds. We were forever broke."

Sam went on to describe a lost childhood. An alcoholic father and a mother worn down by financial hardship left little time for nurturing. As the eldest, she cared for three ungrateful sisters who made fun of her acne. She left home early and after two failed marriages, was working on her third.

"My relationships start off fine," she said. "Then the men self-destruct, just like Dad."

"Did anything good come out of your family?"

Her face brightened. "I escaped to the bush. I fed scraps to the animals and brought wounded creatures home. Dad threw a fit if he was drinking."

Her fingers twisted her wedding ring. "So what about you? Tell me about your family."

I nervously crossed my arms. "My mother met my father on the boat from Poland. They lived in Chicago for 14 years. Then we moved to Australia in '71 when I was six."

"Why the move?"

I shuffled my feet. "To be near relatives."

I omitted the fact that my father wanted to live in a white country (never mind the Aborigines). My mother treated the decision as if she had been given a life sentence like the early settlers. She lost most of her family during World War II and was heartbroken about being uprooted from friends and the land paved with her dreams. By the time my parents flew over Botany Bay, they were prisoners in a relationship, emotionally chained to one another.

"That must have been difficult for you."

I shrugged. "Being the new kid on the block with a different accent wasn't easy."

"Any brothers or sisters?"

Gretchen intervened before I could answer. "Let's stop there for a moment." Clutching a brownie, she instructed us to circle up.

I moved my cushion and glanced around the room. Several women had tear-stained faces while two of the men sat petrified.

"Some of you had painful experiences," said the psychologist. "Let's share them in the group."

Gretchen comforted each person with soothing words, saying it was safe to disclose buried secrets. She turned my way and smiled. "Haven't heard from you, my dear."

I stared at the brown smudge on the crease of her mouth. My heart thumped. Perspiration dotted my forehead and my world began to spin. Crikey! This was no time for a panic attack! My chest tightened and I sucked in air like a vacuum cleaner.

The psychologist hobbled to my side. She rested one arm against the cane while her free hand rubbed my back. "Take deep breaths, my dear." Her gentle strokes moved to my twitching arm. "Breathe. This is a safe place."

It sure as hell didn't feel safe.

Her touch eased the tension. My arms stopped trembling and my breathing slowly returned to normal. The panic lessened—until I opened my eyes and saw the voyeurs.

I wiped my flushed face. "I'm, uh, sorry."

Gretchen patted my shoulder. "Take it easy, dear. Internal conflicts erupt during my workshops. Nothing to worry about, as long as we face those parts that don't want to be here. Who in your family would be upset about your sharing?"

"All of them," I gasped.

"Then let's start with your father. What would he say?"

I fidgeted on the cushion. "He'd probably yell that I wasn't acting like a man."

"Why?"

"He hated weakness."

She rubbed my shoulder like a trainer readying a boxer for the next round. "Look around the room, dear. Do you see anyone yelling at you?"

I scanned the sea of faces. "Well...no."

"Your father isn't here. But he's inside of you, shouting. If you want to strengthen your own voice, you must release his. Will you let us help?"

I reluctantly nodded.

Gretchen addressed the other participants. "Peter's past prevents him from hearing his inner truth. We must cheer him on as he battles the toxic messages. He can replace the old with new proclamations, but we must help him."

She stood in front of me and leaned on her cane. With a loud voice, she pronounced, "Your feelings are welcome here, my dear. The painful ones that were exiled as well as the joyful ones. We welcome your truth."

Gretchen pointed her cane at Sam, who sat next to me. "Let's go around the circle and affirm Peter."

Sam swooped over and gave me a crushing hug. "I'll help you."

The wimpy looking bloke who was next in line seemed lost for words. After a second nudge from Gretchen's cane, he finally blurted, "Mate, you've got balls. If it wasn't for me girlfriend, I wouldn't be here."

Gretchen, acting like a cheerleader, banged her cane on the floor after each affirmation. Surprisingly, my father's voice faded, as did the anxiety and panic.

By the time the psychologist brought the session to a close, I was emotionally spent. We stood in a circle, arms around shoulders, as she delivered a final instruction. "During this weekend, I want everyone to journal. Welcome any thoughts, feelings, dreams, or internal dialogues. Your journal will reveal the residents occupying your inner world. Commit time this weekend to write before you sleep."

The white-haired psychologist then concluded the evening with individual hugs. I eased away from the group. My inner parents told me to go to bed. I was about to follow their advice when Sam corralled me and a few others into a brisk walk to Echo Point.

I reluctantly followed the group to the popular tourist attraction, the Three Sisters. A group of Japanese tourists snapped pictures of the three towering sandstone pinnacles illuminated by large beacons against the backdrop of a black sky.

Sam shared the Aboriginal legend. "Three beautiful sisters from the Katoomba tribe fell in love with three brothers from a neighboring clan. Since tribal law prevented them from marrying, the brothers waged battle. A shaman turned the sisters into stone until the battle was over, but he died during the fight. The women have been imprisoned forever in rock."

We stared at the triple rock formation. Floodlights made them appear like immense spires of burning coal jutting above the valley.

Sam lowered her voice. "Be careful, there may be a bunyip around."

I leaned against the metal railing. "And that is?"

Shadows danced across the craters on her face. "A giant lizard with eyes of fire. The wild creatures in the bush may not be who you think they are."

"Very funny," I scoffed.

She pointed skyward at the cloud of fluttering wings. "Those long-eared bats are snatching insects attracted to the floodlights. But they could be watching us."

"Yeah, sure," I said, in as fearless a voice I could muster.

"Shush. Hear that?"

"What?"

A throaty hiss screeched near the trees.

"Possums," she whispered. "They may be warning us."

I faked a giant yawn. "I've had a long day. Time for bed."

While the others stayed to hear more ghost stories, my roommate, Perry, headed back with me. His hands shook as he lit a cigarette.

"Not sure about this workshop, mate," said the weedy bloke with black, greasy hair, Elvis sideburns, and a gold stud in his left ear. He rubbed the faded gold stars embroidered above the denim pocket. "Me girl signed me up for it," he said, puffing hard on his cigarette. "Tole me I had to come. We had a tiff, if you know what I mean. Didn't wanna get thrown out on the street, mate. I quit using but still get the craving. Me girl tole me this would set me straight..."

He babbled on as we approached the lodge. "Been over a month since I've used. Not easy, if you know what I mean. The other day me mates shared a bong of ice. Had a taste and me girl went off her rocker. Times are tough, mate."

"Sure are." I cringed at the thought of sharing a room with a not-yet-recovered addict. "We're not allowed to smoke inside."

He exhaled outside the building and grumbled, "Guess I'll finish me smoke outside."

I climbed the stairs to the Spartan cell on the second floor. I removed my pajamas and bag of toiletries from the suitcase and placed them on the bed nearest the window. I wanted fresh air.

Perry, reeking of tobacco, stormed into the room. "Let's play some tunes," he shouted. He inserted a disc in his boombox and before I could say, keep it down, "Jailhouse Rock" blared from the speakers.

"People may be sleeping."

"No worries, mate." He lowered the volume a fraction. "I could listen to the King all night."

"Yeah, well, we have an early morning."

"Don't need much sleep. Not me, mate. Have plenty left, if you know what I mean." He grabbed a pair of sunglasses and hitched up an imaginary guitar to impersonate Elvis. "I play the bass guitar in a band and rev up the crowd. Wild, mate. Real wild."

Gretchen's brochure promised a weekend to eliminate stress. She should have promised a money-back guarantee. I sat on the hard bed while guitar man pretended to enthrall an audience. He grabbed a cigarette and was about to light up when I reminded him again about the rule.

"No worries," he said. "Need another smoke to calm me nerves. Take off the edge, if you know what I mean." He lit the cigarette and dashed out.

When he left, I flicked the switch. *Jailhouse* no longer rocked. I showered, cleaned my teeth, then activated my laptop. Although I brought it to play games, I decided to follow Gretchen's suggestion to journal.

It seemed strange, tapping my innermost thoughts on the keyboard once again. After the humiliation of discovering my mother reading my diary with the intimate details of my love life five years ago, I vowed never to incriminate myself again. However, if this workshop offered a chance at inner peace, I was prepared to give journaling another go. I wasn't so sure, however, whether all my experiences would be welcome.

Koo-koo-koo-koo-koo-ka-ka-ka-ka-ka. The raucous laughter of a kookaburra pierced my ears. I woke with a throbbing head and an aching body. I staggered to my feet when I spotted the reinforcements inching their way toward my body. Some leeches had already clambered aboard. Enraged, I searched and destroyed, mashing the mongrels between my fingers. Yanking them off wasn't the best remedy because of the anti-coagulant, but I didn't care. I'd rather a weeping wound than a sucking leech.

Koo-koo-koo-koo-koo-ka-ka-ka-ka-ka. The cacophony of laughter rose once more. I sneered at the bird on the nearby branch. It stared back, defiant. Sam said the Aborigines considered the white-chested kingfisher a protector. The only comfort I found in the kookaburra's haunting laughter was that it ate snakes and lizards.

Drops of rain splashed my face. A downpour seemed imminent. I needed shelter. I found a long branch and broke it in half. Using it for support, I hobbled along the bottom of the gully and kept a sharp lookout for anything that crawled.

When gossamer spider threads brushed against my face, I panicked. I stumbled over slippery wet logs and cursed Sir Walter Scott's words, "Oh what a tangled web we weave." Plodding through the wet scrub, I truly felt deceived.

The drumbeats in my head pounded a rhythm of pain. I frantically scoured the primeval rainforest. Gray eucalyptus trees stood tall in the distance like beckoning ghosts. I could almost feel unseen forces. Were they pushing me toward civilization or deeper into the bush?

A branch cracked beneath my feet. I screamed and tripped into a group of ferns and their clutching leaves. I fought my way free and quickened my pace. Sam and her ghost stories! Giant lizards with eyes of fire. There weren't monsters scavenging the woods for warm bodies. I remained hyper-vigilant, just in case.

Near exhaustion, I spotted an overhanging ledge of sandstone covered with moss. I was about to enter the tiny crawlspace when I noticed black droppings, the size of tiny worms, scattered on the ground. I cautiously poked my stick into a deep crevice at the top of the makeshift cave. A flutter of bats flew out. I cowered as they rustled overhead. When the rain turned into a deluge, I had no choice but to crawl inside. I shuddered at the prospect of sharing this lair with flying rats.

Since I had lost my watch during the tumble down the ravine, I had no way to tell time. It seemed like dusk, but the black clouds overhead made it difficult to determine when night would fall.

Rest in a dry space was welcome, but I now craved food. Without a clue about the bush tucker that sustained Aborigines, I figured it was best to just wait and rest my weary head against the rock face. Before I closed my eyes, I spotted another leech poking out from under a rock. I smashed it with my stick. False alarm. A lizard scurried off, leaving its wiggling tail behind. Not exactly a bunyip with fiery red eyes.

Nestled under the overhanging ledge, I gingerly touched the gash on my head and the sticky crust of blood. I blotted it with the end of my shirt and wondered how Aborigines mended their wounds.

The pelting rain eased into a light shower. I crawled from the overhang to a nearby puddle. I slurped the brackish water, then splashed my face. As I made my way back, I dislodged some rotting timber. A black, hairy funnel web, furious about being disturbed, bared fangs long enough to be legs. The deadly spider attacked my shoe. I kicked back at walking death. He would not be visiting my cave.

I stumbled into my sanctuary and huddled against the sandstone. Ouch! A pinch on the back of my neck made me reach back and grip a tiny tick. I pressed the bastard between my fingers, but its hard shell resisted. I smashed it against a rock. *Pop!* No more tick. No more free meals—for anyone!

A southerly wind brought a cold breeze. The tops of the trees swayed. I shivered at the thought of being alone at night. No matches; no fire. I spotted an ominous shadow darting behind a blue gum tree. Then another dark figure moved behind the ferns. The bunyips were coming to devour me! I clutched my tightening chest and broke into a nervous sweat.

"Get a grip, Pinowski," I trembled. "It's your imagination. Don't have a panic attack now. Take some deep breaths. Help is sure to arrive."

I searched for something, anything to keep my mind from dwelling on the moving shadows, or the ticks and spiders, leeches and snakes. I remembered the workshop. Yesterday—Friday morning.

✦ ✦ ✦ ✦

I woke with a horrible pain in my neck. Perry was snoring loudly. His stinky cigarettes and constant farting made for a dreadful night's sleep. The mattress, stiffer than a surfboard, prevented my head from settling into a comfortable position. As a result, muscle spasms riddled the right side of my neck.

I gingerly climbed out of bed and tilted my head at an angle to ease the pain. I turned on the laptop to record my frightening dream.

I'm a prisoner in old Sydney Town, dressed in dirty crimson. Chained to retarded convicts. Desperate for freedom, I yank the chains. Convicts fight back. We scuffle. I grab an axe. Swing at my leg. Whoosh. I scream. Blood squirting. Leg's gone. But so are the chains. A free man, I hobble, leaning on the axe.

If Gretchen asked for dreams, she could have them. I quickly dressed, packed my computer, and carried it and my wallet to the car. Not trusting Perry, I wanted to secure my valuables.

In the dining area, many of the participants were already eating. Overhearing some of their personal stories, I wondered if we were all emotionally retarded, like the convicts in my dream. Family dysfunction was rampant, like a disease.

I grabbed a plate of eggs and reluctantly sat with Sam when she waved me to join her, Rosie and Alana.

"What happened to your neck?" asked Sam.

"It's crook. Couldn't settle last night. Perry smelled like a cigarette factory."

"Disgustin' habit," snapped Rosie MacBain, a middle-aged, Celtic woman with brassy red hair. "Where's the lout?"

I glanced around the room. "He's still sleeping."

My eyes settled on the next table where an attractive woman with a cream cashmere sweater was sipping tea. Soft golden ringlets fell to her shoulder. Our eyes met. We both smiled. Now, she'd make a fine roommate.

Rosie nudged Sam and sniggered. "If Peter stares any harder, his neck will be more than a wee bit out of shape."

Red-faced, I turned to the picture window and pointed to the veranda. "The birds are hungry."

The king parrots and rainbow lorikeets squawked on the food tray dangling from the rafters.

Rosie stared at the other table. "I think ye'd be wantin' a different form of wildlife."

Alana scowled at Rosie, "Don't embarrass him. You promised to behave."

"How do you know each other?" I asked.

"We work together as social workers in Queenscliffe," said Alana Saunders, a dark, twenty-six-year-old Filipina. She patted Sam's arm. "She's our clinical director."

Sam squeezed Alana's shoulder. "She talked us into coming."

"I just love Gretchen," smiled Alana. "She's my therapist."

She made that statement as if it was a badge of honor. I personally would've kept that kind of badge close to my chest. I assumed that Alana had other badges she wanted to conceal. Whenever she smiled, she hid a chipped front tooth and mottled teeth behind her lips.

Alana and the two other women related more like sisters. Sam, the bush expert, acted the elder, being in her mid-fifties. Her spiked gray hair contrasted with Rosie's brassy redhead. Ten years younger than Sam, Rosie took a provocative role, while Alana with chin-length black hair presented as a melancholic, dependent soul.

"Sam and Rosie are like family," added Alana wistfully. "Better than my own."

Before I knew it, she took a twisting detour down memory lane. She told me that her mother escaped the slums of Manila by coming to Australia as a mail-order bride. Alana's father had owned a cattle station in Queensland and placed the order for a wife who later died during Alana's delivery. The father never forgave Alana or her mother for the damaged goods.

As Alana said, "When I got older, I cooked and cleaned for the men." She choked on the next words. "Plus the extras on the side."

As if to mimic the shift in mood, dark foreboding clouds rumbled in the distance. Rain splashed against the window.

"I was an orphan, like Gretchen," continued Alana. "The Philippines were my mother's land while my father's land brought abuse. I didn't belong to either country." Tears trickled down her cheeks.

Sam placed an arm over her shoulder. "It's okay. Let it out. That's why we're here."

Alana leaned against her shoulder. Her crying shifted to deep sobs. Others around the room noticed the outburst and became silent. I frantically scanned for Gretchen. We desperately needed her and a bucket.

Rosie stirred from her chair and caressed Alana's shoulders. "No one's gonna hurt ye, Lassie."

Gretchen entered the room as lightning illuminated the sky. Booming thunder jolted the earth and howling winds forced the parrots from their perch. Rain pelted the veranda.

The psychologist spotted Alana and hobbled over. She leaned on her cane. "What's wrong, my dear?"

Alana answered with a torrent of tears.

Sam gently stroked her hair. "She was reminiscing about her family."

"Let's move her to the group room," said Gretchen, oozing compassion. She waved for everyone to follow.

Sam and Rosie eased Alana out of the chair and, with Gretchen leading the way, the rest of us walked in solemn procession. My lopsided head begged for a hot compress.

We gathered on cushions around Alana in the cozy conference room, which resembled a spacious living room with a fireplace.

Gretchen eased herself to the floor and pointed around the group. "This is your new family. We're here to comfort you. Look around and see the loving faces."

Alana gazed my way with an embarrassed smile.

Gretchen squeezed Alana's hands. "When you shared your pain, my dear, you were being authentic. That moved us. Your courage inspires others to share their stories. We're ready to go deeper."

Gretchen smothered Alana with a motherly hug. More tears. Rosie and Sam replaced Gretchen, with more hugs. The others followed. I offered an authentic pat on the shoulder.

"We have lots of *home* work to do," emphasized Gretchen. "Before we travel farther on the Yellow Brick Road, let's take the chill out of the air and light a fire. They're forecasting more showers."

She rubbed her tummy. "But first, I'll organize scones and fruit for nourishment. We have to feed the soul *and* the body."

Before I could say, bring on the scones, Gretchen came to an abrupt halt. "Where's Perry?"

Counting him, there should have been ten participants. We were one short. Gretchen pointed her cane at me. "Check if he's upstairs, my dear. We don't want him to miss out."

I dashed to the room to grab Perry and a hot compress for my throbbing neck. I found him packing, with a lit cigarette dangling from his lips. He wore the same denim shirt with faded gold stars.

I swatted at the smoke. "What's going on, Perry?"

He stuffed the boom box into a well-worn khaki duffel bag. "I'm outa here, mate. Can't see this helpin'. Don't need me woman. I've got me friends, if you know what I mean."

"Hang on, Perry. Gretchen wants to see you." And probably stand him in the center of the group.

"Don't think so, mate. I'm outa here." He moved past me and headed for the door.

I followed him to the landing, where he stopped in his tracks. Gretchen stood at the foot of the stairs with a mob at her back. Perry sized up his options—either dash madly through them or stand trial.

Gretchen rested her cane on the bottom step. "What's the problem, my dear?"

He winced at the obvious.

She struggled up one step, then another. "You can go," she said. "But do tell us why you're leaving."

The heads below her bobbed in agreement.

Perry warily eyed her as she reached out a hand. "Can you help me up? My hip replacement is such a bother."

He clutched the duffel bag. "I'm leavin.'"

"Come on, dear," she huffed. "Give an old woman a hand."

He hesitated, then dropped the bag and lifted Gretchen onto the landing.

She straightened her green woolen sweater. "If you tell everyone why you're leaving, you can go in peace. Have you left relationships without an explanation? Surely, we deserve one."

Perry shook his head. "This ain't helpin.'" He checked for another exit. There was none.

Rosie bustled to the first stair. "Walkin' out on us is an act of a coward."

Alana joined her. "I bared my soul to the group. If I can do it, you can too."

A muscular, bald-headed man stepped forward. "There's only four of us blokes here, mate. We need you."

Gretchen grabbed his arm. "Take this opportunity to make new friends and change your life. If you leave now, you'll wander the streets forever."

That realization proved the knockout punch. Perry blinked several times, as if evaluating his options. A departure would signal the end of a relationship and a meal ticket. That meant homelessness and a life on drugs. He reached for his bag and gave a half-hearted, "I'll give it a go."

The crowd cheered. He reacted with a dazed grin. I patted him on the back as others climbed the stairs. Sam and Alana hugged his stinky body. My guess is that he had never received such attention from his family, who probably threw him out on his ass.

While the others celebrated his return, I dashed to the room for a compress. I soaked a washcloth in hot water and applied it to my neck. I checked the mirror and looked at my ridiculous cocked head. I tried stretching the muscles and reeled in pain. Then it dawned on me. The group's victory was my loss. I groaned at the thought of more sleepless nights with Perry.

I returned to the conference room holding the compress. Logs sputtered in the fireplace. Drops of rain trickled down the chimney, causing the flickering flames to hiss. The pitter-patter against the outside windows accentuated the warm, cozy atmosphere. I grabbed a scone before Gretchen's final call.

Our leader swallowed her last morsel. "Circle up."

Her brood quickly responded and nested on soft cushions around her straight back chair. She addressed Perry in a soft hypnotic voice.

"When faced with change, part of you will be terrified. It prefers the trance of the old dance. Your parent's loud voice prevented you from stepping into your true feelings and desires."

She tapped Perry with her cane, "And so, my dear, that's why I couldn't let you leave without a fight. I saw you surrender to the voice of fear. You came here to heal. I'll help you do that." She waved her cane at the rest of us. "So will these loving souls."

As Perry nervously glanced around the room, I wondered what his inner voices were saying.

Gretchen wielded her cane as if it were a sword. "The poet e.e. cummings said, 'To be nobody-but-yourself—in a world which is doing its best, night and day, to make you somebody else—means to fight the hardest battle which any human being can fight; and never stop fighting.'"

Bang! Gretchen thumped the end of her cane against the floor. "Let's begin the courageous fight. Pair off with someone you don't already know."

That's when I got stuck with Carmen Fusco, a rigid, forty-year-old lawyer I didn't want to know. Her chiseled, blunt chestnut hair had edges as sharp as her tongue.

"I guess it's you and me," she said brusquely.

I faced the woman with a smug button nose. Then I caught a whiff of her sickly-sweet perfume that was so powerful she could've been embalmed with it. She wore a black turtleneck with a gold chain dangling an angel with a trumpet. Matching gold earrings reinforced the message: she loved to blow her own horn.

Gretchen called out instructions. "This exercise will bring to light your family roles. You unconsciously recreate them daily. Before you can choose new behaviors, you must first identify your old dance, the default patterns you've been trained to repeat. Complete the following sentence. 'I am a good son or daughter when I...' Speak only in the present tense. Allow five minutes per person."

I rubbed my aching neck. "You go first."

Carmen reacted as if a witch's broom went up her ass. "You didn't confer with me," she bristled.

"Do you want to go first?"

"No."

Carmen gave me another pain-in-the-neck. "Alright," I said, sniffing her awful perfume. I glared at the angels dangling from her ears. "I was a good son when..."

"Excuse me," she interrupted. "Gretchen instructed us to complete the sentence in the present tense. You should say I *am* a good son. Not I *was* a good son."

I stretched my neck muscles. "Was, am, it's not much of a difference."

"It's imperative we follow instructions. I'll ask Gretchen."

I stopped her from flagging our leader. "I'm not going to argue over something so petty." I emphasized my next phrase. "I *am* a good son when I made the family smile."

"You're still talking in the past," lectured Carmen. Her red nails fiddled with a trumpeting angel. "You should say I am a good son when I *make* the family smile."

I wanted to punch her smug button nose. "Let me do this my way. No big deal if I use a present or past verb!"

Before I could stop her, her hand flapped in the air. Great, I thought, here comes the judge.

"What's the problem?" asked Gretchen, limping toward us.

The lawyer pointed her finger at me. "He's not following your instructions. He's using the past tense, not the present."

Gretchen smiled at her. "Be patient, my dear. It can be difficult to make the shift. Why don't you go first and demonstrate."

Before Carmen could protest, Gretchen wandered toward another pair of swaying hands.

With the judge gone, Carmen glanced skyward with an arrogant I-guess-I'll-have-to-show-you-how-to-do-it look. She caressed the angel on her chest and said, "I AM a loving daughter when I AM considerate of my parents. I see them most Sundays. I acknowledge how proud they are of my accomplishments—my law degree, my MBA, my loving husband who happens to be a brilliant chemical engineer and professor at Macquarie University. My parents expect no less than excellence. I haven't disappointed—"

"Hold on Carmen," I interjected. "You just said, 'I haven't. You're supposed to stay in the present." Score one for Pinowski!

Her red nails dug into the medallion. "I DO NOT disappoint my parents. They swell with pride at my success."

By the time she completed her oral argument to this jury of one, I reviewed all the facts—her grandiosity, need for admiration, sense of entitlement, arrogance and superiority. I pronounced my verdict, NPD—narcissistic personality disorder.

She reached for her dangling earring. "It's your turn," she declared. "I hope you were paying attention to how it should be done."

A sharp pain careened up my neck. "Does that medallion remind you to blow your own trumpet?"

She grimaced as if I had stabbed her angel. "That's uncalled for!"

The words tumbled out before I could shut my mouth. "You're pretty sensitive about your horny angel."

Her jaw clenched. Her red face transformed to purple. "I won't take such insolence," she fumed. She bolted from the cushion.

Carmen returned with Gretchen at her side. The lawyer pointed an accusing finger at me. "He made egregious statements, too insulting to repeat."

"She kept correcting me," I said, rubbing my neck. "And I have a muscle spasm which makes it hard to concentrate."

"No excuse for impertinence," she attacked. "Moreover—"

"Hang on, my dear," soothed our adjudicator. "Let's take this one step at a time. Did your parents ever make fun of you or not take you seriously?"

Carmen shook her head so vigorously her earrings danced. "My parents always admired my achievements. Clearly, I was their favorite."

"Who wasn't their favorite?" asked Gretchen.

Carmen's button nose sniffed as if inhaling a skunk. "My younger brother, Russell. He's bi-polar, ADHD, and half a dozen other labels. His favorite sport was tormenting me. Obviously, he was envious of my talents, for he had none. If I practiced the flute, he'd mock me in front of his friends, calling me a flartist. Then he would make disgusting sounds."

"How did that make you feel?"

Carmen grimaced. "I swore I'd never let him or anyone else put me down."

"So you became a lawyer," remarked Gretchen. "A great career to right any wrongs. What you're really fighting for is recognition."

Carmen sniffed, "Possibly."

"Peter acted as a trigger," added the psychologist. "He inadvertently activated a trance state. In your mind, he became another Russell. You fought to defend yourself. Let's work with this, shall we?"

"He's the one who needs help."

"We'll get to Peter in a moment, my dear, but let's work with you first." Gretchen leaned down and patted a cushion. "I'd like you to sit down and relax."

Carmen resisted. "I came here to learn techniques to improve staff relationships. I'd prefer you deal with the real problem—Peter. He acts like my recalcitrant employees."

Gretchen patted the cushion again. "Let's release some resentment, shall we?"

The angel lady glared at me before begrudgingly sitting down.

"Now close your eyes, my dear," instructed our leader. "Very good. Take a deep, cleansing breath and let go of the tension. Now go back in time when you were younger, when you were practicing the flute. Picture that moment. How old are you?"

Carmen clenched her teeth. "Twelve."

"Imagine your brother appearing. How do you feel?"

Her body stiffened. "Humiliated."

Gretchen spoke in a calm voice. "Do you use words to hide or attack?"

"Words protect."

"If you continually defend yourself, you prevent others from knowing you. That's not how you want to live, is it, my dear?"

Her earrings shook ever so slightly.

"Then let's break the trance, shall we? Picture your brother. Send him a bolt of forgiveness. He probably felt stupid and unloved, just like you. He sought attention at your expense. That doesn't condone what he did. But you can shift the internal dialogue and break the default program. You don't have to repeat this dance ever again. See yourself as a scared little girl. You needed protection and love. Send yourself forgiveness."

Gretchen lightly stroked Carmen's shoulders. "Receive the love."

The muscles on the lawyer's face tightened. She fought to control her emotions. A lone tear oozed from one eye.

"That's right, my dear, let the feelings come."

What also came was a loud rumble from my stomach. I moved my cushion further away. My hunger pains growled again.

Carmen opened her eyes and wiggled her nose.

"Don't let Peter's noise disturb you."

"I can't." She straightened her body and glowered at me. "You broke my concentration. I can't continue."

Despite Gretchen's encouragement, Carmen refused to go any further. The exasperated psychologist turned to me and asked. "Is there anything you'd like to say?"

"I'm...uh...sorry. Didn't mean to make fun of you." At least, not that bad. "My neck was hurting, and I felt criticized. That's why I made the joke."

Before Carmen could offer a rebuttal, Gretchen told her, "Remember, Peter isn't Russell. You can either find fault with what he said or you can hear an apology. What would you prefer?"

Before she could answer, I forced a smile and held out my hand. Better to make peace with a lawyer than incur her wrath or a lawsuit. "I hope we can be friends," I lied.

She grudgingly shook hands. Gretchen asked us to seal the pact with a hug. We both resisted, but upon our leader's insistence, complied, ever so briefly.

I asked for a bathroom break.

"In a moment, my dear. We need to address your humor."

Carmen nodded, way too vigorously.

"I said I was sorry."

"You used humor in your family to handle conflict, didn't you?" She tapped my leg with her cane. "Who were you trying to cheer up?"

"My mother enjoyed my jokes."

"Did that make you a good son?"

I glanced at my watch. "I guess."

"And what about your father?"

"He had a weird sense of humor."

"Just like you," scowled Carmen.

I retaliated, "Not as bad as your brother."

"Don't get defensive, my dear," calmed Gretchen. "We're helping you recognize patterns. How did your father make fun of you?"

My stomach grumbled. "As a joke, he called me P.P."

"How'd that make you feel?"

I lied again. "I got over it."

Gretchen peered into my eyes. "Your father's humor belittled you. You get laughs, just like your father, at other people's expense."

"I can vouch for that," retorted Carmen.

I protested. "Laughter's good for the soul."

"Playful laughter, yes," said Gretchen. "But your humor creates a barrier between you and your feelings. It's a form of avoidance. Next time you have an impulse to make a joke, pay attention to what you're feeling."

I felt like making a wisecrack, but thought it best to nod in agreement.

"At least we solved one of your problems," announced Carmen haughtily.

"*We?*"

Gretchen raised her hands. "Be careful. You both are starting to dance old steps." She asked me, "Do you have an older sister?"

"Yeah. Why?"

"Did you and your sister argue?"

"She was bossy. Acted superior."

"You fought back with sarcasm. See how you and Carmen recreate a similar relationship—she with her brother and you with your sister?"

She banged her cane against the floor. "Great work."

I stared in disbelief. "What was so great?"

She rapped my knee with the wooden stick. "You recognized the transference. You projected your issues onto Carmen and re-engaged an old pattern. Inspect, reject, and select," she instructed.

I acted on her message to inspect my thoughts and feelings, reject what I no longer wanted, and select new beliefs and behaviors. I detested Carmen, wanted no part of her, and looked for a quick exit. Fortunately, Gretchen called for a break.

She rubbed her tummy. "I brought homemade chocolate for those of us chocoholics."

I was about to suggest a 12-Step group, but passed on the remark. I rushed to the loo to deal with the increasing pain in my neck. The bathroom offered a temporary respite, or so I thought. Spiraling smoke rose from one of the stalls. Perry also needed a hideout.

The steaming hot cloth acted like soothing balm. I pressed it against my neck and returned to the conference room where I perched myself near the fireplace, away from Carmen Fusco. Watching the flames flicker and crackle, I pondered life without humor.

Koo-koo-koo-koo-koo-ka-ka-ka-ka-ka. Outside the window, the bird's laugh reminded me of the song "Kookaburra" by Marion Sinclair. As a child, I often repeated the lyrics about the bird sitting on the old gum tree.

I hoped Gretchen would bring some laughter when we reconvened. Unfortunately, the opposite occurred.

She dabbed her mouth with a chocolate-stained hanky then talked about the masks we wear. She said we developed false selves as children to protect ourselves from getting hurt. She beckoned us to face our fears and connect with our authentic self.

"Pair off with someone and share your fears," she said. "Take fifteen minutes."

Gretchen materialized a small bar of chocolate from her pocket and removed the wrapper. I watched her take a bite as Thomas approached.

"I need a break from the women," said the bloke with the physique of a wrestler. Bald-headed and clean-shaven, Thomas Barker sported a sweatshirt with a picture of a soaring eagle. His piercing eyes glimmered like two stones of polished lapis lazuli. "Care to pair up?"

"Sure," I said, grateful for anyone but Carmen.

"We're outnumbered."

"Six to four," I added, and that included Perry.

We organized our cushions near the fireplace. I could almost smell Carmen's sickly perfume even though she chatted with another bloke on the other side of the room.

I pointed at her. "Keep clear. She's a lawyer and a bitch."

Thomas winked. "Understood, mate."

Gretchen banged the floor with her cane. "Come on," she called. "Reduce your resistance. Share your fears."

I struck first. "So what are you fearful about?"

His deep blue eyes veered toward the ceiling. "Dying."

"You're worried about dying?" I asked, incredulously. He was in great shape.

"I have HIV."

My immediate impulse was to move back ten paces. I recalled the lyrics, *Gay your life must be.* "Are you, er...dying? I mean, what stage are you at?"

Thomas shook his head. "I have the virus but it hasn't moved into AIDS. I'm on antiretroviral medication."

My fear of rejection quickly transformed into terror. I heard an inner voice—my mother stridently warning me about contracting a disease.

He tapped my arm. "Are you scared?"

I shifted on my cushion. "I, er...don't know anyone personally who has AIDS."

Thomas reacted as if smacked on the head. "I don't have AIDS," he snapped. "People wrongly assume HIV means AIDS. You're diagnosed with AIDS when your T-cell count falls below 200."

"Didn't mean to upset you," I apologized.

His face reddened. "Bet you didn't know that eighty percent of HIV-infected people are not symptomatic and have a near normal CD4 cell count for ten or more years without treatment. With proper treatment, the timeframe extends."

I moved back on my cushion. "Yeah, well, as I said. I didn't mean to offend."

The muscles on his neck became taut like strands of rope. "I'm a health educator and put up with a lot of ignorant, homophobic morons, mate. I hope you're not one of them."

"No way," I said. "I'm a psychologist. I understand what you must be going through. So, shall we move onto other fears? I'm sure Gretchen wants us to compile a list. I'll share some of mine. I'm unemployed and worry about finding a job."

"Why aren't you working?"

"Cutbacks. I was low man on the totem pole. Or the low Pole on the totem," I chuckled, then nervously checked for the joke police.

Thomas leaned forward. "You're uncomfortable, aren't you?"

"Yeah, well, a little," I said, wishing for another partner. "Not sure what to say."

Thomas ran a large paw across his shiny head. "Damn Catholic indoctrination. Still causes me to feel guilty. I used to be a priest."

Christ! It was hard to imagine Thomas in robes. I soon discovered he was ordained for seventeen years. When he fell in love with a parishioner, he came out of the confessional box, so to speak. He later discovered that his male lover was screwing around. That's when he contracted HIV. Thomas initially thought God had punished him for his transgressions, but eventually found redemption when he was hired to educate others about the disease.

"Hope sprang from the seeds of destruction," he said. "But I'm frightened to love another man again."

"Make sure everyone shares," called Gretchen. "Take another minute."

"I've used most of the time, mate," said Thomas. "What else do you fear?" He slapped my knee. "Fears, mate."

Why did he touch me? "I...uh... Where to begin?"

"Do you ever fear castration?"

I crossed my legs. "Don't think so."

"Those of us who were circumcised carry emotional and physical scars. Do you?"

"I guess," I said, wondering why he wanted to know if I was circumcised. I wasn't about to expose myself.

Gretchen's all-too-familiar thump on the floor caught our attention. "Let's try a visualization exercise to deepen the process. Lie down on the floor and make yourselves comfortable."

She hobbled to the windows and closed the curtains. I hesitated before resting my head on the cushion. Thomas sprawled his large frame nearby. Our shoulders brushed. I shifted to avoid further contact.

Gretchen stood near the fire as flickering flames cast eerie shadows. "Close your eyes and bring your awareness to the rain. Let the gentle patter help you relax. Take a deep breath...hold it...exhale. Release any worries."

Easier said than done when lying next to a man with HIV.

"Take another deep breath and exhale the tension."

I stilled my mind but became aware of my throbbing neck. Maybe Perry had the right idea to bolt.

"Now imagine the time when you were inside the womb, suspended in a warm pool of water, bathed in heavenly light. Protected and loved. Without fears. Let the sound of the rain move you deeper inside...deeper still..."

I listened to the rain's hypnotic rap against the window. As a young boy, I'd stare at the yard during a storm and watch puddles form on the grass. I'd sneak out and splash in my bare feet.

Gretchen's soft voice continued. "Recall a time when you were a frightened as a child. Notice when darkness envelops the light."

I hear yelling. My mother's crying. I'm five and terrified. I cry when my father hollers. He tells me to stop acting like a girl. He reaches for the belt. Ma screams, "Leave him alone." His eyes go wild. He throws a glass of vodka at the wall and storms out. He returns later, drunk. I hide under my bed.

Gretchen's words faded in and out. "How did you handle your feelings?"

Have to keep busy, out of harm's way. Acting silly and cracking jokes keeps Pa off guard. Stops me from hating.

"Now imagine a blue healing light pouring over your head, dissolving the darkness. It gives you strength. You don't have to hide anymore. This is a time for renewal, a time to connect with your lost child. Allow your inner light to radiate once more."

No light. Pa's there, and Ma. I'm paralyzed.

"Find your lost child. Ask him or her to speak."

Pa's ghostly figure yells, "Stop listening."

"Let the wisdom of your soul guide you."

I descend down broken stairs into a dark basement, past burnt-out timbers and piles of ash. Remnants of a holocaust. I hear a faint whimper. "Where are you?" I shout. The arm of a small child, buried under debris, reaches through an opening. Frantic, I remove charred wood and rusted steel and haul a bruised and blackened little boy with tattered clothes from the rubble. His frightened, emaciated body recoils. I wrap my arms around the whimpering boy. We climb the stairs together. He winces at the light. Terrified of leaving his asylum, he panics and screams. I hold him tightly.

I hear Gretchen calling me back.

I can't leave without him. I clutch him tighter and mount another step. He wriggles free and grabs my leg to stop my advance. He holds fast, trapping me in the basement.

"Move back to the present," called the faint voice.

I can't dislodge him. "Hurry," I yell. "We'll be late."

"Come back now."

The boy won't budge.

"Come back to the group, Peter," said Gretchen more firmly.

I want to, but if I leave, he'll be trapped.

She touched my shoulder. "What's happening, my dear?"

My eyes remain closed. "The boy's scared. He won't come with me."

She speaks into my ear. "Tell him you won't abandon him. That he can reside in your heart and feel safe, protected and loved. Tell him that."

A torrent of tears spill down his face. It's been a long, long time since he felt truly loved.

Soft hands stroked my shoulders. "That's right, my dear, let it out. Embrace the little boy. Connect with him. Let your soul breathe. Experience the love."

Like a spring thaw, my body melted. Tears cascaded down my face in rivulets. A warm glow surrounded me—until I opened my eyes. And saw the group of staring faces. What would my father say? I quickly wiped my face.

"Don't be ashamed," comforted Gretchen. "You connected with a lost part of your soul."

That lost part looked around at the smiles of Sam, Alana, Rosie, and Thomas. Then I sniffed Carmen's familiar odor. She stood apart from the group and scowled.

"Don't let the critical voices take over," counseled Gretchen. She grabbed my hand and, with amazing strength for a seventy-five-year-old woman with a reconstructed hip, heaved me to my feet.

She instructed the others to stand around me. "Gently pass Peter inside the group. Make sure he doesn't fall."

She nudged my stiff body. "Close your eyes and relax into the outstretched arms. Receive the loving energy. Trust us. We'll catch you."

The group passed me around like a giant beach ball. I peeked to insure I wasn't swaying into the arms of Carmen.

Gretchen told the others to repeat the mantra, "You are safe, protected, and loved."

As I was rocked around the group, my internal chorus of critics resisted. However, the waves of affirming words muted their voices. I finally surrendered into the supporting arms. When my body came to a halt, I felt more relaxed and somewhat safe.

"Great work, my dear," said our leader, triumphantly. "Your breakthrough was inspiring."

I scanned the circle of beaming faces. My eyes avoided Carmen's pout and rested on a beautiful woman I had not yet gotten to know. We both smiled. I was ready for the radiant soul.

↞↞↞↞

Vroom! Vroom! I jumped up and banged my head against the over-hang. The gash re-opened and oozed blood down my face. I dabbed the wound with my red-stained shirt.

Vroom! Vroom! Excited by the sound of a motor, I squinted at the darkened forest. Rescue seemed imminent. I wept for joy—until the lyrebird strolled out of the ferns. Thrusting its long, feathery, silver tail over its head like a canopy, the bird scratched and scrabbled at the ground. The two lyre-shaped feathers shimmered and fluttered as the male bird continued his courting ritual—imitating birds and human sounds to attract a female. The lyrebird thrust its head for-ward. *Vroom! Vroom!*

With hope of discovery dashed, I shivered under the sandstone overhang and cursed the false alarm. I tossed a stone at the bird. It canceled its vocal display and sprinted past a toppled turpentine gum tree. My next rock bounced off the fallen trunk that was pointed toward another eucalyptus, split into a wide V. The formation of the trees created a sculpture of creamy wooden thighs begging for penetration.

I wanted Celeste's hot, curvy body snuggling next to me. Without a fire, I shuddered at the thought of weathering the cold night. To avoid wallowing in fear, I nestled under the ledge and recalled my first encounter with Celeste McCleod.

After the group cradle, I blinked at the sexy apparition. With freckles sprinkled on her nose and only a hint of makeup, her face glowed. Long, blonde hair swayed in golden ringlets as she approached me.

"Wow!" she exclaimed. "That was a powerful exercise!"

I half-nodded and stared transfixed at her foxy, hazel eyes and shapely body. I inhaled a delicate scent of lavender and imagined long, sexy legs beneath tight jeans, and taut breasts under her creamy, cashmere sweater.

She looked puzzled. "What's wrong with your neck?"

"What? Oh, I slept the wrong way. Tilting my head reduces the pain."

"You're in luck. I'm a massage therapist. Let's have a look."

"No worries, it's okay."

"Nonsense," she giggled. "Your body needs an alignment."

We lagged behind while the others filed into the dining area. I settled into a cushion with Celeste at my back. Her slim fingers probed my neck.

"Ouch! That's sore."

"You're really tense."

Like a baker, she began kneading the muscles. "When's the last time you had a massage?"

"Like this? Never!" I groaned as her fingers applied more pressure.

"Relax," she said softly. "I heard you're a psychologist."

I inhaled her lavender scent. "Mmmm."

"I thought of studying it myself, but decided to use my hands."

Her nimble fingers worked my neck and shoulders. "Mmmm," I purred. "You chose the right profession."

She patted my shoulders. "That should do it. How are you feeling?"

I stretched my neck from side to side. Relief! "You have phenomenal hands!" Not to mention a gorgeous body. I turned around.

A few years younger than me, Celeste was clearly the most attractive woman in the group. I hit the jackpot since there was little competition. Thomas and Perry were out of the running, for obvious reasons, which left a middle-aged Englishman.

"Hungry?"

"Ravenous," I said.

With a rejuvenated neck and a throbbing heart, I bounced alongside Celeste into the dining area. However, my exhilaration dissolved when I saw the buffet. Another vegetarian meal.

Celeste drooled. "I love dhal."

She spooned what looked like gray mud onto her plate. Lentils with garlic and coconut made my stomach turn somersaults. What about us carnivores? I settled for a small salad and extra lashings of rhubarb crumble, then found an empty table. There, Celeste and I had a delightful conversation about the workshop, our families, and our careers. When it was time for the afternoon session, we agreed to pair up for the next one-on-one exercise.

Raindrops peppered the roof while I parked my cushion next to Celeste. For the first time, I actually looked forward to the next experience. No matter what Gretchen threw at us, I would relish the opportunity and Celeste's loving hands.

Gretchen warmed herself by the fire, then eased onto her throne. She announced that the group would create two families, who would then establish nurturing environments for members to embrace their true selves. Two volunteers would act as captains. Each would alternate choosing one member at a time. After each selection, new members would then become part of the decision-making process. Gretchen had one rule—anyone could accept or reject a group's request.

Our leader asked for volunteers. "Who wants to play Adam or Eve in Eden?"

Thomas quickly raised his hand. With the specter of death standing at his door, he was more than eager. Not surprisingly, Carmen and her gold angels leapt forward as the second captain.

Gretchen swept her hand around the remaining eight. "Your families will spend considerable time together, so choose wisely."

I wanted to be with Celeste. For that to happen, either Thomas or Carmen had to pick us both. Although I felt uneasy about Thomas, I pinned my hopes on the former priest over the perfumed narcissist.

True to form, Carmen trumpeted first. She announced that she wanted a strong, confident man. Therefore, she chose Winston, an uptight Englishman. He strutted pompously from his cushion. Little did he realize he was about to taste forbidden fruit.

Thomas responded unceremoniously by selecting Alana. My guess is that he reached out to the melancholic soul because she lost her mother at childbirth. Whatever the reason, Alana broke into tears when chosen.

I sadly recalled my feeble attempt at cricket. With my horrendous fielding and hitting, I was always the last one picked. Surely, today would be different. Perry and I were the remaining men, so I figured my bat would be at a premium.

The selection process quickly stalled when Carmen and Winston disagreed. He pointed toward Celeste, or, rather, her breasts, while Carmen vigorously shook her head. She would repel any competition and Celeste's youth and beauty served as a threat. The lawyer must have presented a damn good argument because they eventually chose Rhonda, an overweight woman. In contrast, Thomas and Alana plucked Sam.

Carmen and her team conferred next. Another labored discussion. You'd think the bloody lawyer was charging by the hour! Winston and Rhonda lobbied intensely for Celeste and, to my horror, won.

No! I silently screamed. Not with Carmen. We were supposed to be together.

Celeste hesitated but reluctantly accepted. I was devastated.

Thomas pointed to me. "We'd like you to be part of our family, mate." Alana and Sam nodded.

And just like that, I was chosen. I stared at their warm, smiling faces then glanced at Celeste and her beckoning eyes.

Thomas's group was obviously the better choice. If I refused his offer, I'd end up with Celeste *and* Carmen. Gretchen told us to take responsibility for what we wanted. I didn't want a bugling lawyer, but I definitely desired Celeste.

With my heart pounding, I stared at my feet and stammered, "I'd, uh, really like to, Thomas, but I'd rather be in the other group."

He raised his eyebrows. "You sure, mate?"

Celeste beamed with excitement when I nodded.

Thomas seemed flabbergasted. He shook his befuddled head and consulted with the others. They selected Rosie, the feisty Celt.

Clearly, Carmen wasn't keen on me, but, considering the remaining batsmen and the pressure from Celeste, I was ready to suit up. The group huddled and talked, or rather fought. Celeste pointed my way, but the control freak overruled her. Carmen probably believed, and rightly so, that Celeste and I would be a force to reckon with.

Carmen argued her case as if in court. Winston eventually sided with her, probably because Perry's bat didn't pose a threat to his male ego.

"Don't dither any longer," intervened Gretchen. "Choose."

Rhonda switched her allegiance with Celeste and broke the impasse. Perry was selected, three to one. And just like that, I was without a team.

Rejected, I was ready to grab my bat and go home.

"The two groups must be even," directed Gretchen. Her cane tapped my arm. "Would you reconsider the first group?"

I glanced at them and mumbled, "If they'll have me." I gazed longingly at Celeste, then Thomas. "Can I join your family?"

Rosie huffed in a lilting brogue, "Only if ye'd be wantin' us."

I sucked up my pride. "I really want to."

Sam and Alana each grabbed a hand and pulled me into my new family: Thomas Barker, who passionately embraced a ministry of AIDS education; the dark-skinned Alana Saunders, who carted a truckload of abandonment issues; Sam Woodland, who knew heaps about the bush and men with addictions; and the fiery Rosie MacBain, who enjoyed conflict as much as the Scots loved whisky.

Gretchen instructed us to spend the afternoon identifying values and beliefs we wanted our family to embrace. Once we completed that task, we had to decide on a name to represent us.

As soon as we sat on our cushions, Rosie laid into me. "I can't believe ye'd be choosin' them over us."

"Let's not give him a hard time," pleaded Alana. "He's family now."

Rosie turned on her. "Why didn't ye pick me sooner?"

Sam interjected, "We knew you'd turn down the other group."

"There was no doubt you'd be with us," added Alana. "We wanted Peter, not Perry. So we had to choose him before you."

"He didn't accept, now, did he?" chafed Rosie.

"But he saw the light," added Thomas. He patted my knee. "You're on our team, mate. Glad to have you."

I smiled sheepishly and stole a quick peek across the room. Carmen was already arguing with her family. At least I didn't have the avenging angel.

Thomas assumed the role as captain. "We're supposed to discuss the positive attributes for our group and decide on a name."

We spent the afternoon doing just that. Alana didn't want anyone to feel rejected while Rosie expected togetherness, even during meals. Thomas promoted openness while Sam advocated a caring community. I merely wanted dinner with Celeste but wasn't game to say that. Rosie, still smarting about the selection process, was itching for a fight. I went along with the process and agreed with the others that openness, honesty, acceptance, and mutual support would be the hallmark values for our group. We then proclaimed ourselves, "The Family That Cares."

Frankly, I could've cared less. I pined for Celeste.

When we broke for dinner, I rushed to the loo and found Perry puffing madly on a cigarette while pissing in the urinal. I waved at the smoke.

"Bullshit," he raved. "Me girl tole me this weekend was gonna help. Me and you should get outa here, if you know what I mean."

Not without Celeste. I found her waiting outside.

She grabbed my arm. "I'm sorry, Peter. I tried. I really tried. Carmen was intractable."

"The bitch."

She moved closer and whispered. "That was sweet of you, wanting to be with me." Her cute dimples sprang to life. "Meet me outside after dinner."

The door crashed open and Perry barged out of the bathroom in a cloud of smoke. I spotted Rosie marching down the hall and ended our conversation with a wink and a nod.

In the dining area, the two groups ate on opposite sides of the room, like the Montagues and the Capulets. "The Family that Cares" versus "We're Right and Proud of It."

The pumpkin soup and vegetable casserole offered little comfort, so I doubled up on the peach cobbler. I gobbled it down, then waited for the right exit.

Outside, in a secluded spot near the front entrance, I heard the sweet voice.

"Glad I found you," cooed Celeste.

I melted into a warm embrace. Christ, she felt good. I gazed at her lovely fresh face—the tiny freckles dotting her nose and the soft, golden ringlets brushing her shoulder. I smelled the peach cobbler on her breath and longed to kiss sweet lips. Her mouth opened slightly and our faces inched closer, lips hungry.

"Out here," yelled Rosie. "I think he's out here."

Celeste and I jumped apart before Nosey Rosie appeared to cast a disdainful glance at us. "Peter, ye'd better come along."

Irritated by her intrusion, I asked, "What's the rush?"

"Gretchen's ready to start."

"Be there shortly."

When she left, I hissed, "It's a bloody conspiracy."

"It's so-o-o frustrating," agreed Celeste. Her eyes twinkled mischievously. "Meet me after tonight's session."

"If it's not raining, we can take a walk. Alone."

My co-conspirator giggled, then kissed my lips.

The taste of her peach cobbler made my legs go all wobbly.

"PETER!"

We dashed off before another emissary fetched the wayward children.

With luscious peaches on my mind, I smacked my lips through a series of family bonding exercises. We shared our birth order, the roles we played, our family wounds, and unmet needs. Then we processed—the code word for sharing. Alana wept more about her past, Thomas bared his shame, and Sam and Rosie commiserated about their failed marriages. I had no choice but to contribute.

"You have to be part of our family," said Alana.

"No holding back," added Sam.

"It's okay to share, mate," said Thomas.

"Quit thinkin' about her," grumbled Rosie.

I protested, "Expressing feelings doesn't come easy." I participated as best I could, but my mind wandered.

When Gretchen finally released us, I breathed a welcome sigh. Communicating in The Family That Cares was bloody exhausting.

I yawned. "It's been a long day. I'm going to bed."

Rosie eyed me suspiciously as Alana motioned for a group hug. That prompted Sam to propose a sunrise bush walk.

I groaned. "No thanks. I need a good night's rest."

I wiggled free from the hugging mass and left the others in the conference room along with Gretchen, who was mediating a dispute with the other group. I waited in my room until the rendezvous.

Resting on my bed, I fantasized about Celeste, imagining her as a water nymph emerging from a rock pool, her pink, supple breasts glistening in the sun. I wade into the water and nestle against her naked body. My mouth ravishes her lovely buds while my hands caress her flesh. We descend into the warm water, sinking deeper and deeper. Flesh on flesh.

"I need a smoke, mate," hacked Perry who bolted into the room.

I leapt from the bed. "Is your group finished?"

He rummaged in his duffel bag and removed a pack of cigarettes.

"Dunno, mate. The lawyer's a raving lunatic. Tole her I needed a smoke. Gettin' the craving again, if you know what I mean."

He struck a match.

"Outside."

He transformed into a snarling rat and glowered as if I had snatched his last morsel. "Need it, mate," he hissed. He lit the cigarette and inhaled as if there was no tomorrow.

I coughed. "The room's small. I won't be able to sleep."

"I'll have this one here," he sneered. "Maybe the next outside."

Just what I needed. A second miserable night's sleep. The cause of Perry's ugly transformation was undoubtedly Carmen.

"How's the group?"

He flicked ashes to the floor. "Don't wanna talk no more." He reached for the boom box. "Jailhouse Rock" played once again, louder than ever.

I pushed the window wide open and left. This would be my last night with the cretin. I'd talk with Gretchen tomorrow and demand a room change. My only solace was that Perry and Carmen were stuck together in the "We're Right and Proud of it Family." Served the bastards right.

I hid in the bathroom until I heard the rumble of feet climbing stairs. When doors closed, I crept silently down the hall. I spotted Celeste downstairs waving like an adolescent. The coast was clear.

I eased myself down the stairs and raised a finger. "Shh."

She grabbed my hand and led me to the empty dining area—a perfect hideaway. We were finally alone in the corner of the dark room, away from the others, away from processing. The only light emanated from a half-moon shining through the picture window. It cast a radiant aura over Celeste's face. White teeth glistened; hazel eyes sparkled.

"I wish you were in my family," she whispered.

"Likewise."

Her face inched toward mine. "I'm glad we found each other. Can you feel the tantric connection?"

Before I could answer, she kissed me. Gently, at first. Then her lips pressed hard against mine. Her tongue darted into my mouth and unleashed pent-up desire. Our mouths became ravenous. We consumed each other's peach cobbler. Celeste moaned and reached under my shirt. She stroked my chest. Electricity pulsed down my spine. I stiffened with excitement. It had been quite a while since I felt overwhelming passion.

She took my hands and placed them under her cashmere sweater. She purred and arched her firm breasts. I squeezed. Her breathing quickened. My quivering lips moved under her sweater to pluck a ripe grape.

"Yes," she begged. "Kiss them."

I sucked a juicy nipple until it stiffened.

"Mmmmm. Suck hard," she pleaded.

My mouth devoured her breasts, alternating one with the other. Her breathing quickened. She reached for my thighs and felt my hardness. I squirmed with delight. We collapsed to the polished wood floor.

My nose inhaled the pungent fragrance of sex juice. She directed my hand down to her jeans. "Mmmmm. Touch me there."

She was sopping wet. She beckoned me to climb on top. I wanted those creamy breasts, her darting tongue, her beckoning thighs, but I needed protection. I didn't want to end up like Thomas.

"Anyone here?"

I froze on the floor.

The lights flashed on.

I jumped to my feet. "Who's that?"

"Thought I heard some talking."

Like two teens caught making out, Celeste and I stared wide-eyed at our leader clutching a brightly flowered robe. Thank God, we weren't fully undressed. But then again, it was evident to the wily psychologist we weren't just processing the day's events.

"I was coming down for a midnight snack," she chuckled. "Heard some noise. It's late so I suggest you both get some rest. I'd prefer everyone fresh for tomorrow."

As Celeste struggled to her feet, Gretchen added, "Once the workshop is over, there'll be plenty of time for you to...well...be with each another."

Without saying a word, we sheepishly crept out of the room. We left our leader scrounging for food, but I wondered if she was part of the conspiracy to keep us apart. At the top of the stairs, I stole a sumptuous kiss, then departed. With mother Gretchen lurking about, I didn't want to linger or tempt fate until I was equipped with protection.

Not surprisingly, I didn't sleep. My mind kept drifting from pleasure to pain. From Celeste to Perry. She offered ecstasy; he provided agony. I gave up the struggle to force him to smoke outside and drifted in and out of a disturbed sleep.

Crash! I jumped at the loud thump. Bloody possum! I glared at the red eyes peering at me inside the cave. "Get!" I yelled.

The bush visitor scurried back into the scrub. Night had descended. Tiny, blinking lights flashed like headlights from the black forest. I prayed they were only nocturnal marsupials—kangaroos, wallabies, wombats, and possums. The cold air and the rustling noises in black space made me shiver.

Then came the mosquitoes, like kamikaze fighters. They zoomed around my ears. I stretched my T-shirt into a makeshift tent over my wounded head. Too exhausted to battle anymore, I crouched against the sandstone and closed my eyes, sinking back into a reverie.

I stirred when I heard the thud. Perry picked up the fallen duffle bag.

I rubbed my eyes. "What time is it?"

"Seven," he snarled.

"Why are you packing? It's Saturday. The workshop doesn't end till tomorrow."

With a cigarette dangling from his lips, he stuffed his gear into the khaki bag. "No worries, if you know what I mean."

I doubted if I'd ever know what he meant. I coughed. "Please put out the cigarette."

He said nothing. He packed the boom box, unplugged the clock, and left with a bag much fuller than when he arrived. After realizing the clock belonged to the room, I scurried out of bed to check if he'd pilfered my clothes. The scoundrel had rifled through my suitcase. He left the clothes but stole my cache of strawberry licorice. I checked under my pillow. Thank God, my car keys were there.

I threw on some clothes and rushed to check my laptop and wallet in the car. Yesterday's pre-emptive action to secure my valuables had thwarted a disaster. Perry was nowhere in sight. He was either hightailing it to the train station or hitching a lift back to Sydney.

When I walked into the dining room, Sam waved toward me. "We saved a seat."

I glanced longingly at Celeste encamped with her family on the other side of the room. I smiled at her until I caught Rosie's frown.

She groused, "Ye'd better be payin' attention to us."

The sleepless night made me snap. "Can I pay attention to my breakfast?"

"Testy, are we?"

"Let him be," said Sam. She pointed her fork at the buffet. "Get some tucker and join us."

I grabbed a bowl of muesli, then sat glumly between Thomas and Alana.

"You missed an incredible bush walk," said Alana, way too enthusiastically. She displayed a swatch of yellow flowers above her ear while Sam wore a sprig of eucalyptus leaves.

"Before sunrise, a magical mist covered Jamison Valley in white froth," gushed the bush woman. "Alana and I blessed the new day."

Outside, the sun peeped through gray clouds at the golden sandstone cliffs, which stood majestically above the lush green valley.

On the veranda, a red and blue rosella perched itself on the feeding tray along with a younger bird with olive-green feathers and a gaping mouth.

Alana motioned toward them. "That momma's having a dickens of a time feeding its chick."

I grunted and attacked my meal.

"I wonder if that baby ever feels rejected."

"Birds don't have feelings," I told her.

"That's not true," corrected Sam, assuming the role as chief ornithologist. "Some birds grieve the loss of their mates."

I stole a peek at Celeste. "Probably depends on the mate."

"What a glorious morning," announced Gretchen cheerfully. Dressed in purple slacks and a violet sweater, she shuffled into the dining area. She chuckled, "Some of you stayed up late. Hope you conserved energy."

I averted her gaze and crunched my muesli.

Gretchen launched into the day's itinerary. She instructed us to use breakfast as a planning session for a family excursion after lunch. She suggested a trip into nature, since the rain had stopped.

Carmen raised her hand. "If we prefer indoors, where would you suggest?"

Our leader reached for a banana muffin. "If you want culture, visit the Writer's House at Varuna, the home of Eleanor Dark."

Smarty-pants Carmen quipped, "I read her classic trilogy, *The Timeless Land*."

"Indeed," nodded Gretchen. "Or perhaps you could visit Norman Lindsey's Gallery in Faulconbridge."

That would have been my choice if Celeste and I were together. Norman had an array of nude paintings and sculptures.

"There's so much to see in the Blue Mountains," continued Gretchen. "Alas, you won't find the red waratah, our state flower, this time of year. Don't fret. There are plenty of gorgeous flowers in bloom. Start planning. Meanwhile, I'll check on Perry."

I stopped eating. "He packed and left."

She reacted as if stabbed in the heart. "You should have said something, my dear."

"I just did."

"I'll check." With her cane leading the way, she quickened her pace.

Rosie sipped her tea. "Perry's a ruddy idiot."

"At least I'll get a good night's sleep."

Thomas rapped his spoon on the table. "Let's not get off task. Gretchen asked us to plan an excursion. I'd like to see waterfalls. Any will do—Leura Cascades, Wentworth Falls, or the one in Katoomba. With all the rain, they should be spectacular."

Rosie grimaced. "I'm wantin' to shop and pick up a few prezzies for the kids. We could have tea and scones in town."

Sam had other plans. "We should walk down the Giant Stairway near the Three Sisters."

"That's a steep climb down the face of a cliff to the valley," I protested. "There's millions of steps."

"Less than a thousand," she corrected.

"They'll be slippery as hell." I turned to Rosie for support. "No shops on those treacherous stairs."

"We'll take it slow," reassured Sam.

Rosie grunted. "I'd be votin' for something gentler."

Our Filipina member intervened. "That descent can be difficult. Let's do something we can all enjoy."

Sam huffed, "As long as we're in nature."

I would've preferred time with Celeste. Since the groups were going separate ways, I offered another alternative. "How about the cable car ride over the gorge?"

"If you're looking for a view," said Sam, "it's on the valley floor."

"There are poisonous snakes out there."

She swatted away my comment. "They're shy. Make any noise and they'll scoot out of your way."

Rosie's eyes bulged. "Shoppin's a wee bit safer."

"Oh, for heaven's sake," said Sam, exasperated. "We're meant to be in the bush."

"A bush in the highlands is a beautiful shrub," whined Rosie, "not a forest."

Sam raised her eyebrows. "Well, this is Australia, not Scotland."

Thomas wiped yogurt off his upper lip, then tapped the table with his spoon. "Remember, we're The Family That Cares."

He summarized our interests—visit a waterfall, sightsee, spend time in nature, and shop. He proposed a compromise: take the Scenic Railway down to the valley instead of walking the thousand steps. The path below was well marked and was a short hike to Katoomba Falls. After we returned on the train, we could spend time in the souvenir shop and revolving restaurant. Thomas's suggestion ministered to most of our needs, even though Sam argued for a five-kilometer bush walk, and Rosie and I grumbled about the creepy crawlies.

Gretchen interrupted our debate, looking very distressed. "No sign of Perry," she fretted. "Never had a participant leave. A few threaten to go, but I've always helped them face their fear."

Taking his departure personally, she called us to the conference room to process the loss. Rather than grieving the Elvis wannabe, I secretly celebrated. No more loud music and imaginary guitar playing, and no more cigarette smoke and smelly farts. I had the room to myself, and hopefully, a late night visitor. I planned to stop at a chemist for condoms after the group excursion.

We returned to the cushions and listened to the crestfallen psychologist. "Losing someone triggers rejection. I feel dreadful. Does anyone know why he left?"

Carmen spoke first. "Perry shared a room with Peter. I know firsthand about Peter's penchant for making fun of others."

I glared at her dangling angels. "As a matter of fact, he did complain. About YOU."

"How dare you–"

Gretchen intervened before the fireworks exploded. "Let's redirect our anger, shall we? We're mad that Perry abandoned us."

I was tired and cranky and spoiled for a fight. Bring it on.

Our leader glanced warily at me and Carmen, then made a decision. "Perhaps each family should process this loss. Make sure everyone speaks and is heard. We don't want to lose anyone else."

Gretchen stayed with the other group. The Family That Cares moved to an opposite corner where I ranted about Carmen. We spent the rest of the morning processing our feelings about rejection, abandonment, and loss. By the time we adjourned, I was more than ready for an excursion, as long as it was outside with no processing.

We grabbed an early lunch and received final instructions from Gretchen to return by dinner. We bundled into Sam's Land Cruiser and headed to the popular tourist attraction, Scenic World. Five minutes from the lodge, the Scenic Railway was housed in the same facility as the Skyway and the soon-to-be-finished eighty-passenger Cableway that would cart tourists to the valley floor.

We clambered aboard the railway, a far cry from a typical train. Open-faced like a roller coaster, with a metal screen acting as the roof, the carriage plunged 400 meters in a near-vertical drop through the bush and sandstone rock. I was expecting a scenic ride, not a heart-stopping nose-dive. I held on for dear life!

When the train halted on the valley floor, I staggered off. "The Skyway would've been far better," I sneered.

"Don't be silly," chided Sam. "Imagine the old days. Coal miners used the railway to haul coal and shale."

"I'm not a miner, and I'm not fond of trains in free-fall."

She ignored me and removed her shoes and socks. She pocketed the socks, tied the laces together, then tossed the shoes over her shoulder. The sturdy woman stamped her feet hard against the ground. "When you walk barefoot, the land will guide you."

She removed a yellow bandanna from her neck and wrapped it around her head, leaving a tuft of spiked gray hair sprouting from the center. She plucked leaves off a nearby eucalyptus tree, sniffed them, then stuffed them inside the bandanna. She pocketed her diamond wedding ring.

"No need for material possessions," she said. "Nature provides in her own way."

With Sam's transformation as Earth Mother complete, she stamped her right foot on the ground. "Toward Katoomba Falls."

I waved the brochure in the opposite direction. "There's an elevated boardwalk that way. It passes the coalmine. Let's have a gander."

I wanted to follow the gaggle of tourists on the walkway, but Sam would have none of that.

"We're here to walk *on* the land, not above it." She marched toward the falls.

I could either fall in line or be left behind. I begrudgingly joined Thomas, Alana, and Rosie on the meandering dirt path known as Federal Pass along the base of the escarpment. The bare-footed Sam trudged ahead, oblivious to the stones and twigs. She stopped abruptly at a massive turpentine tree and faced the canopy.

"Do you know why this area's called the Blue Mountains?"

Before anyone could reply, she answered. "Nature colors the bush with a deep shade of blue when the light reflects the dust and oil of the eucalyptus trees."

Earth Mother strolled forward and lectured us about the land formed more than 200 million years ago. She grabbed a waxy leaf from a nearby tree and crushed it in her hand to smell the eucalyptus.

"The trees secrete a gummy sap, hence the name gum trees."

Continuing the bush tour, she pointed out flowers and fallen feathers and the telltale droppings of a wombat. "Won't see them during the day," she said.

When we heard the sound of splashing water, Thomas yelled, "Around the bend."

He lumbered past Sam and rushed to the bridge facing Katoomba Falls. Compared to Niagara or Victoria Falls, it seemed more like spit dribbling over a cliff. A slow, steady stream of water poured down 250 meters and splashed over the weathered gray, orange, and yellow escarpment onto the rocks below, flowing into a creek that fed the Kedumba River. A fine spray baptized us as the afternoon sun peeped through the overcast clouds. Light glistened off the falling water and formed a dazzling rainbow.

"Awesome!" proclaimed Thomas who, like a kid, clambered past the metal railing and down to a foaming pool.

Despite the grim specter of HIV hanging like a guillotine, the gentle giant acted as if there was no tomorrow. He removed his green shirt with the picture of a soaring eagle, then his shoes.

I yelled. "We're supposed to stay on the trail."

He waded into the water. "Nonsense, mate."

I looked around for a sign. The only posted warning cautioned visitors to bring water, wear warm clothes and sturdy shoes, and abstain from fires. Nothing about staying on the track. But there was a clear reminder: last train up at 4:55 p.m.

I stumbled down to the pool where the others splashed their bare feet. Thomas kicked cold water at me.

"Hey," I flinched. "Pick on Rosie."

She scowled. "Ye'd better not."

Alana paddled her feet. "We should've brought snacks and drinks."

"There's plenty of bush tucker around," said Sam. She sipped water from a rock pool. "Ahhh. That's better. Katoomba's an Aboriginal word and means shiny tumbling waters."

I walked over to Rosie who was sitting on a boulder and asked, "Didn't you want souvenirs for your kids?"

Her eyes twinkled. "Aye."

"We have plenty of time," interjected Sam. "There's lots to see."

Thomas slipped on his shoes. "Lead on."

I groused, "Rosie wants to go shopping." Not that I cared, but dark clouds were rolling in. A snug restaurant was far preferable than trundling in the rain.

Sam convinced the others to follow, so I trailed behind them past towering sandstone cliffs and moss-covered rocks through lush rainforest and tall eucalypts. After walking some distance, I was about to demand we turn back when our tour guide did the unthinkable. She veered off the track and descended a steep slope into thick woods.

"Come on," she waved.

Rosie and I halted.

I yelled, "Hold on."

Sam trudged back up and grabbed Rosie's arm. "I know you love flowers. But we have to get off the beaten path to see them. Come, I'll help you down."

Despite Rosie's protests, Sam enlisted the aid of Thomas. They each grabbed an arm and guided Rosie down the slope.

"I'll break a leg for sure."

"I've got you," reassured Thomas.

Alana reached for my hand. I declined her offer, preferring a tall stick to steady myself. I stumbled into a batch of prickly vines and had to disentangle myself. I scrutinized every twig to make sure it wasn't a poisonous snake.

Lagging behind, I called out, "Hold on, don't lose me!"

Sam stopped ahead near a mound of compacted yellow dirt as tall as Thomas.

Puffing hard, I caught up with the others, who listened intently to our guide's lecture.

"Termites were used by the Aborigines to make the didgeridoo."

I cared less about the long, wooden instrument hollowed out by ugly critters. "Sam, can we please go?"

A cackling, bubbling sound startled me. "What's that?"

Sam sighed at my stupidity. "A noisy friarbird. If you hush up, you'll also hear the piping whistles of butcherbirds and yodeling currawongs." She trudged deeper into the woods. "Now look here," she exclaimed. "A mountain devil."

She plucked reddish tubular flowers with two horns off a shrub and offered them around. "Aborigines call it devil flower. Taste the sweet nectar. The honeyeaters love it."

"Mmmm," said Alana, reaching for another.

I was in no sucking mood. The morning's muesli had kicked in and my intestines signaled their intention. Drops of rain spurred me to act.

"We need to get back to the train before it pours."

Ignoring me, she snatched green leaves from a crimson bottle-brush. "Crush these and smell the citrus."

I refused the offer and suppressed another urge. "You go on ahead," I told the group. "I'll catch up with you in a moment."

"Where're you going?" asked Sam.

Did I have to make an announcement? "Nature's calling."

"We'll wait for you."

I waved off the audience. "I'll catch up to you after I...you know."

"If you have to take a dump, grab a stick and dig a hole," she said, more concerned about the bloody environment than my need for relief. If I had asked for tissues, Sam, no doubt, would've instructed me to use leaves.

I scrambled deeper into the dense woods so no one would see my ass hanging over a hole. At a time like this, a bloke needed privacy.

Upon Rosie's insistence to get out of the rain, Sam led the group back up the steep incline. "Don't stray too far," she yelled.

"I'm not a bloody idiot," I hissed. I stumbled downward, away from the voices.

Sam was now spouting Henry Lawson's poem, *The Blue Mountains*:

Above the ashes straight and tall,
Through ferns with moisture dripping,
I climb beneath the sandstone wall,
My feet on mosses slipping.

I cursed her as I slipped on slimy rocks and plodded past ferns and blue gums, deeper into the bush. I tripped over a fallen stringy-bark and righted myself. My bowels groaned. I scratched at the leaves and fallen branches with my stick. This was no time to shit on a snake. With my intestines ready to burst, I dropped my pants. Then I spotted it. The biggest damn python basking itself on a fallen log, several feet away. It flicked its tongue then slithered toward me.

Sam had warned us that diamond pythons were in the area but said we'd never see one. Wrong again! Marked by yellow diamonds, the large snake moved closer. I dumped and jumped. This was no time to bury the past.

I yanked up my pants and backed off into the bush, cautiously scanning for more snakes. Something bit me on the leg. I screamed. Bloody leeches! Crawling up my shoes and ankles. In a panic, I ran recklessly. Nowhere. Anywhere. Just to get away from the sucking bastards. I stomped any leech crossing my path and dashed deeper into the dense forest until I slipped on a moss-covered log and plummeted down the steep ravine. I came to a crashing halt when my head collided against the tree.

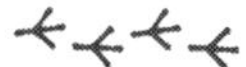

I shivered in the makeshift cave. Exhausted, hungry and cold, I had given up the battle. I rested my woozy head against the sandstone. Images came and went. I was entering another world.

A weathered Aborigine, with a white, scraggy beard and matted hair stands beside me. Wearing only a loincloth, he holds a fiery torch that lights a face marked with white lines and ocher dots. His body is painted in ghostly chalk. He stamps his feet, beating to the rhythm of my throbbing head. He sings a strange incantation.

"Cooee," yelled a voice. "Cooee!"

My mind spins. The eucalyptus trees sway to the rhythm of his song. Kangaroos and hairy-nosed wombats emerge from the dark night. Long-nosed bandicoots and bush rats join echidnas and snakes, lizards and frogs. They gather around the Aborigine. A kookaburra lands on his shoulder with a purple flower in its beak. The Aborigine takes the delicate flower with feathery fringes and places it around my head. He sings another incantation. Words fade. He holds the torch near my eyes.

"Cooee," came the shout. "Cooee!"
The elder pulls at my shirt. "Wake up."
I squinted at the light and trembled. "Who are you?"
"It's me," shouted the figure.
The Aborigine morphed into a face with a yellow bandanna sprouting feathers and flowers.
"I found him. He's over here!" Sam shined a light into the cold night.
Heavy tramping snapped twigs. Thomas's massive frame appeared. He grabbed one of my arms and heaved me from the cave.

"You alright, mate? We'll get you into a warm bed." He removed his jacket and covered my shoulders.

"How did you find me?"

"I finally picked up your tracks," said Sam. She removed her bandanna and fastened it around the gash on my forehead.

"Let's go, mate," said Thomas. He helped me to my feet. "You need a hot meal, and, by the look of it, some stitches."

Sam led the return journey, shining the small light while Thomas half-carried me up the steep incline. When we arrived back on Federal Pass, he grabbed a fallen branch and broke it in half. He handed it to me for support.

"Where are Alana and Rosie?"

"I sent them for help," said Sam. "Fortunately, I ran into a backpacker who gave us his spare light. I hope the batteries hold."

"I thought we'd never find you in the dark," said Thomas. He squeezed my shoulder.

I winced. "That's the last time I take a crap in the bush."

As I trudged along, the pain in my body returned with a vengeance. My skull pounded and my bruised hip throbbed with every step. My scraped elbow and lower arm hurt like hell. While the bandanna protected my forehead, I suspected some of the leech wounds oozed blood. Lightheaded, I tripped on a tree root.

Thomas caught me before I fell. "Easy, mate."

Sam shined the light my way. "You okay?"

"Will be as soon as I'm out of this bloody place."

She moved closer. "Why did you pick the fringe-lilies?"

"What are you talking about?"

"The violet flowers. There were some next to you."

I rubbed the bandanna. "I didn't pick any."

"Someone placed them there."

"Maybe I was delirious and picked them."

"Aborigines place fringe-lilies around the head of someone who suffers a trauma. It's supposed to protect them."

I thought of the Aboriginal elder, but said nothing. I didn't need any of Sam's folklore about bush magic. I needed a doctor, not a shaman.

We said no more and continued our journey through the cold night. I leaned on Thomas and the crude staff, and shuffled along as best I could, stopping periodically to catch my breath. When I spotted twinkling lights ahead, I quickened my pace.

At the foot of the railway, several men gathered with searchlights. Alana bolted from the group and rushed toward me with outstretched arms. "Oh my God, they found you."

"Ouch," I gasped.

She released her hold. "Oops. Sorry. But you're alive. I'd never forgive myself if anything happened."

Hell, if anyone deserved the blame, it was Sam. I shuddered at the prospect of spending a night with noxious creatures.

A burly bloke from Bush Rescue approached. "You okay, mate?"

"I guess."

He eyed my bandaged head. "We were about to set out with a search party."

He called topside and spoke into his walkie-talkie.

"Rosie's at the top," said Alana. "She harassed the staff to stay put until we found you."

The burly bloke ushered us aboard the train. I was grateful my exhausted and bruised body didn't have to climb the near-vertical ascent. As soon as the train wrenched its way to the top, I collapsed into the seat.

↞↞

I stayed overnight in Katoomba hospital. The doctor wanted to make sure there were no complications from the concussion. No broken bones, but I did need seven stitches to close the gash. A nurse found a leech in my sock, engorged with my vintage red. Bloody mongrel!

I lay in bed, surrounded by my companions, and reflected on the fact that Sam and Thomas had scoured the terrain with one small light, and that Rosie and Alana remained vigilant, from top to bottom, alerting bush rescue and maintaining watch. They were truly a family that cared.

Despite their reassurance that it could've happened to anyone, I felt like a bloody fool. I envisioned a headline in the *Herald*: "Bushwalker gets lost with his pants down."

"Ye had a wee bit o' luck down there," said Rosie. "Last month, a young couple went missing for days. The girl was bitten by a snake and died. He barely..."

"Peter needs his sleep," interrupted Sam. She frowned at Rosie. "He doesn't need a bedtime horror story."

Alana stroked my head. "I'm glad you're safe."

"Sure are, mate," said Thomas.

I smiled back at my newfound friends and snuggled under the covers. I closed my eyes and entered dreamland.

FINAL DAY OF WORKSHOP

SUNDAY, FEBRUARY 27

Clapsticks clacking. Didgeridoo droning. Full moon shining. Fire crackles, casting shadows against Aborigine. Scraggly hair and white beard surround a weathered face. He paints white lines and ocher dots on my cheeks, nose, forehead. He smears white clay across my naked body. The wind howls. A didgeridoo drones. The Aborigine claps his hands and stamps his feet. A kookaburra flies from a tree. Into the fire. Hss! Smoke rises from the burning coals. Forms bold letters: B-A-I-A-M-E.

The word flashed in my mind like a neon sign when I woke. I pondered the dream as I waited for Sam. She insisted on collecting me from the hospital to make amends for taking us on the road less traveled.

She handed me a large paper sack. "Thomas grabbed clean clothes from your suitcase."

I changed in the bathroom and cringed at the thought of Thomas packing my underwear. I washed my hands twice. I adjusted the one-armed glasses precariously on my nose and followed Sam to the nursing station to sign the discharge papers. With a stitched forehead, slight concussion, bruised hip, and scraped arms, I felt lucky to be alive.

Sam pulled away in her Land Cruiser and asked how I'd slept.

I hesitated a moment, then blurted about my dream and the word "Baiame."

She stopped abruptly by the curb. Her hawkish brown eyes sparkled. "Has the Koori visited you before?"

"Yesterday, in a dream. He placed fringe-lilies around my head. But I told you last night that I must've picked the flowers. I was disoriented."

"Strange things happen in the bush," she said. "Especially when you're cut off from nature. I saw you arrive at the workshop with an oversized suitcase and a laptop."

"So?" I said defensively.

"Aborigines believe Spirit is always with us. If we don't listen, Spirit creates a crisis or speaks through dreams to get our attention. You experienced both."

"And the message is?" I asked disdainfully.

"Baiame is the great spirit in creation. He's the master of life and death. Your dream is calling you to go within and connect with Spirit."

"What about the kookaburra? It flew into the fire. Does that mean I'm about to get roasted?"

"It's your totem."

"Which is?"

She pulled away from the curb. "An animal that offers wisdom or power."

"Great. I get a laughing jackass."

"A kookaburra is very significant," she said earnestly. "One Aboriginal legend describes how Baiame, after he created the world, hung a bright star in the sky. It's said that the kookaburra laughed before the first ray of light to wake humans from their sleep."

"I'd prefer an eagle."

"Spirit provides what we need. My totem is a goanna. The large lizard reminds me to stay close to Mother Earth."

She parked near the Lodge. "Let's go inside. Gretchen and the others are anxious to see you."

I stepped out of the car and heard the familiar call. *Koo-koo-koo-koo-koo-ka-ka-ka-ka-ka.*

"Remember," said Sam. "When you hear a kookaburra, it's time to wake up."

Unsettled by the bird's eerie laugh, I followed Sam into the conference room. Gretchen and the two groups immediately stopped their processing and applauded my arrival.

Our leader rushed forward and clutched me to her chest. "Thank God, you're safe," she cried. "I couldn't bear to lose another."

I almost lost my glasses in her gripping embrace. I stuffed them in my pocket while I faced the onslaught of hugs from my family. Celeste was next in line and kissed me on the cheek.

"I sent you lots of love," she whispered.

I inhaled lavender and gently squeezed her. "Missed you."

A few others barged in for a welcoming hug. Carmen was the exception. I overheard her tell the Englishman, "It's amazing what he'll do for attention."

I was in no mood for a dust-up. I veered away from the angel lady when Gretchen called us to order.

"Now that Peter has happily returned, let's return to our commitments."

Thomas brought his cushion next to mine. "Before we leave, we're supposed to clarify our goals and commit to change. I decided to forgive Gary and his betrayal, and find my true self."

"I'm not ready to forgive the ex," chafed Rosie. "But a good man would do me just fine. I'm lookin' for love."

"I want to break free from my past," added Sam. "No more enabling. Charles has to give up gambling or else he's history." She squeezed Alana's hand. "And what about you?"

Her deep-set eyes glistened with tears. "I'm saying goodbye to abandonment," said Alana. "I need love and acceptance."

Sam wrapped her arms around her. "I love you just the way you are."

Alana dabbed her eyes. "And I love you." She reached out her hand to me. "I love you too, Peter."

Her words prompted the five of us to huddle close and bask in heartfelt appreciation for one another. Thomas nudged my arm. "What about your goals, mate?"

I glanced at Sam. "Seems that I'm called to wake up and find my way. Finding a job would make it a hell of a lot easier."

"What kind of position are you after?" asked Sam.

"Anything would do, but I'd prefer counseling adults and couples."

Alana, Rosie, and Sam glanced at each other conspiratorially. They nodded in unison.

"As it so happens," said Sam gleefully, "our agency needs a psychologist, and preferably a male to balance the team."

Alana's eyes brightened. "Sam *is* the clinical director."

"Do you think I'd have a chance?"

Sam winked. "I'll put in a good word for you. You are family, so to speak."

Rosie sniggered, "Ye'd better not get lost."

I laughed, "Make sure there are no leeches."

"I'm feeling left out," groused Thomas.

We pulled him into a group embrace. I peeked at the other family and saw Gretchen repairing a rift between Carmen and the Englishman. Celeste caught my eye and glanced heavenward in exasperation. Carmen and her angels were tooting again.

When Gretchen restored order, she beckoned us to gather round. She rested against her wooden cane and gazed lovingly at her brood. "My dears, when you go within, you will never be without. Signs will mysteriously appear and point you home."

She raised the cane like a magic wand and tapped each head. "You explored who you are and your roles and patterns. You uncovered fears, took risks, and faced pain. You discovered needs and wants, and overcame adversity. You created a new family and, with it, a sense of belonging. You forged new goals and opened your hearts to love."

She rested her cane on the floor. "Our time is at an end, my dears. But before you leave, make follow-up plans."

Gretchen told us that we needed ongoing support to battle the negative messages from the past. We were asked to exchange phone numbers and addresses and meet regularly with our group. Each family was supposed to select a person to keep Gretchen informed of our progress. Alana was unanimously chosen for that role. She was so pleased, her broad smile revealed her chipped tooth.

Organizing a follow-up meeting proved to be difficult. Everyone, except me, was heavily booked. Rosie was committed to her children's band, Thomas was organizing a men's conference on AIDS, and Sam and Alana had professional commitments. After considerable negotiation, we agreed to meet in three weeks at Sam's house. A group hug sealed the pact.

Before sending us off, Gretchen herded us into a circle. Like a proud mother, she gave final instructions: *INSPECT* thoughts daily by journaling; REJECT negative thoughts if they pop into mind; SELECT loving and affirming beliefs; PROJECT them into the world with love; EXPECT positive results; ACCEPT victories.

She ran her hand through snow-white hair. "Great victories consist of many smaller ones. Even though the Olympics won't start until September, you already carry the torch. Hold onto the glowing light that resides within. You are my Olympians running the marathon. I cheer you toward the finish line."

Tears welled in her eyes. "We lost one member." She nodded toward me. "We could have lost another. Victories without hardship are hollow and offer little cause for celebration."

She clutched a hand of the person on either side and asked us to follow her lead. "Let us celebrate an ending and a beginning. Join me in song."

We are in this together, we are one.
As we walk on our journey,
From the darkness to the light,
We come home all together, we are one.

We swayed as a group and sang the verse a second time. We finished with hugs. Some of the women cried. Celeste and I languished in a long embrace before exchanging phone numbers. I longed for a passionate kiss. That would come later, without a crowd.

After more goodbyes, I packed my car and drove toward Sydney. Before the workshop, I was unemployed, anxious, and depressed. I was now departing with newfound friends, the prospect of a job, and a budding love relationship. As I wove through traffic, I thought of Dorothy in the *Wizard of Oz* and hummed the tune, "Somewhere over the rainbow."

It was time to return home.

LEAP YEAR

TUESDAY, FEBRUARY 29

Ba-boom, ba-boom.

Woof. Woof. Nesha jumped on my bed and nuzzled my sheets. *Woof. Woof.* Crikey! Two in the morning.

Ba-boom, ba-boom, ba-boom.

I hated my bloody neighbors. When they moved in four months ago, 582 North Steyne turned into a war zone. The adjoining wall on the second floor of a four-flat vibrated.

Ba-boom, ba-boom. The twang of a guitar blared from an electronic percussion box.

I imagined the sweet scent of marijuana permeating the flat. I banged on the wall. He twanged louder. I heard him and his girlfriend laugh. The feral mongrels were a nightmare, sleeping by day, playing at night. I stopped counting the times I awakened to his guitar and their caterwauling.

I had wrongly assumed the emaciated girlfriend would be the sensible one, but she ended up being the most abusive. When I had politely asked her to keep the noise down, she told me to fuck off. Bloody stoners. Hard living, boozing, and drugging had ravaged their thirty-year-old bodies marked with weird tattoos and an array of posts, hoops, and other dangling paraphernalia. His ear lobes had more metal than flesh, and her face looked like a pincushion. My diagnosis: polysubstance dependent with personality disorders up the wazoo.

Woof. Woof.

"You hate them too, don't you, Nesha?"

Twan-g-g-g-g. Ba-boom, ba-boom. Twan-g-g-g-g.

I wasn't going to phone the police again. The last time I called, I found trash dumped across my doorstep the next day and a long, deep scratch on my car door. I couldn't prove it was the morons, so the police did bugger-all.

I once countered by blasting my stereo next to their bedroom wall during the day. No response. They were so stoned or drunk, they were out like the Grateful Dead.

I had complained at the real estate office. The staff was as useless as pockets on underpants. As long as they received the rent and property wasn't destroyed, no action would be taken.

I sought support from Mrs. Faughlin, the elderly neighbor downstairs, but she suffered from an obsessive-compulsive disorder and often forgot to wear her hearing aids. I doubted whether she heard anything while she forever polished her windows.

My only respite came when their hard rock band played at the pubs. During those gigs, they'd stay out late and wouldn't arrive until the morning. By that time, I was able to catch a few winks.

Woof. Woof.

"We'll get them evicted," I told my faithful companion.

A cross between a bull terrier and a shorthaired pointer, Nesha had little bite but his loud bark sometimes acted as a deterrent. This morning I encouraged him. "Bad neighbors."

Woof. Woof.

I banged on the wall again and thought of the sign, "Welcome to the Magic of Manly," which greeted residents and tourists to Sydney's beach suburb. At 2:00 a.m. I wasn't feeling magical nor manly. Moving would solve the problem, but I didn't want to give up a one-bedroom apartment across from the beach.

Then the music, if you'd call it that, stopped. At first, I assumed my last rap on the wall had banged some sense into the cretins. Wrong.

I heard giggling and scuffling. Their bed squeaked and groaned. Since our bedrooms shared a paper-thin wall, I suffered through their vocal display of X-rated sounds. The girlfriend, who fancied herself a singer, rasped, "Suck me!" When her high-pitched voice squealed, I figured he was doing just that!

The fact that I could hear them must have stimulated their frenzied exhibition. "Yes. Faster," she yelled.

Our communal wall shook. I pictured two naked bodies pressing metal against tattooed flesh as he vigorously pumped her.

"Harder," she screamed.

Make it real hard and quick, I wished.

Woof. Woof.

The couple concluded their hard rock rendition of orgasmic music, twanging and ba-booming one another on the squeaking bed. When the heavy breathing and piercing moans finally halted, I slipped back to sleep, only to be disturbed by dreams about getting pierced by my naked, tattooed neighbors.

Clink. Clank. Clang. Bottles clattered! My hand fumbled for the clock. Bloody hell! 5:45. Like clockwork on Tuesday mornings, the garbos emptied the bins of trash and recyclable containers. *CRASH!* I wanted to ignite a rag in a bottle of petrol and toss it at their truck. *Kaboom.* No more garbos!

Nesha pounced on the bed with a shaggy duck in his mouth. I grabbed the raggy toy that quacked when squeezed. *Woof. Woof.* I tossed it to across the room. He bounded after it and returned with it quacking.

Exasperated, I shouted, "Okay, I'm up. Happy now?"

After I returned from my weekend of love and acceptance, Nesha had regressed to the clingy puppy who had once been abandoned to the Royal

Society for the Prevention of Cruelty to Animals. When I collected him from the kennel, he barked excitedly like the first time I spotted him, five years ago. His charcoal body sported large white spots on three of his paws. The cream zigzag on his tail waved like a metronome.

I grabbed my new pair of glasses, threw on a shirt and shorts, then led him across the street to the park overlooking the beach. He immediately found his favorite watering pole, the one with a posted sign: "Dogs allowed on a leash under the effective control of a competent person. Dog feces are to be removed immediately and properly disposed of by the person in control of the dog." Words obviously weren't enough for the city council. The sign showed graphic pictures of the proper way to collect and dispose of dog poo. I was well armed with my plastic bag and scooper.

Having completed his duty, Nesha barked and ran after the seagulls. While he could be a pain at times, he was my best friend. With my loyal companion at my side, I inhaled the salty air and sauntered on the beach, the cool sand beneath my bare feet. I found a piece of driftwood and tossed it into the water. "Fetch."

Nesha dashed into the waves and returned with the stick in his mouth. He pranced on the sand, begging for another throw. Thus began our morning ritual.

As the sun rose over the blue sea, we passed a fisherman trolling for silver tailor. With a burlap bag hitched to his side, he stood in the surf and cast a lure from his beach rod into the frothy ocean. Every cast disturbed the hovering sea gulls.

At that time of the morning, only fishermen, diehard joggers, surfboarders, and dogs with their owners took advantage of the beach. Though I never saw the shark nets floating beneath the ocean, I always wondered if they were secure. I never ventured out far, figuring it'd be my luck to run into a hammerhead.

We finished our morning with a rinse at the outdoor tap. I backed away as Nesha shook himself dry. When we returned to the flat, he immediately rushed to the toilet for his preferred drink. Despite my attempts at behavior modification, I had a hard time getting him to use the water bowl in the kitchen. My only recourse was to make sure I always flushed the toilet.

I patted Nesha dry with a dirty towel from the hamper, then tossed it into the bundle of soiled clothes from the weekend. The Laundromat could not be postponed any longer. My mother would go bonkers if she saw the dirty dishes, piles of papers, and layers of dust. Monet's framed print of a stormy sea, *Rough Weather at Etretat*, sat idle in the corner, waiting to be hung.

I fed Nesha and grabbed a bowl of cereal. I cleared an empty space on the coffee table in the lounge room and plopped on the couch. It faced the sliding glass door to a tiny balcony with a view of the beach. Actually, the balcony was nothing more than a ledge with enough room for some potted plants. Anything more spacious would have cost me dearly.

After breakfast, I checked email. Nothing from my old friend, Surjit Bhullar. The child psychiatrist had once been a mentor on my first job, which eventually had turned out to be a Down Under version of *One Flew over the Cuckoo's Nest* set in a children's psychiatric department. That horrendous experience nearly made me cuckoo forevermore. I tried to keep in touch with Surjit, who now worked in Adelaide. With a quirky, metaphysical bent, he didn't give emails a high priority. I tapped a quick message. "Where the hell are you?"

I updated my résumé, then wrote a covering letter to Dr. Herbert Norton, Director of Queenscliffe Counseling Centre for Change. Following Sam's suggestion, I phoned him yesterday to inquire about a job. He sounded interested and asked me to email the letter and résumé. It was time to take the big leap. As Gretchen put it, a big victory was made up of smaller ones. I pressed the *send* button.

"Wish me luck," I told Nesha. He barked his support.

"Want to go for a ride?"

He immediately bolted for the door.

"Hold on. Let's get the laundry."

As I bagged the dirty clothes, I heard the steady stream coming from the next-door toilet. The cretin was emptying his bladder. The intake of booze made him and his partner frequent visitors to the loo. I had complained about the lack of soundproofing to the realtors, but they said nothing could be done. The building was old; I'd have to live with it.

With laundry bag in hand, I passed Mrs. Faughlin, standing outside in her familiar attire—pink curlers and matching housecoat. She waged a never-ending battle against the sea and sand sprayed against her windows. She scowled as she spritzed the glass with blue cleaner.

Nesha sniffed her bathrobe. I tugged at the leash and yelled, "Get away" before she could spray him.

The Laundromat was packed. I jammed three loads into the two available washing machines. Once the cycle started, I strolled outdoors with Nesha and headed toward the beach. At the south end, an elderly man, tanned and leathered, in skimpy Speedos, baked on the sand near a couple of topless young beauties. He gawked shamelessly at them. I suspected the lifesavers shared his vision. No doubt, they kept a sharper lookout for girls than the dangerous riptides or man-eating sharks. Occasionally, they redirected the splashing swimmers back toward the two red and yellow flags on the beach, standing like goalposts, which marked the safe-to-swim area.

When I returned to the Laundromat, I removed my clothes from the machine and discovered to my horror that I had left a pack of spearmint gum in a shirt pocket. What a mess! I sorted through the wet clothes and plucked off sticky goo. I had no choice but to rewash the bloody lot.

When I finally dumped the clothes in dryers, I treated myself to a cappuccino at an outdoor café with a magnificent view of the beach esplanade. I gazed at the expensive high-rises overlooking the sea. Thus far, my old apartment building wasn't threatened by urban renewal.

I sipped the yummy white froth and watched the swimmers and surfers head for the ocean. Overseas tourists, speaking strange tongues, casually strolled around Norfolk Island pines that must've been a hundred years old. Some shoppers chatted on their mobiles.

"Hey, mate," called a voice.

I turned around and squinted in the sun.

"It's me."

Woof. Woof.

The weedy bloke jumped back.

I gripped Nesha's leash and stroked his head. "Settle down."

"It's me, mate," said the disheveled man with torn jeans, dirty black hair, and long sideburns. Perry still wore the shiny gold stud in his left ear.

He cautiously eyed my dog and reached for a nearby chair. His smelly T-shirt reeked of body odor and cigarettes.

I gagged. "What are you doing here?"

He pulled a bag of tobacco from his pocket and began rolling his own. "Me girl and I broke up, mate. 'Cause I left the fuckin' workshop. Couldn't handle that bullshit, if you know what I mean."

He lit his cigarette and tossed the burning match on the ground. "Listen, mate. I could use a cuppa, if you know what I mean."

Hoping to get rid of him, I rummaged in my pocket and handed him a dollar coin.

"It costs more than this, mate."

"That's the best I can do, Perry. I'm unemployed."

"I need to find work meself. I play in a band with me mates, but the money's ratshit. Need a few quid, if you know what I mean. Can you spare a little more?"

I shook my head.

He went to pet Nesha, who wisely barked.

Perry quickly withdrew his hand.

I pulled Nesha closer to my chair. "He bites."

"Listen, mate. I need a good meal. Times are tough, if you know what I mean. Can you spare an extra quid? I'll pay you back, no worries."

I watched him fidget with the tobacco and wondered if he was on crystal meth or weed, the drugs of choice around here. I gulped the rest of my cappuccino.

"I'd like to help out but I'm low on money. Have some errands," I said, then added sarcastically, "If you know what I mean."

He drew hard on his cigarette. "Live around here?"

Before I could stop myself, my head nodded.

His eyes widened. "I can stop by and say g'day. Where's your digs?"

"I'm planning to move," I lied. The last thing I needed was an addict casing out my place.

"No worries, mate. But I could use a few more coins."

I pulled the leash. "Not today. Have to dash."

He yanked at my sleeve. "Come on, mate. I'm hurtin'."

Without answering, I made a hasty exit, checking that he didn't follow.

With Perry stuck on my mind, I removed the clothes from the dryer. The tell-tale gooey marks on the drum told me I hadn't removed all the gum. Crikey! My best pair of jeans ruined. I plucked out the rest of my clothes and stuffed them in the laundry bag. When a muscle-bound bloke piled his wet clothes into the gum-infested dryer, I made a hasty exit. He wouldn't be in the best of moods if he found spearmint staining his underwear.

I took a long, circuitous route to avoid any contact with Perry. Desperate for cash, he could stake out my place. I shivered at the thought of my home under threat.

GETTING TO KNOW YOU

As I waited in The Healing Touch Salon at Bondi Beach, I watched a pair of angelfish kissing in the aquarium. Celeste was fifteen minutes late. While we had talked numerous times, I hadn't seen her since the workshop. Six long days! Though I had plenty of free time, she was consumed with her massage practice.

She strolled into the lobby and approached me with a wide smile that accentuated her dimples. "Sorry, I'm late," she apologized.

The kiss on my cheek made me quickly forgive.

She was as gorgeous as I remembered. Spirals of golden hair tumbled over her shoulders. Dressed in white slacks, she wore a tight T-shirt displaying a picture of two hands. I yearned to caress those hands.

"That was a bonza massage," announced a bronzed, muscle-bound bloke exiting a room.

"Thanks," blushed Celeste, turning toward Mr. Muscle. "The emu oil will keep working its magic."

He rubbed his thighs. "The soreness is bloody well gone. Do your magical fingers make house calls?" He flashed pearly teeth and winked.

The thought of her stroking Mr. Muscle made my skin crawl. I wanted to smash his face with the bottle of emu oil.

After he left, she rubbed my back. "Don't worry, Peter. It's only business."

"He clearly enjoyed himself. Why did he need a massage?"

"He plays rugby for the Sydney Roosters."

A rooster hanging around my chick!

"I work out the kinks on him and several of his teammates."

Her sexy, sculptured fingers, pressing oily flesh, would probably tighten a man's muscle.

"Interested in some Thai?" she asked.

"As long as we don't bump into footballers."

She slapped my arm. "Don't be silly. I'll go change."

We ate at the Thai Dragon restaurant where the expected custom was to sit shoeless on cushions around a small table. Celeste easily adopted a lotus position while I struggled to get comfortable. I would have preferred eating at Celeste's place. But then again, I wanted to take it slow. I learned my lesson six years ago with my first real love, Theresa Ramadopoulos. With a voracious sexual appetite, she'd pounce on me like a crazed lioness and get me so excited I'd come faster than a cheetah. I was crushed when she ditched me. After Theresa, there were a few flash-in-the-pan romances, but nothing long-lasting. I hoped for something more permanent with Celeste.

I gazed into her hazel eyes and felt an electric current pulsate between my legs. I shifted position to make sure it wasn't obvious.

She licked her lips and leaned forward. "I felt this instant connection when we met."

The connection intensified over our meal of Pad Thai. She said we were destined to teach each other many lessons. With Celeste as a teacher, I was more than willing to be her student. I planned to study hard.

After dinner, Celeste invited me to her place for dessert. Though it was only a short walk to her apartment, I had to restrain myself from running. The gentle sound of the distant surf could be heard as we entered her apartment.

Two cats immediately pounced. She picked up the two felines. "Meet Laksmi." The black and white cat purred in her left arm. "I named her after the Hindu goddess of fortune."

She then kissed the gray tomcat snuggling against her right arm. "And we can't forget Indra, the king of the gods and ruler of heaven."

"That's weird," I said. "I call my dog Nesha after the Hindu elephant god, Ganesha." I removed the gold chain and dangling medallion under my shirt. "My friend, Surjit, gave it to me when I was having a hard time."

"That's incredible!" she said. "A statue of Ganesha sits on my nightstand. He removes obstacles in life." She fondled the medallion depicting a man with an elephant's head. She kissed my forehead. "It's a sign we're meant to be together."

His-s-s-s. The gray tomcat bared his teeth.

"Shhh." She clutched the cat against her chest. "I'll show you around."

Celeste's living room was furnished simply—couch and recliner, bookshelves, entertainment unit, and floor cushions. An orange tablecloth covered a coffee table adorned with a bowl of flowers, candles, incense holder, and picture of a bearded Indian with a red-dotted forehead.

She released the cats and lit an incense stick. "My meditation altar."

"Who's this?" I asked, picking up the picture.

"That's Babaji, my teacher. He transformed my life."

She guided me to the couch. Indra immediately pounced on the spot where I planned sit. Bloody cat!

Celeste placed him on her lap. "Babaji started an ashram in Coogee. He's an amazing guru with a huge following."

"Guru?"

She stroked her cat. "In Sanskrit, the word 'gu' means darkness and 'ru' is that which dispels. He's an enlightened being who teaches self-realization through meditation and chanting. He says the divine exists in everyone."

"It's not a cult, is it?"

Celeste laughed. "No more than Christianity. The peace and joy I experience at the ashram is incredible. You'll see for yourself."

"I'm a recovering Catholic," I joked. "My mother wanted me to join the seminary but, thank God, I saw the light."

She lit a votive candle. "When you embrace Babaji, his light surrounds you. You'll live in the moment."

I replaced his picture on the table. "I'm not into religion."

She stroked my arm. "Don't be closed-minded. When I introduce you to Babaji, you'll see what I mean. Actually, he predicted we would meet."

"What?"

Her eyes twinkled. "He told me I would find someone special at a workshop before the end of February. And here you are!"

I beamed. "Glad his prediction worked. Does he make you fast and give up earthly pleasures?"

"Don't worry," she giggled. "He encourages us to enjoy our bodies. No alcohol and drugs, but he teaches that sex, when harnessed, takes us to a higher spiritual plane."

"That type of religion, I can embrace."

We both laughed. Except Indra who scowled, if cats could do such a thing.

Celeste removed a book from the bookcase. "Have a look."

She handed me *Ananga-Ranga,* an Indian text on love, then played a CD of Ravi Shankar. Sitar music, accompanied by hypnotic chants, ushered in a passage to India. Celeste placed the gray tomcat on the floor and moved close to me. The king of the household was none too happy. The furball leapt back to her lap and nuzzled against her breasts. She spanked his tummy.

"Don't be so possessive."

I turned a page to a graphic picture of a naked Indian couple locked in a yogic embrace. The man supported himself on his knees and penetrated the woman, who arched her back. Her shoulders and head rested on the ground while her legs straddled the man's shoulders.

"That's called the Inverted Wheelbarrow," said Celeste, shamelessly.

"That's heavy duty ranga danga."

She playfully nudged my arm. "*Ananga-Ranga*," she corrected. "Tantric sex awakens kundalini."

"Kunda-what?"

"Kundalini. Serpentine energy that spirals up the spine through seven chakras—energy centers in the body. If they're open during sex, energy flows like an electric current."

I flicked to the next page. A yellow light surrounded a naked couple embraced in ecstatic sexual union.

"The Conjunction of the Sun and Moon," purred Celeste. "Both partners have to be deeply connected to get that kind of rush. It takes practice."

"Practice makes perfect."

Her hot breath moved closer. "Have you experienced tantric sex?"

I shook my head. "But Freddie's a willing student."

"Freddie?"

"My name for, you know."

Celeste touched my thigh. "I like him already. I often think of that missed opportunity in the dining room."

I closed my eyes and felt her wandering fingers. "So do I."

She grabbed my hand. "Cats aren't allowed in the bedroom."

My body resisted as my mind whirled and twirled like a pretzel. We hadn't talked about protection. Did she have herpes or some other disease? Would I be able to perform for my teacher?

Celeste's sensuous kiss stopped me from thinking. "My kundalini's stirring," she breathed. "Join me in the bedroom."

She led me to a queen-size bed that occupied center stage. Speakers, installed on the wall, hummed the sound of sitar and chants. A gentle breeze from the open window tossed orange curtains against a potted bamboo. She closed the door and lit several candles.

Her voice cooed. "How about a massage to relax you?"

I patted my pants pocket. "I have protection."

She reached for a bottle of oil next to the statue of Ganesha on her nightstand. "You're safe with me. Babaji wants us to live in the moment."

She peeled off my shirt and guided me onto her bed, face down. She oiled her hands and touched my shoulders. My skin sizzled.

"Yes-s-s," she whispered. "Let your worries melt away. Ylang ylang and emu oil open the senses. Perfect for a tantric moment."

Her fingers acted like magical wands. Soft feathery strokes floated across my skin.

"How does this feel?"

"Mmmmm."

While the sounds of India played in the background, my anxiety and Catholic guilt faded into limbo.

"Ready to open your chakras?"

I nodded into the pillow. Ready or not, here she comes.

With deft fingers, she kneaded my muscles and pressed my spine at various points. She hummed the chants while her soft hands caressed my skin. My body surrendered.

"Now let's turn you over."

On my back, I gazed at her radiant face. Candlelight flickered off golden hair that twisted seductively across her shoulders. When she smoothed oil across my chest, my skin tingled. My heart thumped. Desire stirred between my legs. I was experiencing kundalinguini!

The sweet smell of ylang ylang brought a rush of passion. I was ravenous. Jiggling breasts under her orange blouse beckoned me. I touched them. Her nipples hardened.

"Release them."

I unbuttoned her blouse and set them free. Around her neck, a chain dangled a wooden mala with a picture of her Swami, nestled between her breasts.

"Kiss them."

My lips tasted sumptuous nipples.

Her breathing shifted into shallow, rapid-fire bursts.

I hesitated.

"No, don't," she pleaded. "Kundalini is rising. Kiss me all over."

With pleasure! I peeled off the rest of her clothes as she tugged at my pants.

"Protection," I whispered.

She opened the drawer in the nightstand. I gasped at the life-size dildo and boxes of condoms. What did she expect? A football team? Had the Roosters nested here?

"Maybe we should talk."

She removed my pants. "Let's raise our energy."

Roosters pecked at my mind. Rugby players could have occupied this bed. Her philosophy was clearly *live in the moment*. Her sexual past could impact my future.

She sensed my anxiety, "Relax, Peter. I usually use condoms." She massaged around my heart. "Stay in the present. Open your chakras."

Her magical fingers helped me surrender, as did the ylang ylang, the chanting, and Celeste's slender, naked, gyrating body. I reached for the condom. I wanted to enter the passage to India.

"Not yet," she moaned. "Kundalini needs stimulation." She placed her hand under my scrotum and gently rubbed. "Do the same to me."

The *same*!

She placed my hand under her pelvis and rocked to the rhythm of the chanting.

Couldn't we make love like normal people?

She guided my head to her breasts. "Kiss them."

That was easy.

"Nibble them."

A taut nipple pressed against my lips.

"Mmmmm," she groaned. "I love that." She breathed more rapid-fire bursts.

Inspired by her passion, I moved from one breast to the other.

"Feel the energy?"

I nodded with an overpowering urge to penetrate.

"I'm ready to join lingham and yoni."

She took a condom and sheathed Freddie. Fully protected, he was now ready to enter the sacred passageway.

She held me tight as we rocked our pelvises back and forth. I didn't care if it was kundalini or raw passion. I welcomed her hard kisses against my lips. My tongue darted into her mouth. She squeezed my bottom and Freddie plunged deep. My body became electrified, as if plugged into a socket. The sitar droned and our chests heaved. Sweat saturated our naked bodies. I thrust deeper, faster and faster.

"Yes," she screamed.

The cats meowed and scratched at the door.

I surrendered to the passionate frenzy and exploded into her holy temple.

"Yes-s-s," she cried. "Love me."

Orgasmic fireworks ignited the bedroom. Celeste kept coming, wave after wave. Relentless, she wanted more. She thrust my head toward her breasts and directed my hands to her pleasure spot.

"Kiss me; touch me." She held my head tight and screamed with ecstasy. "More," she pleaded.

Only after her final orgasm, which seemed forever, did she release her grasp. I collapsed, my head spinning.

We eventually stirred from our semi-comatose state. Celeste kissed me sweetly on the lips. "Next time, I'll have all your chakras whirling."

"Can my circuits handle it?"

She climbed on top of me. "We'll just have to see, won't we? Anyone for seconds?"

BIRTHDAY CELEBRATION

SUNDAY, MARCH 5

Brring, brring.

Woof, woof.

I dashed into the house and picked up the receiver.

"Hello... Wait a minute." I hissed at Nesha, "Calm down," then returned to the phone. "Just walked the dog... Yes, I'll be there at one... Yeah, I got your message yesterday... Was with a friend... You don't know him... No, I didn't attend Mass. I'll talk later. Bye."

I hung up the phone and told Nesha, "Another call from the grand inquisitor."

As an old-time Catholic, my mother believed I was a lost soul. She prayed daily that I'd return to the church, visit her more often, and find a good Polish woman. If she knew I had slept with Celeste last night, she would've invoked every one of her problem-solving techniques—novenas, Masses, the rosary, plus the spritz of holy water.

Even though I moved out five years ago, her interrogations continued. Whenever she phoned, I braced for an onslaught of questions. However, now that I embraced Gretchen's call to be true to myself, I was ready to face the supreme test.

At 1:30, I pulled up in front of 23 Orpington Street, a red brick bungalow in Ashfield. As soon as I let Nesha out, he bolted for the large plaster statue of Mary, gracing my parents' front lawn. I shouted and pointed at a nearby tree. He complied with a whimper. I took several deep breaths and replayed Gretchen's affirmations. "Reject negative thoughts. Victories without hardship are hollow and offer little cause for celebration."

My heart thumped when I opened the front door.

"*Wy jesteście późny*! You're late!" My mother dashed into the living room and crushed me with a bear hug. She immediately felt my ribs. "Not eating enough, Piotr."

I wanted to say she was eating enough for the two of us, but bit my tongue. Years of hardship were etched on her wrinkled, sixty-one-year-old face.

She flashed piercing blue eyes. "You should visit more often."

I handed her a present. "*Szczęśliwy dzień urodzenia*! Happy birthday."

She lifted her apron and wiped her eyes. "You shouldn't." She clutched the present in one of my arms. "Everyone's in the kitchen. *Przybywają*. Come."

Nesha followed me past the picture of Our Lady of Częstochova prominently displayed on the living room wall. My mother prayed often to the Black Madonna marked with a scar on her right cheek. Most prayers went unanswered.

"Piotr," yelled Uncle Janek in a festive mood. "Come celebrate."

My father's older brother grabbed a shot glass and filled it past the rim. He thrust it forward. "*Dobra żytnia*."

"No vodka, thanks."

My hefty uncle tugged at one of his gargantuan ears that sprouted tiny bushes. He scrunched his face into a deep frown. "Take." He waved the glass in my face.

I wanted to pour it over his bowling ball head.

He swigged the vodka. "*Bardzo dobrze*. Very good."

His grin revealed two dark front teeth. The cheapskate never got them capped. The same miserly attitude stopped him from making my father a partner at the garage. He handed the bottle to his brother.

My father happily obliged.

"One shot for Ma," he commanded.

"Not drinking," I told him firmly.

"It's her birthday," he growled. He filled a glass and handed it to me. "Be a man. *Pić.* Drink."

"Józef," scolded my mother. "Leave him."

"Ah-h-h," he grumbled, then saluted me, "*Na zdrowie.*" Already beyond his limit, he downed the vodka.

My father's drinking was a perpetual problem. A chronic workaholic, he stayed late and when he returned home, downloaded alcohol. Even at sixty-four, he could hold his liquor. His white hair and trimmed mustache reminded me of the Gestapo.

"Here he is," shouted my aunt as she emerged from the bathroom. "You're thin," said Adele. She wrapped her beefy arms around me. "Why don't you visit us?"

"Busy," I lied.

"Rubbish!" shouted my father. He guffawed to my uncle. "P.P. does psycho piddle." They both roared.

My aunt pinched my cheek. "Did you ever find a job?"

Smacking her false teeth would've spoiled the party, so I forced a smile. "As a matter of fact, I do have a job."

"About time," bellowed my father.

My mother cried, "The Madonna answered my prayer."

My uncle reached for the bottle. "This calls for a drink. Right, Józef?"

"*Tak!*"

They refilled the glasses and clinked. "*Na zdrowie.*"

My mother snatched the vodka. "No more," she shouted. "*Psiakrew,* it's my birthday."

When my mother hollered, "dog's blood," she was really pissed off. She banged the bottle back in the cabinet. "*To jest czas jeść.* Time to eat."

As we moved toward the table, my heart pounded those all-too-familiar tom-toms. I excused myself, rushed to the bathroom, and clutched my chest. Waves of anxiety rippled through my body with an electric hum. The weekend inoculation of love and acceptance was wearing off. I was slipping back into the black cave. I splashed water on my face and gazed in the mirror at the terrified little boy who used to lock himself in the bathroom. I remembered my mother's broken heart. Though I was only six, I tried desperately to ease her pain of leaving Chicago. My jokes brought an occasional smile to her tortured face. I became a sentry in front of the TV to stop her from watching American programs. They made her worse. My father eventually hid the TV in the garage.

I felt helpless and sought comfort from him, but the Gestapo turned me into his whipping boy. He would occasionally wallop me, but it was his constant belittling and threatening roars that stung like hot lashes. He mocked me for crying.

"If you act like a girl, go play with Stella." As if my older sister wanted me around. He would storm back into the garage and do what real men do—fix things and drink vodka.

My father worked long hours at his brother's garage and left me and my sister as sacrificial lambs. My mother would clutch me, saying I must help her survive. Her dark, ugly moods oppressed the family like thundering clouds. Whenever she suffered, I shared her pain. Eventually, she lapsed into a severe depression and had to be hospitalized. That's when the clouds opened and drenched our home in misery.

My father was brutal. After she was released, he'd scream at her for not getting out of bed. Then he'd bark at us to take over her chores. The despot made us prisoners in the land Down Under. Home became a jail.

He tried to erase all memories of America and constantly belittled good news from overseas. He permitted memorabilia of Poland in the house—a photo of Pope John Paul II in the front hall and Our Lady of Częstochova in the living room—but any remnants of life in Chicago were banned, not even a mug with a picture of the lakefront.

When my mother recovered, we all paid a heavy price, always wondering about a relapse. She fled from the black clouds by frenetically immersing herself in chores. Forever busy, forever active, with no time to sit or think about her tormented soul. She became the lonely bread maker while my father became the sole breadwinner.

When I turned thirty, I escaped to Manly for a life without conflict. However, without me as a buffer, my parents escalated their fighting. My mother would call me in tears while my drunken father yelled in the background. He rarely became physical, but his verbal abuse could make Mount Kocziusko tremble.

Woof. Woof. Nesha scratched at the door. I gazed at my reflection. The frightened little boy morphed back into my adult self. I splashed my face and planted a brave smile. I inoculated myself with fond memories of The Family That Cares. A few more hours, and I'd be free from the hum of anxiety. I opened the door.

Nesha pounced. I stroked his black coat. "Having a tough time?"

He licked my face. I patted his head. "We'll go soon."

I joined the others around the dining room table. It was filled with platters of Polish sausage, sauerkraut, and *pierogi*. My father occupied the head of the table, with my uncle to his right. My aunt and I flanked my mother who, as cook and waitress, spent more time out of her chair at the foot of the table. Platters clattered and hands reached for food. My uncle speared three cheese *pierogi* while my father scooped sauerkraut onto his plate. The brothers swapped demeaning jokes about Asians and other migrants.

"Can you pass the sausage?" I interrupted my uncle, hogging the meat.

I grabbed a small link and cut a piece for Nesha, sitting patiently under my chair. He wolfed it down and barked for more.

"Were you at the Blue Mountains?" asked my aunt. Without waiting for a reply, she said, "Uncle and I visited last year. The prices were horrible. I'll never go back."

I said little during the rest of the meal. I evaded my mother's incessant questions about my job, or rather potential job, and redirected her to the birthday presents. Once she opened them, I was out of there. Unfortunately, a phone call delayed the gift-giving. My sister wasn't content with a brief birthday greeting. She and her family had to say hello to everyone.

When it was my turn, I took the phone. "Hi, Stella... Of course, I'm enjoying myself. Wouldn't you?"

She asked if my father was behaving. I told her, "The usual," then passed the receiver to my aunt.

Forty-five minutes later, the laborious call finally ended.

"Time for presents, Marysia," clapped Adele. She brought them to the table that had already been cleared by the birthday girl.

My aunt passed her the gifts. My mother chose mine first. She carefully unwrapped the paper so it could be reused and removed a burnished wooden plate with an intricate flower pattern.

"*Dziękuje bardzo*. Thank you." Beaming, she kissed my cheek.

Score a genuine acknowledgement. Gretchen did say we should accept small victories.

Like an excited girl, she opened the remaining presents—sets of towels and facecloths from my aunt and uncle, and a new iron and ironing board from my father. She was delighted and kissed everyone a second time.

Before the cake-cutting, Janek grabbed his accordion. He obviously missed playing with the Polka Snots, for he rarely passed up an opportunity to squeeze the box. He pulled hard on the accordion, and we joined in with the traditional

Polish birthday song, albeit sung way too enthusiastically by my father.

Sto lat, sto lat, niech żyje żyje nam.
Sto lat, sto lat, niech żyje żyje nam.
Jeszcze raz, jeszcze raz, niech żyje, żyje nam.
Niech żyje nam!

I thought about the birthday verse: "Good luck, good cheer, may you live a hundred years." That's an eternity, with a husband hooked on vodka.

TANTRA YOGA ASHRAM

Jealousy reared its twisted head. Tormented by images of Celeste kneading Roosters, I battled mental demons. I had plenty of time; she had less. Her massage practice and the ashram consumed her. Given the opportunity, I would've camped out at her office to make sure the rugby players weren't getting more than they needed. Celeste wasn't too keen on the idea. However, she was ecstatic at my offer to visit the ashram. It gave me another evening with her. Besides, I wanted to check out the guru who held her spellbound.

Acting like a little girl anxious to show off her favorite toy, Celeste excitedly directed me to a side street in Coogee.

"At tonight's satsang, Babaji gives Shaktipat."

I parked the car. "Does that mean I'll get a shake and a pat?"

She giggled. "Silly. The word 'pat' means 'descent'. Once Babaji awakens our divine power, we descend into Shakti."

Was love really worth going through this? I hesitated before opening the door. "What will he do?"

"Babaji awakens kundalini. You'll feel a surge of energy."

"Tell me more about Swami Ziprunanda."

"We've been over this, Peter. Address him as Babaji. It's a sign of respect. Keep an open mind. Gretchen told us to find a community that takes us home. This is it."

A couple screeched into the parking space nearby, then ran toward the ashram. Celeste tugged at my arm. "Don't want to be late."

I joined her and the others into a large converted house. Inside the doorway's entrance, rows of wooden shelves were neatly lined with shoes. Celeste immediately removed hers.

"Leave yours here," she instructed.

"But there's a hole in my sock."

"Don't worry about it."

I racked my shoes and followed Celeste into the main meditation hall. Life-size photos of swamis adorned every wall. Devotees faced a platform where a large, orange cushion rested on the stage. Dozens of white carnations in two enormous vases stood as sentries on either side of the platform. Candles and incense burned on a nearby table.

Celeste grabbed one of the cushions stacked on the floor. "Take one," she whispered. "The men sit on the right side."

"We can't sit together?" Without Celeste, I'd feel like a platypus out of water.

"Shhh. Masculine and feminine energies are separated." She grabbed a booklet off a table and handed it to me. "Here are the chants. Follow along."

She kissed my cheek, then strolled to the women's side near the front. She was greeted with hugs and kisses. I walked self-consciously to the men's area and plopped my cushion in the back row. My right toe peeped out of the gaping hole in my sock.

The large room swelled with devotees who huddled together, shoulder to shoulder. The lights dimmed, and a hush fell over the crowd. A man in the front played a harmonium. One hand pumped the bellows of the box-organ while the other pressed keys to create a melodious drone. The group swayed with the music and chanted, "Om Namah Shivaya."

I gawked at the religious revival. At the very least, they could have provided chairs. Sitting cross-legged like the others was bloody uncomfortable. I readjusted my legs and, inadvertently, kicked the man in front of me. He was so caught up in the chanting reverie, he didn't seem to notice.

The pace of the music quickened. Excited heads swayed in anticipation. When the chanting reached a feverish pitch, Swami Ziprunanda made a grand entrance. Dressed in saffron robes, the dark-skinned man with a bushy, white beard scanned the devotees with a toothy smile. His belly bulged like Buddha and a red dot marked his third eye. He strolled toward the front of the stage and settled on the orange cushion. With a flick of his wrist, he waved for the music to stop. The crowd hushed, waiting for his words.

"Focus your mind on the divine," he pronounced with an Indian accent. "Let the energy of Mother Kundalini rise. Let her shower you with grace and show you the path of lightness. We shall now meditate."

On cue, the house lights dimmed and everyone fell into a meditative trance, except me. I planned to stay awake. I amused myself by watching the flickering candles cast shadows on the hanging pictures. I rearranged my legs once again and bumped the bloke in front. He reacted by hyperventilating in short, rapid breaths. Crikey! What had I done! I was ready to shake him awake when a woman on the other side of the room followed suit. Then another. The rapid breathers were having a group panic attack.

Then I recalled Celeste breathing in a similar fashion during sex. Were devotees getting hot and bothered for Mother Kundalini? I hoped it wasn't contagious. While the rhythm of breathing swelled and subsided, I remained hyper-vigilant.

My legs fell asleep. The excruciating pain forced me to shift my feet repeatedly. By the end of the evening, footmarks would be permanently embedded on the bloke in front of me.

Mercifully, the swami came to life. He chanted, "Guru Om. Guru Om," and the lights flickered to life.

Most devotees jubilantly joined him in song. The man in front turned around and scowled at me.

"Sorry," I whispered.

The swami rose and scanned the large hall. As the chanting continued, he stepped down from the stage and walked among the multitude. Starting with the women, he tapped the third eye of each devotee. The women swooned. Some collapsed into the waiting arms of those behind them.

He weaved his way toward the men and touched their foreheads. Some acted as hysterical as the women. One shook as if having an epileptic fit. The swami's shaktipat delivered a powerful punch. Bodies shook, breathing deepened, and chanting escalated.

I panicked when he moved closer. He tapped the third eye of the front bloke, who reacted like spaghetti softening in hot water. He descended backward into my lap!

My pinned legs were dead to the world. It was impossible to remove Mr. Soggy Pasta and escape. I gestured frantically at a staff member. He rushed to support the man who was now *al dente*.

I pushed Mr. Pasta off my legs and quickly went to work on my calves and feet. The swami was fast approaching. I had to start the blood flowing so I could get the hell out of there before getting zapped with the hypnotic device. Then I received the tap. On my third eye. I stared back at Ziprunanda. He grinned and nodded.

I braced myself. Nothing. I felt nothing! I had survived the touch. Then I realized it was all a sham in mass hypnosis. No different than an evangelical revival. Stir the crowd with music and singing, mystical words, and spiritual expectations. Devotees wanted, no, they craved to be moved.

Since I didn't believe in spiritual hocus-pocus, there was nothing to fear. My anxiety receded. I relaxed and smiled. Others smiled back, most likely thinking I had been reborn into spiritual union with the swami. He continued his charade and meandered through the crowd, tapping heads and transforming faces.

I chuckled at the carnival. Everyone looked ridiculous. My belly giggled. The giggles squirmed, begging for release. I closed my eyes and pinched an arm to avoid making a spectacle. But I kept thinking of soggy pasta. The giggles returned, this time with a vengeance. They expanded like bubbles in a shaken bottle of champagne. I squirmed on the cushion to stop myself from laughing. I covered my mouth.

An assistant approached me and touched my shoulder. "Let kundalini out."

The cork popped. My belly emptied the fizzies. Giggles erupted into laughter. Tears streamed from my eyes. Other people turned my way. That made me laugh harder. I clutched my tummy. There was no way to stop the onslaught. Until I felt another tap. The swami struck a second time.

I immediately exhaled and the giggling stopped. A wave of calm spread through my body. I gazed into his eyes. He smiled lovingly, then returned to the crowd.

I spotted Celeste who beamed at me from the other side of the room. She blew me a kiss. She seemed delighted, not angry, that I'd laughed at her guru. This confirmed my suspicion she was under a spell.

When I was with her in bed and she raised kundalini, she entered a trancelike state. Her lust became insatiable, not that I was complaining. I flashed to the last time we had sex. Sweat glistened on her gyrating body. She was boiling hot. When I penetrated her luscious passageway, an electrical charge surged up my spine. Our spinal cords seemed to fuse. I craved her now.

Crikey! Mr. Pasta shifted his butt and sat on my foot. The shock snapped me awake. To my horror, Freddie was also awake. I placed my hands over my lap, hoping no one had noticed. My laughing outburst brought enough attention. Stained pants would be the ultimate humiliation. The icy image of my horrified parents splashed into my mind. Their internal voices berated me for participating in a demonic cult. Freddie wilted like well-done linguini.

Ziprunanda returned to the stage with more spiritual gibberish. I blocked out the message in case he zapped the crowd with a post-hypnotic suggestion. When satsang was over, devotees filed out in ecstasy. At last, the show was over.

I waited by the door as Celeste hugged her way towards me.

She kissed me. "Wasn't that amazing?"

"It was, uh, interesting."

"Interesting?" she said incredulously. "Babaji touched you twice. The energy must've been overwhelming."

I shrugged. "Hard to say what happened."

"Tell me everything. Everything!"

As we collected our shoes, I mentioned my fit of the giggles.

She laughed. "Babaji released the tension. During my first shaktipat, my sexual energy skyrocketed. I channel that better now."

"I found myself lusting for you."

"Mmmm. Getting turned on in a meditation hall can be very frustrating."

"Tell me about it."

She planted a long, sensuous kiss. "I feel your shakti." She hurried me to the car. "My place!"

After enduring agony at the ashram, I was ready to embrace ecstasy with Celeste.

QUEENSCLIFFE COUNSELING CENTRE FOR CHANGE

FRIDAY, MARCH 17

A large poster hanging on the wall dominated the small waiting room. I stared at the caption beneath the graphic picture of a bruised woman holding a crying child—*There's no place for domestic violence!*

"Dr. Norton will see you now."

I followed the officious secretary to a cramped office.

Herbert Norton offered his outstretched hand. The Executive Director, a chubby man in his late sixties, looked more like an absent-minded grandfather than a psychologist. Remnants of powdered sugar smudged his lips and fingers.

"Come in, come in, my boy."

After he closed the door, I deployed the schmooze technique. "Sam told me great things about you and the agency."

He peered over black-rimmed glasses and smiled approvingly. "Yes, indeed, my boy."

He directed me to a chair near his desk where a stack of files sat next to a half-eaten doughnut on a paper plate. The absence of green plants was offset by scores of mounted photos of Herbert: holding a halibut, lifting a string of flathead, landing a tuna.

I said the obvious. "You're a fisherman."

He rested into his leather chair and beamed. "Fishing is good for the soul, my boy." He pointed at the picture of a large marlin. "My trophy fish. Took me two hours to haul it in."

Herbert launched into his own version of Hemingway's *Old Man and the Sea*, describing, in painful detail, the weather conditions, the choice of bait, and the battle of wills between man and fish. Since he was in charge of hiring, I demonstrated my listening skills, hoping to get hooked.

Fortunately, the phone interrupted his story. He took the brief call, then checked the clock.

"Now, where were we?"

"Sam suggested I apply for the job."

"Our Sam's a great therapist," said Herbert. He rummaged. "Ah, here it is!" He removed my letter and résumé and adjusted his glasses. "Says here, you graduated from Sydney University. Your thesis?"

I cleared my throat. "The operant conditioning response with rats subjected to frequent immersions in a water-filled maze."

He reached for the half-eaten doughnut. "A behaviorist, eh?"

"Initially. I used object/relations theory and family therapy when I worked at Royal Prince Andrew Hospital—child and adolescent psychiatry."

I didn't mention that the staff were crazier than the patients.

"Your last job was Pittwater School. Why'd you leave?"

"They downsized, but I was ready for a change. I wanted to work with adults. So when Sam mentioned the job, it sounded like a perfect fit."

"She recommended you highly, my boy," nodded Herbert. "That says a lot."

He took a bite of the doughnut, then moved closer as if to share a private secret. "We handle quite a few cases with domestic violence. Our female therapists are very sensitive about the victims, as they should be. But we could use another man on board to give..." He paused for the right phrase, "...balanced perspective."

He wiped the powdered sugar from his lips. "I'm sure you understand, my boy."

The message was clear; he wanted support. No problem. Once hooked and on board, I'd happily pose for a picture.

Before we finished the interview, Herbert discussed the position, benefits, and salary, then promised to contact me within two weeks. He had several other applicants but made it clear that, because of Sam, I was the front-runner. When he ushered me past the waiting room and the poster of the bruised woman and crying child, I hoped there would be room for another man.

FAMILY BARBECUE

SUNDAY, MARCH 19

Sam welcomed me with a bear hug. "We've been waiting for you."

Her genuine warmth made me feel right at home. I gave her a bottle of merlot and followed her into the living room where she showed me a display of Aboriginal artifacts—boomerangs, bark paintings, and spears. She removed a boomerang from the wall and handed it to me.

"This belongs to you."

My hand traced the carving in the wood of a kookaburra on a branch, clutching a snake in its beak.

"The bird's your totem," said Sam. "The kookaburra is also called the 'bushman's clock' because it greets the morning with a laugh. An alarm clock without a snooze button. It'll remind you to wake up."

I was overwhelmed by her generosity. "I can't take this."

She took it back and rapped it across my shoulder. "It's meant for you. End of discussion." She placed the boomerang on a table. "Take it before you leave. Now let's have a barbecue."

She grabbed my arm and led me to a backyard that had an amazing view of the Tasman Sea. Palm Beach was a northern coastal suburb of Sydney, renowned for its beauty. The afternoon sun sparkled off the whitecaps as surfers rode the waves.

"Over here, mate," called Thomas. He tossed onions on the grill, then gave me a bone-crushing hug.

"Easy does it," I groaned.

"It's about bleedin' time," yelled Rosie. "I'm famished." She clutched her glass while hugging me. "Fancy a wee drop of whiskey?"

Before I could answer, Alana nudged her aside. "What about me?" she pouted. She wrapped her arms around me. "How's your head?

"Stitches are out. Thank God, the scar doesn't resemble a lightning bolt like Harry Potter."

"Glad you're here. The Family that Cares is now complete."

"That calls for a toast," called Rosie. "Our three-week anniversary."

I uncorked my bottle of Kalbarri merlot and noticed the kookaburra on the label. I showed it to Sam. "This should wake us up."

I offered the bottle around, but Rosie declined. She pointed to the Glenfiddich on the table.

"A fine drop," she crooned. "Left over from St. Paddy's day. With dad from Glasgow and mum from Dublin, I celebrate the Scots and the Irish." She emptied her glass. "But I favor the Scots when it comes to fine whiskey." She reached for the bottle. "I'll be wantin' a steak on the pink side, Thomas."

He flipped over a slab of meat. "Yours is already well-charred."

She smacked his arm. "Ye'd better not."

"Alright, children," chided Sam. "Let's eat before Rosie has another whiskey."

Thomas forked sausages and steaks onto a platter while Sam brought out salads and bread. As we gathered around the outdoor table, Sam asked us to hold hands.

"Let's thank Mother Earth for her blessings," she began reverently. "We thank the animals and plants for nourishing us. We're grateful for the meal. The sun is a circle. The moon is a circle. The earth is a circle. And the five of us remain a circle."

I would have been content with, "Rub a dub dub. Thanks for the grub. Yay, God."

Rosie lifted her glass and, in her lilting brogue, offered her favorite grace by the Scottish poet, Robert Burns.

Some hae meat, and canna eat,
And some wad eat that want it;
But we hae meat, and we can eat
And sae the Lord be Thankit.

We clinked our glasses, then filled our plates. As I snagged a steak, Alana asked about the interview.

"Herbert said he'd let me know soon."

Sam passed the bread and winked. "You're in."

"I'm not celebrating until I get the final word."

"What's the word with yer lassie?" asked Rosie, pouring herself another glass.

"We're, uh, enjoying each other."

Rosie sipped her Scotch and tittered, "Ye can tell by his smirk, they're spendin' a wee bit o' time in the loft."

Alana frowned. "Let's not pick on each other."

"Only havin' fun," chortled Rosie.

"Peter's not the only one who's found a lover," confessed Thomas. He speared a sausage. "I met Trent at the Gay Mardi Gras parade a couple of weeks ago. We were helping out with crowd control."

Rosie drained her whiskey. "Ye talked about goin' celibate."

"That was until I met Trent," grinned Thomas. "He's so understanding. Don't worry, we take precautions. I won't pass anything on."

Since Thomas taught others about HIV and AIDS, he'd better know what he was doing. Mind you, I wouldn't be with Celeste if she had a life-threatening virus. Hell, I still felt uneasy hugging Thomas and cringed whenever Sam kissed him on the cheek.

"I'm happy for you," gushed our hostess. "Hold onto the love."

His eyes twinkled like polished lapis lazuli. "We're getting to know each other. We had a blast at Mardi Gras. Despite the wowser ministers' prayers for rain, we had perfect weather. The Man upstairs must be gay."

"I pray *She* looks after you," corrected Sam. "You can never be certain about relationships. I discovered too late about Charles and the ponies. He gambled away our life savings and refused counseling. After Gretchen's workshop, I told him to leave."

"About bleedin' time," bellowed Rosie.

Alana slipped from her chair and wrapped her arms around Sam. "You always have us."

Thomas raised his wine glass. "All for one."

We clinked glasses. "And one for all."

Rosie cleared her throat. "Might as well tell ye. I've started datin'."

Thomas ruffled her red brassy hair. "Good on ya, Rosie. Time to get back on the saddle."

She reached for the Glenfiddich and poured another glass. "I may be gettin' old, but I still have the cravin'. When the kids play in the band, I give the cute fellas a once over."

"Men of Sydney," proclaimed Thomas, "watch out."

We laughed and saluted her new quest, then continued the joyous meal. Alana jumped in with the news that she had volunteered to help out at the upcoming Olympics. Like an excited child, she told us she'd be in the opening ceremony but wouldn't divulge the details, no matter how hard we prodded. She and the other volunteers had signed a letter of secrecy, thereby sealing their lips.

I gave a funny rendition of my ashram experience and imitated Mr. Soggy Pasta, collapsing into Rosie's arms. She laughed so hard she toppled her whiskey. She made a valiant lunge but lost her precious drop. Just as well. She was way past the limit.

After the glazed fruit flan for desert, Sam brought out a purple silk bag and plopped it on the table.

"And what be that?" asked Rosie.

"Runes," answered Sam. "Gretchen said that signs would help us find our way home. Reach into the bag and grab one. It will provide direction."

Alana leapt to the task. She picked a wooden rune etched with an X.

Sam glowed. "That's the rune of gifts. It means a new partnership lies ahead. Possibly a loving relationship."

Alana's smile exposed her mottled, chipped tooth.

Rosie snatched the rune out of Alana's hand. "I'll have that as well!"

"You have to choose from the bag," chastised Sam.

"I'm stickin' with Mr. X."

Despite Sam's protests, Rosie wouldn't budge. Exasperated, Sam grabbed the rune and placed it back in the bag. She shook it, then removed a wooden square marked with an M.

"This is the symbol for the horse," she mused. "Movement or transition is its message. Confirms my decision to give Charles the boot."

She returned the rune to the bag and thrust it toward Thomas. "Your go. And don't pull a Rosie."

He removed a rune etched with an N.

Sam's brow creased into furrows. "That's Hagalaz," she said pensively. "It means disruption. You're asked to prepare your soul for major growth."

Thomas sighed. "I was hoping for the same one as Rosie and Alana."

Sam consoled him. "The signs we desperately seek may not be the ones we're meant to have."

He wasn't comforted. He pushed the bag toward me and grumbled, "Your turn, mate."

I didn't want to ruin a perfect day by snatching a bad omen. Ever so carefully, I lowered my hand into the sack as if anticipating a deadly red-back spider. I delicately plucked a wooden piece and turned it over. The rune looked like the point of an arrow facing right: >.

"Interesting," pondered Sam.

"What?" I asked fearfully.

"Kano is the rune of the torch. It signifies a time to dispel darkness and allow openings. But your rune is reversed."

"The symbol is pointed to the right. So what?"

She turned the rune 180 degrees. "It's supposed to point to the left. Reversed, it means death to the old way of living. You must endure darkness before you can ignite the new torch."

"I'm giving up unemployment. That's a good death."

She examined the symbol as if it were an ancient artifact. "This foretells a radical change to the way you perceive life. Sorry, Peter. There's hardship ahead."

I angrily snatched the piece of wood and thrust it into the bag. "If you're foretelling darkness, I say we wander down to Whale Beach and catch the sunset."

"To be forewarned is to be prepared," she advised. "But Peter's right. If we want to catch the sunset, we should head for the beach."

No disagreement there. We packed away the leftovers and headed downhill toward the sea. The wine and whiskey made us stumble across the sand. We linked arms and faced the falling sun painting the horizon in purple and orange hues. As I stood with the family that cared, I ruminated on that bloody rune. I wanted a bright, sunny life, not impending darkness.

BROKEN DREAMS

SUNDAY, MARCH 26

Scars etch my black body. Boomerang in hand, I stalk the bush. Spot an Aborigine. The woman's digging stick claws at the earth, seeking roots. I toss the boomerang. It lands near her feet. A kookaburra laughs. She smiles. Her black hair waves in the wind. She wipes red earth from her full breasts. Then dusts my chest. Our naked bodies rub together like two sticks. Fire erupts.

Brring... Brring...

Half dreaming, I answered the phone. "Hello?" I wiped my eyes and checked the clock. "Christ! It's 8:00 a.m.!"

Nesha jumped on the bed and barked.

"No, Ma. I didn't go to church... I know Easter's in four weeks... Yes, I'll be there...I know Stella's coming."

Woof, woof.

"I can't come over... Freeze the extra *gołabki*. The cabbage rolls can wait till Easter."

She wouldn't end the conversation until I promised to stop over later in the week. Promises were made to be broken. I planned to be with Celeste.

I fluffed up the pillow, then snuggled next to my *pierzyna*. The cozy eiderdown nestled against my body. I glanced up at the boomerang, now fastened to the wall facing my bed. Sam said it was a symbol for wake-up calls. Unfortunately, my mother had my number.

Nesha bounded onto the bed and held the leash in his mouth. You'd think on Sunday, a bloke could get some rest.

APRIL FOOLS' DAY

Herbert Norton phoned and offered me the job! Score one for Pinowski! I immediately called Celeste and shared the fabulous news with an invitation for a celebration dinner. If ever there was an occasion to max out my last credit card, this was it. A regular paycheck would radically alter my economic outlook. With my bank account on empty and the creditors phoning, I was about to beg my parents for a loan. Herbert's call saved me the humiliation.

I chose the Bennelong restaurant in the Opera House with its spectacular harbor views—the perfect setting for a special occasion. Celeste complained about missing today's satsang, but she eventually succumbed to my persuasive argument. "For dessert, you can feast on the sumptuous coconut crème brûlée, followed by braised kundalini at my place."

How could she resist?

Her only proviso—I had to attend next Thursday's satsang. I wasn't enthralled by the idea, but, hey, it was April Fools' Day.

LOVE NIGHT

Another celebratory dinner—this time at Celeste's. My jitters about starting the job on Monday all but vanished at the sight of Celeste in a blue silk sarong with an orange frangipani blossom tucked in her golden locks. The wild scent of frangipani sent me over the edge.

"I'm ready to defer food and dive into the dessert."

She pinched my cheek. "You'll have to wait. The tofu curry's ready."

My eyes wandered to her pert nipples. So was my kundalini!

Her gray tomcat hissed. Celeste grabbed him. "Indra, come here, you naughty thing." He rubbed against her breasts. "Play with Laksmi," she said sternly, then placed him next to the black and white cat resting on the couch.

Each visit, I had to contend with her jealous tomcat. He clearly detested my intrusion. He scampered onto the table as soon as we began to eat. Thus began Indra's ritual. Wait awhile, jump on the table, suck up to Celeste, and return to the floor.

"Off!" she scolded for the umpteenth time. A kick to the head would've been more effective.

Between interruptions, Celeste talked about last night's visit to the ashram. "I love having you at satsang. Thursday evenings should be our night for spiritual replenishment."

Listening to Ziprunanda rave on about awakening consciousness was not my idea of replenishment. My cup would overflow if Celeste didn't spend so much time with her guru—Thursday and Saturday evenings, plus the periodic weekend seminars. She was obsessed by the swami.

"Babaji can help you achieve Samadhi, a state of Oneness. You must learn to meditate."

I stroked her soft face. "Does meditating on your beauty count?"

She tapped my third eye. "Focus, Peter. That's what Babaji wants. To move past the illusion of ego and merge with Cosmic Spirit."

"If I had a choice between cosmic spirit and sex, I'd vote for the latter."

"Babaji says we can have both. Sexuality is the seat of our creative center. It can take us from separateness to a blissful state of Oneness. But we must concentrate."

I eyed her luscious breasts. "My mind gets too distracted."

She nibbled my neck. "Let's put the dishes away. I'll show you what I mean."

My body shivered. I quickly piled the plates in the sink, then followed Celeste to the bedroom. I knew the scrumptious ritual. Remove clothes. Massage body. Friction makes heat. Heat fires passion.

She lit the candles. "Lie face down. But leave your clothes on."

"Huh?"

"You're ready for the next level," she said with an impish smile. "Focus on the energy centers and avoid thinking about sex."

I stared at her shapely curves. "You're joking."

She spanked my bottom. "Just follow my instructions."

I lay down on her queen-size bed. "This isn't going to be easy."

"Wait a sec. We need the beats of the chakras."

She left the room to start the music. Pulsating drums soon vibrated through the wall speakers. She returned with a rose quartz crystal in her hand and swayed with the drumming.

"The different rhythms activate each chakra. Resonate with the drumming while I balance your energy centers with my crystal. Let's start with the root chakra, Muladhara. Think of the color red."

As soon as she massaged around my coccyx, Freddie stirred. Not thinking about sex was like asking a ravenous python to avoid a scrumptious cat. I struggled with Celeste's instructions. I focused on the color red, but imagined cherry nipples beckoning me.

She chanted "Lam" to the beat of the drums and stroked the base of my spine. Her voice and touch sent my body tingling. A burning sensation pulsed around my perineum.

The rhythm changed, and Celeste whispered that she was moving to Svadisthana, the seat of sexuality. She placed one hand under my belly below the navel while her other hand pressed the crystal on my lower back.

"Think of the color orange."

I immediately flashed to the orange blossom in her hair. I inhaled the wild, fragrant scent. Freddie pressed against the bed.

The rhythm of the beat shifted once more and she moved to my solar plexus. Her left hand massaged my lower rib cage while her right hand rested the crystal at a parallel place on my back. "The third chakra, Manipura, is fire. It increases your willpower. Visualize a whirling vortex of yellow."

As she chanted Ram, I wanted to exercise my will and ram Freddie home.

When the music shifted again, one hand moved to my chest. The point of the crystal touched the middle of my back.

"Surrender to your heart chakra, Anahata. Open and receive loving green."

When she chanted Yam, I felt an arc of energy pulsate from her hand to my chest. It traveled through my heart to the tip of the crystal. My heart opened like a flower in an emerald pool. "Yummm." I entered a land of bliss.

Overwhelmed with sensations—the drumming, chanting, colors, soothing touches—I barely noticed her hands shift to my throat. She mentioned something about the fifth chakra and the color blue, but I was lost in the pool of love.

Another rhythm. Another shift. One finger touched my third eye and the crystal touched the back of my head. "Open your psychic connection. Ajna is the sixth chakra."

When she sang Om, I murmured, "Mmmmm." Purple rays flooded my forehead. My body burned with desire. I turned to touch her.

"Wait," she said. "We're almost at the crown of enlightenment, Sahasrara. Imagine a lotus with a thousand petals surrounded with violet light."

She pressed the crystal on the crown of my head. My body trembled; my breathing quickened. My heart pounded with the beat of drums.

"Surrender to kundalini. Let go," crooned Celeste.

As if I had a choice. The battle was already lost to the pulsating rhythm and an invisible mystical force. My body quivered. Energy electrified my spine.

She gently turned me over and stroked my face. "Your chakras are open. Surrender to love." She removed her sarong. "I balanced my chakras along with yours."

Her naked body glowed in the candlelight. Freddie swayed like a tall cobra.

Celeste wet her lips. "My yoni's ready for union." She sheathed Freddie with a condom. "Let's start with you on top."

My skin erupted in flames when I mounted.

"Slow," she said lovingly.

I kissed her shoulders and stroked her silky hair. Our mouths touched. Lips and tongues tasted with delight. Her hands directed me to her nipples. Both of us groaned.

Love and passion poured from my heart and soul. I felt open, wanted, loved.

"Yes," moaned Celeste. "Let our chakras merge."

I merged deep inside her.

"Open your heart. Let me in," she breathed. "I want to penetrate your chakras."

Then I felt it. A deep piercing connection, as if her psyche entered my body. The two of us were becoming one!

"Yes!" she cried. Sweat poured from her face. "Surrender. I am you and you are me. Say it."

Lost in paradise, I followed her on the road to ecstasy. I repeated, "I am you. You are me."

Our flesh pressed. Our tongues probed. Our minds melded. I could feel her ravenous appetite. She hungered for me. I wanted her.

As she became more aroused, so did I. Each touch heightened the other's. When her breathing quickened, so did mine. When my pelvis thrust, so did hers. We fed off each other.

We repeated the mantra, "I am you and you are me."

I entered her mind, becoming one with her. She felt beautiful. I felt beautiful. Inside her psyche, I felt breasts. I kissed erect nipples. She and I squirmed. She kissed my nipples. I hissed, "Yes."

She was me, and now I was her. I felt her body opening and receiving me. Hot and excited, I felt the juices flowing down my thighs. Her psyche thrust deeper.

She hissed, "I want to come inside of you." We reversed positions, with her on top. Her thighs began thrusting. She pinched my nipples.

A shudder rocketed down my spine. I had become Celeste's squirming flesh. I struggled to corral myself back.

"Surrender," she commanded. "You are me and I am you."

I waved the white flag. I wanted her. All of her. Deep inside.

"Yes," I moaned.

The ache between my thighs burned. I screamed, "Yes! Faster. Faster!"

In a frenzy, she penetrated deeper, deeper. She held onto my nipples as if they were reins.

"Oh my God," I screamed. My body writhed on the bed, causing her to thrust faster and squeeze harder.

"OH MY GOD!"

"YES," she cried.

We both exploded into waves of orgasms pounding us like a raging surf. I was her. She was me. Clutching each other, we shook and gasped for air. Until we could take no more.

We collapsed into each other's arms and hovered in a state of blissful oneness. Until I opened my eyes, unsure who was who.

DAY AFTER

SATURDAY, APRIL 8

In the morning I felt weird, very weird. Had I imagined what happened last night, or had we switched bodies, like the science fiction thriller, *Invasion of the Body Snatchers*?

Celeste tried to calm my anxiety. "When two souls connect like we did last night, they merge together into androgyny."

I didn't like the sound of that. I spent the rest of the day making sure I was back in my body. I spat often, scratched my balls, and grunted loudly like a man.

NEW BEGINNINGS

The drive to Queenscliffe took only five minutes. That meant I could dash home for lunch and take Nesha out for a stroll. That would lessen his feelings of abandonment, though I was sure he'd bark and sulk in protest.

I parked my car in the lot and peered into the rearview mirror to comb my hair and straighten my striped blue tie. In spite of Sam's fortune-telling rune of impending darkness, I prepared myself for a positive beginning. I took a deep breath, grabbed my briefcase, then headed for the red brick house, reconverted to accommodate the executive director, clinical director, four therapists, receptionist/office manager, and waiting area. The conference room with kitchen amenities was an add-on.

Sam greeted me with a heartwarming hug. "Welcome. Herbert asked me to get you settled. I've organized fruit and croissants for morning tea."

"With four-fifths of The Family that Cares, it already feels like home."

"You're a perfect fit. I'll show you the office."

She led me down the hall into a sparsely furnished room with beige walls that smelled of fresh paint. A desk, filing cabinet, and chairs occupied the small space. Windows were noticeably absent.

Sam half-apologized. "It's small, but, with a little ingenuity and a plant or two, you'll transform this into a masterpiece."

Michelangelo would be severely challenged to perform such a feat.

"You can interview couples here, but if you have a boisterous lot, use the conference room. You can book the room with Frieda at the front desk."

I placed my briefcase on the scuffed wooden desk. Muffled voices came from the other side of the wall.

"Soundproofing's a problem," she said, ruefully. "We've tried everything short of erecting an extra wall. The best solution for now is the sound machine."

She flicked the switch of a beige canister on the floor. A soft whoosh echoed like a continual wheeze.

"Turn it on when you have a client. It muffles the chatter."

"Who has the office next to me?"

"Geraldine Hackerman. Her clients can get noisy."

She moved toward the door. "I'll see you at morning tea. Don't forget to complete the forms on your desk. Hand them to..."

"Frieda Hoffenhammer," snapped a large, Germanic woman. She strode into my room like one of Wagner's Valkeries. "I'm the office manager."

More like an amalgam of secretary, receptionist, accountant, and Attila the Hun.

"I'll leave the two of you," said Sam on the way out.

"Has she discussed the paperwork?" asked Frieda.

"NO!" shouted a voice next door.

"You'll get used to Geraldine's role plays," she sniggered. "Frankly, if clients aren't angry before they see her, they're mad as hell afterwards."

"Fuck you!"

"For heaven's sake," barked Frieda. "A woman doesn't have to swear."

I turned up the whooshing machine. It was no match for the voices next door. "Isn't there anything we can do?"

The walls reverberated the answer. "NO! I'm not a victim!"

"We tried insulating the ceiling and installing sound boards. Short of earmuffs, the best solution is the sound machine. We'll eventually reconvert a storage room into an office. That will give us another option."

She marched to my desk and picked up a sheaf of papers. She rifled through the tax declaration, benefits applications, and a bunch of bureaucratic forms. "Complete these before noon," she commanded. "I'll add your name to the kitchen clean-up. Everyone's assigned a week of tidying. I don't tolerate messes."

As if to punctuate her point, she picked up a paperclip from the carpet and placed it on the desk. "Any questions, see me at the front desk."

She marched out the same way she entered. Heavy footsteps led her on the next mission.

Thankfully, my other visitors were far more welcoming. Alana and Rosie arrived later bearing gifts. Alana handed me a mug with a picture of koalas in a tree, and Rosie presented me with a box of Irish tea.

"You look a wee bit strange with yer shirt and tie," said Rosie, adjusting her tartan skirt. "Let's not dilly-dally. Time for morning tea."

They brought me to the conference room where Frieda was compulsively arranging croissants and a fruit platter. Herbert Norton waved a croissant. "Welcome, my boy. At last, another man."

Frieda shoved a paper plate in my hand. "I expect you men to help yourself. No waiting on you here."

She glanced disdainfully at Herbert who had crumbs on his white shirt. "Clean up after yourself," she scolded the tubby Executive Director.

He brushed at the crumbs then reached for a piece of pineapple.

"Where's Geraldine?" asked Sam, entering the room.

"Late as usual," scoffed Rosie.

Just then, Geraldine Hackerman scurried through the doorway. The gaunt thirty-five-year-old psychologist slumped into a chair. She wore her black hair short and her thick eyebrows long.

"Sorry I'm late," she huffed. "I had a horrid session with Nola Cutler."

When she spotted me, the psychologist raised her ominous eyebrows. "I'm Geraldine," she announced in a nasal monotone that sounded as if a wad of cotton was stuck up her nose. "I have the office next to you."

"So I heard."

Everyone laughed, except Geraldine. She smirked, "What's your theoretical orientation?"

"There's ample time to get into that," interjected Sam. She passed around the fruit platter.

Herbert reached for a slice of watermelon. "So who's got tickets for the Olympics? Five months before the games start." His head nodded like a bobble-head doll. "I snagged a couple for fencing."

"I'll not be bravin' those crowds," said Rosie. "By the looks of it, the trains will be cartin' two million a day. I'd rather be off on a holiday."

"That's not the Olympic spirit," said Herbert. He grabbed a handful of strawberries. "I was twenty when the Olympics were held in Melbourne. It was 1956. Dawn Fraser and Lorraine Crapp each took two gold medals for swimming. Murray Rose grabbed three. And what about Betty Cuthbert? Her sprint left the others quaking in her dust. She captured three Olympic golds. They made us proud."

"I wasn't even born," said Alana.

Herbert pointed his fork at her. "This September is your turn for Olympic memories."

He prattled on about the upcoming games while Frieda began clean-up. She handed him a plastic bag for rubbish, but he held onto his plate and passed the bag to me.

"It's a pity," he said, "they don't have fishing as an event."

"Before we get back to work," announced Sam, "let's officially welcome Peter."

"Hear, hear," said Herbert, waving a croissant like an Australian flag.

Alana, Sam, and Rosie clapped while Geraldine stared blankly. Frieda was far too busy cleaning up the crumbs.

⋆⋆⋆⋆

Later in the day, I joined Sam in her office which, to no surprise, was decorated with plants and Aboriginal art. Above her desk, a bark painting depicted a black and yellow lizard protecting her eggs.

"Your totem is everywhere."

She nodded. "Reminds me to stay connected. By the way, what did you think of our Geraldine?"

"Needs a sense of humor."

"She can be intense. I encouraged her to attend Gretchen's workshop, but she rejected the idea. I hope you'll help her lighten up. She over-identifies with her abused clients."

"Is she married?"

"Eight years. Her husband's on the shy side."

No doubt she preferred her men docile.

Sam reached for a bundle of files. "Here are your cases. We've been inundated the past six months. With you on board, we can whittle at the waiting list. You'll get most of the males, but there are a few clients who need urgent care."

I was ready to roll up my sleeves and get to work.

SUPERVISION GROUP

TUESDAY, APRIL 11

In the morning, I scheduled appointments for the next few weeks. I expected motivated adult clients. They'd be far more rewarding than oppositional school kids.

When it was time for the supervision group, I made a quick pit stop. The air freshener, potpourri, hand lotion, and sign, NO SANITARY PADS IN THE TOILET, marked the staff toilet as the domain of women. The floral scent lingered as I made my way toward the conference room.

Alana's face brightened when I entered. "I brought bagels for the meeting." She handed me a plate.

"My second day and a second helping."

Rosie passed the strawberry cream cheese. "A wee bit o' replenishment goes a long way."

"Sorry," gasped Geraldine, rushing to a chair. "Another phone crisis. Nola decompensated after yesterday's session. Triggered her narcissistic injury. I need some time."

Sam turned to me. "We start supervision with a check-in to update our lives. Helps us stay connected. Who wants to start?"

Rosie perched her reading glasses atop her red hair. "Kieran and Bridgett were brilliant," puffed the proud mother. "My son rapped the drums like a demon, and my bonnie daughter, oh how she blew the bagpipes. They came first in the south coast pipe band competition in Wollongong."

Her beaming face shifted to a scowl. "But their mongrel father didn't attend. Cowan never found the time when we were married."

"How old are your children?" I asked.

"Kieran's 18 and Bridgett's 16. They're no bleedin' saints, but they take their music seriously."

Rosie reached for her spectacles. "Must say, I had a ruddy good time in Wollongong. A kindly soul bought me a drink."

"Ah-h," I said. "The plot thickens."

"Nothing serious," she said with a glint in her eye. "But Brodie asked me out for dinner."

"Only for dinner?" I teased.

Our clinical director reeled us in. "Let's move on, shall we. We have lots to cover. What about you, Alana?"

The young social worker shrugged. "I was supposed to go out with friends over the weekend but fell into a funk. Didn't feel like going out."

Rosie tapped her knee. "Ye should have called. Fresh air and music would've done ye the world of good. There were some good-lookin' lads."

Alana blushed. "Thanks, but I wasn't in the mood." She nodded to Geraldine. "You can check-in."

The psychologist dabbed a swatch of cheese on her bagel. "I don't like talking about my husband," she began in her annoying, nasal monotone. "But he refuses to tackle his alexithymia." She glanced my way. "Emotional shutdown. How do men expect to be in a relationship?"

"All men aren't shut down," interjected Sam. "Peter attended Gretchen's workshop."

Geraldine scowled, "You're not going on about that again?"

"Outside connections build a therapeutic community."

When Alana and Rosie nodded their support, I bobbed my head.

Geraldine narrowed her black eyebrows and huffed, "I don't want social encounters outside of work. I prefer clear boundaries." She then jutted her jaw towards me. "It's Peter's turn. But be brief. Nola's in crisis."

"I'm glad to be here. Thanks for making me feel at home."

With the exception of Geraldine. Her teeth gnawed a bagel.

After Sam checked in with an update about her marriage heading toward divorce, we finally moved to the business of supervision. There was no doubt in my mind that if we were a group of men, we'd have skipped the personal stuff and brought out the toolbox to fix any problems with clients.

Sam picked up a folder. "The waiting list is now at two months. With Peter on board, we knocked off a month. Does anyone else have room?"

Alana volunteered. "I can probably take another."

Sam shook her head. "Your Vietnamese bereavement group starts in a week. You'll need time to get that off the ground. I don't want anyone burning out."

Alana patted Sam's arm. "Thanks. I was feeling overwhelmed."

Rosie perched her glasses on her nose. "I'm terminatin' Roxanne and her family. Let's see the list."

Sam passed her the folder. "One person's been waiting a long time. Wants to be seen by a female. You know who I'm talking about."

Rosie groaned. "I'll not be wantin' Madge. Her file is five inches thick. I worked with her before. Always in crisis; never satisfied. Can ye take her, Geraldine?"

She vehemently shook her head. "Can't take another borderline. I have far too many as it is. How about Peter? Surely, he can handle borderlines."

"Madge doesn't want a male," said Sam. "Peter's caseload will soon be filled with narcissistic males, conflictual couples, and the occasional antisocial personality disorder."

What about motivated clients?

Sam eventually talked Rosie into taking the case.

The social worker grumbled. "If she files a complaint, ye better cover me butt. It'd be far easier if we had a part-time doc."

Alana agreed. "Can't we talk to Herbert again?"

"I've been over this," sighed Sam. "We're way over budget."

"Which psychiatrist do you use?" I asked.

"I'm on good terms with Kenneth Kukula," said Geraldine, smugly. "He's an excellent diagnostician."

Rosie chortled. "His social skills are as rare as chicken's teeth."

"But clients don't have a long wait," defended Geraldine.

"Too right. They dart in and out of his office faster than swimmers flee a shark."

"Intake schedule," said Sam, assuming control. She turned my way. "Alana, Rosie, and Geraldine each take a day on intake. On Friday we only take emergencies. That leaves Thursday without coverage."

"I've had Mondays for the past year," whined Geraldine. "Can I switch with Peter?"

Sam cautioned me. "Friday's non-emergency contacts are carried over to Monday. You'll get a double helping."

Hoping to score points for teamwork, I volunteered. "Might as well jump in."

Sam smiled approval. "Thanks, Peter."

"Now can we discuss Nola?" asked Geraldine.

Sam gave a weary nod. Rosie leaned back into her chair and rolled her eyes at Alana.

"As everyone knows, except Peter of course," began the psychologist, "I've worked with Nola Cutler for the past two years. Her cutting has reduced considerably since we first met."

She smiled at her self-congratulatory remark and continued. "She uses scissors on her arms and legs. No suicidal ideation, just surface cutting. This morning, Nola phoned, hysterical. She had re-opened old lacerations. Yesterday's session triggered flashbacks about her mother screaming at her for cutting pictures out of Vogue magazines. When Nola was beaten as a child, she withdrew to the bathroom and scraped her legs with scissors. I spent twenty minutes on the phone calming her down, then scheduled an emergency appointment for tomorrow. Her wounds clearly symbolize emotional trauma inflicted by an abusive mother."

Geraldine became so animated talking about the crisis that her nasal monotone reached a higher octave. My assessment: Geraldine didn't want help; she wanted attention. Diagnosis: histrionic.

Sam and the others helped her process the interview and reinforced the treatment plan of self-soothing techniques. While I didn't say so, I thought Geraldine herself could benefit from the same procedures.

After hearing about the cutting client, I hoped my clients wouldn't be as desperate. Tomorrow I'd find out.

DIVING INTO THE DEEP

A westerly breeze swept across the beach as the sun peeped from the clouds. Nesha scampered across the sand and chased seagulls into the surf. I whistled, then shouted, but my passive-aggressive dog ran farther up the beach. When I pretended to head home and leave him behind, he stopped his pursuit of the birds. He was clearly unhappy about my new schedule. Full-time employment and a relationship meant less time for him.

I tried to offset his feelings of abandonment by coming home during lunch hour, but, whenever I left, his whimpering induced waves of guilt. Still, Nesha remained my trusted companion. No matter how long I was away, he always greeted me with a joyful bark and a wagging tail, proving that a dog is a man's best friend.

Today was my late night. Therefore, I didn't clock in until one. That afforded me breakfast with Celeste. Our different routines presented challenges for our relationship. My free evenings conflicted with her thriving massage practice. Many of her clients wanted her busy fingers after hours or on Saturdays. Complicating our relationship further was her obsession with the ashram. For the moment, I chose to avoid conflict and savor the occasions we could spend together, no matter how brief.

Celeste greeted me at the door with a sumptuous kiss. With only two hours to spare, we headed straight for the bedroom to satisfy ravenous appetites. After a nourishing romp, I tore myself away when she offered seconds. It was only my third day on the job. I couldn't be late.

I wolfed down half a quiche and mango wedges, then, after a lingering sensuous kiss, dashed to the car. Savoring the delicious meal, I broke out in song. "Hi ho. Hi ho. Off to work I go. I love Celeste. And she's the best. Hi ho. Hi ho…"

Then I hit traffic. The Sydney Harbour Tunnel was normally faster than the Harbour Bridge, but a fender bender caused a back up. I turned on the radio for an update. Not surprisingly, the news was abuzz with Sydney's preparations for the Olympics. The Prime Minister assured everyone that, come September, all would be ready. Additional seating was being installed at the Aquatic Centre for more people to catch the big splash. While I was excited about the prospects of Olympic gold in Sydney, I dreaded the horde of tourists clogging major arteries.

Fifteen minutes late meant an immediate interception by Frieda. The office manager officiously pointed at her watch and informed me that my first client had arrived forty-five minutes early for her 1:30 appointment. Frieda had completed the financial paperwork, and, based on the sliding fee, had charged the client five dollars for the visit. She brusquely thrust the file into my hands and returned to her post.

I rushed to my office to check my voicemail. Five messages—four from clients to schedule appointments and one from my mother to tell me the "exciting" news that she finished the *pisanki*. Did I really care about dyed Easter eggs? The family's next gathering would take place in less than two weeks—way too soon for me.

I took a deep breath and focused on the upcoming interview. I reviewed the file then, like a diver springing from a board, plunged into my first session.

In the waiting room, I introduced myself to the short, wispy woman sitting under the poster of the abused woman. Bonnie

Kilbourne wore jeans and an oversized T-shirt with a picture of two dolphins splashing in water. Sprinkles of gray in black hair and a tanned, leathered face made her appear much older than her thirty-two years. Protruding eyes brightened when I introduced myself.

"Thanks for seein' me, Doctor Pin... That's a hard name."

"It's Pinowski."

She returned a half-smile. "Mind if I call ya Doctor P? It's easier."

"Sure," I said. "Follow me."

When she entered my office, she scanned the room and furrowed her brow. "This is kinda depressing. No windows," she said. "Ya need some plants."

What was she expecting, a botanical garden? I pointed to a chair near the desk. "We'll have to make do."

She sat down and waved at the bare walls. "Don't ya like pictures?"

I slouched into my swivel chair. "I'm working on that." I opened the intake file and said, "I'd like to get some background..."

"Sorry, Doctor P," she interrupted. "I'm not doin' so good." She reached for the tissues on the desk. "Me boyfriend left." She pulled a wad of tissues and sniffled. "I can't live without him."

"Take it easy, Bonnie."

She whimpered, "Why did he have ta leave me?"

"I don't know. But let's work together on this, shall we?"

"The bed's empty. I can't go on."

"Are you thinking of hurting yourself?"

Sniff, sniff. "I don't wanna wake up in the morning. Not without Perry." Tears trickled down to the swimming dolphins. "We were soul mates."

"When did he leave?"

"Three weeks ago." Sniff, sniff. "Said he didn't need me."

She blew her nose.

I handed her the trash bin. "How long were you together?"

She tossed the wad into the bin. "Four years. We fought a lot. I don't wanna live without him."

"Are you thinking about taking your life?"

She began to sob uncontrollably. Tears splashed her dolphins. She caught her breath and whimpered, "Perry's left before and come back. But now, I don't know. He took his clothes and some of me stuff. If he doesn't return, I don't wanna live."

I wheeled my chair closer. "I'll help you get through this, but I need to know if you're planning on killing yourself."

She dabbed her watery eyes. "Why?"

"If you're serious about suicide, you'll need intensive treatment at the hospital."

The wispy woman vehemently shook her head. "I don't wanna go ta hospital."

"I want to make sure you're safe."

She brushed bits of tissue from her oversized T-shirt. "I'm not gonna do nothin'."

"If you did, how would you do it?"

The tanned-leathered face creased into a scowl. "Goin' ta hospital won't help. It didn't for Perry."

"He was hospitalized?"

"Ta get off drugs."

"What did this Perry look like?"

"He wasn't the best but he had a heart of gold when he wasn't usin'. He played guitar and pretended he was Elvis. Made me laugh."

Crikey! The chain-smoking Elvis wannabe?

"Did he ever, uh, receive help, like attend a group workshop?" I asked.

Bonnie sighed. "I tried tough love. Threatened ta kick him out if he didn't go ta a weekend group. I even paid. He dropped out and went back ta being a druggo. Stole things again. I couldn't have that. Tole him ta leave. But I didn't really want him ta go."

"Bonnie," I consoled. "You're in a lot of pain. It's important to get on with your life."

She pulled the last tissue from the box. "Perry left me...all alone." She wailed, "I need him. He'll be back. He has ta."

I removed fresh tissues from the bottom drawer. "Take a few breaths," I said, handing her the box. "Calm yourself."

She blew her nose. "I love the bastard. We used ta have good sex. When he's not usin', he can be nice. When he's drinkin' or usin' ice, he turns into a monster."

"He took methamphetamine?"

She nodded. "Bad stuff. When he's usin', he calls me stupid and ugly. Says I'm the one who's psycho." She wiped her eyes. "Guess he's right."

"The best thing you can do is get better," I said. "Are you on medication?"

She scrunched the tissues into a ball and tossed them in the trash. "I don't want no medication."

"Anti-depressants can help. I'll refer you to a psychiatrist for an evaluation."

She stamped her foot on the carpet. "No drugs. I don't wanna be like Perry or me dad."

"Your father was an addict?"

She shrugged. "Cocaine. But he was a good dad when he wasn't usin.'"

I stared at the dolphins now swimming in tears. Bonnie was hooked on helping addicts, seeking the love she never received. If she could realize this, she might take better care of herself.

I leaned forward. "You're in pain and need plenty of support. I'll provide individual therapy but you'll need a women's group..."

"No group," she pouted. "And no drugs."

Nothing like a cooperative client to start the day. "Let's take it one step at a time," I said calmly. "Will you work with me?"

Her wide eyes glanced around the room. "Ya need plants and pictures. And can't ya get a window?"

"Not unless I break a hole in the wall," I teased. "But I think a plant and picture would definitely help."

I spotted a hint of a smile.

"You'll get through this," I assured her. "But let's talk about your support system. Do you have any friends or family?"

She shook her head. "Perry was me friend, and me mum and sis are in Queensland. Don't talk ta 'em."

"What about your job. Says in the intake, you work part-time as a waitress."

"Missed a couple of days. They may not want me back."

"Listen, Bonnie. Even if you don't want medication or a group, you still have to eat. Working will keep you connected to others as well as provide an income. You need the job."

"It's only a coffee shop."

I picked up my mug with the picture of koalas. "Nothing wrong with a cappuccino."

She half-smiled. "Guess I can go there after we're done."

"That's the spirit."

"Can I see ya Friday?"

"Well, uh, that may be a bit soon." I reached for my appointment book. "How about Monday afternoon?"

She grimaced. "Can't wait that long."

I snatched a tissue and wiped my forehead. "Monday's only five days away. If you're having a difficult time before then, you can call me."

Her face softened. "Ya won't be busy?"

I tapped my pen on her file. "Not too busy to help you take care of yourself."

She hesitated a moment, then said, "Thanks."

I completed the assessment session and discussed the treatment plan. It included a no-suicide contract and a commitment to get help if she contemplated self-injury. While one can never be totally sure about a suicidal risk, I believed she grabbed hold of the counseling lifeline to drag herself to shore. Attached to therapy, she had a better chance at overcoming turbulent waves.

I would have to wade through her transference, as she'd likely project her longing for a father figure onto me. That would come later. My immediate concern was to instill a purpose for living.

KOOKABURRA SIGHTINGS

Koo-koo-koo-koo-koo-ka-ka-ka-ka-ka.

I rolled over and checked the clock. 6:00 a.m. Bloody bird! The eerie laughter erupted again and prompted Nesha to bark his way to the front of the apartment. I found him staring through the sliding glass door at my balcony railing. A perched kookaburra clicked its large beak. The white head and brown band around its eyes reminded me of a bandit. I rushed toward the door, forcing the bird to take flight.

"I'll have the last laugh!" I yelled victoriously to Nesha. "That'll teach him to wake us up."

Nesha ran for his shaggy duck and returned with it clutched tight in his jaws. When he shook it, the duck wheezed instead of quacked.

"That's the fourth toy you've broken."

Woof. Woof.

"Oh, what the hell. Let's go to the beach."

Nesha jubilantly led the way across the street toward his favorite post, the one with dog poo removal instructions. I chuckled every time he left a deposit. Fortunately, we had an early start, which meant more time at the beach. That didn't stop Nesha from barking disapproval when I tried to corral him back home. After many failed attempts, I attached the leash and dragged him indoors. We found the kookaburra back on the balcony, this time with a tiny lizard wriggling in its beak. No sense chasing the damn bird. I was already late for work.

With two minutes to spare, I rushed into the office. Frieda immediately handed me a message.

"Bonnie Kilbourne called twice," she pronounced. "Wants you to call ASAP."

I hurried to my office. Bonnie picked up after the first ring.

"It's Dr. Pinowski."

"I'm sorry for causin' ya trouble, but I'm feelin' real bad. Can I come and see ya today?"

I took a deep breath. "Has anything happened?"

I heard muffled tears, then silence.

"Bonnie?"

"I'm...sorry," she sniffled. "Don't know if I can go on like this."

"Do you feel like hurting yourself?"

More silence. My heart sank. "Bonnie, talk to me."

"I'm sorry, Doctor P. Ya told me ta call if I was feelin' bad."

"That's right, Bonnie. Are you feeling bad enough to kill yourself?" I held my breath.

"Don't wanna talk on the phone. Can I come in?"

"I can see you later this morning, but I need to know if you're thinking of hurting yourself."

"If I can talk, that might make me feel better."

"Alright. Come in at 11:30." I wondered if she was emotionally desperate or desperately dependent.

Not surprisingly, Bonnie arrived twenty-five minutes early. Whatever her emotional state, she needed clear boundaries. I waited until our set time, then collected her. She wore the same splashing dolphins T-shirt.

"Still no plants or pictures."

"Yeah, well, hopefully by your next session. You said you needed to talk."

"I feel bad without Perry. Like I don't wanna live. But after our talk, I thought about what ya said. I wanna follow your advice, Doctor P, but the weekend's gonna be hard. What if Perry doesn't come back?"

Tears trickled down her cheeks. She came prepared with a hanky.

"It may be hard to imagine life without him, but we're working together, right?"

She wiped her eyes. "It's hard without him."

"It's harder if you're not on your own side."

She crinkled her nose. "What do ya mean?"

"I may be asking a lot, but you have to put your life first."

She blew into the hanky. "Ya make it sound easy. When I left here Wednesday, I felt better. But the bad thoughts came back."

"About killing yourself?"

She frowned. "I don't wanna do it, but there's nothin' to live for."

"If you won't be safe over the weekend, I can organize a stay at the hospital."

She flinched. "Don't ya start talkin' about that hospital. I'm not goin'. They'll put drugs in me. Can't I call ya on the weekend?"

I shook my head. "We're not set up for after hours. Emergencies are referred to the ER."

"What if someone really needs ta talk?" she asked desperately.

"Are you working this weekend?"

Bonnie gave a half-hearted shrug. "Maybe."

"Listen, Bonnie," I said sternly. "You can't stay at home and wait for Perry. Go to your job. You'll be with other people. And you'll earn money."

"I'm NOT a victim!"

Bonnie and I both jumped.

Crikey! This was not the time for Geraldine's empowering techniques. I heard her shout, "Say it louder!"

Bonnie nervously glanced around the room at the next, "I AM NOT A VICTIM!"

"I'm sorry. Bad soundproofing." I turned on the sound machine. The wheezing dampened the noise, but a woman's muffled voice could still be heard.

Bonnie blew her nose then became self-conscious about her honking. "Maybe they can hear us."

"Only if we're shouting."

Even with the bloody machine, we heard, "I AM NOT!"

Bonnie frantically glared at the bare wall. "Someone's getting yelled at. Ya have ta do somethin', Doctor P."

I reassured her, "It's okay. They're role-playing. Let's refocus. Is there anyone you can talk to over the weekend?"

Her eyes darted from me to the wall. "Can we have a different room?"

"Not right now."

"I can't talk with someone shoutin'."

"Next time you come, I'll make sure the room's quiet."

"How about this afternoon?"

I gritted my teeth and cursed Geraldine. "I'll do something about the noise before Monday. Let's tough it out and talk about the weekend. Do you have any friends?"

A muffled "You bastard" echoed in the background.

Bonnie stood up. "I won't be botherin' no one. And I hope ya don't have any more yellin' on Monday."

"If you're feeling bad and think about harming..."

"I can't take the yellin'," she scowled.

With Geraldine's client bellowing next door, it was useless to dissuade a disgruntled Bonnie from leaving. Her parting words, "If I come on Monday, no more yellin'."

⟵⟵⟵⟵

When Geraldine finished her session, I rapped on her open door.

She turned from her desk and squared her jaw. "I'm pressed for time. What is it?"

I seethed. "I had to cut a session short with a depressed woman. She was traumatized by your client's venting."

Geraldine bared her teeth. "Herbert hasn't taken my advice to get off his fat bum and turn the storage room into an extra office. But since you're a man, he may listen to you. In the meantime, I will not stop empowering my clients."

"I'm not asking you to change what you're doing," I hissed. "I don't want a fragile client blown out of the room. The least you can do is let me know when your clients will practice their newfound power."

Geraldine's nasal voice pierced the room. "I can't plan those sessions. And I don't like your caustic comments."

I wasn't about to get into a flaming argument, not now, anyway. "Imagine if one of your female clients was suicidal and depressed, and I had a couple in my office screaming at one another. Surely, you'd be upset."

Her eyebrows twitched. "Tell Herbert we need that extra office. I can use the support."

To avoid a raging battle during my first week at work, I decided on diplomacy and pleaded my case. "My client had an abusive boyfriend. She's hyper-sensitive to loud noises. You're the expert on victimized women. You know the symptoms."

She relaxed her eyebrows. "When will you see her?"

"Monday afternoon. 2:30."

She reluctantly checked her schedule. "That should work. I'm teaching a client relaxation techniques."

"My client will appreciate it. I'll book her future appointments at the same time."

As I turned to leave, Geraldine called out, "Don't forget to talk to Herbert. When that office is finished, we won't have to juggle schedules."

"He'll definitely hear from me." And it wasn't about moving to a reconverted storage room.

Unfortunately, his door was closed. I left him a voicemail complaining about Geraldine's noise. In the meantime, I decided on my own course of action.

SHARK ATTACK

SATURDAY, APRIL 15

Celeste and I trundled down to Shelly Beach, south of Manly in Cabbage Tree Bay. The aquatic reserve offered a small, protected beach that attracted families and anyone interested in marine life. As we walked along the sand, several scuba divers surfaced in the bay.

Since Celeste was gung ho on snorkeling, I purchased a mask fitted with prescription lenses. I didn't want to swim blind among the dangerous creatures lurking beneath the surface—venomous blue-ringed octopi, barb-tailed stingrays, and man-eating sharks.

The other animal I was concerned about was Celeste. Like some of the buff, well-tanned women on Bondi Beach, she preferred to go topless. While that suited me fine when we were alone, I was embarrassed by her public exposure. She called me a prude, but I hated the fact that horny blokes leered at her breasts when she baked on the sand.

Today, she saved me the discomfort and kept her top on. A small yellow triangle barely covered her left breast while a red triangle covered the right one. The colors were the same as the flags marking the swimmers' safety zone, policed by lifeguards. Mind you, I would have preferred swimming between Celeste's red and yellow flags rather than jeopardizing my life underwater.

Because of her work schedule, we couldn't snorkel until late in the day. That made me queasy, since sunset was only a few hours away, when fish hunted for their evening meal. Celeste reassured me we were well protected in the bay. She pointed to the cloudless sky and the sun shimmering off the water like sparkling diamonds.

"Let's go while there's still light." She donned her flippers and mask and moved gracefully into the ocean.

I stepped gingerly into the shallow water. Br-r-r-r. A helicopter hovered down the coast, probably checking for sharks. I was ready to return to the warm sand when Celeste surfaced.

"You'll get used to it," she yelled, then like a mermaid, disappeared under the surface.

I fastened the mask and snorkel and poked my face underwater. The prescription lenses made the underwater world crystal clear. Too clear. A school of small bream startled me. I surfaced.

Celeste waved an arm. "Out here!" She cried. "Incredible fish."

I gazed at her beckoning flags and waded waist deep. Slowly, cautiously, my shivering body swam toward her. Then she disappeared under water. I nervously looked around, then felt a tug on my swimmers. They dropped to my knees. I screamed when a hand jiggled Freddie. Panicking, I grabbed for my shorts to prevent a carnivorous fish from attacking the dangling bait. Celeste surfaced and laughed uproariously.

I sputtered into the snorkel. "DON'T."

Before I could scold her, she dove again. I kept her in sight as I paddled nearer the shore. Periodically, I peered underwater, searching for predators. When none could be found, I breathed more easily. I spotted baby squid, a large cuttlefish, and a seahorse. Then I came upon a four-foot blue grouper. The large, slow-moving creature seemed oblivious to me. No wonder the dumb fish was protected. A dumber spear fisherman would incur an $11,000 fine or three months' prison time if caught with one.

I waved my arm to catch Celeste's attention and show her the fish. When she saw me, she yelled for me to come quick. Preparing myself for another prank, I approached her warily, with one hand clutching my shorts.

When I reached her, she dove. Her flippers kicked up a spray. I backed off and peered underwater. Beneath the surface, my mermaid gently kicked her fins and left a trail of golden hair floating behind her. She pointed excitedly at a stingray stirring up the sand. She returned to the surface for air and dove again, this time toward a speckled gray and brown rock. I swam closer. It moved! The rock turned into a six-foot wobbegong shark with beady eyes. Celeste recklessly swam toward the sand shark and startled it. It darted away from her but headed straight toward me. Its ugly, whiskered mouth opened. Shark attack!

The adrenaline kicked in. I flailed my arms to escape. In the process, I knocked the snorkel out of my mouth and gulped air and salt water. Coughing and spluttering, I thrashed madly toward the shore, believing that at any minute the shark's mouth would chomp a leg. Terror drove me forward until I beached myself like a whale.

Exhausted, I coughed out water and cleared my lungs. I collapsed on the sand and trembled about nearly losing a limb.

When I heard the sound of flip flops, I opened my eyes and saw Celeste in her flippers.

"You okay?" she said, half concerned, half laughing. "I've never seen you move so fast."

"I could've been killed," I spluttered.

"It was only a harmless sand shark," she giggled.

"This one attacked me!"

She knelt down beside me and tickled my ribs. "I'm the only one who wants to attack you."

I wasn't amused. I grabbed my mask from the sand. No more snorkeling. As far as I was concerned, the beach was closed.

PALM SUNDAY

APRIL 16

Palm reader at psychic fair. Her one good eye scans my hands. She cackles, "Relationships. Double trouble." Her boney finger traces my palm. Leaves yellow, sticky slime. I jerk my hand away. An alarm bell rings. She seizes my hand. Jams it in her mouth. Bites hard. The bell rings again.

I pulled my hand out of Nesha's slobbering mouth and stumbled for the ringing phone.

"Hello?... You woke me up... No, I haven't gone to church... I know it's Palm Sunday... Go ahead, pray for me."

Woof! Woof!

"Have to take Nesha out before he pees on the carpet... No, I can't pick up the *gołabki*. I have other plans. Got to go. 'Bye."

Celeste stretched her arms and yawned. "Who's that?"

"My mother. Don't ask."

She grabbed my hand and tugged me toward the bed. "Where're you going?"

Nesha scratched at the front door.

"He has to go. Keep the bed toasty."

She caught hold of one of my fingers and sucked hard. She released it and cooed, "I'll be waiting."

I threw on clothes and herded Nesha through his morning ritual. "Hurry," I said. "I'm freezing."

He bounded toward the beach. I tugged hard on the leash. Shivering from the cold drizzle, I marshaled him back home. I poured his food, then leapt back into the warm bed.

Celeste screamed. "Ag-g-g-h! The iceman cometh."

I rubbed against her. "Payback for yesterday."

"You're not putting a coldsicle inside me."

I kissed her hands. "Palm Sunday. Time for worship." My lips moved up her arms to her neck, then her luscious lips. I brushed her blonde curls and kissed her passionately. "Are you ready for the resurrection?"

I reached between her thighs. They were already thawing.

"Hey!" I pushed Nesha and his licking tongue away from my face. I picked up his shaggy duck and tossed it out the bedroom. As soon as he scampered after it, I closed the door.

Woof! Woof! Jealous that Celeste and the smell of her cats had taken over my bed, he scratched at the door. Last night, I'd had to let him back in.

"Pets are like children," said Celeste. "They can't stand being neglected."

I ignored the barking. "Now where were we? Ready for a hotsicle?"

"Mmmmm."

Thus began our day of worship.

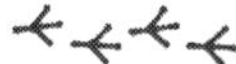

Later in the day, I prepared a salad while Celeste added veggies to the pizza before popping it in the oven.

"I was hoping you'd join me for a special satsang tonight."

I groaned at the mere mention of the ashram. "I thought we'd take in a movie."

She wrapped her arms around my waist. "Babaji is better than a movie. Come with me."

"I can't sit next to you."

She kissed my neck. "You're next to me now."

I gazed into her twinkling hazel eyes. I kissed the freckles on her nose, then the dimples on her smiling face. How could I resist? Seems my mother's prayers would be answered. I'd be attending a service after all.

INTAKE

I now understood why Elizabeth was so keen on switching intake days. In addition to handling the backlog from Friday, I had today's requests for service. My job was to screen out the druggies and chronically mentally ill who needed to be referred to other treatment programs. The most distressing part of the job was informing callers about the three-month waiting list. The dismal news left prospective clients more depressed than before the call. Fortunately, there were no suicidal or homicidal threats. However, one bastard wouldn't take no for an answer.

"I need to be seen today," he barked on the phone.

"As I said, you're not at risk, so you have to wait until an appointment is available."

"If I don't talk to someone," he yelled, "who knows what I'll do."

I scanned my notes: Cedric Crossan, twenty-nine-year-old truck driver, married one year with no children, mandated by his employer to seek therapy.

"You said you weren't planning on hurting anyone."

"That was before I found out I had to wait. What the hell's wrong with you?"

"Cedric, you told me you were laid off work because you swore at your boss."

"It's not me problem he's an asshole. He won't let me back till I get counseling."

"If you need immediate help, I can provide the names of private therapists."

"Do you know how much they cost?" he yelped. "I'm not paying those prices. You have a sliding fee."

"But we also have a waiting list."

He screamed, "I'll lose me job if I don't see someone! Do you want that on your head?"

I scribbled *Intermittent Explosive Disorder* on the intake form. "We'll call you if there's a cancellation."

"I don't have to take this shit," he growled. "Who's your boss?"

"W-why do you want to speak with her?"

"Since you won't help, someone else will. Gimme your boss."

Crikey! A complaint on my first day of intake. I squeezed the phone. "Cedric, I'm sure we can work this out."

"You're damn right. Gimme the boss."

"Alright," I acquiesced. "Hold on a sec." I placed the call on hold and waited thirty seconds. "Sorry, Cedric, she's not available. But I'll tell you what I can do, since you're so distressed. I checked my schedule. There was a cancellation tomorrow at two. I can see you then."

Silence. Then a grumble. "I'm busy at two. Can you make it eleven."

The bastard! No way could I skip supervision.

"I'm booked solid. Since it's important to get back to work, surely, you can change your plans."

More silence. Then, "What else do you have?"

So much for the urgency. "That's it, Cedric. Two o'clock and that's because of a cancellation. If you don't want to go on the waiting list, take this slot."

And stop wasting my time!

He hemmed a bit, then groused, "I guess I can meet me mate later. Tomorrow, then."

I gave the bastard directions and slammed the receiver down. Sam will obviously want to know why he jumped queue. What could I say? He was an asshole!

⤺⤺⤺⤺

Not surprisingly, Bonnie appeared twenty minutes early. I waited before collecting her for our third session. When she walked into my office, her eyes brightened at the sight of the potted plant in the corner. She fondled the red and green woolly flowers that resembled tiny paws.

"One of me favorites. Kangaroo paws."

"I bought it over the weekend." I tapped the start button of the CD player on my desk. "Soothing music should help today." Tony O'Connor's haunting bush music played in the background.

She glared at the wall. "Hope there's no more yellin'."

"Shouldn't be." As long as Elizabeth kept her word.

She touched the wall and checked for vibrations. "That's better." She rested in the chair and, with a childish grin, asked, "Can I bring in *ABBA*?"

Their popular song came to mind, "Gimme, Gimme, Gimme."

"Sure. How are you feeling?"

Her eyes dropped to the floor. "Perry's back."

"Perry? What happened?"

"He's usin' again. Wanted money. I begged him ta come here. If you'd talk ta him, he might listen."

I doubted that. "Is he still with you?"

Her eyes watered. "He stayed Saturday night and left the next day with the stereo. I don't sleep well when he's usin'. I worry he'll do bad things. He must've put somethin' in me drink, 'cause I slept till noon."

"Perry sounds dangerous."

"You can help him."

"I don't think he wants help."

She sniffled. "Why did he have ta take me stereo? I can't play ABBA."

I handed the bereft woman the tissues. "Your relationship with Perry isn't healthy. He's used and abused you. You have to let him go and care for yourself."

Her dark brown eyes bulged. "I don't want him ta go."

"When he's with you, he treats you like crap and steals your things."

"Not all the time," she protested.

"He makes you feel like he cares, then hurts and intimidates you. You hope he'll change but he doesn't. You become helpless and powerless."

She stamped her foot. "What are ya talkin' about?"

I drew a large square on my writing pad and sketched a picture of a rat inside the square. I showed it to her. "When I was in graduate school, I studied rats. One was put in a cage and given electric shocks. After a while, it became immobilized, unable to move. Even when the door to the cage was open, it acted helpless and did nothing. It learned to be helpless. That's why you stay in this abusive relationship. It's as if you have no power over your life. You see Perry as the one who'll make you happy."

She crossed her arms and sulked.

"The rat that was shocked into helplessness was eventually taught to regain its power. A string was tied to its paw and an electric shock was administered to the cage. When the string pulled the paw upward, the electric current stopped. This was repeated until the rat learned to move its legs by itself. That was the only way to stop the pain and walk again."

I echoed Gretchen's message. "It's time to wake up and find your way home."

Her body quivered, then erupted into sobs. The realization sank in that she wouldn't find love or happiness with Perry.

"Keep breathing through the pain."

She wept while a droning didgeridoo played in the background. The best I could do at the moment was witness her suffering—the hardest part of the job.

She grabbed more tissues and wiped her dribbling nose. "You're right, Doctor P. Perry's a druggo. He won't come back till he needs money."

"Better to realize that now than later. You can build a life without him."

She peered through soggy, brown eyes. "How do I do that? Can't even play me ABBA."

"See me individually and attend a women's group."

She twisted her head from side to side. "No group."

"You need friends and people who care about you."

"I can see you."

"That's not enough," I said. "You need healthy relationships."

Her eyes leaked again. "Not now."

I tried another tack. "What about a pet? I have a dog. He's a wonderful companion."

That piqued her interest. "What kinda dog?"

"A cross between a bull terrier and a short-haired pointer. He can be a pain, but he's loyal and affectionate."

"Don't ya have a girlfriend?"

I shifted uneasily. "It's not appropriate to talk about my personal life."

She crinkled her nose. "I'm not wantin' to be your girlfriend. Just wanna know if you ever had the same problem."

I reached for a tissue and mopped my head. "Everyone has problems in relationships."

She persisted. "Did anyone ya love ever leave?"

"Listen, Bonnie. What's important is that we focus on taking care of you. That means creating a safe home. That's what our work is about."

"When will I see ya next?"

I checked the calendar and the Easter holiday break. "We're closed Good Friday, Easter Monday, and Tuesday, which is Anzac Day."

She yelped, "Can't wait till the middle of next week. I need ta see ya before Easter."

Either I saw her in three days, on Holy Thursday, or in nine days, on the Wednesday following Easter. With Perry lurking around, this wasn't a good time for a long break.

"Okay," I agreed. "Let's meet Thursday afternoon. Making requests is one way to look after yourself."

She smiled coyly. "I'll follow your suggestions." She reached over and patted my arm. "Thanks, Doctor P."

I wanted to create an emotional home, but without me as a permanent fixture. Awkward about her touch, I picked up her file and used my best professional voice. "Let's talk further about self care."

TRADITION

TUESDAY, APRIL 18

Tradition created regularity. So did bran muffins. The tradition during supervision was to eat and discuss clients. Adhering to the custom, I brought the muffins to the conference room where Alana was brewing tea. Sam arranged the wedges of watermelon on a platter while Rosie sliced homemade banana nut bread. Geraldine arrived late with a sense of urgency on her plate. The bulging case file under her armpit indicated another crisis.

Alana poured tea and offered a cup with a generous smile. More than anyone else at the agency, she went out of her way to make me feel at home. She was ten years younger and had a sweet face and nice figure, but kept it hidden, like her mottled teeth. I wondered whether her attentiveness was a genuine desire to make me feel comfortable or whether she had a crush.

"Grab your food," called Sam. "Let's start."

As per tradition, we checked-in with personal updates. I kept mine brief but spoke glowingly about my relationship with Celeste. Rosie puffed like a mother hen and mentioned her children's highland band was cutting a CD. Alana shared that her therapy with Gretchen had incorporated breath-work to release blocked energy. Geraldine bitterly complained that her husband, like many men, refused to attend couple's therapy. The most alarming news, however, came from Sam, who dropped a bombshell. The Board of Directors was pressuring Herbert to retire.

"The Board should leave us be," seethed Rosie, who shook her fist so hard, her reading glasses plopped from her head. "They'd bugger up a tin of soup."

"My friend on the Board confided in me," said Sam. "Herbert is sixty-seven, and slowing down. They want dynamic leadership."

So much for tradition!

"Sam!" exclaimed Alana. "You should apply for the position."

She wagged her head. "I'm strictly clinical. But we're getting ahead of ourselves. He hasn't retired yet. I'll update everyone when I hear more." She reached for her yellow pad. "Let's move to cases. Who needs help?"

We all raised our hands. Alana wanted to discuss her group of grieving Vietnamese; Rosie needed to report on Madge, the borderline; Geraldine, not surprisingly, had to process another session with her cutter; and I needed time for Bonnie.

Sam gave me the nod. "Since you haven't presented yet, you can start."

On my left, Geraldine folded her arms and jutted out her jaw, upset she couldn't go first.

I turned away from her and faced the more receptive audience. I told them about Bonnie and her relationship with Perry.

"A ruddy scoundrel," snarled Rosie. "Knew it the first time I laid eyes on him."

"How many sessions have you had?" asked Sam.

"I saw her in crisis twice last week and then yesterday. She's depressed, with some suicidal ideation. Thus far, no real intent or plan. She resisted my recommendation for a psychiatric evaluation and possible medication."

"So what kind of help are you looking for?" interjected Geraldine, clutching her thick file.

I glared at her. "If you recall, she's the one who was traumatized by your role play. I had a hell of a time calming her down."

"That's not my fault," she glowered. "You should have worked that out with me before you saw her. Did you talk with Herbert?"

Sam intervened. "Construction on the new room will begin in a couple of months. But let's get back to Peter's client." She asked me, "What's your assessment?"

"She has features of a dependent personality disorder. She arrives early and has a difficult time leaving. She became agitated about the prospect of waiting more than a week for the next session."

Our clinical director offered cautionary advice. "She wants you to take care of her. She may interpret any attempt to set limits as neglect or rejection. Be caring and firm, just like you would with a child, but establish clear boundaries. When she's able to trust you, she can heal her distrust about being loved."

Rosie reached for the banana nut bread and passed it around. "She's a hungry bird with her mouth wide open."

"And make sure you and Geraldine work out your schedule," counseled Sam. "She's hyper-vigilant, so make her feel safe. You model a man who's nurturing and caring, in contrast to the men in her life who were abusive and rejecting. She may idealize you as the good parent and become a compliant child in the hope you'll satisfy her dependency needs. Be warned, she'll test you. She'll anticipate abandonment. If she senses it, be prepared for rage and withdrawal."

Rosie nibbled on the bread. "I teach clients to pamper themselves when feeling lonely or neglected." She patted Alana's knee. "She'd be great for yer women's group."

Alana beamed. "The women are needy but can be very giving. She'd fit right in."

"Bonnie resisted that suggestion," I said. "Maybe after more individual work."

Geraldine raised her dark eyebrows and sniffled. "What about your counter-transference?"

Sam nodded. "Didn't you look after your mother when she was depressed?"

"Uh, yes," I answered, uneasily.

"Bonnie may provoke similar emotions you had as a child. As therapists, we often face old wounds that are triggered by clients. Be aware of any feelings about caring for a dependent woman."

Geraldine jutted her jaw. "Is it easier for you if the woman is passive or in control?"

"I prefer it when there's more of a balance, don't you?" I snapped. She clearly preferred being on top.

Before Geraldine could play queen of the mountain, Sam interceded. "Our dependency issues are worth exploring, but we have plenty of cases to discuss."

Geraldine tapped her watch. "Nola's phoning after supervision. I need to discuss her."

"Thanks for the input." I avoided Geraldine's pouty face. "I'll keep everyone up to date."

Alana patted my arm. "Bonnie's fortunate to have you on her side."

"Yeah, well, I appreciate the support."

↞↞

After supervision, Alana caught me in the corridor. "Want to go out for lunch?"

"I have to head home and let my dog out."

"I can keep you company." She smiled with anticipation.

"Maybe another time," I said awkwardly. "I'll grab a quick bite and let him loose on the beach."

Alana's smile turned upside down. Her dejected face made me feel dreadful. I assuaged my guilt by promising lunch next week. While that appeased her, it made me realize the intricacy of staff relations, especially if Alana wanted more than friendship. Fortunately, Nesha provided a ready-made excuse for an escape during lunch.

I returned an hour later for my two o'clock appointment. Cedric Crossan arrived fifteen minutes late with barely an apology.

"I need a letter for me boss," began the truck driver. He reminded me of a beer barrel polka, minus the polka. With a bulbous nose and a belly hanging over his khaki shorts, Cedric wore a T-shirt inscribed with a slogan, *A Beer Never Disagrees With You*. He ran beefy hands over the top of his buzz-sawed head.

"How long is this gonna take?"

I smelled the hint of brew on his breath. "Normally, the first session is an hour," I said. "But since you arrived late, we only have 45 minutes."

"As long as me boss gets a letter."

"He wants to know you're in treatment?"

Cedric winced. "I'm not here for treatment. I was told to take anger classes."

"Because you were laid off for calling your boss an asshole?"

He chuckled. "I was the only one who had the balls to say that to his face."

"How often do you get mad?"

He tugged at his belt. "Only when the other bloke deserves it!"

I reviewed the intake form. "You're twenty-nine and have been married one year. Has your wife ever complained about your temper?"

"Listen, mate," he roared. "Me wife and I get along fine. Never hit her, if that's what you're tryin' to say."

"Bear with me, Cedric," I said. "I'm just trying to assess your situation. Does your wife think you have a problem with anger?"

He scratched his thumb up his bulbous nose. "She'd say I yell sometimes. But I've never touched her."

"So she might complain about your temper?"

"All wives complain."

"Does she ever say anything about your drinking?"

He guffawed. "She has a few beers with me every night."

I doubted they drank only a few. Since he delivered kegs to pubs, he probably took advantage of the leftovers.

"What other complaints does your boss have about you?"

"Listen, mate. The boss is on me ass for taking too long with deliveries. Hell, he doesn't have to push barrels around." He pointed to his scraped legs. "They get dinged up from pushin' kegs while he sits in a bloody air-conditioned office. I had enough of his shit. Tole him to stick it up his ass. Then I called him an asshole."

Cedric glanced at the wall clock. "So when do I get me letter?"

"After the assessment. But we have to decide on a plan." I scribbled on my notepad.

The human beer keg cracked his knuckles. "Listen, mate. I don't need any help. I won't be causin' any more trouble. Me job's too important. Call me a one-session cure."

I tapped my pen. "Right now, all I can write is that we've started treatment, I mean, anger management classes." I gazed at his bulging knuckles. "Have you ever hurt anyone on the job?"

He leaned forward. "This confidential?"

"Absolutely."

His thumb reached for the inside of his nostril. "I once tossed a beer keg at one of the blokes. But it was empty and he started it."

"What happened?"

"Nuthin' really. A few bruises. But he didn't have to be makin' fun of me, now did he?"

I eyed his massive hands. "Have you ever punched anyone or anything?"

"Put a few holes in walls but, I swear, haven't hit anyone in a while."

"And the last time was?"

He scratched the brown stubble atop his head. "Dunno. Maybe three months ago. A bloke in a pub poked fun at me wife. Had to defend her, now didn't I? All in good sport. He even apologized to me missus when it was over."

I imagined Cedric stomping his head. "Any blood?"

He shrugged. "He tripped over a table. Maybe a bloody nose."

I jotted my diagnosis, *Intermittent Explosive Disorder*. "You obviously have a problem with anger. When you were a boy, did you get into fights?"

"Hang on," he fumed. "Every boy fights. Well, maybe not you. But me dad taught me never to take any funny stuff. And if I did, he'd take me to the shed."

He proudly puffed out his chest and the T-shirt with *A Beer Never Disagrees with You*. "I was taught to be a man, not a gay poofter. I hope you're not one of 'em."

"I'm not," I protested. "And besides, that doesn't make any difference whether I can help. What's clear is that your temper affects your work. You called your boss a name and threw a beer keg at a worker."

"It was empty."

"The real issue," I said, raising my voice, "is your anger. You want to keep your job, don't you?"

He slapped his thigh hard. "That's why I'm here."

I wanted to scream, *then work with me, for Christ sake*. I clenched my teeth. "We'll have to work on controlling our emotions."

Cedric sneered, "Will you write the letter?"

"I can confirm that you've attended one session and will continue with treatment." His clenched fist made me correct myself. "Anger management classes."

I plodded through the assessment and was relieved when our time was up. As I scheduled his next session, he snarled, "Where's me letter?"

"You can pick it up tomorrow or wait till next week."

His thumb scratched the inside of his nose once again. "Me boss won't let me back without one. I can't lose me job."

I wanted to punch the bastard's nose and, in the process, break his finger. I had let the ingrate jump the waiting list queue. In addition to arriving late, he demanded immediate attention. No wonder he had problems!

I picked up his file and stood up. "I have another appointment. I'll have it done by the end of the day."

He didn't budge. "How about now? Won't take but a sec. Saves me from comin' back."

I plopped the file back on the desk. "This isn't the best way for us to work together."

He squeezed the armrests so tightly, I thought he'd etch permanent grooves. His face steamed. "Let me speak to your boss."

Demands and threats would have to be dealt with later. In the meantime, I typed the goddamn letter with one sentence. "Cedric Crossan attended counseling today and has agreed to return for another session."

I wanted to add my diagnosis but figured I'd lose a chair. I would tackle his threatening behavior in the next session. I could hardly wait!

⫷⫷⫷⫷

As I typed the assessment, Celeste called with bad news. She was off to the ashram on an emergency mission. The swami was having back spasms and needed a massage.

"What about dinner?"

"Sorry, Babaji is holding a special satsang this evening. He has to be in good shape."

"I've had a long day. I'd love a massage."

She sought to make amends. "Tomorrow night. I'll love you all over."

"That's my late night," I pouted. "Won't get home till after nine."

"Then come to the ashram tonight. We can spend time afterwards."

I snapped, "Chanting with strangers isn't my idea of relaxing at the end of a tough day."

"Don't get so huffy."

"Why shouldn't I? I've been dumped for a swami."

Celeste's voice was cold and detached. "Call me tomorrow after you've cooled down."

Then she hung up. I slammed down the receiver. A fucking great way to end the day!

⟵⟵⟵⟵

When I arrived home, Nesha pounced on me. I brushed him aside. He'd have to wait. I was still stewing about Celeste. She was over-involved with a balmy swami, and I was the odd man out.

When I took Nesha out, a northeasterly was blowing. It whipped the surf into a wild froth. Warning flags on the beach flapped wildly in the wind, and scores of bluebottles had been washed ashore. I shouted at Nesha when he sniffed at the poisonous jellyfish, also known as the Portuguese man-o'-war. Before I could grab him, he nudged the translucent air sac and yelped. One of the long, stringy tentacles had grazed his nose. I quickly wiped sand on his snout, then dragged him by the collar to rinse his face at the water's edge. In the process, I stepped on another bluebottle. The stinging tentacles seared my skin. I snatched a nearby shell and scraped it off. When I washed my foot in the sea, an angry red mark was left on my ankle. Nesha and I scurried indoors to escape the horde of jellyfish and the whipping sand.

I cooked spaghetti and fumed about the swami getting massaged by Celeste. I reached down to my wounded foot and gave it a rub.

After dinner I checked Ziprunanda's website. Nothing but propaganda bullshit. "Believe and be enlightened." The only thing enlightening was that Celeste was caught in the tentacles of a cult.

Nesha nipped at my feet.

"Leave me alone," I shouted and hurled a shoe across the room. It left a black scuff on the wall. Nesha cowered.

"Sorry," I said. "It's not you; it's the swami. He's an asshole."

HOLY THURSDAY

APRIL 20

Thanks to Jesus and Anzac Day, Australia was about to launch a five-day weekend. I could never understand why Good Friday, Easter Monday, and the commemoration of war deserved special holidays, but I wasn't complaining. After nine days on the job, I rejoiced, "Halleluiah!" Extra time with Celeste.

Frieda handed me files for the day and issued orders that she'd be closing the doors promptly at five, so no dawdling. I saluted her and bounced to my office, singing, "Here Comes Peter Cottontail."

On my desk, a chocolate Easter egg rested near a bag of jelly beans. Before I could drop my briefcase, Alana bounded in. "Like the prezzies?"

I blushed. "From you?"

"Sam gave everyone the jelly beans. I bought the egg." She gave a big hug. "After all, you're part of our family."

"I didn't know we're supposed to give stuff."

Alana pouted. "Don't you like the egg?"

"No, it's not that," I said. "I love chocolate, I really do. It's just that I feel awkward getting something and not giving anything back."

Her dark face softened. "I'll take a thank you."

I returned a hug. "When I eat the egg, I'll think of you."

She squeezed back. "The Family That Cares has another reunion this Tuesday. Can't wait."

Brring. Brring. I picked up the phone and listened to Frieda tell me to get to work.

"My client's arrived," I told Alana. "Thanks for the sweets."

After she left, I shifted my attention from chocolate to sex.

Albert Schweinfurt, aged thirty-two, glumly pulled at the tuft of blond hair on his chin. "I screwed up again. The wife's not happy."

I could just imagine. The computer salesman had a compulsion for phone sex. He was easily seduced into long, erotic conversations with beguiling women who charged three dollars a minute. When his wife found out and threatened divorce, Albert finally responded to the wake-up call.

What I found particularly eerie was the laughing purple kookaburra tattooed on his left arm. I couldn't take my eyes off it. "What happened?" I asked.

"She searched the computer and found pictures of naked women dressed as Easter bunnies. Went ballistic about the phone sex."

"That cost you four thousand dollars?"

He shook his sorry head. "At least. Dana raged about our credit card debt. It's over 35K."

"You didn't mention that at our first session."

He rubbed his tattoo. "The main problem's the phone sex."

"What about women online?"

He winked at me. "Surely, Pete, you've had a peek at the websites."

I confronted his steely blue eyes. "You're having more than a peek, Albert. If you want me to help you, you'll have to come clean."

He rubbed his arm again. "So I've sent a few messages to women. No harm done. The wife's not interested in sex. They wanted some; I did, too. So they sent pictures of themselves in exotic positions. They asked me what I liked. I told them. Thank God, Dana didn't find those pictures."

"Are you still in contact with them?"

"Only when I'm at work. Don't want Dana to catch a whiff."

"Selling computers gives you access all day." And plenty of whiffs!

With a devilish grin, he pulled his chin whiskers. "Yeah. The boss likes porn, too. He knows I'm a tits man. They drive me wild."

"Does he know about your problem?"

"Hell, yes! Says I should dump Dana."

A mobile gyrated in Albert's pocket. He whipped out the phone as it played the stripper's theme song. "Hello?... Can't talk now. I'll call later."

He shoved the phone into his pocket. "Sorry. Business call."

I suspected he was giving me the business. "Listen, Albert," I said. "You need counseling and a twelve-step program."

"Whoa! Might as well ask me to cut off my nuts. I told you last time, I don't want anyone knowing my business. Besides, I'm not much different than other blokes. So I sneak a peek and send a message or two. My problem is I got caught."

I pointed out that phone sex and online women were affecting his marriage. If he didn't tackle his internal addictive software, he'd find himself divorced.

"Yeah, well. I don't want that," he sighed. "Been married seven years. Don't want to leave little Albie. Dana doesn't want another kid until we sort ourselves out. How can we do that if we're not having sex? That's the real problem."

"If you want to save your marriage, you have to work on yourself."

His phone gyrated again, making it sound like we were in a strip club. Another so-called business call. He reluctantly complied with my request to turn it off.

When he stroked the tattoo on his left arm, I wondered why he chose a bird instead of a naked woman.

"Why the kookaburra?" I asked.

He smiled coyly and played with his chin hair. "My first love was a foxy lady. She had a thing for kookaburras. Adored them. After one too many beers, I had one planted on my arm, hoping she'd nest with me. In the end, she flew off with another bloke. Never told Dana. She believes I love the bird. In my heart, I still do."

During lunch break, I removed Nesha's leash. Foolish mistake. He bolted down the beach after the gulls. I ran the length of a soccer field before I could tackle him. He barked playfully, wanting another run. And run we did, all the way home.

I was twenty minutes late for Bonnie's interview.

"Where were you?" fretted the frail woman. "I kept askin' the secretary about ya."

I apologized as I ushered her into the office. "I went home for lunch and my dog took off on the beach. Sorry."

She cradled her dolphin T-shirt and sat down. "Ya live nearby?"

"Uh...yeah," I answered evasively. "So how are you doing?"

"Whereabouts?"

"Close enough."

She handed me a CD. "I brought ABBA."

Considering that I had arrived late, I wasn't about to argue over her choice of relaxing music. I inserted the disc.

"Live by the beach?"

"Yep," I said. "So tell me about you."

"I hope I get a full session."

"You'll have fifty minutes." Paying five dollars on the sliding scale meant she would definitely get her money's worth.

When ABBA's "Dancing Queen" played in the background, Bonnie began to giggle. The song must've triggered fond memories.

"You seem in a chipper mood."

She giggled again.

Then I noticed it. The dolphins on her shirt shifted. I rubbed my eyes, then stared at her chest. One dolphin swelled over the left breast. She squirmed.

Mesmerized by the undulating mammals, I asked, "What's going on?"

She laughed and reached under her shirt. She removed a furry creature. "I took your recommendation, Doctor P. One of the cooks at the restaurant had a sugar glider. He didn't want him and gave him ta me."

The glider crawled over her shoulder.

"Come 'ere. Quit fussin', Doc."

"Doc?"

She sniggered. "Since it was your idea ta get a pet, I named him Doc. Cute little bugger, eh?"

I stared at the gray marsupial with black saucer eyes. When it climbed over her shoulder, she laughed and ABBA sang the song, "Knowing Me, Knowing You."

I remained speechless as my namesake pawed his way over her chest.

"He sleeps with me. We have loads of fun in bed."

I didn't want to go there!

She grabbed the hyperactive sugar glider and showed me the flaps of skin along each side. "When he jumps, he can almost fly," she squealed. "Wanna see?"

I raised my hands in a stop sign. "I don't want to chase another pet today."

Bonnie reached into her pocket and removed a plastic bag. "Doc's real friendly. He eats nuts and berries right outa me hand. Watch."

Our session could well have been a visit at Taronga Zoo. Though I wasn't happy about the sugar glider in my office, I was pleased she found a healthier replacement for Perry. I wished she had chosen a different name.

Another emergency massage for the swami! Celeste canceled our dinner in favor of a guru rubdown. Her atonement was a promise to cook tomorrow night. When I reminded her that I could be with her during the day, she curtly informed me that she had to work Good Friday. Clients wanted massages before Easter.

I spent the night alone with Nesha, just like Bonnie and her pet. Since there was nothing worth watching on the telly, I logged onto the Internet. Albert and his entertaining ways flashed to mind. To better understand him, I decided to conduct some research. Indeed, there were plenty of x-rated websites.

GOOD FRIDAY

APRIL 21

Green-eyed Grim Reaper. Flails bloody sickle at my naked chest.
Slices flesh. Bony hands reach for my heart. I scream

"Ah-h-h-h!" I clutched my chest and gasped for air. Then I realized my nightmare was raging next door. The cretins were at it again with drums and guitars at one-thirty in the morning. Nesha barked loudly. I called reinforcements.

The police arrived while the music blared.

"Yes!" I shouted. "Get the bastards." Haul the druggies to jail and end the nightmare.

I placed my ear to the wall and heard the morons argue with the men in blue. The music stopped. The front door closed. I rushed to the balcony. Horrified, I watched the coppers drive away without anyone in cuffs!

Thump! Thump! Against the wall.

"We know you called 'em," cried a demented woman. "You're fucked."

A man screamed, "Dead meat." He jarred the wall with thunderous kicks.

Crikey! I reached for the phone, then hesitated. Another visit from the coppers would reinforce their rage. I imagined the crazed couple, pierced with all fashions of metal, snorting, smoking, and plotting. I anxiously crept into bed, knowing that a long blade could penetrate the bedroom wall.

I tossed and turned until sunrise, then crept out of the apartment for Nesha's morning walk. Slimy, rotting garbage had been scattered outside my door. I fetched a plastic bag and retched as I scooped up a putrid fish head. The mess was so foul even Nesha steered clear.

I fumed the rest of the day and plotted revenge—a timely call to the police when the smell of weed saturated the air, or a well-placed dent into their beat-up van. For the moment, I decided to lie low. This evening I would rest in Celeste's comforting arms at her place.

⟵ ⟵ ⟵ ⟵

6:30 p.m. I scampered to my car and froze. The windows on my Mitsubishi were busted. Glass shards littered the street.

"They threatened me last night," I yelled to the officer who responded to my call.

"Settle down," he said, jotting notes on a form. "Can't leave your car on the street. I'll radio a tow truck."

"What about the neighbors?" I cried. "They're psychopaths."

He peered into my car and wrote down the identification number. "We'll take care of it."

"I need protection," I pleaded. "They're on drugs, for Christ sake. They destroyed my car and left a fish head at my door. Oh my God. That's what happened in *The Godfather.*"

The copper tapped his clipboard and told me tersely, "No witnesses. Nothing to fingerprint. Could be an unrelated case of vandalism. Anything missing from your car?"

"Windows!" I screamed.

"No need to shout," he said sternly. "File a complaint. We'll visit them and talk it over. That should stop any retaliation."

I pointed to their apartment. "Those people are demons. They're out to get me. Arrest them!"

He scribbled a note. "All we have is your word against theirs." He completed his report and handed me a duplicate. "You'll need this copy to file a claim with the insurance."

I snatched the paper. Who the fuck knew what the animals would do once the police started an investigation. I felt exposed, a victim without protection.

The officer left as soon as the flashing lights of a tow truck appeared. The driver stepped onto the pavement and surveyed my car.

"Bad time for busted windows, mate. Most places are closed, it being the holidays. I can tow it to a friend's garage. They'll take care of you next week."

On the verge of tears, I told him, "My father's a mechanic. I'll call him."

While he hitched up the car, I punched the numbers into my mobile.

"Ma, I've had car trouble. Is Pa there?... I'll talk about it later. Right now, I need to get it fixed... No, I wasn't in an accident. Vandals broke the windows... No, I wasn't in the car... Can you please get Pa?... Yes, I'll see you Easter."

My father's voice made it clear he was already celebrating. "I told you to r-r-rent a garage," he slurred after I briefed him.

No time for an argument with a pickled brain. "Can you repair the windows?"

"Don't f-f-fix glass. S-s-send the car to Teddy's."

"Where?"

"Ash-sh-field. Parramatta r-r-road."

"Hold on." I borrowed a pen and paper from the truck driver and wrote the address. Before I could hang up, my father put my mother on the phone.

"What happened?" she shrieked.

"Tow truck's here. Have to go." I ended the conversation before she could reply.

The driver whistled when I showed him the address. "That's on the other side of the city, mate. It'll cost heaps. My friend's garage is ten minutes away. Fast and cheap. I can get you a discount."

I'd never hear the last of it from my father. "Thanks," I said. "It has to be Teddy's. Drop it off in the lot."

He calculated the mileage and did, in fact, charge heaps. I figured, when it came to cars, my father wouldn't lead me astray. I paid by credit card, then phoned the repair shop. The recorded message announced that they were closed till after the holidays and wished me Happy Easter.

I called Celeste with another update. I was supposed to be with her two hours ago.

"You poor thing," she consoled. "You sound exhausted."

"I'll feel much better when I see you tonight. Can you drive over?"

She moaned. "I know you've had a tough day, Peter, but I've had a rough one myself. It's a long drive. My back and shoulders are throbbing. And I'm heavily booked tomorrow."

"Everyone has off on Holy Saturday."

"To get massages," she sighed. "I'll come over as soon as I'm finished."

"What time?"

"Seven. The Roosters booked the afternoon."

"Footballers?"

"They need me."

"I need you too," I snapped.

"I'll make up for it tomorrow," she said, unconvincingly. "I'll pick up Chinese for dinner."

"I'd rather have you tonight."

"Let's talk later."

"Thanks, Celeste. Happy Good Friday!"

HOLY SATURDAY

APRIL 22

Storm clouds blackened the sky; the surf crashed against the beach. Still smarting from last night's incident, I wanted to be outdoors, away from the vandals. When it started drizzling, Nesha tugged at the leash. He wanted to head back, but I dragged my feet. I was about to cross the street when I heard a familiar voice.

"Hi, Doctor P."

I stopped in my tracks. "Uh...hello. What are you doing here?"

Bonnie gave a sheepish grin. "I was takin' a walk. Thought it was ya."

Nesha sniffed her worn jeans. She reached down and petted him. "Nice dog."

Damn if he didn't lick her hand. This was not the time to be friendly. I tugged at the leash. "Better be off. See you next week."

Bonnie squealed in delight. "Doc, quit fussin'." She reached inside her faded red jacket and removed the sugar glider.

Like a hyperactive tourist, the sugar glider bobbed its head every which way, with curious black eyes scanning the terrain. It scurried inside her jacket, creating a bulge wherever it moved. Bonnie squeaked.

I pulled at Nesha. "Better get him indoors before it pours."

She pointed toward my building. "That where ya live?"

"I'd...uh...rather not say," I said. "Professional boundaries."

She paid no attention. "Bet it's the top one on the end, the one with the bird on the balcony."

I spotted the kookaburra. How the hell did she know? I squinted at her protruding eyes and her grinning face.

"I have to get going. Let's talk about this at our next session."

I jerked Nesha away from her and walked briskly up the street away from my building. My bloody dog kept lurching toward the apartment, but I struggled to keep him moving.

When I turned the corner, I checked that she had left, then circled the block again before returning home. Bonnie obviously had nothing better to do over the Holidays than to stalk her therapist. That would be the first order of business at our next appointment.

My place no longer felt safe. The neighbors from Hell stirred indoors while Bonnie roamed outdoors. I remained hyper-vigilant and ruminated on every possible calamity. Then I remembered my mother's favorite saying—when worried, get busy. Listening to the patter of rain bouncing off the roof, I cleaned windows, scrubbed the bathroom, and brought out the white tablecloth. Nesha tilted his head and gave me a quizzical look, as if I was a man possessed.

I completed the chores in time for Celeste's arrival. Though we ended on a sour note last night, I hoped to remedy that with a romantic dinner and an injection of love. I lit the candles when I heard a knock.

Celeste stood at the door with a soggy bag of Chinese takeaway. She was soaked. I took her parcel and moved for a kiss.

She cut me short. "I'm bushed." She removed her sopping raincoat and grumbled, "Eight massages, starting at seven-thirty this morning."

I followed her to the balcony door where she stared at the rain splashing against the glass.

"The only parking space was two blocks away. Your neighbors better leave my car alone."

"If they do anything, they'll answer to me," I said with bravado. I rubbed her wet shoulders and kissed her cheek. "I should have made dinner."

She bristled. "You were awful last night."

I stroked her droopy hair.

"Sorry. I had an awful day." I guided her to the couch. "I'll make it up to you. Stay here and I'll prepare everything."

I opened the cartons and dished out vegetables in garlic and tofu with cashews. The menu meant she was pissed off. On a good day, she would have brought me a beef dish. I uncorked a bottle of wine and poured two glasses."

She moved to the table and gulped half the glass.

"You must've had a bummer of a day."

She drained her wine and reached for the bottle.

"I'm sorry about yesterday," I said contritely. "My car's out of commission and the coppers did squat. And when I couldn't be with you..." I kissed her on the neck. Then I spotted it. "What's that?"

She turned away. "It's nothing."

My head pounded like the surf outside. "Nothing? That's a love bite. From a Rooster?"

She glumly sat down and reached for the rice. "I'm tired and hungry. Let's eat, and talk later."

"Are you making out with your clients?"

She glared at me. "You won't understand."

I fumed. "What is it I'm supposed to understand?"

She banged her glass on the table, spilling wine on the tablecloth. "Babaji teaches us love isn't possessive."

"Does that mean loving two men at the same time?"

She stormed from the table.

I followed her to the living room. "I thought you loved me."

She turned and faced me. "I do. But I also have love to share with others."

"Others!"

The wind howled and whipped against the balcony door. The metal frame shook. Nesha growled and nuzzled against my leg.

Others? How many? I clutched my chest. Couldn't breathe. I had to leave and get fresh air. I grabbed the leash and bolted outside with Nesha close behind.

The rain pelted me as I wandered aimlessly down the street, staggering from the blow of betrayal, the kiss of Judas. Celeste was my love, my hope, my salvation. She had just ripped my heart out. I imagined others sharing her body. I leaned against a trash bin and heaved.

Nesha nuzzled my arm. I bent down and clutched his black fur. Forsaken, I wept in my own Gethsemane. Alone, except for my companion. He licked the tears on my face then tugged at the leash. We splashed through puddles and meandered along the promenade, past the closed shops.

When Nesha led me home, I wanted Celeste to be gone. But she had remained. She wiped her tear-stained face and approached me.

"I didn't mean to hurt you," she wept. "I wanted to tell you for some time." She wrapped her arms around me.

I wrenched myself away. "Tell me about the others."

Her eyes watered. "I will, but let's get dry clothes on you."

A puddle formed around my feet. "I'd rather know now."

She returned to the couch and pleaded with me. "I want you to understand. I'm compelled to share my love. It's not dirty. It's beautiful."

"Who were the others?" I seethed. "Was it the swami?"

She shook her weary head. "He only wanted my spiritual love. When I felt his spirit flood my body, I couldn't contain the love. I shared it with you. But I had more to give. My clients felt the energy. It pulsated in my hands. They wanted to share their love as well."

I kicked my wet shoes at the wall. "So it was the Roosters."

She didn't answer. I shook her shoulders. "It was them, wasn't it?"

Tears trickled down her cheeks. "Only some."

"To the highest bidders?" I screamed.

She jerked away. "I knew you'd act like this. You're making something beautiful seem ugly. That's why I never told you. It has nothing to do with money. It's about sharing love with those who need it."

"I needed your love. Wasn't I enough?"

She stroked my face. "Of course you're enough. You're my special lover. But you can't possess me."

My heart throbbed with pain. I collapsed on the couch, totally dejected. "I can't share you with others."

Celeste moved next to me. "Shhh. Let me make you feel better."

She unbuttoned my wet shirt and touched my quivering chest. Heat radiated from her soft hands. Healing strokes sent shivers down my spine. Her lips whispered into my ear, "Let's make love."

My frozen heart began to melt. She removed my sopping pants, then her own clothes. When she straddled my legs, Freddie woke. He wanted to thrust, but visions of sweaty Roosters tensed my body.

"I want you," moaned Celeste.

I wanted her, too. But so did the others.

She eased me off the couch, led me to the bed, and closed the door on Nesha. While we had become lax with condoms, this was one night I demanded protection. As we made love, disturbing images flooded my mind. Men crowing about their prowess. Celeste fucking in a frenzy.

I thrust hard. Harder still, to erase the mental pictures of naked men on the massage table, begging for love. I grunted and plunged deeper. I pictured Celeste servicing with her hands, moving from one to another. Then her mouth. And women?

"No!" I yelled, overwhelmed with visions of wild orgies.

"Yes," she groaned. "I'm coming." She clutched my waist and pumped her hips hard against me. She screamed wildly as we both came in a frenzy.

Sweaty and exhausted, I collapsed next to her, unsure who was on her mind.

I knew, for certain, what was on mine.

EASTER SUNDAY

APRIL 23

The dream woke me in the middle of the night. I felt Celeste's hand stroking my erection. I flashed to the black hoods and turned over.

In the morning, she wanted to talk. I needed to retreat. She asked me to spend Easter with her. I declined. For once, a visit with my parents became a priority.

She suggested we meet again.

I told her I'd call.

"When?"

I wouldn't say. The door to my heart had closed. I couldn't bear the pain of betrayal, so I avoided Celeste and her jangling sensual keys that could tempt the door open. When she left, we both knew the relationship basket held an egg fractured like Humpty Dumpty.

Without a car, I had to leave Nesha behind. Neither of us wanted to part. I hugged my faithful buddy goodbye, then caught a ferry to Circular Quay. A bench on the open deck offered me solace. A stiff breeze blew off the ocean as we passed the headlands. A bloke in a passing yacht saluted the ferry with a bottle of champagne in one hand and an arm around a sexy babe. I went inside and found a young couple making out. My heart ruptured with images of Celeste and her Roosters. I sat glumly during the rest of the trip. The ferry chugged past the Opera House with shadows casting an eerie pall over the white porcelain tiles. Once the ship berthed, I hurried past the bustling crowd.

"Read and be saved," shouted a lanky man with a scraggly beard. He thrust a pamphlet at me with the headline, *Repent. Jesus saves sinners.*

I tossed it back. Celeste needed this, not me.

The train ride to Ashfield, though uneventful, raised my anxiety. Anticipating more dysfunction, I prepared myself for the questions about the car and my relationship with Celeste.

My mother was the first to greet me. Her tight embrace held me prisoner. "Piotr, what happened? Where's the car?"

"Let him breathe," called my older sister. Stella pried me away and gave me a quick hug. "How are you?"

Before I could answer, my fifteen-year-old niece blurted, "Hi, Uncle Peter." Krystyna's grin revealed a mouthful of braces.

"Where'd you get that dress?" I asked, glancing at my mother and her lack of taste.

Krystyna made a horrible face about the poofy, pink dress. "Babcia gave it for Easter." Then with a whisper, "Mum made me wear it. Danka refused to wear hers."

"No way," announced her defiant, older sister who wore designer jeans and matching jacket. Silver earrings dangled with ebony beads. The seventeen-year-old returned to her mobile phone and her texting.

My father, Aunt Adele, Uncle Janek, and my brother-in-law, Stanley Leśniowski, gathered in the living room.

"*Wesołych Świąt Wielkanocnych,*" gushed my aunt.

"And a Happy Easter to you," I said.

Since she never had children, my aunt doted on me and my sister. I would have preferred if she had given my share to Stella.

My father moved in with a shot glass and bottle and saluted me, "*Na zdrowie*," then guzzled his drink.

"Józef!" scolded my mother. She grabbed the bottle and placed it on the coffee table. "We have church."

"Hold on," I said. "You were supposed to attend the early Mass."

My mother smacked my shoulder. "On Easter, we pray together."

"I'm not going," I protested. "I had a hard week. The sermon by Father Czarnecki will make it worse."

My mother bristled. "Everyone must go. And Józef!" She slapped my father's hand when he grabbed the vodka. "No more."

Under the spotlight, he begrudgingly put down the bottle.

Stella sidled next to me with her older sister act. "Come on," she pleaded. "It'll make Ma feel good."

I remained defiant. "Take Danka and Krystyna."

The two girls groaned. Stella shot them a menacing look, then pulled out her favorite strategy—guilt.

"If Stan and I could fly in from Melbourne, you could at least give up an hour."

My mobile rang. All conversation stopped. I immediately thought of Celeste and checked the phone. "C U thair." A text from Danka.

I corrected the brat. "It's spelled t-h-e-r-e."

"Put that away," scolded her mom.

Danka stamped her foot. "OMG. I was only havin' fun."

"In our family," I told her, "the only fun is in dysfunction."

"Not funny," chided Stella.

My chubby aunt grabbed my face with her puffy hands. "*Proszę.* Please. Sit next to me at church."

"Oh, for Christ's sake," I said. "As long as everyone leaves me alone."

She kissed my cheek. "*Dziękuje bardzo.* Thank you."

My mother kissed her fingers and planted them on the picture of the Black Madonna. "My prayers are answered."

We arrived at St. Vincent's in two cars for one o'clock Mass. A few remaining spaces dotted the packed church, so we split up. I ended up between my mother and aunt, who acted as guards. My father disappeared once he parked the car.

Father Czarnecki, having celebrated his golden jubilee years ago, stood like an ancient relic, dressed in white chasuble and tunic. I gazed at the words on the front wall. *Ego Sum Nolite Timere.* I am without fear. If only that were true. The upcoming family meal terrified me.

During Mass, my mother fingered rosary beads and mumbled prayers while the silver-haired priest, his hands shaking, consecrated the bread and wine. Soon thereafter, he and a deacon passed Holy Communion while two women offered chalices to the queue of believers. My mother pushed me out of the pew to receive the body and blood of Christ. Bowing reverently, she approached the priest and stuck out her tongue. She preferred to receive the host the old way, just like she was taught as a child. The priest's trembling hand placed the wafer on the tip of her tongue. My second grade teacher, Sister Margaret, told me, "Tiny Jesus visits your mouth, then slides into your tummy." I swallowed a lot of nonsense when I was a kid.

My father appeared out of nowhere and faced a solemn woman holding a gold goblet of wine. To her dismay, he took a large gulp. Sharing germs from a chalice was not my idea of a holy experience.

Back in the pew, my mother's arm tugged at me to get on the hardwood kneelers. My butt didn't budge. I sat during the rest of the service but was the first one on my feet when the Mass was over. On the way out, my mother stopped at the holy water font and blessed herself. Her fingers returned for seconds and splashed my face.

"Cut that out," I said angrily. "I don't want to be blessed."

Back at the homestead, Stella and her daughters joined my aunt and mother in the kitchen while my father played bartender to the men. He broke out the vodka and poured shots for my uncle and brother-in-law. Normally, I avoided drinking with the family. Today, I threw caution to the wind. Still reeling about Celeste, I needed extra help to get through Easter.

When I asked for a glass, my father shouted with surprise. "*Ja!*" In his eyes, I was acting like a real man. He cheerily clinked his glass against mine. "*Na zdrowie.*"

He swallowed his vodka, then stabbed his finger at my chest. "You're too weak," he said. "With neighbors, you must fight back."

I snatched the bottle before he could refill his glass and offered my own advice. "You've had enough. We haven't eaten."

He winked at my uncle and Stanley, who chuckled along with my father. "I handle my liquor better than Piotr handles neighbors." He balled his rough, callused hand into a fist. "I'd give them this."

"That'd really solve the problem," I said. "Listen, Pa. The car's at Teddys. Can you put in a good word? I need it ASAP."

My uncle slapped my father's arm. "Customers want quick service and a better price, right Józef?"

My father laughed. "Remember that fat, ugly Asian? Purple hatchback needing a muffler. She demanded a discount. Told her to talk to the boss."

"You scoundrel," said his brother. "She was worse than Adele on a bad night!"

Both men guffawed so hard my uncle's bald head turned beet red and my father staggered against a chair.

Mercifully, my mother intervened. "*Usiąć!* Take a seat!"

As the patriarch of the family, my father took the chair at the head of the table while my mother sat at the opposite end, a marital habit well established over forty-three years. He liked to bark orders and make decisions. This often created problems with his older brother. Although they were amiable drinking buddies, my father and Janek argued frequently about running the garage. My uncle had the final word, since he owned the business. But in his home, my father had to be the boss. He directed my uncle and aunt to sit on his left and Stanley and Stella on his right. When Krystyna asked to be next to her mom, my father pointed at the vacant chair next to Stella.

"Danka's older. She sits there."

I was positioned near my mother and winked at Krystyna, who sulked across from me.

"Don't worry," I said. "It's more fun at this end." I pressed a spoon against my nose. "Koala bear."

She smiled back. A conspiracy was born.

"Let's pray," said my mother. She led us in the Lord's prayer. "*Ojcze Nasz, któryś jest...*"

I nudged Krystyna's knee under the table and made a face at my father's bowed head. She crossed her eyes and giggled.

After grace, my mother passed around the *opłatek*, a meaningless tradition carried over from Christmas. Everyone offered their white wafer, the size of a small envelope, to each other and wished success.

My aunt broke a piece from my *opłatek*. "*Powodzenia.*"

I snapped off part of hers. "And good luck to you."

Krystyna offered me her wafer and giggled. "Hope your girlfriend's cute."

I winced. "May you find a studly boyfriend."

My mother reminded everyone to break off a piece for my father's sister, Elżbieta, now recovering from a knee replacement in Melbourne. With the wafers consumed, we ripped into the food—baked ham decorated with cloves in the sign of a cross, sauerkraut, creamed peas, mashed potatoes, and a blessed basket with farmer's cheese, hardboiled eggs, rye bread, and Polish sausage.

"Why do we always have ham on Easter?" whined Krystyna.

My father chuckled, "'Cause it keeps the Jews away."

"Don't listen to him," I told my niece, then turned toward my father. "It's Easter, for Christ's sake. For one day, can you be kind?"

"Don't tell me what I can and can't do!"

My aunt quickly passed the rolls and changed the topic. "So, Piotr, where's your girlfriend?"

"He's never brought her here," complained my mother.

"One of these days." I shuddered at the thought.

"Is she Polish?" asked Adele.

"No, and it doesn't really matter."

She pinched my cheek. "A Polish woman makes a good wife. You're thirty-five. Time to settle down." She offered me a platter. "Try my homemade nut bread."

I grabbed a slice. "I don't need a wife and kids to be happy."

"Now you can talk," she said. "When you get old, you'll see what I mean. Your parents have you and your sister. Janek and I have no one who'll look after us."

"A-a-a-h!"

Everyone at the table stopped eating.

I ignored their stares and spat into my hand. The fragment of a walnut shell sat next to a broken piece of tooth.

My aunt spotted the shell and yelled at her husband. "I told you to be careful when cracking the nuts."

He shrugged apologetically. I glared at the bushes sprouting from his large ears and envisioned using a weed whacker. Bloody fool! I dashed to the bathroom to survey the damage in the mirror. Part of my lower back tooth had been sheared off, near a large filling. While there was little pain, I groaned at the tortuous thought of visiting a dentist.

I returned to the table and found my father waving his fork with a slab of ham. "The Asians are taking over. And you can never understand them."

My uncle's bald head bobbed. "You and Frankiewicz are the only reliable men. New workers want benefits without hard work."

I entered the fray. "We were all once migrants," I argued. "Remember, I was born in Chicago."

"We never hear from our friends," said my mother wistfully.

"No reason to," snapped my father. "That door's closed."

Stella gave me the evil eye. I had opened the unmentionable door—Chicago. We weren't supposed to talk about the place, even though Stella and I were born there.

"We could've owned a business on Milwaukee Avenue," grumbled my mother, churning a resentful memory. Though she treated my uncle respectfully, she never quite forgave him for luring us to Australia to make my father a hired hand.

My aunt, seeking to ease the tension, picked up a decorated egg with an intricate design of a fish. "Marysia, such beautiful *pisanki*. How do you do it?"

My mother's egg ritual was another painstaking task that she gladly suffered. She would prick a tiny pinhole on both ends of an egg, blow out the insides, create homemade dye out of onionskin, then with a fine brush, paint elaborate crosses on a dozen eggs. My mother had carried plenty of crosses.

She didn't answer, her mind wallowing in the past. My father and sister scowled at me. I would pay dearly for opening the unmentionable door.

"I want to text Stacey," burped Danka.

"Not until you've finished eating," berated her mom. "You hardly touched your food."

"OMG, I'm not hungry!"

"I told you not to eat that chocolate bunny."

"Make room for lamb's cake," said Adele. She nervously faced my mother. "Marysia, your cake looks beautiful. Marysia?"

My mother snapped out of her trance and smiled weakly.

Guilt flooded my veins like hot searing lava. I berated myself for picking at the ugly scar of my mother's depression. Memories of Chicago triggered the pain of losing friends and a life once established in America. I made amends by returning to the role of a comic.

Placing two olives in front of my eyes, I looked at Krystyna. "Here's looking at you."

She giggled. "You're silly."

I felt bloody silly trying to erase my mistake by lightening the mood with stupid jokes. After the meal, my father relegated me to clean up with the women, my punishment for bringing up the past. When I finished kitchen duty, I joined the others in the living room. My father, Janek, and Stanley shared drinks and racist jokes. I steered clear and chatted with Krystyna.

My father drained another shot and pointed the bottle toward me. "Take thish and shmash your neighbor.

Krystyna whispered, "Dziadziu's drunk."

"Hush," scolded her mom.

It was time for an announcement. "I have a train to catch."

"Stay," pleaded my mother. "Pa will drive you back tomorrow."

Krystyna chimed in. "Please stay, Uncle Peter. It's boring without you."

"Shtay and drink," slurred my father.

My mother hissed, "Józef, stop!" She grabbed my arm. "I've made the bed for you."

"Nesha needs me. I'll come by next week when I pick up the car."

"*Na zdrowie!*" answered my father.

My mother grabbed the bottle from him. "*Więcej nie!* No more!" She pleaded with my uncle. "Do something!"

That was like asking a sinking ship to rescue the Titanic. Janek wobbled unsteadily toward my father and pointed toward the couch. "Sit."

"You're not boss." He reached for the bottle and stumbled to the floor. "One lasht drink."

Then it happened. Before I could shut my mouth, words escaped like a clap of thunder. "Give the drunk his fucking vodka!"

Everyone froze, including myself. I had opened another unmentionable door. Krystyna whimpered and moved toward her mom. My father staggered to his feet and snatched the bottle from my stunned mother. He sloshed booze on the floor, trying to refill his glass.

I grabbed my jacket. "Have to go." This time no one protested.

Stella pulled me aside. "His drinking's gotten worse. Ever since you moved out."

I seethed, "Forget the guilt trip."

"You're the psychologist. Can't you get him into treatment?"

I glanced at my father and his bulging gut, now resting on the couch, his eyes half-closed.

"Talk to him tomorrow when he's sober. He might listen to you. I'm just his dumb son."

I said my goodbyes while my mother organized a bag with leftovers. She shoved the parcel in my arm. "Take it," she said, tearfully. "Come visit when you get your car. We talk then."

With care package in hand, I waved farewell and trudged slowly toward the train. The bracing wind chafed my cheeks. I choked back tears. Happy Easter!

EASTER MONDAY

APRIL 24

"Hello?... No, I wasn't awake... I know Stella's leaving tomorrow...
Can't come, Ma. I'll call her later."

I stopped answering the phone. Stella left several messages begging me to drop by. My mother went on a rampage last night, hunting down bottles as if they were vermin. I'd witnessed it countless times. My father would storm out in a rage and get sozzled at the pub. He'd return with reinforcements and hide them in the garage. She'd eventually give up and the unmentionable door would close. Everything would return to normal, if you could call it that.

I hunkered down in my cave and ruminated about yesterday's disaster. I cursed my father, my aunt's nut cake, and Celeste. My tongue kept flicking across the sharp edge of my broken tooth. I cringed at the prospect of a dentist wielding a tiny pickaxe.

Only for a brief moment did I connect with the outside world. I checked my email and ignored two messages—one from Celeste with a plea to call her ASAP and the other from my psychiatrist friend who wrote one of his longer, cryptic messages: *All is not as it seems. Will write later. Surjit.*

When Nesha and I popped outdoors, I made sure the streets were clear of Bonnie and the druggies next door. After I returned home, I rolled the stone across the entrance to my cave.

ANZAC DAY

TUESDAY, APRIL 25

Today's holiday commemorated the 1915 massacre of 7,600 Australians and 2,500 New Zealanders at Gallipoli. The actual wounded were twice those numbers. The yearly parade down George Street would finish at Hyde Park. Lest we forget. Yet that seemed to be exactly what world leaders did. Forget the emotional impact on families and communities when soldiers were sent to strange places with a group of strangers to commit strange acts of violence—all for some worthy cause.

I followed a weatherworn man in uniform, hobbling across the ferry's ramp at Circular Quay. He disappeared into the crowd bustling with warriors from the past, families with children, and tourists snapping pictures. I pushed my way through a throng of onlookers captivated by the music of three Aborigines. Smeared with white streaks on their faces and naked torsos, the men wore red loincloths and played didgeridoos and clap-sticks. They stamped their feet in traditional dance on the pavement and pointed occasionally to the basket littered with coins.

When a tourist snapped a picture, a skinny Aborigine yelled, "Ow 'bout some money, eh?"

The man with the camera disappeared into the sea of faces.

"Turn your back on us kooris, eh?" glared the Aborigine. He banged hard on his clap-sticks.

I wove my way past other buskers—jugglers, magicians, and guitar players. By the time I arrived at Surry Hills, I was bushed. The sight of the gentle giant greeting me at the door with a "G'day, mate" and a crushing bear hug eased my weariness. Thomas directed me inside his small terrace house where Sam and Alana sat in the living room, munching on chips and cheese. Their faces brightened as soon as I entered. We shared a round of heartfelt hugs. Although I had seen them a mere five days ago, I missed The Family that Cares, especially after the Easter fiasco.

"Everybody and their sister must've been at the Quay," I said. "Where's Rosie?"

"Bad news," frowned Sam. "Her son was in a car accident a few days ago. He's okay," she added quickly. "Kieran suffered a dislocated shoulder. He was driving his girlfriend home, and someone ran a red light. Rosie wanted to stay with him."

"It's crazy out there." I told them about the neighbors busting my car windows.

"That's brutal, mate," said Thomas.

Alana clutched my arm and peered at me with her soulful eyes. "Be careful."

"I placed my dog on guard duty."

Sam handed me the cheese platter. "You need to clear their negative energy. I could perform a bush cleansing at your place."

I grabbed a slice of Gouda. "Like an exorcism?" I imagined flailing bodies and spinning heads.

"More of a ritual," corrected the earth mother. "Used it to get rid of Charles." She winked. "He never knew what hit him."

"I'll let the police handle it," I said. "The investigation may pressure them to leave."

The kitchen timer ended our discussion as Thomas leapt from the couch. "Dinner's ready."

We gathered around a mahogany dining table laid out with paper plates and plastic cutlery. Thomas apologized for not using the family silver. "Hope you don't mind," he said. "Less trouble this way."

No difference to me, I was famished. He poured red wine, then served spinach lasagna along with salad and garlic bread. After Sam led us into another earth prayer, we dug in. I made easy work of my meal and grabbed seconds.

"Where'd you get the collection?" I asked, scanning an array of masks. African faces, Chinese dragons, even a carved Buddha adorned his green walls.

He wiped lasagna from his lower lip, then reached for the mask of a ferocious dragon baring white teeth and a red protruding tongue. "This came from a friend in Panama. He told me it brings courage." He placed his plastic fork on the plate. "I need that more than ever."

"What's wrong?" asked Sam.

Thomas wiped perspiration from his smooth scalp. He hesitated, then spoke. "I wanted to tell you after dinner. My T-cell count has fallen below 200. Means I have AIDS."

Bang! A door slammed in my head. I stared at the robust, broad figure. The ex-priest looked as if he could single-handedly subdue a wild boar. I sat transfixed while Sam moved in for a hug. She eased him out of the chair and stroked his face. He buried his face in her shoulders and began to sob. Alana left her chair and wrapped her arms around them. I wanted to reach out. I really did. Yet I sat there frozen to my chair, worried that I had eaten a meal prepared by him. Now that he had AIDS, the risk of infection had multiplied. Was that why he brought out the paper plates and plastic forks? My gut wrenched in conflict—console him or protect myself. Alana and Sam, seemingly, had no such concerns.

I eventually joined them and patted his shoulder. He was, after all, part of our family. We stood around Thomas.

"We're here for you," said Sam lovingly.

He pulled out a handkerchief and wiped his eyes. "I needed to hear that." He blew his nose then said, "Let's go to the living room."

We followed him in a solemn procession and sat with him on the carpet, huddled in a circle.

Alana dabbed her eyes. "When did you find out?"

He sniffled, "Last week. I thought the antiretroviral therapy would protect me. Guess I'm not invincible."

Images of my own mortality flashed to mind—my blood infected by his food, his fluids, his touch. An open casket swallowed me with its giant jaws.

Thomas squeezed my wrist. "You're afraid of me, mate. I see it in your eyes."

Before I could protest, he said, "I want you to feel at home with me. To speak your truth, as Gretchen suggested. We're family. It's better to be honest, even if it hurts."

Sitting next to me, Alana grabbed my hand. "I'm afraid, too, Peter. I ask myself what I would do if I had AIDS." She faced Thomas. "I'm frightened."

He caressed her face. I would have recoiled at his touch. Alana gently kissed each finger. Those kisses taught me to courageously step forward and dissolve the barriers of fear.

"I'm also scared," I confessed. "I've never been close to someone with AIDS. I'm worried about catching it. But I want to be here for you, Thomas. You've treated me better than my own family."

Tears spattered his shirt. "I don't want to waste my life," he said. "This is a huge wake-up call. I have to follow the advice I tell others. Live the moment. I suggest we do the same."

We all began to lower our walls. Sam talked about the pain of her failed marriages and the childhood wounds inflicted by her father's drinking. She was through rescuing alcoholic men. It was time to reclaim her life.

Alana pointed to her mottled teeth and shared her shame. Her father never took her to the dentist because he didn't want to waste money. The tragedy was that she believed she wasn't worth much. She desperately wanted to change that horrible belief so she could experience true love.

Everyone's openness dissolved my resistance to talk about Celeste and her cheating, and my drunken father. Unearthing buried secrets and despair eased my burdens. The genuine caring and loving acceptance of my friends acted like healing balm on festering wounds.

Throughout the day, we bonded with greater openness, genuine sharing, more hugs, and plenty of tears. We stayed well into the night. Reluctant to say goodbye, we eventually parted ways, emotionally nourished and ever so grateful for a family that truly cared.

BOUNDARIES

WEDNESDAY, APRIL 26

Late at night I stumble in bush cabin. Hear whimpering noise. I peek behind curtain. Spot piercing red eyes, blood-matted brown fur. A trembling wallaby crouches on its side. A broken arrow lodged in its heart. A paw scratches at my fingers, beckons me. I remove the arrow. The marsupial winces then smiles. Healing begins. I smile, then wince. Its injury becomes mine. Pain thumps in my chest. The wallaby gains strength. I weaken. Dragged through curtain of death, I shriek, HELP!

The bizarre dream stayed with me like a bad case of indigestion. The message was clear—stay clear of wounded animals.

Since today was my late night at work, I hoped the one o'clock start would make for an easier transition to seeing clients. My car was still in the shop, so I took the bus with plenty of time to spare for Bonnie's session at one-thirty. To my chagrin, she was already waiting when I arrived.

Boundaries were high on my agenda, so I let the minutes tick away until the imaginary bell clanged. When I collected her, she walked like a pregnant woman, carrying her sugar glider beneath her bulging shirt.

"Doc's sleeping," she said softly. "He won't be botherin' us."

Her pet didn't concern me, but the picture on her T-shirt gave me the shivers. A kangaroo grazing at twilight reminded me of my eerie dream.

"How was Easter?" she asked as she took her seat.

I forced a smile. "Fine. And yours?"

She stroked her tummy. "Doc kept me company. We didn't have anywhere ta go." She handed me ABBA. "Did ya visit family?"

Her creased, leathered face and her protruding eyes, along with her short black hair, reminded me of a pixie gone astray.

I took the CD and placed it on the desk. "We need to discuss boundaries."

"What do ya mean?"

"You visited my home on Saturday. My private life must be kept separate from therapy. Surely, you understand."

The bulge under her shirt stirred. She clutched her stomach. "You sayin' I can't act friendly toward ya?"

"I'm here to help you, Bonnie. My personal life can't be part of the conversation. And we shouldn't have contact outside sessions."

She furrowed her brow. "Doc and I needed fresh air. No harm done. I didn't ask ta visit, even though I kinda wondered about your place. Mine's depressing. You're lucky ya live near the beach. And your dog liked me."

Nesha also needed a lesson in boundaries. So did her pet. It crawled over her left breast.

"Appropriate boundaries make our work more effective."

Doc popped its tiny head out of Bonnie's sleeve. His saucer eyes darted around the room. She grabbed him and held him in a protective grasp. "Ya tellin' me, ya don't wanna see me no more?"

I waved my hands. "No, Bonnie. I'm not saying that. It's important you come here. We have lots of work. I want to—"

Doc jumped out of her hands and pounced on my desk. The marsupial stretched the flaps of its skin and sailed to the opposite side of the room. It landed on my potted plant. The kangaroo paws crashed to the floor, spilling the soil and red and green woolly flowers.

"Hey!" cried Bonnie. She pulled a plastic bag from her pocket and withdrew a dried apricot. Her pet jumped at the treat. She snatched the glider and held it to her belly while it munched the piece of fruit.

"No one's gonna hurt ya," she crooned.

I picked up the plant and scooped the dirt into the pot. "It's important we discuss this."

"What's ta discuss?" she pouted. "Ya don't wanna see me. Doc and me don't have ta come." She whispered into its ear, "We can take care of each other."

"Look at me, Bonnie," I said, returning to my chair. "I want to help you."

She lifted her sorrowful eyes. "Seems more like ya wanna dump me and Doc."

"You do want my help, don't you?"

She shrugged. "Thought I did, till ya said ya didn't wanna see me."

I gave an exasperated sigh.

"You're tired of seein' me."

"I'm just frustrated you're taking it the wrong way. I triggered your abandonment issues. You feel rejected. That's why it's important we talk about this. When your parents were intoxicated or on drugs, they didn't teach you about boundaries."

I pointed at the sugar glider with its head buried in the bag of treats. "Your pet needs to feel protected, safe, and cared for. We all do. I'm trying to create a safe place for you to sort through your feelings and learn to take better care of yourself."

"Seems like ya don't wanna see me." The glider sniffed Bonnie's hand and licked her fingers.

"I'm bringing up boundaries so we can be clear about our relationship. I'm here to focus on you. That's what you're paying me for." At five dollars a session, she was getting a bargain. "We must resolve this," I pressed. "I put aside my personal life and devote the time for you."

She reached into the bag and gave her pet a nut. "Does that mean I can't go ta Manly 'cause I might see ya?"

I shifted uneasily. "It means we can only see each other in the office. If we bump into one another, and it can't be helped, no worries."

Her face softened. "So ya still wanna see me?"

"Absolutely," I said emphatically. "I have you down for Wednesdays at 1:30." I was about to raise the issue of her early arrivals but decided to save that till later.

"What if I need ta talk?" She fondled her pet. "I only have Doc."

"If there's an emergency or you need to talk, call me. I may be in session, but I will get back to you as soon as I'm available."

"Your secretary's mean. Always tells me you're busy."

"You need others besides me. I told you about our women's group."

"No group," she protested.

"It's important to connect with others. A group provides you with support."

She clutched the glider. "Doc and I have each other. And if ya don't wanna see me..."

I raised my voice. "You're not listening."

She recoiled. "Don't have ta yell at me."

"Sorry, Bonnie," I said, softening my tone. "Please trust me."

Doc burrowed under her shirt. She giggled. "Quit ticklin'."

I would've preferred that she left her hyperactive pet at home. That would be another future agenda item. For now, I was content to address boundaries, which, undoubtedly, would remain an ongoing issue.

I shifted the conversation to her family. Bonnie talked about her father, who died from cirrhosis of the liver. Her older brother overdosed on heroin. Addictions were an integral part of her upbringing. Not surprisingly, she hooked up with Perry, a friend of her brother. Perry offered Bonnie an escape from her alcoholic mother and sister who lived together in a caravan park, somewhere in Brisbane. The escape turned into an emotional prison.

When it was time to wrap up the session, Bonnie, as expected, avoided closure.

"I had a strange dream last night, Doctor P. Didn't get a chance ta tell it."

I stood up. "We can discuss it next week."

She grabbed the CD from my desk. "But it was about a man who looked like ya. He shot an arrow and hit a kangaroo."

I stopped in my tracks and glanced at the kangaroo on her shirt. "Was it dying?"

She nodded. "What does it mean?"

Hell if I knew.

⟵⟵⟵⟵

During a break, I grabbed a cup of coffee and sought out Rosie. Her door was closed, but the muffled voices behind it sounded like Sam and Alana. I gave a gentle rap.

Rosie opened the door. "Speakin' o' the devil."

She squeezed me affectionately and brought me into her office where Alana and Sam were sitting.

"Looks like they filled you in about yesterday's meal," I said. "How's your son?"

Rosie pushed a chair toward me. "The poor darlin'. He's a wee bit better since takin' the pain meds. The judge should throw the book at the ruddy idiot. He went through a red light and totaled Kieran's car. I'm grateful he only has a dislocated shoulder. Could've been killed."

"Drunk driver?"

"Nay," she snapped. "He was yappin' on a mobile."

As if on cue, my mobile buzzed. I removed it from my pocket and turned off Celeste. I wasn't ready for reconciliation.

"I heard about Thomas," said Rosie. "Poor lad. I'll visit him tomorrow."

"There's more bad news," Alana told me.

"No! He looked fine yesterday."

"Not Thomas," corrected Sam. "It's Herbert. He resigned."

All three women nodded in unison.

"When? Why?"

"The official word is that he's retiring," answered Sam. "Unofficially, he was forced out. Herbert's putting on a good face but I know he's upset. We were planning to celebrate his sixty-eighth birthday. Now it'll be his farewell party."

"You should apply," I told her.

"The Board wants someone with a corporate image." She ruffled her spiky gray hair. "I don't fit the description."

"What will happen to the agency?" fretted Alana.

"I'm still clinical director," reassured Sam. "We'll place clients first like we always do."

Rosie's defiant voice boomed. "Whoever takes over must reckon with us."

Like four musketeers, all for one and one for all, we promised to stand together, no matter who took over as director.

CLIENTS IN DEMAND

THURSDAY, APRIL 27

With an ashen face, Herbert remained in his chair next to me in the staff room. Everyone had finished morning tea. His chubby hands cradled a mug. The dejected man rambled about his forced retirement. He had worked dutifully at the center for over twenty years, first as a psychologist, then as clinical director, and finally at the helm.

"Money was tight the past few years," he confided. "I did an admirable job, if I do say so myself, but the Board wanted fresh blood." He clutched his cup. "I had a few more good years before retiring with my wife to our cottage in Port Stevens." He was far from enthusiastic.

I offered him the plastic container with my mother's Easter *kolaczkis*. He grabbed another poppy seed pastry covered in powdered sugar. For a brief moment, a smile graced his face. Then it disappeared.

"They're searching for my replacement, my boy."

"Why were you forced out?"

He finished his *kolaczki* and reached for another. He glanced around the empty room as if checking for a spy, then placed a stubby finger to his lips, leaving a trace of white powder. "Our staff is mostly women," he said. "The Board wants one to replace me."

"One of the staff?"

"No, no," he corrected. "A woman from the outside. Someone prepared to, um, implement new policies."

"Like what?"

"Shhh." He moved closer. "An employee complained to the Board. They wouldn't tell me who."

"Why would anyone complain?" I asked angrily.

He waved for me to keep my voice down. "I know it wasn't you," he whispered. "Information was shared well before you were hired. I have my suspicions. Frieda never liked my free-and-easy style, and then there's Geraldine. She's been riding me about that new office. And Rosie, she and I have had our share of battles."

I rose to her defense. "Rosie's not a backstabber." She was a musketeer.

Herbert snatched another pastry. "I shouldn't be telling you this, my boy. Watch your back." He tapped his lips with a forefinger covered in sugar. "Mum about our conversation."

⥈⥈⥈⥈

My Intermittent Explosive Disorder was late again. Cedric rested ham-like hands on an overhanging belly. Today, the slogan on his T-shirt shouted, *Don't Call Me Stout. Give Me A Stout.*

"Are you back to work?"

"Yup," he said smugly. "Me union forced the boss to take me back 'cause I had your letter. He'd cop it big if he kept me off work. But he said I had to keep seein' you. So let's get on with it."

I doubted whether I could help this hostile truckie who, at twenty-nine, relished the free samples during beer deliveries. Nonetheless, it was time to get on with it, as Cedric said.

"I'd like you to come on time for your sessions."

He smoothed his wrinkled khaki shorts. "Was only a few minutes late. No harm done."

"Actually, it was twenty minutes. And the first session, you arrived fifteen minutes late."

"Means you have less work to do."

"You don't want to be here, Cedric. But if you need another letter from me, you have to make a commitment to treatment."

His eyes narrowed as he raised his voice. "You know I don't like that word. I'm here for anger classes."

I stared at the massive claws gripping the arms of my chair. "Are you aware that you're raising your voice? Look at your knuckles. They're turning red."

He glanced at his hands. "So?"

"You're angry, aren't you?"

"So?"

I squeezed my pen. "If you want to manage your anger, you have to be aware of the physical signals."

He rubbed his bulging knuckles. "What are you sayin'?"

"That you're angry. Your voice is raised, you're rubbing your hands, and you're frowning." I wasn't game to mention that his bulbous nose was turning as bright as Rudolf the reindeer.

He made a half-hearted attempt to lower his voice. "What's the point?"

The point of my pen tapped my notepad. "You intimidate others with your anger. After all, you're a pretty strong bloke."

He flexed the trunk of his arm. "They know not to mess with me."

"How about your wife?" I asked. "Does she get frightened?"

He growled, "She's not scared of me."

"There you go, Cedric. See how pissed off you are?"

"You would be too if I talked about your wife." He glanced at my ring-less fingers. "If you could find one."

I rapped my pen again. "You're not in control of your life."

He scratched his buzz-cut hair. "What are you talkin' about?"

"Your anger got you in trouble with your boss. You called him an asshole."

"He deserved it," he snorted.

"But there were other incidents at work. You threw a beer keg at a co-worker."

"I told you, it was empty. And the bloke made fun of me."

"These incidents showed that you can't control your temper. You want to keep your job, don't you?"

He rubbed his banged-up shins. "I don't like me boss. He gives me grunt work. Pushing kegs ain't what you think. All *you* do is sit in a chair and talk. Not really man's work, is it?"

He sounded like my father. A man wasn't a man unless he used his hands. It was useless talking to a brick wall. I closed his file. "We're wasting our time."

Cedric tugged at his belt. "Listen, mate. I know I can be a bit rough, but I do need me job. I need another letter sayin' I've completed anger classes. If comin' on time is important, I'll be here."

His job must've been on the line. "Alright," I sighed. "But you have to work the program. That means learning about managing your anger."

He shuffled his brown boots. "As long as I get me letter."

"I can't write a letter unless you follow my recommendations."

His thumb scratched the inside of his nose. "Like what?"

He wasn't happy to hear that he had to accept responsibility for his behavior and complete homework. His first assignment was to ask his wife and friends for their observations about his behavior. My letter provided an incentive to follow through, but, as I gazed at his intimidating bulk, I wondered whether I'd be up for the task.

⊹⊹⊹⊹

"Alright, Frieda," I groaned. "I'll take it."

I punched the button. "Hi, Bonnie. What's up?"

Plain and simple, she wanted to talk. The pendulum had swung from Cedric's resistance to Bonnie's dependence. I gave her ten minutes. During that time, she chastised me for making a fuss about boundaries, complained about being lonely, but most importantly, needed reassurance.

Containing her emotions was like holding back a tidal swell. I checked the clock. "Listen, Bonnie. I'm late for a client and have to go. Write down any feelings in a journal. Bring it to Wednesday's session and we'll review it together... No, I'm not mad at you... I know you miss Perry... Let's talk about that on Wednesday... Yes, I'll be on time."

No sooner had I hung up when Frieda phoned to announce my next appointment.

↞↞

Albert Schweinfurt sat like a stunned mullet. "Dana wants a divorce. She found my porn videos in the garage. Says it's over. Why did she have to go snooping?"

"What about marriage counseling?"

The salesman scratched the kookaburra tattoo on his arm. "She won't come," he said woefully. "I'll do anything to save the marriage. I can't leave my son. Little Albie's only six. He needs me."

"You have to come clean with the phone sex, online relationships, and porn."

"I'm done with all that, Pete."

No sooner said than the stripper's theme song gyrated in his pocket.

I watched him suspiciously as he checked the caller I.D., then turned off the phone. He shoved it back in his pants. "Where were we?"

"When's the last time you went online for sex?"

He pulled his blond chin hair and avoided my gaze.

"Albert?"

"Uh…maybe two days ago. But I told them we had to stop."

My mind flashed to Celeste and her Roosters. I ignored her texts. Part of me wanted her out of my life; the other part longed to snuggle in her arms. But so did the others.

"I can't let my seven-year marriage go down the tube. You believe me, Pete, don't you?" pleaded Albert.

The kookaburra caught my eye. "This is a wake-up call to tackle sex addiction."

"I wouldn't call it that."

"Your behavior has threatened your marriage and put you in debt. Still you can't stop yourself. That's addictive behavior."

"I don't think—"

"If you want to save your marriage, Albert, you have to face the massive hole you've dug. You'll probably discover emptiness and shame. If you're honest, Dana might give you a chance."

With resignation, he sighed, "What do I do?"

"In addition to counseling, you should attend a sex addicts' group."

He reacted as if told to be celibate. "Out of the question."

"You said you'd do anything to save the marriage. A 12-step group sends Dana the message that you're serious."

He stared blankly at the wall. Even though a bird representing wake-up calls was permanently etched on his left arm, he resisted answering the call. However, with the pain of an ugly divorce looming, he might wake up.

When I walked him out the office, I wondered about Celeste. Would she change? I was ready for an answer.

WOUNDED IN ACTION

SATURDAY, APRIL 29

My mother stood at the stove, frying *kiszka.*

I grabbed a chair. "Pa working?"

"*Tak.*"

As it turned out, my father either didn't have much influence, or chose not to use it, to speed up the repairs on my car. Regrettably, I had promised to visit my mother after I picked it up. She turned off the stove and served blood sausage, fried onions, and potatoes.

"*Jeść.* Eat."

I picked at the food as my mother bounded repeatedly from chair to refrigerator. She brought out dill pickles, then returned for cheese.

"His drinking gets worse," she said. "I worry."

After she placed the kettle on the stove, I grabbed her arm and made her sit. "He's not going to stop."

"You must talk with him."

I stared at her incredulously. "Talk? You saw what happened on Easter."

The kettle whistled. "*Herbata?*"

"Don't want tea."

She removed two cups from the cabinet and dropped in tea bags. She poured hot water and placed a cup in front of me.

"I hide the bottles. He buys more."

I'd heard this litany countless times. She enabled as much as he drank. Made me crazy hearing about it. I bit hard on the kiszka and felt a sickening crunch. No! My tongue found a piece of bone, the size of a splinter. "Christ! First Auntie's nut bread and now the sausage."

I squinted at the white sliver between my fingers and rubbed my jaw. "It's the same bloody tooth."

My mother snatched the bone fragment and eyed it as if I was responsible for conjuring it. "Podgorski makes good *kiszka*."

"Not this one. Now I *have* to see a dentist."

"Dr. Skrzypczak will fix it."

I grimaced at the mere mention of the sadist. "Remember the time he pointed the drill at my nose and told me to be still or he'd make a third nostril. I was only ten!"

"Dentists cost money. Skrzypczak is cheap."

"I'd rather lose my teeth." I sipped the hot tea. The left side of my jaw screamed. "AGH!"

My mother rushed from the table and returned with a tiny bottle of clove oil and a cotton swab. She ministered to the broken tooth. The pain slowly subsided as the gums went numb.

"Better?"

I nodded.

She reached for the phone. "Skrzypczak will fix."

"No!" I grabbed the oil and pocketed it. "Have to go," I said, rising from the chair. "I'm meeting a friend."

"Please," she begged. "Sit. We talk.

My mother usually employed a host of strategies to get me to stay—guilt, anger, pleas, and threats. But this time, she was more vulnerable, desperate to reach out.

I stared at the wrinkles on her puffy face, her graying hair and slumped shoulders. "What's wrong?"

She grabbed a dish towel off a chair and wiped the plastic table cloth. She spoke more to the table. "Janek told me Pa's drinking at work. Makes mistakes."

I grabbed the cloth. "Pa has two problems: drinking and denial. He won't listen."

"You can make him."

"The best thing you can do is get help for yourself. I've told you many times—attend Al-Anon."

"That won't help him."

I tossed her the towel. "You're as stubborn as Pa."

She slapped the damp cloth at my chest. "If you visit more, that will help. You have no time for us. And you never bring your girlfriend."

Before the guilt trip took a nasty turn, I walked toward the door.

She grabbed my arm. "You help people. That's your job."

"How many times do I have to tell you? You're enabling Pa's drinking and getting more depressed. You need counseling."

My mother waved off my request as if it was a pesky fly. "I keep busy. That helps."

"Yeah, sure. Got to go."

"Wait. Take *ciastka* for your girlfriend." She rushed to the counter and wrapped the cake. She handed me a brown paper bag and kissed my cheek.

"Please, Ma," I said. "Call the therapist. You have the number."

I drove out of sight, leaving my mother and her despair staring out the window. Disengaging from family dysfunction was a constant battle. There was always the temptation to intervene as the white knight on a steed, only to be slammed off my saddle. No more would I leave their house with dented armor and a lame horse.

Recurring images of footballers getting special treatment tormented my mind. As I approached Celeste's place, I planned to keep my armor on. However, when she opened the door, wearing a white tank top and shorts, I wanted to toss my defenses aside and sink into a tender embrace. She welcomed me with an awkward kiss.

We said little as I entered her apartment. The aroma of curry and exotic spices filled the air while Indian chanting droned in the background. When we sat on the couch, the gray tomcat jumped on Celeste's lap and hissed at me.

"I'm glad you came for dinner," she began. "I've done a lot of thinking, especially when you didn't return my calls."

"I was pissed off."

She placed a finger over my mouth. "I know you're mad. I'm sad you're hurt. We both need healing. Babaji teaches us to let go of pain."

She placed the cat on the floor and lit a candle on the nearby table. "We need to release our pain, Peter," she said softly. "I'm prepared to listen. Can you let go of the anger?"

I stared at the tiny freckles on her nose, the dimples on her cheeks, and those hazel eyes. The gentle rhythm of her breathing radiated peace. Yet her stillness stirred my gut as if ugly, black millipedes were gnawing at my intestines.

"I thought we had something special," I said. "I trusted you. I still can't believe you were fucking clients."

My words struck like a whip. Her breathing quickened, yet she sat in silence. I wanted to shake her, let her feel the devastation. The burrowing insects forced me to lash out. "I don't know if I can ever get over what you did with the Roosters, and God knows who else."

Tears welled in her eyes. "I'm listening."

"You have a sex addiction," I said harshly. "You rationalize it with a dispensation from a swami who encourages free love. It's a crock of shit."

Celeste recoiled. Her body shook. Tears fell to her shirt. "Is there more?"

There was heaps more. But I deserved an answer. "Can you be faithful to me? Can you be monogamous?"

She wiped her eyes. "Can you listen without interrupting?"

"I'm not sure," I fumed.

She reached out and took my hands. "I know this isn't easy. All I ask is that you hear me out."

I watched the trickle cascade down her cheeks. "Alright," I said. "I'll try."

She closed her eyes and took several deep breaths. "I'm sorry I hurt you," she said, her eyes shut. "I knew you wouldn't understand. So I kept it hidden. That was wrong. I wanted to talk about it, but knew you wouldn't be open."

I planted my arms around my chest. "Open to what?" I blurted. "You screwing around?"

Her eyes flinched open. Where there was once calm, fire now blazed. "Yell or shout afterwards, but let me have my say."

My stomach felt like hundreds of millipedes were ripping my flesh. "You know how much you hurt me?"

"I'm hurting too," she shrieked. "If we can't let go of the pain, there's no hope for us. Now you've gotten me off balance. I can't talk right now. I need to breathe."

She closed her eyes and disappeared behind her breath. I didn't give a fuck. I wanted to vent my rage and release the scrambling beasts gnawing at my entrails before they pierced my heart.

She spoke, as if in a trance. "My parents made me suppress any sensual or sexual desire. Said it was sinful, satanic. When I met Babaji, he taught that divine essence flowed within. He said I would live in harmony only after I found myself."

She opened her eyes. "I know you don't believe in past lives, but I know we've been together. Something powerful drew us to one another. I cherish that. But I need to own my truth. I'm a sensual being. I'm compelled to share myself with others. I've talked to Babaji about this."

I jeered, "Is the balmy swami your god?"

"Don't make fun," she pounced. "He and the ashram are my family. When you reject them, you reject me."

"Your ashram doesn't work for me."

She bolted upright. "This isn't working, Peter. You don't want to let go; you want to attack."

Her tomcat jumped on the couch and hissed.

I had to ask the question before the black millipedes consumed my heart. "Can you be monogamous?"

She averted my gaze. "It's complicated. My sexual chakra is opening."

I blinked in disbelief. "Meaning no?"

She answered coldly. "You're just like my parents. Angry and judgmental." She nodded toward the kitchen. "Let's have something to eat. We can talk later."

"I'd prefer finishing our conversation."

Her nostrils flared. "You're more interested in possessing my body than in loving me. If Babaji doesn't see a problem with me expressing myself, I don't either."

My insides crawled. Was she telling me it was over? Her cat crept toward my hand and sniffed. I angrily swatted him away. He pounced on my wrist and sank his teeth.

I screeched. Blood oozed from the puncture.

"Indra," shouted Celeste. "Bad boy." She shoved him off the couch and berated me. "You shouldn't have attacked him."

"He bit me!"

She inspected the wound. "We better clean this before it gets infected." She led me to the bathroom and placed my hand in the sink. She rummaged in the cabinet and took out a small bottle and syringe.

I panicked. "What's that?"

"Need to flush out the wound with a strong antiseptic."

"No needle!"

"There's none on this syringe." She inserted it into the bottle and filled it. She seized my hand and squirted the broken skin. I screamed and lurched away. "Why didn't you tell me it was going to hurt?"

"Because you'd do exactly what you did. I have to apply it once more so the wound doesn't get septic."

I howled while she cleaned the bite. After she bandaged my wrist, I told her, "It's been a hard week. Better go."

"Can we share a meal?"

I was in no mood for sharing—food or otherwise. "It's best I leave."

She didn't protest. "This didn't turn out as I had hoped."

I said no more and left with an injured wrist, battered armor, and a wounded heart.

DIS-EASE

SUNDAY, APRIL 30

I swabbed the broken tooth with oil of clove and moped on the couch in front of the telly. A nature show featured a six-inch African millipede, thicker than a pen. Made me squirm, especially since the internal swarm of insects tunneled their way through my heart.

I rubbed my injured wrist. Images flickered across my mind like a slide show. Celeste naked, massaging a sweaty footballer. *Click*. Both moaning and screaming. *Click*. Fucking and sucking. *Click*.

To block the mental pictures, I took Nesha for a long walk to North Head, high above the beach, and watched the whitecaps cresting the waves. Between that northern point and South Head, ships found safe passage to Sydney Harbour. We strolled past the Quarantine Station, established in 1832 to hold passengers carrying disease. Closed since 1984, the station was now a historical site that offered tours. An amorous couple, arm-in-arm, kissed before ducking inside. Their affectionate touches triggered the start button. *Click*. Tormenting images flashed once more. *Click. Click.*

FOGGY TUESDAY

MAY 2

On the way to work, I walked three blocks to collect my car. I could've parked closer but didn't want to risk another round of vandalism from the cretins next door.

The mobile rang. I checked caller I.D. "Thomas. What's up?"

"You free tonight, mate? Thought we might catch a meal."

"Now's not a good time."

"Why?"

"Problems with Celeste. I'm not good company."

"That makes two of us. Thought you could help me with my pity party. And if you're down and out, mate, all the better. I won't be alone."

Misery loved company. We planned to rendezvous at Cockle Bay.

⋖⋖⋖⋖

Preoccupied with Celeste, I wanted to skip the supervision group and remain hidden in the fog. An impossible feat with three observant musketeers. Alana quickly sensed something was wrong.

"Don't want to talk about it," I told her as we settled into the group.

"Better to clear the cobwebs before you counsel anyone," said Sam.

"Maybe later."

Alana patted my arm. "We're here for you, Peter. Now's as good as later."

Rather than argue, I cut straight to the chase. "My relationship with Celeste is probably over."

"Did you have a fight?" asked Alana.

Geraldine's bushy eyebrows twitched excitedly. She spoke in her grating, nasal voice. "Did you hit her?"

I sneered at the psychologist. "Not all fights end up with a man battering a woman."

She pointed at my bandaged wrist. "Then what happened there?"

"Her cat bit me."

She glanced suspiciously at the bandage.

I held out my arm. "Do you want to check the wound, or maybe you think I'm cutting like your clients."

"What's your problem?" she huffed.

"You!"

"A fight's a-brewin'," clucked Rosie. "Shall I bring out the broadswords?"

"Settle down," intervened Sam. "Let's look at the real issues."

The theme for the remainder of supervision was conflict and the way we handled it. I acknowledged that I was upset with Celeste and probably displaced some of the anger onto Geraldine who, true to form, was less forthcoming. Everyone knew her laundry list of complaints about her husband, and every man for that matter, but she wouldn't assume any responsibility for her part. No wonder she irritated the hell out of me. If it weren't for the musketeers, I would've given her the broadsword.

⟵⟵⟵⟵

We sidled into a booth at the Shark's Nest restaurant.

"Schooners, mate?"

"That'll do just fine," I said. "Had a rough day."

The waiter brought us Fosters. We clinked glasses. "Cheers."

My eyes drifted to the feature attraction that gave the restaurant its name. An enormous circular tank in the center of the room housed small reef sharks swimming around living coral. Bright, colorful fish in an array of yellow and blue hues stayed out of harm's way. To complete the décor, a waterfall cascaded over rocks at the far end of the restaurant.

"Glad you came, mate," said Thomas. He lowered his voice and leaned across the table. "When you have AIDS, you find out who your real friends are. Trent dropped me for another bloke."

"The bastard!"

"Just when I needed him. The last group of treatments don't seem to be working. They switched to another medication. The side effects suck. Muscle aches, fatigue, occasional fever. But hey, who's complaining. I'm alive."

For how long? The overhanging light shimmered off his head, casting an eerie shadow.

"Thanks for being here, mate. It means a lot."

"You're part of the family."

Another round of schooners arrived and we placed our orders. Thomas took a large swig while I sipped my cold beer. The regular applications of clove oil had stopped the pain, but any radical temperature change made my tooth throb. I was prolonging the dreaded call to a dentist.

I told Thomas about my other pain, Celeste, and recounted the aborted meal.

"Sorry, mate," said the ex-priest.

"I can't bear the thought of her being with others and can't bear being without her. Any advice, Father?"

"Do you love her?"

"I thought I did. Not so sure anymore."

He swirled the beer in his schooner. "Life may be short for me, so here's my theory. Know what you want and fight for it. The two of you got on like fire. If she's wrestling with her sexuality, maybe you can help her."

"But she's with other blokes!"

"Listen, mate. You're pissed off, but maybe you can salvage something. You didn't give her much of a chance. She wanted to talk, but you shut her down."

"I couldn't listen to her shit."

"Relationships can be brutal, mate. One did me in. Yet I opened up again and still got hurt. No sense brooding."

He waved for the waiter and ordered another round. It arrived with our meal—grilled shark.

He smacked his lips. "This is worth living. A fantastic meal and wonderful company."

We attacked our meal and drank our schooners. My body relaxed and the rumbling insects in my gut stopped gnawing. Even my tooth behaved.

Thomas leaned across the booth. "Listen, mate. I really like you. If you weren't so straight, I think we could've had something. Then you could tell Celeste you were also wrestling with your sexuality."

The alcohol clouded my mind. Crikey! Was this a come-on?

He slapped my shoulder and guffawed. "Your face looks like it met one of the sharks. I was playing with you, mate. We're friends, nothing more. So stash the terror."

"I don't want to send any wrong signals," I said nervously.

Thomas waved me off with his huge paw. "The only signal you sent was that you cared enough to spend time with me when my friends let me down. Celeste's a foolish woman to let you get away."

"If only she knew."

He pushed aside his plate. "Sorry I poked fun, mate. Couldn't stop myself from stroking your homophobia. You're wound tighter than a nun's ass. Maybe that's a problem for Celeste."

I bristled. "What do you mean?"

"Don't take this personally, mate. Maybe she needs variety and you're not giving it to her."

"That's no reason to cheat," I argued. Other patrons glanced our way.

"Calm down," said Thomas. "I'm not excusing her. But if you know what you want, then fight for it. Unless you don't want her."

"Of course I want her, but so does a football team."

"Talk to her. Work it out. Tell her you'll introduce variety. Loosen up."

My mind spun 360 degrees. "How am I going to do that?"

With a mischievous grin, he suggested, "Imagination. Get a few sex books. Improvise." He chuckled, "I'd lend you mine but don't think they'd work for you."

"Damn right." I said, reaching for my draft. "But you may have something. If I give Celeste what she's missing, she might not want the Roosters. Hell, it's worth a visit to the bookstore."

He slapped my back. "That's the fighting spirit. That's what I'd want from my lover."

The glow on his face faded. His shoulders slumped as if crushed by an invisible weight.

"Sorry, Thomas," I said. "I've been so caught up with Celeste, I haven't, well, I can't even imagine how I'd handle what you're going through. Is there anything I can do?"

"Being with you is the best medicine, mate. I've been depressed, reminiscing about mistakes. Have to stop feeling sorry for myself." He lifted his schooner. "Time to live each day as if it's the last." He clinked my glass. "To life."

We spent the rest of the evening talking, laughing, and watching the sharks swim lazily in the tank. When we said our goodbyes, Thomas gave his patented bear hug.

I squeezed back. "Thanks for the advice."

"By the way, Alana has a thing for you," he said, playfully. "So if it doesn't work out with Celeste..."

I stopped him short. "Don't even go there. Alana's fantastic but I don't want to wreck a good friendship."

"You're a babe magnet."

"And you're a bullshitter. You must've served whopping sermons!"

We laughed heartily, then went our separate ways. Strangely, I had bonded with a man I once feared. And just as amazing, the fog lifted.

POLISH INDEPENDENCE DAY

I listened to my mother's phone messages. One reminded me it was Polish Independence Day; the other complained about my father.

I returned the call. "What're you doing there?" I asked. "It's noon."

"Came for lunch," he answered sharply.

More like a liquid meal. "You usually eat at the garage."

"Today, I eat at home. Aren't you working?"

"I start late today. Where's Ma?"

"She went to church. Novena."

That's why he slipped home for a drink. Not a good sign. I burst through the unmentionable door. "Ma's concerned about your drinking. You need help, Pa. You'll end up killing yourself."

"Don't you worry," came the stiff reply. "How's the car?"

"Your drinking's worse. Get some help."

Silence.

"Pa?"

"Can't talk," he barked. "Have to work."

"It's Independence Day. Free yourself from vodka."

He hung up. The stubborn old fool! I could never please him. Used to believe something was wrong with me. Then I realized he was an alcoholic and workaholic. Those two became his favorite sons. When he helped me move out five years ago, he was more interested in getting me out of his house and his life.

At our sixth session, Bonnie couldn't contain her excitement. "I saw him today!"

"Who?"

"Perry."

"You were supposed to move on without him."

She cradled the sugar glider. "He's serious about stoppin' drugs."

My stomach sank. "Has he moved into your place?"

"Perry likes Doc." She took out a plastic bag and gave it a treat. "He's gonna get himself sorted out."

"What about boundaries?" I chided. "He was supposed to be drug free and in counseling before you'd take him back. The last time, he stole your stereo."

Her eyes bulged. "He's gonna buy me a new one."

"Drug addicts promise the world."

"I was missin' him bad," she whined. "Doc's good company, but I need me Perry." She stroked her glider happily chomping on fruit. "With Perry back, I won't be botherin' ya as much."

I seriously doubted that. "Let's take this one step at a time."

"I brought me diary like ya asked." She handed me a binder. "ABBA's inside. Can ya play it?"

I wasn't in the mood for ABBA but didn't want to add rejection to the growing list of issues. I tossed the CD into the player, then checked Bonnie's single page. It looked like Sanskrit. "I'll need some help here."

"Can't ya read?" She grabbed the binder and pointed to each word as she read.

Friday. I'm mad. Doc P. doesn't like me.

Saturday. Still mad. Maybe I won't see him. He won't care.

Sunday. Called Doc P. Got his stupid voice mail. He should answer his calls. Doc and I went for a walk.

Monday. This is stupid.

Tuesday. Feel bad. Called Doc P. lots of times. Busy as usual. He doesn't care.

She shrugged. "Didn't write today."

"Yes, well, at least it's a start. You'll soon get used to it."

She complained, "Don't like keepin' a diary."

"What you wrote was fine. There are no grades." Although an "F" would've been kindhearted.

Clearly, she was pissed off I was unavailable. At least she had a forum to express her emotions. With practice, she'd write more, but I wouldn't count on another Jane Austen.

I offered encouragement. "Imagine that the journal is another way to communicate with me. When you're mad, get it out. I can read it at the session. Okay?"

She grunted, "I prefer talkin'. Ya never answer when I call. Now that me Perry's back, I can talk ta him."

"What about drugs?"

She averted my gaze. "He's gonna get help."

"Where?"

"Didn't say. But he promised."

She was in as much denial as Perry.

"You have to protect yourself," I cautioned her. "He'll rip you off again."

Her eyes begged forgiveness. "I was lonely, Doctor P. Ya don't know what it's like. I need a man. If he gets help, we can have us a good life."

I spent the rest of the session preparing her for the eventual. Having found a place to crash, he'd grab some grub and cash. Bonnie objected, but listened to my request to be vigilant, set clear boundaries, and have a safety plan in case of violence. Based on her history, I doubted whether she'd follow through. But she did agree to continue writing.

When we ended, I removed ABBA mid-song, "Thank You for the Music," and handed her the CD. No doubt, she would be hearing Perry's familiar tune, "Gimme, Gimme, Gimme."

LITERARY RESEARCH

THURSDAY, MAY 4

Thomas's advice resounded in my mind—know what you want and fight for it. I was lonely, and, contrary to what Bonnie assumed, knew what it was like to be without someone who made my heart sing. I craved for the healing touch and warm embrace of Celeste. If she needed variety, I could provide it.

After work, I browsed the sexuality section at Angus and Robertson books. Several titles popped off the shelf: *Titillating Tricks for Ardent Lovers; Magical Monogamy;* and *Kinky Can be Normal.* Like a novice delving into the forbidden, I flipped through chapters on lurid fantasy, creative bondage, exotic positions, and sex toys. In the end, I selected *Tantric Sex,* which seemed safer than whips. Hopefully, it would thrust me onto the same page with Celeste, who was highly skilled in Tantric principles. Variety might make monogamy work.

"What do you have there?" asked a high-pitched voice belonging to a curvaceous redhead, who was at least ten years older than I was.

She reached for the book. "May I?"

Not waiting for a reply, she flipped through the pages and found a graphic pose of a naked woman straddling an erect penis. She licked her glossy, red lips and drooled. "Very yummy." She wiggled her bottom, tightly wrapped in pink shorts. "Do you recommend this position?"

Drawn like a magnet, my eyes veered to the pink blouse that bulged with ripe grapefruits.

I cleared my throat. "I-I don't work here."

"I hope not," she squealed. She pointed to the picture. "You need a partner to practice this position."

"I-I'm buying this for a friend."

The brazen redhead feigned surprise. "I'm sorry. I didn't see a ring." She gazed hypnotically at my eyes as her right hand unfastened a button on her blouse, revealing more cleavage. "Let's cut to the chase, shall we. If your place is nearby, we can have some fun." Her hand reached for my thigh and squeezed. "What's your name, honey?"

Charmed by the cobra, I stared at her tongue flicking moist lips, then at the luscious grapefruits begging to be plucked... What the hell was I doing? I wanted Celeste, not a floozy.

"I have a girlfriend," I said, grabbing the book. Without looking back, I bolted toward check-out. Australia had some of the most poisonous snakes in the world but I never thought I'd find one in a bookstore.

I returned home and slipped into bed with *Tantric Sex* in hand. Thomas was right. Life was too short to let opportunities slip by. I would visit the ashram tomorrow night and surprise Celeste. Cradling the book, I imagined her tantalizing, naked body performing wild, erotic Tantric acts. However, the curvaceous redhead kept wiggling into the fantasy.

WHAT A SURPRISE

FRIDAY, MAY 5

I grabbed the files from Frieda and smiled. "Good morning!"

She leered at me. "Your dirty cup's in the sink. Clean up after yourself."

"I'm onto that," I said, determined not to let Pruneface dampen my spirits. Celeste and I would be together this evening.

I found Frieda's post-it note plastered on my mug—PETER'S MESS. Hell, everyone knew my cup had the koalas. I gave it a rinse and poured coffee. Thank God it was Friday.

My first appointment found Albert Schweinfurt with unexpected company—an enraged wife. A fiery brunette with a pixie haircut, Dana waved her fists in the air, revealing eucalyptus leaves, shaped in a wreath, tattooed across both wrists. "I want to know what Al's been telling you. The bastard's a con artist."

Before I could inform her about confidentiality, she smacked his arm and the purple kookaburra tattoo. "He's out of control."

"Hold on," I said. "No violence here."

"He spent $6,000 on sex calls!"

Far more than he told me. Before I could ask about the discrepancy, Albert went on the attack.

"She's gone bonkers, Pete."

"Hold on!" I shouted. "Time out."

Dana turned her wrath on me. "Did he tell you about the women online and the porno pictures? One slut held a dildo with Albert's name marked in purple. She was shoving it up—"

"Stop!" I yelled. "We can't get anywhere like this."

"She won't listen to reason," sniped Albert.

"No more lies and cheating," she blasted. "You've been telling those women you're single and want to fuck their brains out."

"Calm down," I said, interrupting the tirade.

"He'll con the socks off you," she screamed. "Our son's only six. I can't have him around a pervert."

He pulled angrily at the blond chin-hair. "If you'd give me some at home, I wouldn't be looking elsewhere."

"Blame me?" she screeched. "I gave you plenty! You're never satisfied. I watched porn with you, even went to the strip joint at Kings Cross. You wanted more. Talked about a threesome. You're as fucked up as your boss. He hits on me every time—"

I leapt to my feet and acted as a barricade. I shouted, "I can't help you if you're yelling at each other."

They both stared at me as if I was the problem.

"I know you're upset," I said to Dana. "If you can't be in the same room, I'll have to separate you. Albert needs help. That's why he's here."

The brunette huffed, "He's a liar."

"I have a good picture of what's going on," I said. "If Albert overcomes his sex addiction, would you work on the marriage?"

"I don't trust him."

"See what I mean, Pete?"

I glared at him. "If you want your wife and son, you'll have to fight for them. If you don't, your marriage is over."

"You've got that right," bellowed Dana. The eucalyptus leaves on her wrists swished through the air. "I'm through with this sicko."

I turned on her. "You're making it hard for me to do my job. If you can't contain yourself, please go to the waiting room."

She dropped her arms and sulked. "I won't say another word."

I returned to my seat. "Fighting for your family, Albert, means stopping any contact with women, continuing with therapy, and attending group meetings. You have to demonstrate that you mean business."

"Yeah," she agreed, then caught my eye. "Oops."

He scratched his tattoo. "She has to trust me."

"She won't trust you if don't tell the truth. You have to come clean."

"Yeah!" she shouted.

I pointed toward the door.

"Won't say another word. Promise."

I re-focused on Albert. "You have to give it your best shot. And I'd encourage both of you to get marriage counseling."

"Not until Al proves he's faithful. Otherwise, I'm getting a divorce."

"Let's take it one step at a time," I said. "Albert, can you make a commitment, no contact with women?"

He looked as if I was crazy. "I sell computers to them."

"You know what I mean."

"Yeah, okay. I don't want a divorce." He glared at Dana. "I love you."

She huffed, "Prove it."

Albert would have to demonstrate his true intentions. By the time we finished the turbulent session, the couple staggered out of my office, a bit more civil. For how long was anyone's guess.

✦ ✦ ✦ ✦

I rushed home after work and quickly changed clothes. I originally planned to arrive at the end of meditation, but decided otherwise. My surprise visit would demonstrate my love and acceptance for Celeste. While I might never feel comfortable in the ashram, I could acknowledge it as Celeste's home.

Battling the weekend traffic, I arrived 15 minutes late. I placed my shoes in the rack and crept toward the large, darkened room that had swelled with devotees, shoulder to shoulder, sitting cross-legged on their cushions, swaying to Om Namah Shivaya. I stumbled toward the back of the men's area and found a vacant piece of carpet.

I craned my neck over the chanting crowd towards the women. With the packed house and dimmed lights, it was difficult to spot Celeste, who normally sat in the front row. If she wasn't here, tonight's surprise would be on me.

I endured the evening of chanting and waited impatiently for the lights to flicker back to life. I alternated my aching legs as the singing reached its crescendo. Then there was silence.

The room brightened and Ziprunanda, dressed in saffron, made his grand entrance like a rock star. He strolled through the sea of devotees and touched their bowed heads as he slowly made his way toward the stage. Behind him walked a woman, also in saffron robes. I remained transfixed on the figure in prayerful pose strolling behind him. As if struck by a thunderclap, I jolted into realization. Celeste's spiraling blonde locks had been shorn like a sheep stripped of its fleece.

My shock gave way to rage. The swami must've drugged her or made her his sex slave. My body shook with fury. I wanted to stab the red dot that marked his third eye.

A hush fell over the crowd. The dark-skinned swami with the bushy white beard and fat belly sat cross-legged on the orange cushion. He nodded to Celeste.

On cue, she announced, "Today, I have embraced sadhana, the practice of spiritual discipline." She bowed reverently to her guru. "I accepted Babaji's invitation. Hereafter, I shall be called Bhakta, devotee of God."

Everyone clapped, except me. She bowed to the audience and moved to the front row where she was heartily greeted by the women.

I wanted to snatch her brainwashed body and reveal the lunacy of this extreme makeover.

"Spiritual discipline requires an inward journey," lectured the swami. "Renunciation of worldly possessions is the first step to attain oneness with the divine."

I seethed as the swami babbled about the joy of surrendering. There was no joy in losing Celeste. When it was time for silent meditation, I made a swift exit. No mass hypnosis today during satsang. I hurried past the devotees, not before stepping on someone's ankle. I escaped the hall, grabbed my shoes, and rushed outside, away from the bloody nightmare.

I sucked in the cool night's air. My mind cleared. It was time to fight and seize Celeste so she could her reclaim her identity. I waited until the devotees streamed from the ashram, then made my way to the small room where tea was being served. A throng of admirers surrounded Celeste. Before I could approach her, a woman offered me a cup of chai. Without thinking, I accepted the creamy cinnamon tea and took a sip. Crikey! The tea could be spiked. I was about to empty my cup into a potted plant when I heard that familiar voice.

"Peter? Is that you?" Celeste rushed toward me and hugged tightly. "I asked for a sign and you showed up."

"I wanted to surprise you," I said, frowning at her shorn head. "What a surprise."

She laughed and hugged me again. "You don't know what it means to have you here. I felt so bad after you left my place. I spoke to Babaji. He suggested sadhana to purify my intentions. I decided to let go of attachments and open myself to divine truth. Your presence is a sign I made the right choice."

She embraced me again. A small crowd gathered. "This is Peter," she said to everyone. "He answered my call to join Babaji."

The others smiled and bobbed their heads, probably drugged out on special chai. It was pointless to argue with crazed devotees, so I played along. "I'd like to hear more. Can we meet privately, Celeste."

"My name is now Bhakta," she corrected me. "And I'm moving into the ashram."

"W-what?"

"Tomorrow," she beamed. "I've given away most of my possessions."

"Where will you stay?"

"There's a small room with a bed and dresser. Babaji says we clutter our lives with stuff." She rubbed her hand over her crew cut. "I'm letting go, detaching."

I clutched my tightening chest. Her detachment ripped at my heart. "What about us?"

"Whenever you're here, I'll make time for you."

I tugged at her saffron robes. "Does that mean we won't be able to...be together?"

She pulled me away from the smiling devotees and stroked my cheek. "Not like before," she whispered. "When you left me, I had to look at myself. I hurt you, and probably others. I realized that I had become attached to physical pleasures. Babaji encouraged me to seek spiritual bliss. He said that detachment from worldly desires accelerates spiritual union."

I smelled the tea and the strong odor of cinnamon. As if reading my mind, she said, "I'm not taking drugs. I know this is all very sudden."

"Like practically overnight."

She led me to a quiet corner where we sat on the carpet. She sipped her tea and spoke in a soft voice. "I had been considering sadhana for some time, but rejected the spiritual practice because it meant giving up sex. After we fought, I thought about what you said. I was addicted to pleasure. My body fed men's cravings. I had to let the suffering go. I meditated with Babaji and received the call for sadhana and selfless service."

She beamed at me. "I'm grateful to you for awakening me to my spiritual home."

"I don't think that's what Gretchen had in mind," I argued. "Hell, we had such a good thing. I'm prepared to change, to come your way. That's why I came tonight."

"Funny, isn't it," she said wistfully. "Change happened, but not exactly as we planned."

Two saffron-robed women approached us. "Time to clear up the kitchen," instructed the elder.

No longer Celeste, Bhakta bowed to the women. She kissed my cheek and eased herself off the carpet. "My spiritual practice calls. Come back. There's so much to share. Babaji will change your life." She turned away and disappeared into the kitchen.

I rose to my feet and, in the process, knocked over my cup of tea. The swami's legions could clean it up! They had blissfully imprisoned themselves to service the ashram. The guru's gateway to nirvana led to ongoing adulation, free labor, and personal massages, to boot.

MORNING VISITOR

Knock. Knock.

"Who's there?"

More loud banging.

Woof. Woof.

"Who the bloody hell?" I buttoned a shirt and opened the door. No! "What are you doing here?"

"Sorry to bother ya, mate," said Perry. He extended his right hand while the other held a half-smoked cigarette. "I thought I'd stop by, if you know what I mean."

I didn't shake hands.

His greasy, black hair and tattered clothes reeked of tobacco. "Me Bonnie told me you lived here. Can I come in?" He peered into my apartment. His gaunt face and glazed eyes told me he was whacked. The gold stud that adorned Perry's ear was conspicuously missing. Like Elvis, he had descended into a black hole of drugs.

I stepped outside and shut the door. "I'm on my way out," I said. "What can I do for you?" So much for Bonnie respecting my boundaries! She would cop heaps at our next session.

His smelly face edged closer. "Bonnie says you tole her not to give me money. Why would you go and do that?"

I backed against the door. "You have to ask her. I can't talk about clients."

He hissed like a snake. "She says you tole her not to support me."

Nesha scratched at the door, wanting to play outside. *Woof. Woof.* "He's a vicious watchdog," I warned Perry. "What do you want?"

The howling unsettled the addict, and his demeanor shifted. His mouth widened into a smile. "No worries," he said, as if he was now apologizing for disturbing me at nine in the morning.

He took a huge drag on his cigarette. A cut on his left thumb oozed blood as he pointed to the holes in his shirt. "Listen, mate. I'm short of cash, if you know what I mean. Thought you could help out a mate."

Drug addicts were tenacious and highly adaptive, especially when it came to feeding a habit. When intimidation didn't work, begging became another alternative. And if that didn't satisfy their next fix, robbery would. With Perry on my doorstep, thievery was waiting to happen. Once he discovered Nesha wasn't a watchdog, he'd have no problem breaking in, even with my extra deadbolt.

"I can't give you money," I said firmly. "If you need a meal, clothes, or a referral to a drug program, I can help you."

His grin evaporated as quickly as it appeared. He wiped the bleeding thumb on his filthy jeans. "Need the cash, mate," he said maliciously. "If you hadn't tole Bonnie, I wouldn't be here. Need somethin' to tide me over, if you know what I mean. I'll pay you back."

Payback was exactly what I was worried about. "I don't keep money here," I lied again. "Let's go for a walk. I'll buy you a meal. We can talk."

He didn't budge. "Don't need food," he growled. "Can get that from Bonnie. And I sure as hell don't wanna walk."

Time for the showdown. "You need to get off drugs," I told him. "I'll help out in other ways, but I'm not going to support your habit."

He reacted as if I'd stolen his drugs. His eyes flashed wild. "I need cash and you owe me," he screamed. "Me mates and I know where you live."

I grabbed the doorknob, ready for retreat. "I'm calling the coppers." I jiggled the doorknob and shouted at Nesha, "Bad man. Attack!"

The fierce barking caused Perry to storm down the stairs. He tripped at the bottom and cursed, "Don't mess with me woman. I know what you're after."

He disappeared out of sight. I fled inside and bolted the locks as Nesha jumped on me, ready to play. Watchdog, indeed!

With my home under threat again, I reached for the phone but quickly rescinded the decision. The last time I involved the police, my car was vandalized. The coppers wouldn't do anything except antagonize Perry. Then he'd bring reinforcements. And what the hell did he mean, "I know what you're after." Was he delusional, thinking I was after Bonnie? She told me he had used methamphetamines, so I assumed drug-induced paranoia.

I examined my second-floor apartment for break-in points. The easiest entry was the tiny front balcony. Although it was nothing more than a ledge with space for plants, it faced toward the beach and could easily be scaled. A bloke standing on a shoulder could reach up for the ledge. The sliding glass door offered little protection from a brick. Short of installing steel bars in front of the window, there was little I could do.

Throughout the day, I checked the front balcony for intruders. With the double threat of Perry and the "Rocky Horror Show" next door, I had no choice but to relocate. The only positive note, if you could call it that, was that Celeste/Bhakta fell from my rumination list. Safety and survival dominated as top priority.

Later, Thomas called for an update on Celeste. I shared my woes and listened to his words of comfort. However, I felt a boatload of guilt because I hadn't phoned him to check on his health. He was clearly the better friend. After I said goodbye, I promised to call him within a week. That was the least I could do.

Bang! I jumped at the clatter on the balcony. A kookaburra landed hard on the railing and rubbed its beak against the metal. I rapped on the glass door and chased it away. Then it came in a flash. I needed protection. I would answer the wake-up call and defend my home.

ANOTHER MORNING VISITOR

Knock. Knock. Knock. Knock.

Nesha ran to the door and barked at the frantic rapping.

I grabbed the cricket bat I bought yesterday and crept toward the door, prepared for Perry and his mates.

"W-who's there?"

"It's me," squeaked a voice.

"Me who?"

"Bonnie."

My heart sank. Boundaries meant nothing. I yanked at the door, ready to vent my rage. I choked on the emotions as soon as I saw the sobbing woman. In the palm of her hand sat the little sugar glider—dead.

"I'm s-sorry, Doctor. P," she cried. "Didn't mean ta let Perry know. He forced it outa me. Threatened to kill Doc." She glanced forlornly at her lifeless pet, then collapsed on my doorstep with heaving sobs.

Nesha nudged his way past me. He nuzzled her face and licked her wet cheeks. I pushed him back with the cricket bat and gently lifted her to her feet.

"What happened?"

She caressed the listless creature and sobbed. "I t-tried callin' ya yesterday after he left. Got your v-voice message. Tried ta w-warn ya."

I checked the stairs to make sure he wasn't lurking nearby. "He wanted money."

She whimpered. "T-took mine. Wasn't enough. Asked me where ya lived." Her watery eyes pleaded. "I didn't wanna tell him. Ya gotta believe me. But he grabbed Doc and squeezed."

She convulsed into a wail. Tears splashed on my naked feet.

"Calm down." I wanted her to leave me in peace, but I couldn't send her off in her emotional state.

"Wait here."

I retreated inside, grabbed my sandals, then leashed Nesha. I returned to find her stroking the glider as if it were still alive.

"Let's go for a walk," I said. "We can sit on the beach and talk."

Bonnie snuffled her dribbling nose on her spare hand and followed me and Nesha across the street. In my vigilance to check for Perry, I missed the wad of pink chewing gum on the pavement. Like a leech, it clung to my sandal. I tried scraping it off, but the sticky stuff held fast, like the current emotional crisis. I removed the sandals and plodded with Bonnie toward the beach.

I gave Nesha free reign. Rather than scamper after the gulls, like he normally did, he followed us to the patch of sand where we parked ourselves. He sniffed at Bonnie's pet, then licked her face.

I pushed him toward the beach. "Go chase the birds."

His paws stood firm. Stubborn dog. I turned to the sniffling woman.

"What happened?"

She stared at the crashing surf. "I shouldn't have come, but I had ta warn ya."

A southeasterly blew across the sand. In the distance, a small sail boat capsized from the blustery wind.

"Perry was agitated, probably desperate for drugs," I said. "When I didn't give him money, he left in a rage."

"He came home last night. I wasn't gonna let him in, he was so mad. But he kicked at the door. Didn't want the neighbors ta hear. So I let him in. Bad mistake, Doctor P. He grabbed Doc outa the cage and said he'd kill him this time if I didn't give him the money."

She fondled the pet. "He was crazy," she cried. "Gettin' more edgy. Asked what I was doin' with ya. Said I was holdin' out. I tole him I had no more. He wouldn't listen. He squeezed Doc, tellin' me ta quit lyin'. I screamed at him ta take anything and let Doc go. He squeezed hard, too h-hard."

Her body convulsed into sobs. Nesha licked her face. Bonnie's free hand rubbed his fur. He nuzzled her back.

"Perry was mad at Doc cause he bit him yesterday morning."

I recalled the sight of Perry's bloody thumb.

She wiped her eyes. "Sorry, Doctor P."

I was sorry, too. If I had given him some cash, Doc might still be alive. Perry would have gotten his fix and left Bonnie alone last night.

"He'll return," I warned. "Who knows what state he'll be in. Can you stay with a friend?"

Her protruding eyes faced the gusting wind. She spoke coldly, resolutely. "He won't come back. After he killed me Doc, I didn't care what happened. Grabbed a knife from the kitchen. Wanted ta kill him. I chased him down the street, but he was too fast. I want him ta come back. Ta give him what he gave Doc."

Bonnie had fallen into a raging cesspool.

"You can't kill him," I said. "He's not worth it."

She grabbed Nesha's collar. "What would ya do if he killed your dog?"

I cringed. "I'd feel like killing the bastard, but I wouldn't. And you can't either. Right now, you're upset about losing Doc and rightly so. But it's over with Perry. Finished. It's a wake-up call to get on with your life."

Her sorrowful eyes welled with tears. "I tole Doc my troubles. He made me laugh. Perry took that away. Don't wanna go home. Not without Doc."

"We'll get through this together."

She snuffled. "Thought you'd be mad I came."

"I don't like Sunday dramas," I confessed. "But I do want the best for you. So let's get your ship back in the water."

She patted my wrist. "Thanks, Doctor P. With me pet gone, you're all I've got."

"Let's talk more tomorrow. I can see you in the office at three."

"Boundaries, huh?"

I nodded. "Best that way. The police should be called."

She batted away the stinging sand. "They'll do nuthin'. Just tell me ta call if he shows." The scrappy woman glanced at her pet. "We'll take care of Perry."

"That's what I'm worried about," I said, anxious about a possible homicide. "Promise me you won't let him in. I don't want a stabbing on my conscience."

She stared blankly into the lashing wind. "I won't go lookin' for him."

"Please, Bonnie," I begged. "If he shows, call the police. Doc wouldn't want you to go to jail."

She lifted his little body. "What should I do with him? He needs a proper sendoff."

"We'll come up with something. In the meantime, promise me you won't do anything foolish."

She brushed sand off her face. "Don't wanna upset ya."

"Great answer," I said. "Don't let Perry in. We'll work out a plan tomorrow."

"Can I see you in the mornin'?"

I shook my head. "I'll be swamped with intake."

She grumbled. "Guess I have ta fit your schedule."

I stretched my legs. "I'm taking Nesha for a walk. Remember, if he comes, call the police."

She waved me off. "Ya already tole me."

She rose from the beach and, still cradling the glider, slowly ambled away. I watched the sorrowful figure trudge through the biting sand whipped by the southeasterly. Though Perry may not have the good sense to stay away, I hoped Bonnie would exercise better judgment and put away the knives.

AFTERMATH

MONDAY, MAY 8

Intake was full-on. Frieda marched into my room with another stack of phone messages. All of Sydney seemed in crisis. Individuals contemplating suicide, couples threatening divorce, and the ridiculous, like the bloke who told me he had so much shit in his head, he tried flushing it down the toilet. His was an easy fix. I sent him to the plumber, or so I told him, as I facilitated a referral to a psych ward.

The last call was from a distraught husband whose wife flew to Cairns over the weekend to take up with a man she met on the Internet. Another relationship fallen apart. I related to the husband's pain, for I still longed for Celeste and her gentle, healing hands. Her sensuous clothes and golden spirals of hair had been replaced with a shorn Bhakta in saffron robes. The woman I loved was gone forever.

It was time to follow my mother's advice—when depressed, get busy. Weary from the weekend, I braced myself for the post-crisis session. As usual, Bonnie arrived early, but with a cigar box in hand. Her face was puffy and her large, mournful eyes gazed nowhere. Like her sugar glider, life had been squeezed from her small body.

Consumed with grief, she opened the wooden box on my desk. A putrid stench filled the room. Decaying bodies don't do well in the heat, and today's sun was a scorcher.

She lifted the rigid carcass. I gagged.

"He was me best friend," she sniffled. "Have ta give him a proper burial."

239

I moved my chair back. "Is there any land by your apartment?"

"Not much."

"What about a park?"

She caressed the smelly marsupial. "Hinkler Park's nearby."

"You should be able to find a small patch for a burial."

She nestled him near her belly. Tears fell. "I don't wanna let him go."

We sat in painful silence, she from grief, I from nausea. When Bonnie kissed Doc's head, I handed her the box.

"Let him go," I pleaded. "Plant some fragrant flowers next to him."

She replaced the carcass into the wooden coffin.

I pressed the lid on the box and breathed a sigh of relief. "When one door closes," I said, "another will open."

The remainder of the session seemed more like a wake. Bonnie went through a box of tissues while she reminisced about her pet. She talked about Doc gliding around the apartment, making all kinds of mischief. He had kept her company at night. Now she had no one. And Perry, well, he had better stay clear. Hell hath no fury like a woman whose beloved pet was slain.

When it was time to end, I reminded Bonnie that our regular session was in two days.

She remained glued to the chair. "I can't pay," she said. "Perry took me money. Won't get paid till Friday."

I told her not to worry. We'd work something out.

We said our goodbyes, and like a pallbearer, I solemnly escorted her and the little coffin down the hall.

THE TORCH

WEDNESDAY, MAY 10

Stumbling in pitch black cave, I scramble over sharp rocks. Hear clinking, clanking. Wham! Struck on the head. Bony hand clutches my throat. I flail my arms. More hands appear. Pin me to stone wall. I spot a torch. Floating mid-air. Drawing nearer. Revealing all. I shriek at the bleeding skeleton holding the torch. Clinking and Clanking. He forces me to drink a goblet. Filled with blood and crushed bones. I choke and swallow. My body convulses, shape shifts. Into skeleton man.

⤙⤙⤙⤙

Alana bounced into the staff room with the *Sydney Morning Herald* clutched to her waving hand. "The torch is heading home!" she exclaimed.

I flashed to the morning's dream and spilled my coffee. "What torch?"

She pointed to the newspaper. "The Olympic Torch, silly. It says that the flame will be lit in Athens today. It'll travel around Greece for ten days. Then we'll take possession on May 20. Should arrive here the eighth of June."

I grabbed a towel and mopped up my mess. "What's with all the excitement? The Olympics doesn't start until September. And frankly, I'm not too keen when the torch visits Manly. The traffic will be horrific."

"A pity it didn't visit outer space. Poor weather canceled the trip from Cape Canaveral." She turned a page and showed me the paper. "Great design, don't you think?"

I glanced at the ultra-modern torch. "Doesn't look anything like the ones in ancient Greece."

She puffed her chest and gushed, "This one represents Australia. They've put a lot of thought into it." She outlined the picture with her finger. "The torch has the curve of a boomerang and the sails of the Opera House. It has three layers to represent fire, earth, and water. The inner layer is sea blue, my favorite color."

Alana's enthusiasm amused me. Her mother was born in the Philippines, and her Australian father abused her, yet here she was, a diehard Aussie, practically singing "Waltzing Matilda."

"Seems a bloody waste of money."

"Don't be a party pooper," said Alana, more animated than ever. "Become a volunteer like me. The Olympics and Paralympics need 50,000 volunteers."

The intercom crackled. "Peter, are you there?"

"Yes, Frieda."

"Bonnie's here."

I rinsed my cup, lest Frieda publicly chide me, and told Alana, "If the Olympics make you happy, I won't knock it. But battling millions of visitors doesn't turn me on. I have a hard enough time dealing with one difficult client."

"You're not getting off that easy," she said cheerily. "Volunteering will take your mind off the problems."

Alana was well aware of my relationship saga. While sympathetic, she seemed a bit too pleased that Celeste was ensconced in the ashram. I was now fair game.

She playfully swatted me with the paper. "I'll pester you till you say yes."

I saluted. "Yes, Olympic organizer. But if you'll excuse me, I have to run the twenty-five meter-dash to the waiting room."

Bonnie had called three times yesterday. Without Doc and Perry, she had become more dependent on me. The advice from the supervision group was clear: support her through the crisis, establish a safety plan, refer her to a psychiatrist for medication, suggest the women's group, set firm limits, and avoid contact out of the office, as if I had much say about that.

Bonnie slumped in her chair and stared at the wall as if there was a window. She didn't bring in her journal or ABBA and had stopped showing up for work.

"There's nuthin' ta live for," she said, her eyes dry as a bone. "I wanted Perry. He's gone. Doc made me happy. He's dead. You're the only friend I have, Doctor P. And if ya weren't seein' me, I might as well not be here."

Drawn into her bleak, depressing world, I felt like a mountain climber offering her a rope. I could push hospitalization, but she would probably reject the help and sever our connection, the only thing keeping her from plummeting to the abyss. She resisted when I pointed out the tiny footholds, but eventually grasped my lifeline. Our shared time on Sunday had established a closer bond, without which she would have surely let go. I remained steadfast and encouraged her to hold on and continue the upward climb.

When I concluded the difficult session, I promised her that we would reach the top of the mountain. I even surprised myself by mentioning the Olympic torch, telling her that it symbolized victory and giving it your best shot. For good measure, I parroted Gretchen's words, "Victories without hardship are hollow and offer little cause for celebration."

Although she continued to refuse my advice for medication or a group, she agreed to restart her diary, call me tomorrow, and return to work. She offered a flicker of light when she said, "I'll try and not let ya down."

I planned to keep the same promise.

TORCHED

THURSDAY, MAY 11

In the afternoon, Alana found me on the computer. "Did you catch the torch on the telly last night?"

I turned from the screen. "I crashed after work. But I heard the radio this morning. Seems it didn't go as planned."

Clouds had dampened the lighting ceremony in Athens. A concave mirror was set up to catch the sun's reflection and ignite the flame. Without bright sun, they had to jump-start the torch for its long-distance journey.

"What are you doing after work?" she asked cheerily.

"The usual. Nothing much."

"Want to go out for a bite?"

"Thanks all the same," I said. "I'm pooped and not in the mood for company."

She pulled up a chair and faced me. "I know you're hurting, Peter. We're here for you—Sam, Rosie, Thomas, and me. Don't push us away. We're family."

I gazed at the smiling Filipina. She was younger than Celeste and not nearly as attractive, but her pretty face and warm smile oozed compassion. I chose my words carefully. "I really appreciate you being here. But I'm not ready for another relationship."

"Who says I'm asking for romance?" she said defensively. "Can't we share a meal after work? I'm not asking to get involved. Just deepen our friendship. And I won't take no for an answer."

Usually more passive and soft-spoken, Alana exuded more confidence than usual. Or was it that I had sunk so low?

"You seem different. What's going on?"

She grinned. "Must be the body work with Gretchen. She wants me to be seen and heard. Says that's the only way I'll feel at home with myself."

"Gretchen strikes again."

"I've lots more to share over dinner."

One part resisted. The other part wanted to escape the lonely skeletons clanking inside.

"Oh, what the hell."

She jumped up from the chair and squeezed me. "Fantastic. How about Thai?"

I moaned, "Anything but that. Celeste and I had our first date at the Thai Dragon."

"Pick somewhere close. Let's leave after work." She hugged me again, then skipped merrily out of my office.

After she left, the clinking skeletons banged against my heart. I picked up the phone and called The Healing Touch Salon. I wanted to hear Celeste's voice once more, even if it was a recording. A woman with an Indian accent answered and brusquely informed me she had bought the business. Celeste had severed another attachment. The only consolation was that the Roosters had lost their golden hen.

⟵⟵⟵⟵

Dinner with Alana didn't go well. She was excited; I was depressed. She wanted an emotionally intense dinner with heaps of sharing; I wanted a superficial meal without dessert. She wanted to discuss the torch; I wanted darkness.

Alana tried valiantly to pull me out of my cave, but I couldn't let go of the painful memories. I apologized for being glum. Ever so understanding, she told me to call if I needed a shoulder. I wanted one, but it belonged to Celeste.

RAGING

FRIDAY, MAY 12

The fucking neighbors were at it again, partying until 3:00 a.m. I clutched the cricket bat and pounded the wall. They laughed and taunted me from the other side. I wanted to storm into their apartment and bash their heads like cricket balls, but the thought of prison flushed the idea down the drain. I stewed until six in the morning, when the noise finally abated. By then, it was too late for sleep. I arrived at work, exhausted.

Cedric sat with his left hand wrapped in a white cast. My Intermittent Explosive Disorder was no longer intermittent. The truck driver's sleeveless shirt and black shorts revealed purple bruises on his muscular arms and legs.

"What happened?"

"You should've seen the other bloke," he grumbled. Today his bright green shirt pronounced, *Your Best Friend Is A Keg.*

"You were supposed to manage your anger."

"Don't blame me. It was the fuckin' bloke on the job. I was mindin' me own business when he threw a beer keg at me. I had to throw it back."

"Empty or full?"

"Empty. I'm not daft."

Could have fooled me.

"The bugger's always on me case. Cause he's bigger than me. Kept goin' about me wife. Said she was humpin' someone else. If someone said that about your missus, would you take it?"

"Who threw the keg first?" I asked, waving off his question.

"He shoved. I pushed back. One keg was thrown, then another. I went after him and punched him clean in the face. The bastard called me missus a whore, then pushed a keg on me leg, the rotten sod. I threw a left. The fuckin' coward ducked, and I hit the beer keg behind him. Broke me hand instead of his jaw."

"And your job?"

"No worries. They'll pay me wages until the union sorts it out. Me boss tole me to find another job once me hand gets fixed. I'm not sure I wanna go."

"What about our last session? You were supposed to imagine a dial moving from green to yellow to orange and finally to the danger zone, red. I told you to practice cooling down techniques when you got angry and get back to green. Did you forget?"

"When he first mouthed off, he was yellow. Then he started talkin' rubbish about me wife. I forgot orange and saw red. I wasn't gonna take his guff."

I pointed at his massive left paw surrounded by plaster. "That's a wake-up call, Cedric. If you don't manage your anger, it'll lead to rage. Rage can lead to prison. Do you want to go to jail?"

He shook his head as if clearing away blowflies. "That won't happen."

"It will if you keep getting into fights. Were you drinking?"

He scratched his bulbous nose. "I had some grog with me sandwich at lunch. Nuthin' wrong with that."

"Alcohol plays a big part in your life. Every time you've been here, you've worn a different shirt, each promoting drinking."

He chuckled. "Me mate gives them to me for free at the other job."

"What other job?"

"Part time on the weekends. I help me mate with his pub tours. Holds them in the Rocks. Bet you didn't know the oldest pubs are there."

"The Rocks was, after all, the site of the first settlement," I said smugly.

Cedric swelled his barrel chest. "Yeah, well, we give the tourists a bit of history. Make 'em proud of Australia. About the convicts and soldiers arriving with a mighty thirst. Pulling together to build the pubs."

His revisionist history was getting us nowhere. "The First Fleet arrived in 1788, and if there was any pulling together, it occurred at gunpoint and not to build taverns. So let's get back—"

"If you're so smart," snapped Cedric. "Why did the pubs have oval counters and brass rails?"

"Is this really important?"

"Too right. Tourists want to know." He proudly pointed to his shirt. "They look to me and me mate to set 'em straight. They want to know that an oval counter allows more blokes to be served. And the brass rail was built to get around a law that said no more drinks to anyone not standin'. So the blokes undid their belts and fastened them to the rail. Clever way to stay on their feet."

"Well, let's fasten our belts and focus—"

"They fixed ceramic tiles to the outside walls," he said, as if giving the tour. "That's 'cause it was easier to wash the piss and puke after the stonkered buggers relieved themselves."

"Stop! Let's get back to anger. Alcohol lowers self- control."

"Don't you like a pint or two?"

"Yes," I said. "But I don't break my hand in a fist fight."

He rubbed the bruised knuckles. "Yeah, and you probably wouldn't protect your missus."

His verbal blow caught me in the chest. I had, indeed, allowed the Swami to take Celeste without even a punch.

"Do you want my help?" I asked, wishing he would say no.

"Me boss said he'd fire me if I stopped. But once me hand gets better, we can call it a day." He squeezed the cast. "I don't think the classes are helpin.'"

Neither did I, since Cedric's best friend was a keg.

MOTHER'S DAY

SUNDAY, MAY 14

A honeyeater, flapping wings, sucks nectar from a flower. A cage drops and captures the bird. Frantic, it bangs against the metal frame. Crushes its head.

With the strange dream fluttering in my mind, I snuggled against my *pierzyna*. The soft comfort of the eiderdown lulled me back to sleep. Then the phone rang. And rang. The constant ringing forced me out of bed.

"It's Pa!"

My mother's voice jolted me awake. "What's wrong?"

"*Przyjść szybko*. Come quickly," she wailed.

"What happened?"

"Wait, they're here..."

Agonizing minutes ticked by until she returned breathless. "The ambulance is here. We're going to the hospital. *Przyjść szybko*."

I didn't get much else from my distraught mother other than that my father was unconscious. With adrenaline pumping, I threw on some clothes, rushed Nesha through his paces, then dashed several blocks to my car. On my trip to Ashfield, I got pulled over for speeding. Despite my plea for an emergency escort, the heartless copper refused and even threw in a ticket.

When I arrived at the emergency room, I frantically scanned the wounded—those in wheelchairs or with makeshift bandages.

Neither parent was there. My gut wrenched. The nurse behind the counter directed me to another waiting room for families of patients undergoing operations.

I found my mother sitting with Aunt Adele and Uncle Janek. The women were dabbing their eyes with hankies.

"What happened?" I asked, still reeling with shock.

My mother stood and collapsed into my arms. "They're operating."

Between sobs, she told me that my father had complained of a headache when he got out of bed. He had trouble remembering, and stumbled around the kitchen. She initially thought it was the vodka, since she found a half-filled bottle hidden in the bathroom. She was about to leave for nine o'clock Mass when he collapsed on the floor, and his face turned deathly white. Her screams for help brought the next-door neighbor who called the ambulance.

My aunt moved from the couch and hugged me. "Janek and I were leaving for church when your mother phoned."

I kissed my aunt's cheek. "*Dziękuję za nadchodzący*. Thanks for coming."

My mother choked back tears. "I called Stella. She'll be here tonight." She clutched my hand. "What if Pa doesn't make it?"

My aunt patted her shoulder. "Don't talk that way, Marysia. Josef will make it. *Mocny mężczyzna*. Strong man."

I eased my mother's large frame toward the couch where my uncle remained sitting. Lost for words, he somberly offered a handshake.

Anxious to fill in the pieces, I asked my mother, "Did the staff say why they were operating or how long it would take?"

She babbled on about a head injury. I cut her short. "I'll talk with the staff."

A nurse behind the counter, typing on a computer, informed me that my father was having an operation to relieve the pressure in the skull. She couldn't answer my barrage of questions until she heard from the surgeon. She offered the standard hospital jargon,

"Make yourself comfortable; the coffee shop is down corridor B; you'll receive an update as soon as we get one."

Hell, I just wanted to know if he was going to survive. We didn't have much of a relationship, but he was my father.

I returned to the waiting room and repeated the somber update. In the background, a television was broadcasting a special about Mother's Day. Just as well I didn't bring the mushroom-making kit I had bought for my mother. She was lost in the crisis, shaking with tears of self-recrimination. She chastised herself for not forcing my father to see a doctor. His drinking binges had worsened. Last week, he fell hard against the kitchen floor and banged his head. After that, he never seemed his old self. He was forgetful, and nice instead of ornery. A clear sign something was wrong. But he refused to see the doctor.

My mother said that if he died, it would be her fault. Neither my aunt nor I could convince her otherwise. She knew something was wrong and should have acted. I reminded her of the countless times my father rejected help. She would not be consoled. She preferred penance and pulled out her rosary. My aunt followed suit. They both fingered their beads with a Hail Mary. *"Zdrowaś Maryja, łaskiś pełna..."*

⤝⤝⤝⤝

The surgeon, still dressed in blue scrubs, appeared around noon. He approached my mother and announced, "I'm Doctor Ringel. Your husband's been moved to intensive care. He's had a difficult time."

My mother clutched my arm. "Will he live?"

The tall doctor took off his blue cap and nervously fiddled with it. He avoided eye contact while choosing his words carefully. "There was a subdural hematoma in the skull. We had to operate and drain the blood to relieve pressure on the brain."

"*Jezus, Marja,*" cried my mother. She convulsed against my shoulder.

My aunt touched her back and whispered, "Be strong, Marysia. Josef will make it."

I wasn't so sure. I peppered the surgeon. "Any damage to the brain? Will he be normal again?"

Before the surgeon could answer, my mother dissolved into hysterical sobs. The other families in the waiting room looked up with alarm.

To prevent further hysteria, the doctor pulled me aside. He stared at his blue cap. "I'm sure you understand how serious this can be. We had to cut a hole in the skull to relieve the pressure and suction out the clot. Fortunately, the hematoma was between the skull and the membrane protecting the brain. While we exercised extreme caution, we can't yet tell the results."

My body stood frozen in time. "How big was the blood clot?"

"Very large. About the size of a small banana, on the CAT scan."

"Did you get it all out?"

"As much as we could. We had to be careful not to damage the brain."

I pictured my father lying on the operating table and the surgeon peering at a monitor, probing my father's skull.

"How do you avoid damaging the brain when you're sticking a suction tube inside his head?"

He rotated his cap. "We're extremely careful. Your father's lucky to be alive. Has he recently suffered a head injury?"

"My mother said he fell and banged his head on the floor a week ago."

"Was he drinking?"

In a strange sort of way, I felt ashamed, as if his problem was mine. Vodka had affected my father's job and relationships, and, most likely, his liver.

"He's been drinking heavily, practically every day."

The surgeon frowned. "He didn't get help?"

I shook my head. "He believed more in the bottle than in doctors. Rarely saw one, unless he was practically dying." I realized the irony of my statement. "Will there be brain damage?"

For the first time, he looked me squarely in the eyes. "I don't know. But that possibility exists. Your father was unconscious when he arrived. If he moves out of the danger zone, he may be able to regain many of his faculties. Again, which ones, we won't know for a while. You'll have to prepare your mother."

His words acted like a tsunami crashing against my psyche. "Does that mean he'll be disabled—not walk or talk?"

"Calling Doctor Ringel," blared the intercom.

The surgeon glanced toward a phone at the far end of the room. "I have to answer that," he said. "Right now, I don't know the outcome. Your father's in critical condition. We'll do everything we can to insure he's stable. I don't want to complicate his situation with a seizure as he withdraws from alcohol, so I'll give him something to minimize the withdrawal. We'll monitor him closely in the recovery room."

"Will he be disabled?"

"Doctor Ringel, phone call," boomed the loud voice.

He moved toward the phone. "You should be able to spend a few minutes with your father later today. In the meantime, make yourself comfortable. There's a coffee shop down corridor B. I'll give you an update as soon as I get one."

I watched, as if in slow motion, the surgeon answer the phone, then disappear down a hallway. The trance was broken by my uncle's hand. He gently shook my shoulder.

"Your mother wants you."

I followed him back to the couch where my aunt and mother dutifully prayed their rosaries.

At 2:30 p.m., Dr. Ringel, now dressed in a white coat and accompanied by a young intern, told us we could see my father. However, since he was in critical condition, we had to limit visitors. My aunt and uncle remained in the waiting area while my mother and I followed the doctor into a sterile intensive-care room with a bed in the middle, surrounded by equipment. We warily walked toward my father.

A heavily bandaged head rested on a pillow. Outside the turban of bandages sat a plastic bottle filled with pink fluid draining from his head. An oxygen mask covered my father's nose and mouth. Drips, tubes, and wires dangled from his body while machines beeped and clicked to monitor heart rate and breathing. Undoubtedly, there was a catheter lodged in his penis. My father would be mortified. Thank God he was unconscious.

Rarely had I witnessed him in such a vulnerable state. Sure, I had seen him drunk, staggering around the house, but he always held his swagger. In the hospital bed he was helpless, a soldier fallen in life's battle. Having abused alcohol and those he loved, he was now caged in a limp body. I wanted to touch him, to know he was alive.

My mother had the same idea. She slowly reached out. Before she could touch his face, the doctor grabbed her arm. "Don't want to risk infection."

My mother closed her eyes and wobbled. I caught her before she collapsed. The intern came to my aid. We eased her out of the room.

My uncle and aunt invited us to their house for a meal. My mother refused, choosing to stand vigil near my father. After asking my uncle to pick up Stella from the airport, she returned with me to the intensive-care room. We made ourselves as comfortable as possible, not an easy task with machines bleeping and red, yellow, and white lines undulating on the monitor.

Reinforcements would arrive when Stella flew in from Melbourne. When facing the shadow of death, family can provide consoling support or terrible heartache. No doubt, I'd experience both, but, at the moment, I welcomed support.

DAY TWO IN HOSPITAL

MONDAY, MAY 15

Pa's lifeless body. Wrapped in rubber tubing like a cocoon. Suspended from a ceiling by a cord. His white eyes open, unseeing. The cord stretches, breaks. He crashes onto the bed. Blood and limbs splatter. Tubes wriggle like snakes, reaching out for me. Seeking another victim.

I woke up from the nightmare and nervously checked around the bed for anything that moved. Nesha was sound asleep on the floor of my old room. Then I remembered last night. Shortly after Stella appeared, I drove home to pack a bag and collect Nesha and my laptop. I returned to my parents' home to catch a few hours' sleep. Stella stayed with my mother. They both held vigil at the hospital.

I called the office and told Sam about my father, then asked that Frieda cancel my appointments. Before rushing back to the hospital, I took Nesha out for a brief walk, then locked him in the house. He wailed incessantly as I drove away.

I found my father alone in the room. A note from Stella told me she had taken my mother to the coffee shop for breakfast. Before joining them, I watched the unconscious man breathe through the tube in his nose. He mustn't die, not like this. I remembered my spooky dream and wondered how my father would survive as an invalid. I said a silent prayer, but doubted anyone was listening.

In the coffee shop, I kissed my exhausted mother on the cheek. "How are you?"

"She's not eating," answered Stella. She pushed a plate toward my mother. "One piece of toast."

"What will I do if he dies?"

My sister and I glanced at each other, thinking the same thing. If my father died, we'd have to face my mother and her grief. If he became disabled, we'd have to deal with her and my father's rage about losing his functions. Only if he fully recovered would we be off the hook.

As usual, Stella took charge. "I took off from work. A substitute teacher's filling in for a week, but Danka and Krystyna need me back home." She handed out my instructions. "When I'm in Melbourne, stay with Ma and help her out."

"Hold on," I said. "We're moving too fast." I planned to escape from Manly and my crazy neighbors, but returning home wasn't what I had in mind. "We should wait and see whether Pa improves."

My sister was adamant. "I don't want Ma left alone. Not at a time like this."

The rubber cords of responsibility slithered around my ankles and wound their way up my legs, threatening my independence. It took a heroic feat to break away from my parents five years ago. I could not rubber band back home. It was hard enough dealing with the weekly barrage of phone calls from the grand inquisitor. I couldn't survive with her and, God forbid, an invalid.

"We can talk about this later," I told her. I wasn't a child anymore. Stella would have to accept that. "Did you see Dr. Ringel?" I asked.

She sipped her juice. "He's coming by later."

"I checked some websites before going to bed. Pa was lucky. A subdural hematoma meant that blood formed between the skull and the brain. It would have been far worse if he'd had a cerebral hemorrhage, which meant the bleeding occurred inside the brain.

However, any blood clot pressing on the brain could lead to a loss of consciousness, memory loss, and confusion."

I didn't share that it could also lead to paralysis, coma, even death. I kept it positive and mentioned that with prompt treatment, recovery was more possible since the clot didn't touch the brain tissue directly.

That calmed my mother, but only slightly. She again blamed herself for not taking my father to the doctor after the fall. Stella rushed in with consoling words. I stayed clear of that futile conversation.

After breakfast, we returned to my father's room and set up camp. My mother withdrew her rosary for the litany of prayers. When the nurses arrived to check the machines and monitor blood pressure, Stella and I pounced on them for any progress. They were as non-committal as Dr. Ringel. No one wanted to say if, or when, my father would recover.

In the afternoon, Stella and I left my mother's prayerful drone and returned to the coffee shop for a private conversation. Over bagels and tea, we discussed the contingency plan.

"If Pa recovers, you should move back and take care of them."

I gagged on my bagel. "No way. Ma treats me like a kid; Pa treats me like a joke."

"If I was living here," she chastised, "I'd gladly help out. But I have two daughters, a class to run, and a husband who received a promotion."

"It's easy for you to give orders. You live in another city."

"I know it's hard," she said, softening her tone. "I'll be here this week and will come back other weekends. But we can't leave her alone."

I pulled out my handkerchief and wiped a smudge off my lenses. I didn't want to discuss the possibility that my mother could sink into another black hole of depression. I replaced my glasses and stared at my sister. Although she was blood, I didn't much care for the favored one. When my mother became depressed, Stella took over as the woman in charge. My mother craved my emotional support, my father needed a whipping boy, and Stella wanted a slave. Even after I completed my doctorate, she received the praise for becoming a teacher, marrying a Pole, and starting a family.

"I'm not moving back," I said defiantly. "I'll organize the levels of care. But I won't give up my independence."

She slammed her half-eaten bagel on the table. "You're plain selfish. After all they've done for you. Alright, I'll visit every weekend."

Guilt gripped my chest like a tight rubber band. "I never said I wasn't going to help. I just can't live with them. There's always Janek and Adele."

She pushed her bagel at me. "What if Pa doesn't recover? Ma would never take him off life support. I wouldn't either." She rose and slammed the chair against the table. "I doubt you'd even care."

Before I could reply, she stormed out. I waited several minutes to calm down. I returned to my father's room where my mother vigilantly fingered the rosary. Stella scowled whenever our eyes met. So much for families pulling together.

Fortunately, I brought my laptop to type journal entries and play games. However, the day dragged on as Stella continued the silent treatment, my mother prayed to Our Lady, and my father remained unconscious.

The surgeon and his stooge appeared briefly and broke the monotony. As Dr. Ringel checked my father, I asked about alcohol withdrawal.

"I have him on Librium."

"That's a benzodiazepine."

He nodded. "The central nervous system will recognize it as a form of alcohol. Prevents the body from withdrawal. Once he progresses, I'll wean him off the medication."

"Will he recover?" I nervously asked.

The surgeon shifted uneasily and spoke with a detached, professional voice. "We're doing the best we can. In the meantime, make yourself comfortable."

He was about to step out the door when he caught my aunt entering with a shopping bag. He admonished her for entering. Visitors were limited to three at a time. And no eating in the intensive care room. I volunteered to keep watch and suggested that my aunt take my sister and mother out for something to eat. Adele grabbed my mother's arm and practically dragged her to the coffee shop.

Strangely, I welcomed the time alone with my father. He was never one for father/son bonding unless he needed help in the garage. He kept his holy temple immaculate. The floor was spotless, and his tools were reverently positioned on shelves in neat, tidy rows. Even his altar, the workbench, remained uncluttered. Whenever I became his altar boy, I could never get it right. He'd sneer, "You're too slow," or "Wrong tool, dummy." Eventually, he'd vanquish me. "Go help your mother."

I once snuck into the garage to borrow a hammer. When he found out, I got a beating. Taking tools without permission was a sacrilege. I hated the place for what it meant. He repeatedly told me, real men use their hands. Since I was never good at fixing things, I was not "real men" material.

I gazed at my injured father, his eyes shut, his breathing shallow. Our squandered relationship was, in many ways, like the man lying in bed—unconscious. He offered little praise but plenty of criticism. As a boy, I retreated into a world of imagination, picturing myself a super hero, fighting an alien invading Earth. I discovered later, my father was the alien. He now slept before me, a mere mortal, and I had no power to heal. I reached for his shoulder and touched him lightly. Eyelids slowly flickered.

"Pa? Can you hear me? Can you see me?"

Not a sound. But he squinted into the light.

My excited voice rose. "Talk to me."

Again, no response, but there were signs of life. We might yet have a second chance. I rang for the nurse. She rushed into the room and checked his condition. She called the doctor. When he arrived, he examined the patient. Upon hearing the news that my father was, indeed, regaining consciousness, I bolted for the door.

The three women were sitting in the coffee shop around a table piled with my aunt's potato salad, coleslaw, and sandwiches. My mother hadn't eaten.

"Come quick," I shouted. "He opened his eyes."

They stared in disbelief, then, as the words registered, leapt to their feet.

My mother clasped her hands together and praised, "Our Lady."

My aunt packed up the food while the rest of us hurried to the room where a nurse was busy monitoring the vitals.

"Józef, you gave us a bad scare," spoke my mother, as if he had woken up from a bad dream.

"He can't talk," said the nurse. She scribbled on the chart. "We hope he'll recover more functions. If you notice any change, call us." She placed the chart in the rack over the bed and left.

My excited mother touched his arm. "I need you home. Get better. We can visit your sister in Melbourne, and Stella and her family. But no more vodka."

I smiled at Stella. She placed her arm around me. "Sorry about earlier."

"Me too."

And to think, all it took was a flicker of an eyelid. The ice thawed between me and my sister. We chatted to each other and the patient, though he couldn't speak. There was some recognition we were there, but he was clearly drugged from all the medication.

My aunt snuck in and handed my mother a small bottle. She opened it and anointed my father's bandaged forehead. Holy water was her magic elixir to speed his recovery.

Later that evening, I turned on my mobile and was shocked to receive five messages. In the past, most calls were from my mother or Celeste. Today, it was the family that cared. The shower of support from Alana, Rosie, Sam, and Thomas made me realize how much I cherished their friendship. At the same time, I recognized my self-absorption. I hadn't called Thomas as promised, and I had spoiled a meal with Alana. My father's near-death experience provided yet another wake-up call. I promised, hereafter, to take better care of my friends.

The fifth message was a long one from Frieda. She had canceled today's appointments and wanted to know about the rest of the week. She also mentioned that Bonnie had phoned several times and insisted on speaking to me. She was quite agitated and refused Frieda's suggestion to talk with Sam. I was sure Bonnie would take it personally that I had my own crisis.

I returned the calls and apologized to Thomas. He was a trouper. "No worries, mate," he told me. "You had more pressing matters."

No more pressing than AIDS.

I stayed at the hospital for night duty. Stella and I tried to convince my mother to return home and sleep in her own bed. She held up her rosary and was resolute. "These beads keep Pa company."

Stella drove my car back to the house and promised to look after Nesha. He hated being away from home without me and would surely have a panic attack. Hopefully, he'd stop howling and settle down. At least he had a soft carpet. I had to endure a long night in a stiff chair.

A THOUSAND QUESTIONS

TUESDAY, MAY 16

At one in the morning, I shifted my creaking bones out of a pretzel position. The bloody chair offered no comfort for my sore back and stiff neck. I imagined Stella sleeping soundly in a soft bed and prayed for her early arrival. I wanted to pass the baton and head to the house for a shower and much-needed change of clothes.

Both my parents were sound asleep. My mother's rosary dangled precariously from her fingers as she sprawled out in a chair near his bed. She remained vigilant even while asleep. A nurse crept into the room and monitored the machines, changed the IV drip, and took blood pressure and temperature. After she left, I stretched my body and experimented with numerous contortions before curling up in a fetal position.

When Stella arrived, she was in a foul mood. "Your dog howled all night," she growled. "You said he was trained."

"He's trained to be treated nicely," I grumbled.

I left sour puss with my mother, who was busy working the beads, and drove to the house. Nesha lunged at me as soon as I opened the door, but, in his excitement, released his bladder. I cursed Stella for not taking him for a longer walk. Knowing my mother's sensitive sniffer would detect an accident, I vigorously scrubbed the carpet to remove the odor.

Before leaving, I calmed Nesha. "Be a good boy," I said, ruffling his fur. "I'll be back soon. No more messes."

At the hospital, we fell into a routine. Stella and I conferred regularly with the staff, my mother prayed for divine intervention, and my aunt ferried freshly cooked meals to keep our bodies well-nourished.

During that late afternoon, the prayers were answered.

"Józef," cried my jubilant mother, standing next to his bed.

My father's head moved; his eyes blinked. His lips quivered, and he spoke with a faint gurgle. "E-E-E."

He was trying to communicate! His eyes darted from my mother, to Stella, then to me.

"E-E-E," he gurgled again.

I pressed the button to alert staff. A nurse appeared and verified that my father was trying to talk, as if we didn't know that. She encouraged him to speak. Clearly, he was trying to say something but couldn't find the words. The best he could do was babble, "E-E-E-YU."

He slowly lifted his swollen right hand and pointed in the air.

"Does it have to do with the hospital?" I asked.

He shook his head, then nodded.

"Is it in the room?" asked my mother.

Again, he nodded, then frowned.

"Is that a yes or a no?" asked my sister.

He shook his head.

I pulled out a sheet of paper from my briefcase and wrote YES on one side and NO on the other. I showed it to him. "Point to the answer. Do you want something?"

He pointed to YES.

"The doctor?" asked my mother.

He tapped NO.

Thus began our version of a thousand questions. Was he in pain and needed medication? Was he hungry? Did he need the nurse or have to go to the toilet? After posing countless scenarios, it was clear he wanted none of the above. We were stumped.

I grabbed another sheet of paper and scribbled the letters of the alphabet. I instructed my father to point to letters and spell a word. He slowly placed a finger on the letter W.

Excited, I asked, "Does it start with a W?"

Flustered, he nodded. "E-E-E-YU."

The three of us huddled around his bed and peppered him with questions, as if we were about to uncover a great secret. Could he perhaps be telling us he missed us?

The answer finally came as he painstakingly pointed out the letters—W-A-L-L-E-T.

"Is that what you want?" I asked incredulously. "Your wallet?"

His eyes beamed recognition. He pointed YES. The three of us cheered as if we had just won Olympic gold. Mind you, it took us nearly two hours. After more letter pointing and pantomimes, we discovered that he wanted to make sure his wallet wasn't stolen.

I spent the rest of the day acting like Agatha Christie's Hercule Poirot, deciphering cryptic messages. My father sought to know where he was and how long he had been in the hospital. Though I couldn't understand his gibberish, I was grateful communication had been established.

"I'm glad you're with us," I told him.

He smiled as if to reassure me he wasn't ready to die. I thought of another question that remained unanswered. Would he return fully able or partially disabled?

A DAY OF VISITORS

WEDNESDAY, MAY 17

Though it was the fourth day at the hospital, it seemed more like the fourth week. Time elongated; minutes turned into hours. Each tiny improvement seemed like a monumental breakthrough. My father was eating, albeit with help from my mother because of his swollen right hand. He was gaining control over his body, but his speech remained unrecognizable. I did hear him utter, "N-I-E," when my mother proclaimed the power of prayer and anointed him with holy water.

Later in the day, the chaplain dropped by and listened to my mother's request for a Mass to insure my father's recovery. The priest solemnly assured her that all was in God's hands. My mother raised her beads. "Our Lady helps."

Ever the skeptic, I walked away from the spiritual support group. Why did God get the credit when life improved, yet received no blame for disasters? And if my mother's prayers were so effective, why didn't they stop my father from drinking?

After lunch, Doctor Ringel arrived with a coterie of assistants who carried a tray of bandages, ointment, and medical instruments. Stella ushered my mother out of the room to avoid hysterics while I remained at his bedside.

Not one to trust doctors, my father's eyes flashed with terror when the surgeon removed the gauze and tape. The right side of his head was encircled in tubing that drained into a plastic bottle.

Near the drainage hole in the skull was a three-inch cut. It had been stitched together after the doctor had surgically replaced the jig-sawed piece of cranium that was removed to drain the blood and repair the damage. The doctor explained that the flap of skin was stitched firmly in place to keep the skull intact. The small drainage hole would remain unprotected by bone under the skin. Therefore, it was imperative that the side of the head never be injured. He also said the brain had shifted because of the pressure of the hematoma, but he was pleased with the recent CAT scan. It showed that the swelling had decreased.

The doctor cleaned the wound. "No sign of infection," he told the intern.

He removed the tubing and stitched the skin over the drainage hole, then left it to the assistant to apply fresh bandages.

"What's the next stage?" I asked.

He took off the rubber gloves and handed them to a nurse. "The symptoms of aphasia should abate. A speech therapist will come by later and help your father communicate. Physiotherapy and speech therapy should help him regain more functions."

"How long will he be here?"

Dr. Ringel moved toward the door. "Another week and a half, depending on his progress. Tomorrow we'll move him out of intensive care. He might need a rehab center. Let's wait and see how he does over the next week or so. He'll have to give up alcohol. I'm weaning him off the Librium. He's already on a lot of medication."

"Like what?"

The surgeon waved his hand as if shooing a fruit fly. "Not for you to be concerned about—meds to decrease brain swelling, antibiotics, stool softeners, etc. However, once he's drug-free for seven to ten days and without withdrawal symptoms, we'll start Naltrexone to curb his desire for alcohol. In the meantime, he could experience intense cravings."

Of the two recoveries, abstinence would be the most challenging. My father had a chance to dry out in the hospital and, hopefully, maintain sobriety once he returned home.

As soon as the doctor left, my mother and sister rushed back for an update. I reinforced the message: no more drinking.

My mother kissed her hands towards heaven. "No more," she rejoiced. She grabbed the bottle of holy water and spritzed my father. When she said, "You're in good hands," she wasn't referring to the doctor.

My aunt dropped by with another shopping bag filled with provisions. Food, for the Poles, showed concern for the heart and, just as important, the stomach. We ate rye bread and homemade oxtail soup in the coffee shop while my aunt prattled about my uncle being swamped at work. Maybe now he'd appreciate my father's contribution at the garage and make him a partner.

Our next visitor was a florist bearing a plant and a large basket of fruit. We showed my father the card from his sister, Elżbieta. Her recent knee replacement prevented her from traveling, but she phoned daily. I called her and thanked her for the gift, then placed the phone to my father's ear. Although he said nothing, it was clear my aunt's words struck a chord. He rubbed his misting eyes.

↞↞

The last visitor of the day was a speech therapist, Duong Nguyen, a small, wiry Vietnamese with sparkling eyes and an impish smile. Wearing a white hospital jacket, he carried a notebook and folder and approached my father. He removed a sheet with words and pointed to the page. "Can you read?"

My father scowled and shook his head.

Duong pointed at the word DOG. "Read, please."

Again my father shook his head.

The speech therapist smiled politely and slowly enunciated, "CAN...YOU...SPEAK?"

My father opened his mouth and gurgled, "D-D-A."

"Very good," he praised. "Say, HEL-LO," he encouraged in a sing-song rhythm. "Repeat, please."

My father struggled with the sound, "E-H-H...HO."

"Very, very good," he commended with a broad grin.

I thought of the irony as Duong lavished encouragement every time his flustered patient sounded a word. My father had bitterly complained about Asians not speaking English. Now he had to swallow his prejudice.

I spoke to Duong. "On behalf of my father, we're grateful for your help."

The Vietnamese beamed a toothy smile and bowed. "Very well we work together."

He told us he'd return daily for speech lessons. My father grunted and closed his eyes. He had seen enough visitors for one day.

BACK TO WORK

My father steadily improved, and life assumed a degree of normalcy, if you could call it that. My mother, albeit reluctantly, agreed to bring her rosary home while she slept at night in her own bed. Nesha and I also returned to our own place. The broken sleep and emotional turmoil had taken its toll. I welcomed the sound of the crashing surf soothing my soul.

When I arrived at work, Sam, Alana, and Rosie overwhelmed me with hugs. Their genuine concern touched me deeply. Alana had placed a large bag of mints and a note on my desk. Ever so sweet, she wrote:

This Saturday the Olympic torch starts the journey home to Australia. When you're feeling down, The Family That Cares will brighten your day like a torch.

Geraldine offered awkward condolences on her way to her office for an emergency call. And true to form, Frieda shoved a pile of files into my arms, accompanied with a long list of scheduled appointments, most of them back to back without even a pee break.

First on the list was Bonnie. She showed up in a nasty mood.

"I wasn't gonna come," she pouted. "Ya didn't return my calls."

"I'm really sorry, but there was a family emergency."

"What kinda emergency?" she asked suspiciously. "Ya tryin' ta get rid of me again?"

"My father was hospitalized. I was with the family."

Instead of sympathy, she attacked. "Ya coulda called and tole me."

"Frieda suggested you talk with Sam, our clinical director."

"Didn't wanna talk with no one else," she glowered. "Ya said you'd be there for me."

I took a deep breath. "You're right, Bonnie. I wasn't here for you this week, but the other therapists could've helped."

Like a pouting child, she folded her arms.

"YOU BASTARD. I HATE YOU!"

I jumped. So did Bonnie. A bloody role play! Frieda hadn't conferred with Geraldine.

"YOU WON'T HURT ME EVER AGAIN. DO YOU HEAR?"

We both heard, loud and clear.

"Did you bring your ABBA album?" I asked.

"That wasn't supposed ta happen," she said angrily.

"It wasn't." I wanted to bang on Geraldine's wall and tell her and her client to shut the fuck up. Instead, I gritted my teeth, started the sound machine, and played a CD of ocean waves.

"I can understand you're pissed off with me," I said above the din. "You've lost Perry and Doc and probably thought I was abandoning you. I haven't. My father almost died and is in critical condition. I couldn't be at work and had to count on my colleagues to back me up. You must realize others can help you."

"FUCK YOU!"

I cringed at the voice next door. "I promise, this won't happen again."

"Ya won't cancel no more sessions?" she asked, half pleading, half fuming.

"Let me take care of the noise."

I called the front desk and asked Frieda to patch me through to Geraldine. "I know she's in session," I said. "This is an emergency."

After numerous rings, Geraldine picked up. She was royally pissed off for the interruption. So was I! I asked her to *please* lower the noise. She huffed and she puffed, but she reluctantly agreed not to blow the house down.

I returned to Bonnie. "That should help," I said. "And no, I'm not planning on canceling future sessions. But my father's still in the hospital. Another therapist will step in if I'm called out on an emergency."

Her face softened. "Sorry about your dad, Doctor P. He must be a good man. Mine died an alkie."

I wondered if my father would end up the same.

"What hospital is he at?"

Before I could stop myself, I told her, then quickly added, "I'm sure you'll respect my privacy."

She glared. "I'm not gonna visit him."

"I'm sorry," I said. "It's been a tough week." I picked up her file. "Let's talk about you, shall we? No journal?"

"Forgot it. I'd rather talk than write."

"Journaling clears my mind. It'd do the same for you."

"Who reads yours?"

"No one. I write for myself. Give it a go, Bonnie."

"My spellin's not good."

"Neither is mine. Thank God for Spellcheck."

"Spell what?"

"The computer automatically...never mind. The most important thing is to keep writing, especially when you're upset."

"Will ya read it?"

"Every word," I promised, figuring she'd write no more than a page.

Bonnie resisted many of my recommendations, but she still gripped the frayed rope of connection. My absence had triggered a rockslide. We sorted through the rubble to reach a secure ledge. She remained attached to the therapeutic lifeline and, barring no more crises, would continue her climb up the mountain.

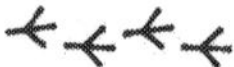

I called Stella for an update. My father was now sitting up in bed and moving his limbs. His speech hadn't returned, but that didn't stop him from signaling my uncle, when he stopped by at lunch, to sneak in a bottle. My mother flew into a rage and told both men that if she caught sight of any alcohol, there would be World War III. Without the use of words, my father could hardly protest.

EXHAUSTED

My father moved out of intensive care into a surgical ward, but not without drama. He initially shared a room with a cricket player recuperating from knee surgery. However, when his mates crowded around the telly to watch a game, my mother stormed the nursing station. The staff quelled her fury by switching rooms. My father's new roommate was an elderly man who, unlike the injured knee patient, turned out *not* to be a pain in the ass, even though he was convalescing from a hemorrhoid operation.

My father's ongoing progress brought its own form of frustration. He became increasingly agitated about staying in the hospital, learning to speak, and being without his friend, the bottle. Even though he loathed his Vietnamese therapist, he was improving. Duong Nguyen said that since the speech center of the brain had been affected, the patient would need plenty of practice. My father spent plenty of time practicing the word, "*Nie.*"

With the hospital visits, family encounters, and a packed schedule of clients, I was exhausted—not the best state to see clients, especially Cedric.

The truck driver's left hand remained in a white cast, but the faint purple bruising on his arms and legs had almost healed. He wore yet another slogan, *Beer Heals All Wounds.*

"The bastard's tryin' to get me fired." He said, then pointed to his cast. "How the fuckin' hell does he think I can work?"

"Have you talked to the union?"

"Are you daft?" he snarled. "Of course I talked to 'em. Their hands are tied 'cause me injury happened over a fight. They're all crooks. The other bloke made a deal with the president. I wasn't gonna let that go, now was I?"

I shook my weary head. "Tell me you didn't have a fight with the union president."

He placed his ham-like hands over his bulging belly and smirked. "Not what you'd call a fight. Just an understanding. I told him I better not lose me job. I had friends at work and we could cause trouble."

"You threatened him?"

He pointed a finger at my chest. "Did I say that?" he asked, accusingly. "No threats. An understanding."

"What happened?"

"Said he didn't want trouble. He'd talk to me boss but tole me to keep seein' you. I need a letter sayin' I passed the anger classes."

I stifled a yawn. "Doesn't seem like you're learning much."

His voice grumbled. "Frankly, mate, you're not that good a teacher."

I should've flunked the student. "Have you been monitoring your anger meter, like we discussed?"

He rubbed his knuckles. "That hasn't worked."

I yawned. "Obviously."

"Am I borin' you?" he asked belligerently. "You've been half asleep since I've been here. No wonder I'm not learnin'."

I valiantly stifled another yawn. "Sorry, Cedric. I've had a family emergency. It has nothing to do with you."

"If you're gonna sleep, I might as well go. Next time take some wake-up pills. I'll see you next week."

When he rose to leave, part of me was grateful to end the class. The other part tried to reason with the recalcitrant student.

"We still have time. Let's review our strategies."

He grabbed the doorknob. "I don't wanna interrupt your sleep."

"I can't write a letter if you don't complete the program."

He paused, then with an ugly grimace, approached me with his good hand balled into a fist. "Are you threatening me?"

I bolted upright from a dose of Cedric's wake-up pills. "No!" I shouted, halting his advance. "I just wanted to have, what did you call it? An understanding."

He rubbed his bulbous nose as if in thought. He then widened his mouth into a grin. "Think you're clever, don't you? Guess it won't hurt none if I finish today's class."

The human barrel keg returned to his chair.

Lucky me.

STELLA'S DEPARTURE

In the black cave once more. A goblet of blood and crushed bones touches my mouth. One sip and my body convulses. Shape shifts into skeleton man. I slink deeper into a cavern. Clinking and Clanking. Through narrow passageway. Into another world—a desert. A pack of dingoes sniffs my bones. They fetch rabbits. Ravenous, I feed. Flesh returns. I shape shift into a dingo. I nuzzle my golden brown coat. Then join others. We eat, mate, and sleep. Nourished, satisfied, I return to the cave. And shift shapes once more. Now a full-bodied man. A skeleton passes me the torch. I kiss his white skull. Friends forever.

Skeletons reappeared in my dreams, some more terrifying than others. I kept the images from clanking inside my mind by staying busy. Not a difficult task, considering the hectic pace from juggling work with visits to the hospital.

My father's room had become a hive of activity. When my mother wasn't praying to the statue of Our Lady brought from home, she hounded the nursing staff. Stella and I concentrated on my father's reading and speaking skills. We encouraged him to sound words aloud and practice word recognition. I bought a children's book in Polish about an elephant eating mushrooms. It seemed easier for him to recall words in his native tongue. He quickly recognized "*grzyby.*" Mushrooms were one of his favorite dishes.

To overcome his frustration about learning to speak and read all over again, Stella and I praised him for mounting the tiniest of hurdles. A major milestone was his first English phrase, "W-want go h-home."

Before returning home, he had to gain better control over his body. He was relieved to have the catheter removed. The first piss without an obstruction was an experience he would never forget. A physiotherapist worked with him to become ambulatory. With his verbal skills slow to return, my father devoted his energy on a quest for mobility. He used the hall as his training ground to prepare his escape from the hospital.

When we weren't walking next him or helping with his speech, Stella and I took turns reading the *Sydney Morning Herald* aloud and quizzing him about the articles. Stella showed him a picture of Olympic Park and read from the paper.

"They're going green at the Olympic site, Pa. The Athletes' Village near Homebush Bay will be the world's largest solar-powered suburb with solar panels fitted to 665 houses. Photovoltaic solar cells are installed on the nineteen light towers along Olympic Boulevard. These 'Towers of Power' will provide twenty percent of the energy for the Olympic buildings. And the SuperDome, Australia's largest indoor sports center, has its entire roof built as a solar collector."

My sister breathed an impressive sigh. "We'll be lighting up the world with state-of-the-art technology. Did you hear that, Pa?"

Not caring much for the greenies, he grunted, "*Nie.*"

She turned the page. "Listen to this. The Olympic Stadium will hold 110,000 people during the Games!"

"Your house is only fifteen minutes away," she said excitedly. "Stan and I could fly in with the girls for the opening ceremony on September 15. You'll be back to normal by then. We could all go."

She turned to me. "Can you buy tickets for the family?"

"I doubt it," I said. "Those tickets have been selling faster than *pierogi* at Klub Polski."

"Pa would love to go."

My father shook his head. "*Nie.*"

Shocked that he actually supported me, I asked him point blank, "Do you want to attend the Olympics?"

His gruff voice was clear. "*Nie.*"

"When you're feeling better, Pa, you'll want to go," added my sister. She pleaded her case to my mother. "You'd attend the Opening Ceremony, wouldn't you?"

My mother clutched her rosary and bobbed her head compliantly.

"It's settled," announced my triumphant sister. "We'll all go."

"Pa said no," I fumed.

"That's because he's feeling bad about being here," she huffed. "If you're not prepared to get tickets, I'll have Stan do it."

"They're projecting 50,000 people moving in and out of Olympic Park Station per hour. Count me out."

She glared at me for pissing on her parade, then returned to the newspaper.

"They're extending the seating at the Aquatic Centre," she told my father. "There are four competition and leisure pools, plus a water slide. You and Ma could join us..."

I left the room and headed down corridor B for another cup of coffee and some fresh air.

⊰⊰⊰⊰

After an early dinner, Stella hugged my parents goodbye. I glanced at the hemorrhoidal patient sleeping in the other bed. My sister could be a royal pain.

"I'll collect the car and meet you at the front door."

"You're spending the night with Ma, aren't you?" she asked curtly.

"Can't. Have to get up early for work."

She enlisted support. "You could use the company, right, Ma?"

"*Tak*. Spend the night, Piotr," pleaded my mother. "I'll wake you early. Make a big breakfast. Like old times."

Rather than get embroiled in another argument, I acquiesced. "Make it a quick breakfast. I have to drop Nesha off before work."

Stella kissed my cheek. "Thanks. I asked Aunty to spend a couple of nights later in the week."

"I'll get the car."

Not before she stopped me with another request. "Make sure you visit Pa after work."

"You don't have to control everything," I griped.

"Don't be snippy. I'll fly back soon with one of the girls."

So she could boss someone else around. I dashed out before receiving further orders. I knew there'd be plenty more on the drive to the airport.

BREAK-IN

MONDAY, MAY 22

My mother served what she called a light breakfast—eggs and sausage, oatmeal and toast, grapefruit and muffins, cold cereal and coffee cake. She wrapped the leftovers and handed me a parcel. I dropped her off at the hospital, then drove like a madman to Manly. The first stop was my apartment.

Nesha lumbered up the stairs and barked fiercely.

"Calm down," I yelled, bringing up the rear.

As soon as I entered the living room, I spotted the balcony. The door had been jarred open. My TV was gone.

I cautiously entered each room. No damage to the furniture or walls, but the DVD player, microwave, stereo, and printer were gone. The desk drawers and cabinets had been searched for cash. The bastards would've left without a penny. Thank God, I had taken my laptop! I shuddered at the thought of someone reading my journal. Stella deserved some blame. If I had returned last night, I could've prevented the robbery.

The police arrived and said it was probably druggies. I told them about the main suspect—Perry. Then again, the cretins next door may have noticed my absence. I asked about fingerprints. The coppers quickly dismissed the idea. It wasn't worth the trouble. Their advice: secure the balcony door.

"If I installed a deadbolt, anyone could smash the glass."

"Righto," nodded the officer.

My naked apartment made me feel exposed, unprotected. The bastards even stole my best CDs and left an unwanted pile behind. *The Swirling Polkas* obviously wouldn't fetch much on the black market. I thought of plastering a notice on my balcony, "Attack dog on premises," then decided otherwise. It would merely act as a neon sign for criminals.

I grabbed my laptop and briefcase and instructed Nesha to bark and bite. Unfortunately, his bark was worse than his bite.

✦✦✦✦

Frieda was in a fury when I arrived late. She angrily thrust a pile of new files at me. "You're on intake. We start at nine, in case you forgot. Bonnie phoned three times, and there's a man in crisis on line one."

"Thanks," I said, and added, "For nothing," under my breath.

The crisis involved a paranoid man who had barricaded himself in his house. He believed drug lords had placed cameras everywhere and were out to get him. I referred him to community mental health and suggested he alert the police. Since he lived in my neighborhood, he had every right to be paranoid.

After dealing with him, I called Bonnie.

She picked up on the first ring. "Doctor P?"

"Yes, it's me."

"It was horrible," came the terrified voice.

"Slow down," I said. "Was Perry there?"

"How did ya know? He came last night wantin' money. I didn't let him in, like ya tole me. He banged on the door. I tole him ta go away or I'd call ya."

Great, I thought. Steer him to me. "Did you call the police?"

"No. But when I wouldn't open the door, he left real mad."

"Why did you tell him you were going to call me?"

"I dunno. You were the first one I thought of."

With clients like her, I didn't need enemies. "He robbed my place."

Silence.

"Bonnie?"

"Did ya see him?"

"I wasn't home. Someone jimmied the balcony door. Must've been Perry."

"It's my fault, Doctor P," she berated herself. "If I hadn't tole him where ya lived."

"There's nothing we can do about it now. If you find out where he is, call me. I'll contact the police. Anyway, I have to go. I'll see you on Wednesday."

"I'm scared, Doctor P. Can I see ya today?"

"I'm booked solid."

"What if Perry comes? Remember what he did ta Doc?"

Conflicted about remaining firm with boundaries, yet compelled to reduce her terror and insure a safety plan, I went with the latter. I squeezed Bonnie in tomorrow. As long as I was treating her, Perry Winkler was sure to be lurking nearby.

⭠⭠⭠⭠

At the end of an exhausting day, I called the hospital for a progress report. According to my mother, the patient was agitated and grumpy. That meant he was getting back to normal.

Alana found me packing up. "Your door's been closed all day," she said.

I told her about the break-in. She was horrified. "Is it safe to go home?"

"Nesha will protect me," I said, unconvincingly. "Besides, there's not much else to take."

"I have a spare couch," she offered. "And your dog's welcome."

Touched by her generosity, I gave her a hug. "Thanks. But I'd feel better keeping watch." I grabbed my laptop. "When my life settles down, let's have a proper dinner. My treat."

Her eyes twinkled. "I'd like that. Don't run yourself down. I don't want you sleeping during the meal."

I closed my eyes and emitted a loud snore. Alana playfully pinched my arm.

"Ouch!"

"You'll cry even more when I tell you the horrible news. Carmen Fusco was hired to replace Herbert."

"Crikey! The angel lady from the workshop?"

She nodded solemnly. "She's attending Herbert's farewell this Friday."

It hit me like a ton of bat droppings. "How the hell did she get the job?"

"Sam said she knew a Board member. Carmen's law degree, MBA, and psych credits convinced the Board she would turn the agency around."

It was now my turn to be horrified. I plopped in my chair. "Celeste told me her family group, 'We're Right and Proud of it,' disbanded after the workshop. No one could stand Carmen. She's a self-righteous control freak. We're screwed."

"We have numbers on our side," consoled Alana.

"Numbers don't count with a narcissistic personality disorder."

The potential disaster weighed heavily as I dragged myself home to feed and walk Nesha. The apartment was safe. After checking outside for Perry, I left for the hospital, making sure I wasn't followed. It was better to be safely paranoid than sorry.

BONNIE'S TENTH SESSION

She stared at her weather-beaten gym shoes. "Did Perry take much?"

"Just the good stuff."

"It's my fault."

"Don't blame yourself," I said, though in fact, I did blame her. "Do you know where he's at?"

Bonnie shook her head wearily. "He'll climb into a hole like a wombat till he needs money. I feel real bad, Doctor P. You probably don't wanna see me."

It was hard to remain angry at the brittle woman.

"Let's put it behind us," I said in a forgiving tone. "But if Perry ever returns, call the police. Promise?"

She lifted her head. "Promise."

"So let's get to work. I'm glad you brought the journal. Can I have a look?"

She handed me the spiral notebook. "Been writin' more, like ya asked."

I flipped it open. My jaw dropped.

"What's this?" I removed an orange flyer.

"A customer at the restaurant gave it ta me. Said I should go."

I stared at the piece of paper. Bold words announced: *OPEN YOUR HEART TO LOVE. A lecture by Babaji Ziprunanda.*

The contact person was Bhakta! Was she opening more than her heart to the swami?

"Doctor P?" fretted Bonnie. She reached for the flyer. "What's wrong?"

She scrutinized the orange page to find the cause of my disturbance. Finding none, she told me, "The customer at the restaurant was real nice. Said this man changed her life, and he'd change mine, too."

I'm sure he would. In a short time, Bonnie would be wearing saffron robes, chanting merrily at the ashram, and changing her name to Bookta.

"Be careful," I warned. "It's a come-on to indoctrinate people."

"You tole me ta make friends. The lady left me a nice tip and was real friendly."

"As was the spider to the fly. I know someone who joined their ashram and gave up everything—home, business, *and* relationship."

"I take it ya won't be going."

"Absolutely not." Ziprunanda had ripped my love from my heart.

Bonnie folded the flyer and shoved it in her pocket. "I was hopin' you'd go with me."

"Don't you remember our conversation about boundaries?"

She gazed back at her shoes. "It's only a talk."

I was about to launch into a stern lecture about boundaries, but stopped myself short. Instead, I proposed the women's group. "You will make new friends there."

"Maybe later." She pointed to the notebook. "Do ya wanna read my diary?"

I squinted at her scribbling and brooded about the flyer. Open your heart to love? My chest still throbbed from the pain of lost love.

LAZARUS

WEDNESDAY, MAY 24

I stepped into a puddle as I held the umbrella over my mother. We scurried into the car, and I pulled out of the driveway with the wipers swinging like an out of control pendulum. I didn't want my mother driving in the torrential rain this morning. My aunt would chauffeur her back in the evening.

We found my father practicing his steps in the hallway. His mobility had improved far more than his speech, though he was now using short sentences.

I kissed his forehead. "Good work, Pa."

He smiled. Despite being cantankerous about the hospital confinement and alcohol abstinence, he occasionally dropped his tough exterior. At first, I put it down to sedation from pain medication, but then realized something more was happening.

"*Jak się pan ma*? How are you?" I asked.

He spoke haltingly. "*Dobrze*. W-want go home."

"You'll stay here until the doctors release you," chastised my mother. "One or two more weeks."

He grimaced. "*Nie.*"

"You'll be out of here in no time," I said. "You're getting the stitches out today."

The right side of his head was still bandaged, but he was convalescing well. He was eating full meals, and the color had returned to his face. His mustache had been neatly trimmed by my mother, who also combed the tufts of white hair peeking from the bandage.

I walked him back to the room, chatting about the rain and the traffic congestion on the Harbour Bridge. When I asked about his speech therapy, he grumbled. Apparently, Duong Nguyen made him read children's books in English. I considered it a bloody miracle that an Asian had succeeded in helping my racist father pass the first grade reading test.

"*Dzień dobry*," called my aunt who sauntered into the room. She showered us with kisses.

"And good morning to you," I said. "What? No food?"

She blushed. "The coffee shop has a special on Wednesdays. Fresh scones with strawberry jam and cream. Come, I'll buy."

"We're supposed to wait for the doctor," I said. "Take Ma. I'll stay."

My aunt tugged at my mother. "Come, Marysia."

I nudged the women out the door. Like two excited schoolgirls, they hurried down the hall.

Alone with my father, I flicked on the telly and channel surfed. "Want to watch anything?"

"*Nie.*"

I turned it off. "Shall we practice your reading?"

He frowned and shook his head. "*Nie.*" He paced the room and stopped occasionally to stretch his legs.

He was a doer, not a talker. When alone with him, I never had long conversations. His dominating and abusive manner taught me to reveal little, lest I get belittled. I was so used to his vodka-fueled outbursts that I half-expected a verbal attack any moment. The alcohol-free environment of the hospital brought some relief from the haunting fears.

"Have you talked with Stella?" I asked, breaking the silence.

He nodded. "L-last night."

"Want anything?"

"*Nie.*"

I checked the clock. "Today's my late night at work. I have to leave before noon."

He stopped pacing and stared at me, funny like. He moved a chair closer and sat next to me.

"You g-good boy," came his raspy voice.

I gazed into his blue eyes. "You alright?"

"I almost d-die." He grasped my wrist and stumbled over his words. "W-was mean. W-wanted you strong. I wrong. You g-good boy."

His eyes misted. "I change. You s-see."

I sat mesmerized by the lone tear dribbling down his cheek. This wasn't the face of a father who had inflicted many wounds, the one who taught me to erect a sandstone mountain for protection.

Emotions flooded my psyche. Why did he have to wait until I was thirty-five to tell me I was good? I would have clung to those words as a child. I desperately wanted him to be proud of me, to know that he loved me—hell, that he even liked me. Instead, I endured alcoholic binges and constant ridicule. And created a well-defended mountain he could never scale.

My mind struggled to keep him out. He was recovering from a near-death experience and wanted to make peace, in case he died. Soon he would return to his old ways, accompanied by his friend, the bottle, not giving a damn about me or the family. I didn't trust his epiphany. It was too late for redemption.

I cursed the tears. I didn't want him to die, yet I didn't want hope to be born again. The countless, stinging rebukes had stripped flesh from my bones. He didn't raise a good boy. He crushed one.

I had learned to stuff my feelings and hide in my imaginary mountain, ready to retreat in the face of danger. If it wasn't his drinking or abuse, it was my mother's emotional tirades. The only safe place was a secret cave where I felt protected from intruders.

Safe, yet unseen. My haven shielded me, but also prevented others from knowing me. I longed for deep friendships, yet was terrified of getting hurt.

"I s-sorry," said my father, choking on tears.

His words blasted a hole in the sandstone, sending tremors through my psyche. Years of pain begged for release. I valiantly held back the deluge, but a small trickle dribbled down my cheek. I joined my father in a baptism of water.

That's when my mother and aunt walked in, chattering and laughing. My father and I froze as if caught in the act of something shameful. We shut down the aqueducts and immediately moved from our chairs. Wanting no witnesses, we wiped our eyes to clear the evidence.

"What?" asked my mother, sensing something was wrong.

I retreated to the sandstone mountain. "Nothing," I said. "Everything's fine."

She seized my father's arm. "Józef, what's wrong? Bad news from the doctor?"

He shook his bandaged head.

"We had a father/son talk," I told her. "Lazarus has risen."

Bewildered, she looked at me, then my father. "What are you saying?"

I reached for my briefcase. "Sometimes it takes a bang to the head." I faced my father. "Right?"

He nodded and smiled.

I left for work, knowing my mother would interrogate him later. I doubted that she'd get much. I expected a call later for details.

✦✦✦✦

Oblivious to the traffic, I swerved through the pelting rain.

Honk! Honk!

I narrowly avoided the beeping truck and clutched the steering wheel to regain control.

The widening crack split me open. Though my newfound friends had accepted me and made me feel that I no longer had to hide, hiding was all too familiar. Abandoning the cave meant exposing hideous emotions. I knew, deep down, it was the only way to stand tall like a man.

A FRANTIC PACE

FRIDAY, JUNE 2

Rusty copper wires in my head. Short circuiting the mental computer. Each eye turns an opposite way. Right leg forward, left leg back. Body twitches. Limbs out of sync. Discordant mental messages. Skull splits open. Spaghetti wires smolder. Defective brain. Needs transplant.

Frightening childhood memories haunted my mind. My internal orphan, blackened with neglect, shame, and self-hatred, peeped out of his hideout. I wanted to reassure him he was safe, but fear of another break-in kept me on guard. Sounds that had never disturbed me before startled me awake. My brain was getting fried. Dreams came and went, as did my ability to enter deep sleep.

I could have benefited from a few days off work, but since I had been at my job less than two months and had used my sick days during the hospital crisis, I had to tough it out. Besides, with Herbert retiring, the agency was heading into a black hole. His farewell luncheon promised a regime change fraught with apprehension.

⤛⤛⤛

The staff room was outfitted with extra tables and plastic tablecloths, not exactly an expensive send-off for an executive director who recently turned sixty-eight, many of those years devoted to the counseling agency. I grabbed a paper plate and snagged chicken wings and pasta. Nearby, Herbert was chatting with his replacement, power-dressed in red slacks and black jacket.

His pudgy hand grabbed my arm. "Peter, my boy. Meet Carmen Fusco."

The forty-year-old lawyer had substituted bold, gold earrings for her heralding angels but kept the same hairstyle—bluntly chiseled with angular edges. The overpowering fragrance of her sweet perfume made me gag.

"Hello, Peter," she said coolly. She extended a rigid hand. "We meet again."

With both my hands occupied, one with a plate, the other with root beer, I cradled the cup next to my chest so I could offer my right hand. "Congratulations."

She shook my hand like a man. The cup slipped. Before I could snatch it, the root beer hurtled to the floor with a loud bang. It splashed in her direction. Horror-struck, I stared at the legs of the new Executive Director, her red pants splattered with root beer. All chatter stopped.

"Oh my God. I'm sorry," I blathered.

Carmen snatched a cloth nearby and angrily dabbed at the stains. I dumped my plate on the table and reached for paper towels.

"I'm so sorry," I reiterated, feverishly mopping the floor.

Everyone in the room gathered round, not so much to help but to gape at the disaster. Herbert was the first to comment.

"I was hoping this wouldn't be a boring farewell," he chuckled. "My dear Carmen, please accept Peter's apologies. I'm sure he didn't do it on purpose."

"Of course I didn't do it on purpose!"

She wiped her pants and glared at the dark brown stains. "The cleaning bill shouldn't be too expensive, Peter."

I nervously laughed, then realized she wasn't joking. "Yeah, sure," I said. "The least I could do is clean your pants."

"Surely you're not suggesting she hand them to you now?" asked Herbert, clearly enjoying the entertainment.

Everyone giggled, except Carmen and me. Sam moved to my rescue. She offered her new boss a dish towel. "One thing's for sure, you've made a splash at the first meeting."

Carmen willfully forced her frown into a smile. "Next time, we'll serve water. But please excuse me while I visit the lady's room."

And off she went.

Herbert slapped my back and chortled, "You'd better be careful with her, my boy, especially with the drinks."

I wiped my brow and whispered to him. "You're leaving me alone with all the women—and Carmen."

When she returned, she took the seat next to Herbert at the head table. She addressed the staff and offered faint praise for her predecessor, who chuckled every time he peered at her stained pants. The Board, no doubt, would hear about his and my performance.

After the speeches and presentation of a farewell plaque, I excused myself to counsel a client.

Battling flashbacks of root beer and Carmen's appalled face at splash-down, I tackled Albert.

"What do you mean, you moved out?"

"Dana filed for divorce. My boss had an extra room."

"Isn't he heavy into porn?"

He nervously fiddled with his candy-striped tie. "I needed a place."

"You'll be like an alcoholic bunking at a brewery."

"Dana made life hell," groused Albert. "She stopped me from seeing little Albie. Said I was a bad influence. So I hired a lawyer on Macquarie Street. Told him to fight back."

"Weren't you supposed to fight *for* her?"

"I'm not begging. If she doesn't want me, there are plenty of women who do."

I suspected the answer, but asked the question anyway. "You're back online, aren't you?"

"What if I am? I'm not with Dana anymore."

"What about the sex addicts' group?

He recoiled as if smelling a rotten egg. "Total waste of time. Three of us showed up. One was heavy into bondage—wanted his nuts squeezed in a clamping device. Sick shit. The other dirty bastard wanted to bang his mother. I left wondering why the fuck I was there."

"Not all groups are like that."

"How do you know? Have you been to one?"

"N-no," I sputtered. "I'm sure there's a better one."

Albert leaned back in his chair. "If you find one, Pete, let me know. Anyway, since I'm not with Dana, that's not a problem. The ladies online don't think so either." He stroked his blond goatee. "I found a real hottie in Perth."

As if on cue, his mobile gyrated to the stripper's theme song. He licked his chops. "Probably her. She likes strutting her stuff on camera. Fantastic tits. Drives me wild. Told her to look me up if she's ever in Sydney."

"Hold on," I said, reining him in. "You met a stranger online and asked her to visit you because she has great tits?"

"You hold on," he retorted. "I may be shallow, but she has personality. We email and call each other. And it's not all about sex," he added quickly. "She's thirty-four and divorced, no kids, and works as a hairdresser. But get this. She has a tattoo of a blue-tongued lizard above her left breast. I told her it was a sign."

"Of what?"

He pointed to the tattoo on his left arm. "Kookaburras love lizards."

If the bird could speak, it would laugh uproariously.

"So you're telling me, it's love at first bite."

He snickered. "Good one, Pete. I'll tell that to Roxy."

I flagged the speeding locomotive. "You're out of control. What about your son?"

His cheerful demeanor soured. "Yeah, well, I don't want to lose him."

"He's six, right?"

"And he needs a father. Dana says I'll corrupt him."

"She won't let you see him?"

He angrily crumpled his tie. "She said her lawyer wants my visits supervised. Can you believe that? Little Albie with a bodyguard? Christ! I'm his father. I deserve joint custody. Dana's a vindictive bitch. She hired another one as her lawyer."

I thought of Carmen and her splattered pants. Without a doubt, lawyers could be merciless.

"Can you talk with Dana?"

He scoffed, "You kidding? She only communicates by email. Then she palms off my requests to her lawyer. Costs me an arm and both legs every time the lawyers talk. Which reminds me, mine may want a report from you."

No wonder he returned for our seventh session.

"What kind of report?"

Albert shifted into the role of salesman, except this time he wasn't selling computers. "You could write that I'm a devoted father and my son needs me. Anything to support my case for joint custody. Should be a piece of cake, Pete."

Frankly, I wasn't sure what I could comfortably. "We can talk about that later. In the meantime, I'd suggest you keep yourself out of trouble."

He loosened his tie. "I need to get in the house to remove stuff from the computer."

"What stuff?"

He rubbed his tattoo, a telltale sign he was up to something. "You know, stuff Dana shouldn't be seeing."

"What's going on?"

"Nothing, Pete."

"You wouldn't hack into her computer?"

He bristled. "It's *our* computer. And I'd only retrieve *my* files."

His files, no doubt, contained incriminating evidence.

HOSPITAL FAREWELL

"Come back," I shouted.

Oppositional when I needed compliance, Nesha chased the gulls as they took flight over the breaking waves. He romped after them into the surf. I shivered on the beach. The Australian winter welcomed the cold currents. After a few bobs in the freezing sea, Nesha bolted back to land. Even the handful of surfies in wetsuits called it quits.

I unfurled the towel and held it in front for protection. He vigorously shook his coat and sprayed water and sand. I stepped backward, then heard and felt the sickening crunch. I raised my left foot off a broken shard of glass embedded in the sand. Drops of blood plopped on the sand. Crikey! Wounded from head to foot. My broken tooth still begged repair. The only consolation was that I hadn't stepped on a druggie's needle submerged in the sand.

Trailing splotches of blood, I hobbled to the outdoor shower tap. I rinsed Nesha and my wound—a one-inch gash on the side of my foot. Although the cut wasn't deep, I could've used a stitch or two. I had the same aversion as my father to the men in white coats, so I returned home to treat the injury.

I bandaged the wound, hoping my last tetanus shot still offered protection. I gingerly stepped into my sandals and stuffed my laptop into the briefcase, along with some extra bandages. I commanded Nesha to stand guard while I checked the balcony for shifty characters—the routine since the break-in. The coast was clear. I stepped out the door, very carefully.

⸗⸗⸗⸗

After three weeks in the hospital, my father was anxious to bolt from prison. He was already dressed and sitting in a wheelchair when I limped into the room. His belongings were packed, as was the statue of Our Lady. My mother was busy making the bed. For her, tidiness was next to godliness.

She looked up. "What's wrong with your foot?"

I waved her off. "A small cut."

She reached for my sandal. "Show me."

I stepped aside. "It's nothing."

"You sure?"

"I'm positive," I lied. "Are you ready?"

When my father stood up, my mother scolded him. "*Usiąć*. Sit. The nurse said you must leave in the wheel chair. Hospital rules."

He grumbled and reluctantly sat down. He took charge of the wheels and guided himself out the door. His prognosis looked good. Both the physical therapy and speech therapy had helped immensely. My father could walk without a cane, speak more fluently, albeit in short sentences, and read at a second grade level. Duong Nguyen recommended more speech therapy, but my father refused. He would not resume English classes with the Vietnamese.

Dr. Ringel said it could take up to a year for a full recovery. The fifth CAT scan showed my father's brain still swollen but without complications. He continued with the medications, but the one he resisted most was Naltrexone, to curb his craving. My mother and I reiterated the doctor's warning against alcohol. As the surgeon said, the small hole in the skull was protected under the scalp, but any damage to the area could be catastrophic.

My mother would exert all her power to prevent another drunken fall. She harbored bags of guilt about my father's injury and was fiercely determined to keep him sober.

When I parked the car in the garage, my mother insisted I watch my father. She had already scoured the area for contraband, but suspected a few hidden bottles somewhere in the garage. My mission: locate and destroy.

On the pretense of keeping him company, I hobbled after him as he inspected his sanctuary. He turned on the garage lights and immediately grabbed a rag. He lovingly dusted the workbench and straightened a wrench on the shelf. When he reached for a heavy box, I grabbed it, despite his objections. He desperately wanted to feel productive and return to work. Sadly, he didn't consider working on his recovery part of his job description.

"Let's go eat," I said. "Ma made borsht."

He lingered for a while, then licked his chops. Beet soup was one of his favorites. Over lunch, he mentioned that Janek needed help at the garage.

"No work until the doctor says it's okay," barked my mother.

I reinforced her message. "You need the doctor's clearance. Uncle would be liable if something happened."

My father grumbled, but avoided an argument. Maybe it was because he was outnumbered, didn't have full speech, or wanted to avoid a battle on his first day home. Whatever the reason, I was grateful for a meal without a squabble.

TORCH TOUCHDOWN

THURSDAY, JUNE 8

Nova Peris-Kneebone, the first Aborigine to win an Olympic medal, carried the torch off the aircraft. It seemed fitting to have her bring the Olympic flame onto Australian soil at Uluru, the monolithic outcropping previously called Ayers Rock. It would've been more significant if the government had formally apologized for stealing their land. The Prime Minister remained steadfast in his refusal to say, "I'm sorry" for the tragedy inflicted on the Aborigines. Ironically, Nova's grandmother was one of the many children stolen from tribes. In the late 1800s, the Aborigines' Protection Board decreed that children of mixed descent had to be removed from their families and sent to missions, believing that "whiter" Aborigines would assimilate better into white culture. Rather than liberating indigenous people, that policy destroyed ancestral roots and inflicted a horrifying sense of hopelessness and despair on the tribal groups. Generations suffered. It's no wonder Aborigines endured the worst poverty in Australia. Their health was similar to those from third world countries.

Nonetheless, keeping in line with the motif for the world to watch, the organizers chose Aboriginal food for the ceremonial meal. Not sure how many politicians actually ate the grilled crocodile. They were more comfortable dishing out the croc.

THE FAMILY THAT CARES
ABOUT THOMAS

SATURDAY, JUNE 10

When Alana opened the door to her one-bedroom apartment, she was crying. She hugged me tightly. "Prepare yourself."

Clutching my bag of bread rolls, I followed her into the living room. Rosie and Sam were solemnly parked on a couch with Thomas between them.

He saluted me with a glass of red. "We were waiting for you, mate."

I cringed at his physical transformation. He had lost considerable weight since I last saw him a month ago, but it was the lesions on his face that made me recoil. Dark red blotches marked his bald head. A crusty brown scab formed on his cheek and lower lip. I felt ashamed at my revulsion.

"Glad your father's better," said Thomas. He struggled to his feet. "I would've visited you in the hospital, mate, but figured, in my condition, it was better to stay away. Am I too scary for a hug?"

Even though the answer was yes, I dropped the rolls on the table and grabbed my gentle friend. This time, he complained when I squeezed.

"Easy, mate."

"Sorry," I said, releasing my hold. "It's, uh, great to see you."

"I look like shit, eh?" He eased himself onto the couch and ran a hand over the lesion on his lip. "Kaposi's sarcoma kicked me in the head."

"What about the medication?"

"I take a delicious drug cocktail," he said cynically. "Nucleoside analogues and protease inhibitors."

"Aren't they helping?"

"For some reason, mate, they're not. My T cells are dropping, and the viral load is increasing. In short, I may not be around for Christmas presents."

Alana, sitting on the carpet, wiped her eyes. She reached for his hand. "You can't leave us."

He stroked her fingers and smiled bravely. "There'll be ample time for grieving. When I talk to those with AIDS, I tell them to live life without fear." He gently patted her hand. "What's for dinner? I bet the rest of you are starving."

Alana stood up and grabbed his hand. "Let's move to the table. I made vegetable soup with eight types of beans."

"By the end of the evening we'll be root-a-tooting," joked Thomas. No one laughed.

"Come on," he said. "Lighten up."

We gathered around the table, and Alana served the soup. Thomas pulled a plastic spoon from his pocket but was quickly reprimanded.

"Put that away," chided Alana. She pushed the silver spoon toward him. "I'm not afraid of you using it."

I thought just the opposite. If he ate at my place, I'd soak his utensils in bleach.

Sam poured the wine. The ex-priest passed around the bread rolls, our version of Holy Communion. He asked us to hold hands and give thanks for our fellowship. He peered intensely at each of us. "You mean the world to me. I love you."

"We love you," the rest of us said. Sam and Alana pulled out hankies; Rosie and I remained stoic.

The mood was melancholic. Gone was the light banter, even from Rosie. Authentic sharing took top priority. I talked about my father's epiphany and my turbulent childhood memories. Sam spoke of her ongoing divorce, feeling both free and alone, yet fearful she might succumb to her husband's desperate plea to reconcile. Alana, with the help of Gretchen, was learning to love her body and expand her senses. Rosie was the only one who provided a dash of frivolity. She described a flourishing, passionate relationship with Brodie that included hot sex. But ultimately, the conversation returned to Thomas.

He talked candidly about the pain of his family's rejection. As staunch Catholics, his parents were devastated when he left the priesthood. When they found out he was gay, they treated him like a leper and, after hearing the news about AIDS, terminated contact. They didn't want any contamination from his sinful blood. His only sibling, an older sister, issued the ultimate rejection—he was no longer her brother.

Without his biological family, Thomas was alone, except for The Family That Cares. He had an assortment of friends and acquaintances, but once he was diagnosed with AIDS, his world changed radically. His recent lover bolted, leaving Thomas to fend for himself.

Sam lovingly stroked his head. "We're here for you."

Alana and I nodded our support as Rosie asked, "Will ye be needin' help?"

The broad man toyed with his spoon in soup that was hardly touched. "I can manage for now. I've arranged for home help if I become incapacitated. I'm hopeful that a different cocktail of medicines will do the trick. I've seen it happen before. I have to be positive. After all, it's only a life-threatening illness."

Sam spoke in a motherly tone. "You're a true inspiration. But you need to eat and get your strength back."

"Don't you like the soup?" frowned Alana.

"When I eat, it goes right through. So don't get offended. Being with the three of you is nourishing enough."

I stared at his haggard jowls and the ugly lesions. His blue eyes still sparkled like polished stones of lapis lazuli.

He dipped his spoon into the bowl. "Eat up," he encouraged. "Alana will be upset if you don't request seconds." After a tiny slurp, he hammed it up. "Absolutely delicious."

I playfully tossed a piece of bread at his chest. He mimicked rage and grabbed a bread roll. He ripped off a piece and bounced it off my arm onto the table. *Smack*! Alana's wild throw hit me in the eye.

"Sorry," she said. "I didn't mean to hit your face."

I brushed the crumbs into my hand, then sprinkled it over her black hair. She screeched and snatched another bread roll. The fight turned ugly. Crusts flew everywhere. Sam and Rosie stayed out until bread pummeled their chests. Both retaliated. No one was left unscathed. With the place littered with crumbs, Alana finally called a truce.

"So much for our Eucharistic feast," laughed Thomas. "Shall we move to the wine?"

"Don't you dare," yelled Alana. She lifted a butter knife. "Anyone who thinks about it, and that includes you, Thomas, will get this."

He lifted his glass. "I'll drink to that."

Alana tossed the knife on the table. "You're hopeless. Look at my place."

We scanned the damage—crumbs littered everywhere. Then we burst into laughter. The fear of death faded as uncontrollable laughter brought us back to life. We giggled so hard our bellies ached. And it all began with a bread roll. Alana told us she wasn't going to bring out Sam's pavlova until we behaved ourselves. Sweeping bread crumbs was one thing, but cleaning up oodles of meringue, whipped cream, and passion fruit was off limits.

We stayed well into the night, a family that refused to say good-bye, especially to Thomas.

MANAGED PATIENT CARE

TUESDAY, JUNE 13

"Yesterday, the torch was carried along the beach at Surfers Paradise."

I stifled a yawn. "Yippee for the Queenslanders."

Alana's update screeched to a halt as soon as we entered the group room. Sam and Rosie were whispering, their bagels left untouched.

"What's going on?" I asked.

Rosie removed her glasses and angrily speared them in the air. "Carmen will be joinin' us."

"During supervision?" asked Alana. "What for?"

Sam wearily shook her head. "We'll find out."

"The Board must be daft," sneered Rosie. "A lawyer runnin' a counseling agency is like havin' a vulture on a life raft."

The bird entered the room with a flourish. "I'm glad everyone's here," she announced.

Geraldine followed close behind, as if she had escorted the queen into the royal chambers. Carmen positioned herself ceremoniously on a chair and placed a bulky folder on her lap. A gold chain dangled around her black turtleneck, but the ornamental angels were missing in action. Not so the trumpets. Shiny gold ones dangled from her earlobes.

Geraldine sat next to the director and offered her the plate of bagels. "Would you care for one?" asked the sycophant. She must've been the mole who snitched to the Board about Herbert.

Carmen beamed at Geraldine and politely refused. "No thank you. Mixing meals and meetings can be dangerous. Right, Peter?"

I feigned an act of contrition. "Sorry about the root beer."

"That reminds me." She removed a receipt from a folder. "Here's the cleaning bill. Cash will do nicely."

Geraldine giggled when I checked the amount. Crikey! Sixty dollars. She must've sent her clothes to Tasmania. I pulled out my wallet and reluctantly handed her two twenties. "I'll pay the rest later."

Without even a thank you, she snatched the money. She then cleared her throat. "I hope everyone enjoyed the day off yesterday. On the Queen's Birthday, I chose to review the statistics. I must say, I was disturbed by the results. You'll be pleased to know that my strategic plan will correct the deficiencies."

"What deficiencies?" bristled Sam. "We pride ourselves on our services. We have an excellent reputation in the community."

Carmen responded with a condescending grin. "I'm sure you do, Samantha. However, the Board asked me to develop a strategic plan to increase productivity. They were clearly impressed by the glowing results at my previous agency."

"We don't need a bleedin'—"

Sam raised her hand at Rosie. She wanted Carmen one-on-one.

"Legal aid is very different from counseling," she argued.

Carmen fussed momentarily with her chestnut hair before carving out her position. "Nevertheless, when I implemented my strategic plan, client numbers and contact hours increased exponentially. I plan to reverse the pathetic numbers and reduce the waiting list."

Sam's spiked gray hair shook with rage. Her face flushed and her voice boomed. "We service a difficult population. They need intensive therapy. We don't use billable hours like lawyers."

"And we don't ruddy well charge their fees," snapped Rosie.

"I'm not expecting you to be lawyers," countered Carmen. "Merely professionals."

"What did you have in mind?" Sam asked tersely.

Carmen reached for a bagel. "I think I'll have one of these after all. Geraldine, can you pass the cream cheese?"

She slowly spread her bagel while enunciating the words, "MPC. Managed Patient Care."

Sam reacted as if hit with a life sentence. "You don't mean that?"

"Heaven forbid," cried Rosie. "The vultures have descended."

Our director poised her bagel for a bite. "Excellent care is managed patient care. By regulating the cost and utilization of services, my strategic plan will increase efficiency and serve more patients. You'll be happy to know, the Board fully endorses MPC."

She smiled then bit the bagel. Smacking her lips, she delivered the next harsh sentence.

"I've read the research on patient outcomes. Most progress occurs within the first twelve interviews. Brief treatment provides a rapid turnover of patients. Our target will be eight to ten sessions per client, with a maximum of twelve. The three-month waiting list will be eliminated, thereby demonstrating the efficacy of MPC."

Sam was incensed. "Those studies about short-term treatment exclude borderlines and other personality disorders, multiple diagnoses, the suicidally depressed, and dual diagnoses with addictions. That's who we see!"

Like an annoyed magistrate dismissing an objection, Carmen swatted the air. "Nevertheless, I'll address those concerns in due time. You are, after all, the service providers."

Service providers? We were no longer therapists? I raised my hand.

"You have a question?"

I imagined Bonnie's reaction to a quota of twelve sessions. "What about trauma victims who need longer treatment?"

Alana and Rosie nodded vigorously while Sam fumed.

Carmen nibbled on her bagel, seemingly lost in thought. She finally replied. "With MPC, patients will be assessed and referred for medication. As they improve, they will either be terminated or referred for group treatment. We'll establish more groups at the agency, which, in turn, will increase our patients' statistics. Of course, if anyone needs longer work, we'll provide them with referrals. There are plenty of twelve-step programs in the community."

Sam rose from the chair. "I object! As clinical director, I'm in charge of the client's welfare. What you're suggesting is that we neglect and abandon clients. It's unethical!"

I half-expected Carmen to bang a gavel and cry, "Overruled!" Instead, she calmly placed her bagel on the table, opened the bulky folder, and removed a bundle of papers.

"You may sit down, Samantha," said Carmen dismissively. "No need for theatrics."

She passed each of us a packet with the cover sheet entitled, to no surprise, "Excellent Care is Managed Patient Care."

"I've put together a Protocol Manual, PM for short, which complies with clinical practice procedures set down by psychologists and social workers."

I flipped through the protocols for short-term treatment, clinical practice, medication management, and individual and group services. There were also new forms for assessments, progress notes, treatment outcomes, and productivity reviews.

Before anyone could respond to the voluminous manual, Carmen's voice echoed in the room. "To insure that your work is effective and efficient, I ordered special software that tracks treatment outcomes. I want MPC to be IMVS—identifiable, measurable, verifiable, and shareable. I can assure you, the new software and forms will make your lives easier."

Sam clutched her packet so tight her knuckles turned white. Her voice shook. "You should have consulted your clinical director and staff."

Carmen fondled her gold chain. "I consulted the Board, Samantha. They hired me, not you. Frankly, you should be grateful I'm upgrading the services."

"I was hired to direct the clinical program. I'm responsible for client services."

Carmen smiled and clutched at the chain. "Why, yes, Samantha. I don't see a problem. The Board gave me a mandate to institute a strategic plan. I've created one. Now I pass it to you. Please ensure that everyone follows the procedures."

Rosie tapped her glasses at the manual. "What's this MM?" she asked. "Says we're gettin' a bleedin' psychiatrist. That'll be as easy as spearin' an eel with a bent spoon."

Geraldine cleared her throat and jutted out her jaw. "MM is for Medication Management. Carmen is hiring a part-time psychiatrist."

I glowered. "How do you know?"

Carmen smiled at the fawning psychologist. "Geraldine approached me last week with the name of a psychiatrist who's willing to work for us. I scheduled a meeting with Dr. Kenneth Kukula later in the week."

Rosie pointed her glasses at Geraldine. "Dr. Kukula?! His clients call him 'no eyes.' The ruddy idiot never looks at clients."

Carmen nodded to Geraldine who raised her thick, black eyebrows. She sniffed into a stuffy nose. "Kenneth is an excellent diagnostician."

"Are you daft?" said Rosie. "A blind turtle makes better eye contact! And where will ye put him?"

"We don't need much space," said Geraldine in her nasal monotone. "Kenneth will dispense medication, not psychotherapy. Carmen will have the storage room converted into an office. Herbert was full of promises and poor follow-through."

"I should have been consulted," seethed Sam.

Alana burst into tears. "I can't work like this. My clients depend on me."

Sam reached for Alana's hand and glared at our director. "If this is your twisted way to get us to resign, you're doing a fabulous job."

Carmen closed the folder. Her lower lip twitched. "I hoped you would be more open, Samantha. Obviously, you're not. Let me make this perfectly clear. If any of you finds the change too stressful, there is…" She paused for emphasis. "…employment elsewhere."

Carmen lowered the gauntlet. Follow her strategic plan or plan a strategic exit. The only one unperturbed was Geraldine, who was firmly encamped with the enemy. But hell, there were four musketeers. I glanced at Alana, Rosie, and our leader. Sam sent the three of us a signal. With a slight shake of her head, she informed us this wasn't the time for battle.

She clenched her teeth. "I have to conduct the supervision group. Is there anything else?"

Carmen widened her mouth, as if tasting victory. Her words dripped with saccharine. "Why yes, Samantha. Thank you. There is one small item."

She passed out a final form. "Contrary to what some of you may think, I'm not heartless. I value your time. Therefore, I created a simple productivity sheet. In the blank spaces, write every activity of the day along with the allotted time. Please complete the list before you leave each day and hand it to Frieda. She'll input the data into the computer. The results will help me determine appropriate workloads for my service providers."

What's next? Uniforms with MPC badges? I was about to ask whether bathroom breaks had to be recorded, but respected Sam's call to retreat.

Carmen picked up her bagel. "I'll finish this in my room." She licked her finger and stood up. "Have a productive session."

A broomstick in the right place would've been too good for her. The narcissistic personality disorder walked briskly out of the room. Needing fuel for grandiosity, she'd use MPC as her signature statement. Services would be nothing more than numbers on the docket in a grand courtroom where she could blow her trumpet to the Board. Clients would get a quick fix with medication and a few sessions, then get dumped back into the community. Carmen Fusco's strategic plan was to build an empire mired in acronyms.

This called for another strategic plan.

COUNTER CONSPIRACY

The four musketeers met for lunch at the local fish and chips place. We huddled around the table for our own version of MPC—Musketeers Pulverizing Carmen.

Sam shared a conversation she had with her friend on the Board. "Carmen has the other board members wrapped around her manipulative finger. They're impressed with her strategic plan, something Herbert lacked."

Rosie lifted her knife. "My great-ancestor was Gillies MacBain. A giant of a man, he was a formidable fighter in the Highland army. At the battle of Culloden in 1746, Gillies dropped fourteen English with his broadsword before he was taken."

She stabbed her fish. "I'll not be goin' down without a fight. Carmen won't be gettin' away with skullduggery."

I choked on my chips. "Easy, Rosie. This isn't the Scottish Highlands."

"Carmen's like the English," she snorted. "She plans to eliminate us. She may have the Board on side, but as my father said, 'The blood of MacBain flows in our veins.'"

"We don't need to wield the sword quite yet," declared Sam. "I'll ask to speak at the next board meeting about an alternative plan. Our voices will be heard."

"No!" cried Alana. "I can't believe it."

We followed her wide-eyed stare out the window. Carmen and Geraldine were approaching the shop. Upon entering, Carmen caught sight of us and froze. She offered a nervous smile. "Staff eating together? A morale booster, I'm sure."

Sam planted a smile. "We needed some fresh air."

"Lunch with the boss?" I asked the turncoat.

Geraldine's jaw went slack. Before she could flap her gums, Carmen intervened.

"Let's not be snippy," she chastised. "Geraldine was kind enough to invite me." She pointed to a table in the corner. "That one's free," she told the brown-noser. "Shall we?"

When Carmen turned her back, I stuck out my tongue at Geraldine. She scowled and turned abruptly to follow the leader.

"That was childish," smirked Sam. "She'll tell on you."

"I'm already in the doghouse. I still owe Carmen twenty dollars."

Rosie swallowed her fish. "We may have lost the battle at Culloden. We won't be losin' this one."

We all agreed. Battle plans would be formulated later.

THE NECTAR OF THE SOUL

Instead of his usual bone-crushing hug, Thomas wrapped his long arms around me in a tender embrace. "Glad you came, mate. You missed Rosie. Left an hour ago."

The Family that Cares was rotating visits to let him know we cared.

I handed Thomas two mangoes. "Fresh from the market."

He led me to the kitchen. Vials of medication lined a counter. "Looks like a pharmacy."

"They put me on another trial. I'm staying positive."

Though crusty lesions remained on his face, Thomas appeared more cheerful and energetic. He handed me a cutting board. "Do me the honors."

I sliced the mangoes and gazed at the vials that would, hopefully, offer a reprieve from the death sentence. He handed me a paper plate, telling me it saved us from washing dishes. Always considerate, he rightly guessed I'd be uncomfortable eating from one of his plates. Why *did* bad things happen to good people?

I brought the dish of mangoes to the table and we sat down. He munched on a mango wedge, a good sign that his appetite was returning.

"I'm been writing," he said. "I don't have children. Words are my legacy."

"I journal on my computer. Clears my mind. What are you writing?"

He wiped his mouth. "Poems, mate. They're the nectar of the soul. Care to read one?"

Without waiting for a response, he retrieved a page from the living room. He presented it to me as if it was precious parchment.

I wiped my hands on a paper towel, then read his poem.

I retreat into prison
Fearful of an empty hole.
My body moves to slumber,
The dark night of the soul.

I stumble in the caverns,
While demons gnaw my skin.
Alone and dejected,
I'm punished for my sin.

My wretched soul cries aloud,
"Where's your compassion?
"Your love and protection?"
God replies in a fashion.

With silence.

After finishing the poem, I, like God, remained silent, overwhelmed with despair.

Thomas eventually spoke. "I was depressed as hell when I wrote that. Felt better once I printed it. There's more nectar to come. AIDS is a potent muse."

"I should've been there for you," I said. "I got caught up with Celeste and my father."

"No worries, mate. You're here now. That's what matters."

It also mattered to me. A close friend, Thomas needed my support more than ever. I stayed until the evening, when Sam and Alana arrived for their turn to care. I left with the poem lingering in my mind. Would God break the silence?

BONNIE'S PROGRESS

WEDNESDAY, JUNE 21

I pored over her journal while ABBA played in the background. Bonnie had passed her twelfth session. According to Carmen's policy of Managed Patient Care, she should get the boot. Although she continued to ruminate about Perry, she had accepted the fact he was no longer in her life. She increased her hours at the restaurant, and was less depressed. However, her journal alerted me to trouble with a capital Z. Despite my warning, she attended the lecture by Ziprunanda.

"A nice lady picked me up," she gushed. "Baba Z made me think of ya, Doctor P."

I practically gagged. "We're very, very different."

Her bulging eyes sparkled. "He tole us we can change, just like ya always say to me. But we have ta open our hearts. So I'm gonna try. The lady asked me ta come again tomorrow. She's gonna drive."

"Did she have orange clothes and short hair?"

Bonnie cocked her head with a quizzical look. "No. But there's other ladies like that with Baba Z. Why?"

The spiritual charlatan! I issued another warning. "They're a cult, Bonnie."

She smiled. "Don't worry, Doctor P. I'm followin' my heart."

Had she sipped the chai?

"How's your dad?"

I wanted to hammer my point about the swami, but decided that would merely raise her resistance. So I thanked her for her concern and told her my father was doing better. In fact, his health was improving. The same couldn't be said for the marriage. No surprise there. He was hankering for a drink. My mother held her resolve. She refused to hand over the car keys until he was fully recovered.

"So what do ya think of me diary?" asked Bonnie, bringing me back to the session.

"Great," I said. "Congratulations."

She beamed. "I'm gettin' good, ain't I?"

To her credit, she had written two pages. "If you keep this up, you'll become another Henry Lawson."

"Who?"

"The famous Aussie writer. Oh, never mind. You're doing great."

But she better hurry up. Managed Patient Care was breathing down my neck.

BATTLE PLANS

The musketeers huddled during supervision.

"I can't believe Carmen would be so blatant. If anyone should accompany her, it should be you, Sam."

"Actually, Peter. I'm relieved," said Sam. She ran her hand through her spiked hair. "If Geraldine wants to play host and introduce Carmen to community agencies, let her. I don't want to traipse around with Carmen."

"She has no right to miss supervision," complained Alana.

"Good riddance," snorted Rosie. She removed the reading glasses perched on her head and angrily planted them on the bridge of her nose. "Did ye read this bleedin' memo?" She strangled the page. "A sign-in/sign-out sheet!" She crumpled the paper and threw it in the trash. "This isn't a ruddy factory."

Alana turned to Sam. "Any luck with the Board?"

Sam told us that Carmen found out about her conversation with a friend on the Board. She pre-empted Sam's request to speak at the next meeting by arranging a strategic plan update for the board members. That meant Sam couldn't lay out our case until the following month.

"That's way too long!" cried Alana.

"Carmen's reign of terror is out of control," added Rosie.

"I'm countering most of her memos with written objections," reported Sam. "Clinical decisions must involve clinicians. I now send copies to Carmen *and* the Board. She's livid. She'll only respond to me by email or memo. I think she wants a paper trail to gather any evidence of insubordination."

"Remember Culloden!" exclaimed Rosie, her eyes ablaze with fury. She jabbed her glasses like a weapon. "It's time for the broadsword. Strike now before it's too late."

"What did you have in mind?" I asked nervously. Her ancestor lost his life in battle.

She adjusted her skirt as if it was a tartan kilt. "A simple plan. We have contacts in every bleedin' agency. We must call them and muster a groundswell of support for Sam and the clinical program. If the ruddy lawyer won't listen to us, she'll listen to the Board when it's bombarded with complaints. Heaps of them. Get ready for battle."

Sam heaved a sigh. "Watch out for the MacBains."

While I would have preferred a truce, Alana warmed to Rosie's plan.

"Let's contact our friends at every agency. They can write letters," said Alana passionately. "Tell them our patients need their help."

"We'll have to do this on our own time," cautioned Sam. "I don't want this interfering with our client services."

"It's already interfering," groused Rosie. "Fillin' out the ruddy forms takes hours that should be spent with clients."

"I know," consoled Sam. "Once the letters and calls start pouring in…"

"The shit will hit the fan," I said.

"Too right!" shouted Rosie.

As the others discussed plans to call in the reserves, I worried about becoming a casualty of war. I didn't want to join the unemployed, especially with my credit card debt. Yet, I couldn't let the musketeers down. It was now time for battle fatigues.

CEDRIC'S GOODBYE

With the added burden of mounting paperwork and lunchtime phone calls to agencies, the musketeers kept a hectic pace. This suited Frieda, who loved the rule of order. The office manager was happy as a clam to be delegated custodian of forms. She monitored the sign-in sheets at the front desk and hounded us for productivity forms at the end of the day.

Never satisfied, Carmen demanded an increase in client hours and statistics to demonstrate the effectiveness of MPC. According to her latest directive, all phone contacts had to be recorded as a minimum of ten minutes, even if we only left a message. Five of these phone contacts translated into fifty minutes on the productivity sheet. It replicated the legal paradigm where saying hello to clients meant hello to money. Every hello padded our statistics.

Alana rushed past me in the hall. "The torch rides a camel today in the Northern Territory. Marks the twenty-third day of the relay. Seventy-three more days till it reaches Sydney."

Despite the added stress, Alana kept up with the torch's bizarre journey around Australia. She was enthralled by Tuesday's dive in the Barrier Reef. The country had gone bonkers. The torch had been transported by sky rail, barge, even camel, but constructing a waterproof container to show off the Barrier Reef was going off the deep end.

I returned to my desk and the pile of unfinished work. Though we weren't allowed to bring client files home, I planned to sneak a few into my briefcase to catch up on assessments over the week-end. Overwhelmed and exhausted, I prepared for the last session of the day.

Cedric's left hand remained in a cast that was no longer white. After consuming a case of Foster's, his mates had gone wild with black and blue markers, scribbling unintelligible signatures over the entire cast. Despite the chill of winter, Cedric wore his signature shorts and a sleeveless T-shirt with a new motto plastered across his chest—*A Beer Is There When You Need It.*

He was one of the few clients who actually fit Carmen's edict for Managed Patient Care. Today's session was his eighth, not includ-ing his cancellations. Since his only goal was to complete an anger management course, he would've been thrilled to conclude after one meeting.

"Still planning to remain at the brewery?"

He raised his broken left hand. "Don't have much of a choice, now do I? Once I'm off disability, me boss will try and get me fired. After I complete the classes, he can't hang that over me head. If he does, he'll reckon with me and the union."

I doubted that he'd learned anything about impulse control. The best predictor of violence was excessive drinking, previous violent history, and past childhood abuse. While Cedric fit the bill on the first two, I had my suspicions about the third. He refused to discuss his childhood, but mentioned in passing that his father punished him by taking him to the shed.

"You wouldn't do anything foolish to your boss, would you?"

He dug a thumb into his nose then wiped a huge snot on his shorts. "Not worth it. I learned me lesson. Put that down in your notes. And say that I completed the classes."

"You still have problems, especially when you're drinking."

"Bullshit," he barked. "You keep tellin' me I shouldn't get mad, even if an asshole calls me wife a whore."

"I've merely said there's a better way to handle your anger than throwing a punch or a beer keg."

He ran his beefy hands over his stubbly scalp. "Your bloody idea of an anger meter with colors made no fuckin' sense. Just give me a fuckin' letter, and I'll be off. I'm not comin' back."

Forget the feedback, insight, re-education, skills training, or cognitive theory. None of them worked. With short-term MPC, I could say that he accomplished one goal. He attended anger classes. If I was totally honest, I'd give my student a failing grade. I stared at the barrel-chested bloke angrily scratching his nostril. I shook my head and turned to the computer.

With arms folded across his protruding belly, he issued a final order. "Make sure it says I completed *eight* classes."

I typed the letter with a KIS—keeping it simple.

To whom it may concern,

Per Cedric Crossan's request, I'm writing to state that he attended eight sessions to address anger management. At this point, no further appointments are scheduled.

Sincerely,

Peter Pinowski, PhD

I expected a fierce argument when I showed it to him. Surprisingly, he said, "Bloody oath. That might do it." Then, as if purchasing a case of beer, he said, "I'll take it."

He bolted from the office, clutching the letter with the protruding fingers from his cast acting like pincers. Good riddance.

I filled out the day's productivity sheet and marked: *3:30 p.m. Cedric Crossan's 8th session, terminated.* A recent directive stipulated that we now had to indicate the interview number plus the dispo-sition—Carmen's way of keeping tabs on length of treatment. Brief meant no more than twelve. I had been at the agency less than three months which meant that, apart from Bonnie, my clients still hovered in the brief range—but not for long.

Under Frieda's watchful eye I handed her today's productivity sheet and signed out. The grueling week made me more than ready for drinks with the musketeers at the local pub. Hopefully, Cedric wouldn't be there to celebrate the end of class.

WOUNDS OF MY FATHER

SATURDAY, JULY 1

"*Nie*!" she screamed.

I rushed into the house and found my parents yelling at each other.

My mother pointed an accusing finger. "No drinking."

My father shook his fist. "I'm no child. If I want a taste, I can have one."

I quickly intervened. "You've been out of the hospital a week, Pa. You're talking better and getting around. Your brain's still swollen, and you're taking medications. The Naltrexone is supposed to curb the craving."

"He doesn't take it," scowled my mother.

He paced the floor like an agitated dingo. "Makes me nervous. Can't sleep. I want one drink."

I stepped toward the moving target. "The doctor can give you something."

"I take too many pills."

I caught my father's arm, stopping him in his tracks. "Don't start drinking," I pleaded. "One vodka will lead to another and another. You'll be staggering around the house. If you fall down drunk, you could end up dead."

Our eyes connected for a brief moment. When my mother shouted, "Listen to him, Józef," he pushed me away.

"You know nothing. Nothing!"

I yelled back. "Wake up, for Christ sake. The next blow to your head will kill you."

Before my father could retaliate, I stormed outside. Away from conflict, alcoholism, and dysfunction. I inhaled the chilled air and walked. Nowhere in particular. But somewhere to quiet my swirling mind. I thought of Thomas, who embraced life in the face of death. My father, on the other hand, was prepared to squander life for the sake of a bottle. So much for epiphanies. If he wanted to drink himself to death, so be it.

I walked and self-talked for an hour, then returned to the house. He was in the garage, waxing the Ford Holden. I grabbed an old towel and started buffing the car door. We both said nothing while we waxed and polished in my father's sacred temple until the job was complete. The Holden gleamed.

I hung my towel on a hook jutting from the wall. "Nice job."

He nodded. "*Tak.*" He grabbed a stool and sat down to wipe his calloused hands with a rag. "You think I'm mean," he said. "You should have met my pa."

I turned over an empty bucket to make myself a seat. "What was he like?"

My father buffed car wax off his hands. "Not kind like me," he said. "Never did I talk back. Not like you. I would have been beaten."

I knew only fragments of his early childhood. His mother died giving birth to his sister when he was two. The middle child of three, he was raised by his father until he married again.

"You never talk about him. How mean was he?"

My father stared at the rag as if in trance.

"Pa?"

"There were many cats on the farm," he said, staring at the con-crete floor. "My favorite was Kasha. She was brown with speckles. I'd sneak food to her in the barn. One time I stole a piece of meat from the kitchen. I didn't see him in the corner of the barn, with his vodka. He beat me for feeding her. Said cats must catch their own food.

"The next day, I couldn't find Kasha. I whistled. No Kasha. Later, I asked my pa. He told me there was no place on a farm for a cat who didn't work. I never saw her again. But I found blood on his pitchfork."

He looked at me. "After that, I worked hard. All the time. But I made a promise. No more cats."

"You never told me about that."

"Some stories are left with the dead." He threw the rag into an empty bucket. "Come. Lunch."

We returned to the kitchen and found plates waiting for us on the table. While we said grace, I glanced at my father's bowed head. His weathered face, white thinning hair and mustache, and wrinkled brow displayed pain and hardship. He survived a brutal, alcoholic father and no real mother. He lost a score of relatives in World War II. He didn't talk about that, either. Seeking a safe, secure home, he migrated twice and learned a new language and culture. His hands, hard work, and vodka became tools of survival. My grandfather trained him well.

The rare glimpse of the past revealed in the garage told me unspeakable stories had been hidden away, yet not quite forgotten. A survivor of a terrifying life in Poland, without a mother, in a war-torn country, my father learned to steel himself against pain. No talking, no feeling, no crying, not even a whimper. However, the silence, suppression, and denial sowed seeds of destruction. With poison embedded in his heart, my father developed a life-long pattern of avoiding pain and relying on alcohol as an anesthetic.

I wondered if he'd ever be open to real healing. It required courage and dedication, a willingness to be awakened from a numbed existence. He'd have to break the silence and share the stories. I, myself, knew how tortuous the work was, and I had the benefit of being a therapist with a surrogate family that cared.

My father relied on his hands, not words. He may not have been capable of telling me what I craved to hear—that I was loved and respected. However, after my brief peek into his secret chamber, it was easier to forgive.

SKELETON MAN

SUNDAY, JULY 2

A disemboweled, bleeding body. Putrefied skin, shed like discarded clothes. Exposing muscles and tendons. Eyeballs rotate in faceless skull. Bony hands reach for the skin. Stretch it over skeleton. A face takes shape.

Another frightening dream to greet the day. I wrenched myself out of bed and dressed for the visit. I picked up a ham and cheese quiche, several bananas, and a bottle of orange juice. I wanted Thomas to have a hearty breakfast.

The musketeers continued to take turns visiting our sick comrade. Today, he painted a brave face, but I knew he was in considerable pain. The new cocktail of drugs was having an adverse effect. Food wouldn't stay down.

"Eat up, mate," he pleaded with a labored breath. "No sense you going hungry."

Though I'd lost my appetite, I picked at the quiche. "Are the meds helping?"

He wagged a tired head. "They make me feel like a zombie. Tomorrow I see the doc. Get the toxicology report."

"Is there anything I can do?" I asked, feeling utterly helpless.

"No, mate." He shifted his legs and winced. "I'm not the best today."

"What about your poems?"

A spark of life flashed in his eyes. "I finished one two days ago."

"Let's have a read. Where is it?"

He pointed to the computer.

I found several sheets on the printer and brought them back to the table. I read the title and gasped. "Skeleton Man? Christ, that's spooky. My dreams are haunted by skeletons. They give me the shivers."

"Then the poem is meant for both of us, mate. Read it."

With trepidation I recited it aloud.

I walk the burnt and blistered desert,
Seeking a home.
Plodding, sometimes crawling,
My decimated body hangs limp, exhausted.
Flesh tormented, again and again.
I walk no more and surrender, a skeleton man.

Now clanking to the whims of the wind,
My skeleton lies in wait,
Bones bleached by the scorching sun.
My skull, home to the scorpions of the night.
I wait—listening, praying—I wait
For a whisper of hope.

Days bleed into nights.
Hope gives way to despair.
My clinking bones chime with the wind,
Sounding a toll.
A toll warning travelers,
Beware of forgotten souls.

Time turns into eternity.
A windswept mound entombs my bones,
Harboring deathly silence.

An empty socket peeps through the sand.
It remains open to the sky
And the scorpions of the night.

When the moon spins black, a she-snake stirs.
Gliding on ebony skin, she scours the desert.
Cautious, yet ferocious, she slithers into a skull,
Only to be met by a scorpion—her first meal.
She burrows deeper where sand gives way to a spine.
A mate has been found!

Hungry for love,
She encircles the vertebrae.
Caressing the spine, she writhes in ecstasy.
She receives no response,
Not even a tremor.
Never before has she been so ignored.

She shovels through sand, fangs at the ready,
Attacking the lifeless serpent.
A two-pronged bite punctures the coccyx.
Venom of black ink mixes with marrow
Causing the bones to shudder
And skeleton man to stir.

Pain, a deep resounding pain,
Thumps up the vertebrae
Till a rhythm of drum beats pound in my skull.
The pain of unmet needs and desires
Pierces my soul with a vision
And transmutes an awakening.

The marrow transfuses life.
Organs appear, arteries pump red blood.
Flesh begets sumptuous flesh.
I rise from the desert tomb
With a new appendage –
An ebony snake dangling between my legs.

With my spirit transformed
I breathe my first breath.
I walk my first step into the light of day.
Courage surges through my bones.
The sand falls from my eyes; I can see.
My God, you have not forsaken me.

When I finished the poem, I faced Thomas and the lone tear dribbling down his cheek. He choked on the words, "I found the road home."

I gripped my friend's hands in solidarity. My fears about sharing a meal or contracting the disease had vanished. We were two brothers facing death and redemption.

SHOWDOWN

TUESDAY, JULY 4

Yesterday, the Olympic torch visited the Tall Trees in Walpole—430 kilometers south of Perth, Western Australia. Torchbearers carried the flame along the world's longest and highest elevated walkway through the giant Tingle and Karri trees.

Meanwhile, at work I was having difficulty seeing the forest for the trees. Carmen's onslaught of memos elaborated her unfolding strategic plan. Over Sam's objection, she invited herself to the supervision group. She pranced into the conference room with Geraldine at her side. Dressed in a yellow blazer and black pants, Carmen carried another thick file. She never arrived empty-handed.

Sitting erect on her throne, she pronounced, "I'll be brief. The new software program is almost complete. We are going paperless. No need for bulky files. All data will be accessed with a tap of a finger."

I wanted to give her a rat-a-tap-tap with *the* finger.

"Don't fret," she said in a sweet, patronizing voice. "You'll soon receive training in PED—the Provider Efficiency Database. It will collate statistics and evaluate progress, all necessary for future funding. PED will incorporate IMVS to make goals identifiable, measurable, verifiable, and shareable. As well, PED will alert you to stay on target with clinical hours and treatment objectives. I'm bringing state-of-the-art technology to therapy."

Rosie scowled. "When are we supposed to type this on the ruddy computer?"

"How's PUD going to help us catch up with progress notes?" I asked.

"It's P-E-D," snapped Carmen, wielding the authority of the acronym police.

"I'm buried in paperwork," added Alana.

Our director offered a supercilious smile. "There's an easy solution to that, isn't there?"

"Which is?" asked Sam, red faced, ready to blow.

"It's obvious isn't it? CR."

"Which is?"

"Concurrent recording. Type your notes during the session. Saves precious time. CR will reassure your patients that notes will be accurate."

"But not empathetic," bridled Sam. "The relationship is the healing medium, not the keyboard."

Carmen waved off the objection. "Lawyers take notes during meetings. There's no reason you can't."

"I'm not a ruddy lawyer," snorted Rosie. "I'm here to help clients, not bludgeon them with bleedin' paperwork."

"No need to get testy," said Carmen indignantly. "I offered a constructive suggestion to reduce the workload. If you prefer not to record during sessions, then end them five minutes early. That should afford you plenty of time."

She gestured dismissively toward Sam. "Work out those clinical issues with Samantha. I have another important matter."

She opened her folder and passed out information sheets. Sitting straight as a board, she announced, "As you know, MPC is about brief treatment. We will be expanding our services to include DMS—Divorce Mediation Settlements. When I was director of the legal aid program, I established a mediation bureau with raving success. A noble cause, mediation saved divorcing couples time and money. Disputes about custody and finances were quickly resolved.

The benefits are laid out in my handout. Of course, I'll provide you with specialized training."

She straightened her yellow blazer. "DMS is brief and effective and complies with IMVS. Mediation can be completed within six to ten hours of face-to-face time."

She beamed. "This adds another revenue stream. Statistics will soar. DMS will expand our versatility; PED will increase accountability. The Board was exceptionally enthusiastic."

Most of us, however, were not. Rosie crumpled the handout. "Ye'd be askin' us to train for mediation plus learn a ruddy computer program? When? Weekends?"

With a devilish grin, Carmen replied, "Why, yes. One that would be convenient for everyone."

Sam's face looked like the head of a thermometer in heat. "Do you want me to remain as your clinical director?"

Carmen arched her stiff back. "I don't see a reason for you to leave right now, Samantha, unless you do."

"I can't sit idle while you dismantle my clinical program," she blurted. "You've completely disregarded my recommendations."

Carmen eyed Sam, then scanned the rest of us. Her lapdog, Geraldine, shifted uneasily at the showdown.

The director brushed off her jacket, as if removing dandruff. "As I told you privately, Samantha, the Board wants new direction. MPC, PED, and DMS provide that. Accept the inevitable."

"Sam's not the only one," interrupted Rosie boisterously. She turned on Geraldine. "What about Nola? Have ye told her she'll be havin' to stop cuttin' herself because therapy's takin' too long?"

Geraldine squirmed as if a slew of cicadas fluttered up her dress. "I support Carmen a hundred percent," came the nasal voice.

"So ye'll be dumpin' Nola?"

"How could you?" asked Alana scornfully.

Geraldine looked to Carmen for a reassuring smile. Receiving a nod, she puffed up with newfound confidence. "I'm reducing Nola's dependence. She'll have psychiatric back-up when Kenneth begins next month. Once stable, she'll join a support group."

"And if she refuses?" I interjected.

Carmen held up her hands in protest. "I want to assure you, as I reassured a few disgruntled callers from the community, that we will manage every patient with the highest professional standard."

"Whose standards?" cried Rosie, working up a lather.

"I won't abandon my clients," added Alana.

"I suggest you implement those noble mediation skills on your staff," derided Sam. "Thus far, they've been missing in action."

Carmen tugged fiercely at her jacket. She pursed her lips as if sucking a lime. "I won't take this impudence, Samantha."

That didn't stop our musketeer. "I've worked hard to establish quality care for our clients," declared Sam. "You're turning them into numbers with a cookie-cutter approach. Short-term treatment works well, but not with everyone. We need flexibility and compassion. I won't accept anything less."

Carmen's face flushed. "If you won't comply with the strategic plan," she hissed, "I can find others who will."

She rose from her throne and made a hasty exit. There would be no mediation today.

THE FACTORY

WEDNESDAY, JULY 5

The four musketeers intensified the campaign. We contacted agencies before and after work and during lunch. We solicited and begged psychologists, social workers, ministers, doctors—anyone who would respond to our call to action for letters and phone calls to express outrage about the Strategic Plan. We wanted to get the word out fast before Carmen bombarded us with more acronyms.

Like a jaguar, she prowled the premises. Her probing eyes scrutinized productivity forms and sign-in sheets. With Frieda deputized as the sign-in police, anyone arriving late was reported and written up.

Sam talked of resigning, but Alana, Rosie, and I convinced her to stay on board. She was the only one who could prevent our agency from morphing into a factory. With the pressure to fill every slot, I felt like a worker on an assembly line, processing clients, completing paperwork, and making phone calls to set up appointments to process more clients. I began to view therapy less as an intimate exchange and more as a conveyor belt. If I didn't keep pace, I'd be trampled by the acronym police.

Five clients serviced. Next...

FAITHFUL COMPANION

FRIDAY, JULY 7

Before leaving for work, I dashed outside with Nesha. As I trudged along the sand, a couple slowly approached. A gray-haired, over-weight man, probably in his fifties, snuggled arm-in-arm with a slim, attractive brunette in her twenties. They looked more like father and daughter, yet the way they lavished affection toward each other demonstrated otherwise.

I watched their love-struck gazes, clenched arms, and gentle laughter pass by, oblivious to my existence. The only way that bloke could score was to be a powerful, rich bastard with a yacht and man-sion overlooking the beach—attractive lures for any nubile beauty craving power and security.

The sight of them made me long for love. I wanted someone to lean on who could, in turn, lean on me. The pangs of loneliness overwhelmed me. A chasm ached to be filled.

Nesha nudged my leg with a piece of driftwood clenched between his teeth. He dropped it and pranced around the sand.

"Not today."

He barked angrily.

"One throw. Can't be late."

I tossed the stick. He scurried through the sand. Thank God for my faithful companion.

BIRTHDAY PARTIES

SATURDAY, JULY 8

Yesterday, my father turned sixty-four. Today we planned to celebrate. I drove to the airport and picked up Stella and her family. My nieces squirmed uncomfortably next to their mom in the back seat, each cradling a carry-on in their lap. Up front, my brother-in-law's lanky legs straddled a small suitcase.

My sister leaned forward. "How's Pa?"

I peered at the rearview mirror. "Making progress. He's now reading at the fifth grade level."

Danka tapped a text message, then pushed her sister. "Mum. Krystyna's taking too much room."

"I AM NOT," retaliated her younger sister. "The car's too small. You need a bigger car like us, Uncle Peter."

"It's big enough for me."

The fifteen-year-old grimaced. "I'm squashed."

"Sit still," yelled her mom. She poked her daughter in the ribs for good measure. "We'll be there any minute." She tapped me on the shoulder. "You should've driven Pa's Holden. It has more room."

Stan turned toward his family. "Next time we'll rent a car."

"If you want me to drop you off at a rental place, I'll take you there now."

"Don't be so snippy," chided Stella. "It's crowded back here with the extra luggage."

"Thanks for the appreciation."

"Oh, for heaven's sake. Don't start with the pouting."

My neck muscles tensed. "We're almost there." I could hardly wait!

When we arrived, the car doors burst open. Bags and crabby passengers poured onto the front lawn. I opened the boot and removed four suitcases. You'd think they were staying a month instead of a weekend.

My mother and aunt rushed out of the house and smothered everyone with hugs. I yelled to Stan for help when my father arrived and picked up a suitcase.

"We'll take care of it," I said.

"I'm not an invalid," he protested. He heaved two large suitcases and carried them indoors. He wanted to show everyone he was healthy. Stan and I grabbed the remaining luggage and followed him inside while my mother and aunt fussed over the girls. To short-circuit any harassment to spend the night, I left Nesha at home. He provided my exit strategy. Besides, I needed a sentry to mind the apartment.

Our luncheon feast was *gołąbki*. Stuffed cabbage rolls was one of my father's favorites and, since it was his party, my mother aimed to please. After his fourth *gołąbki*, my father patted his stomach and burped.

"Janek needs me at the garage," he said. "If I was there, we could've closed early."

"No work until the doctor says it's okay," echoed my mother's emphatic voice.

"Hmmph," he grunted. "What does he know?"

And on it went during the meal.

When my uncle arrived, he slapped his brother on the back and whispered something in his ear. My father's eyes lit up like Christmas lights.

My mother squinted, then pounced upon the bulge in Janek's back pocket.

"Did you bring a bottle?" she screeched.

Like a boy caught sneaking a gherkin from the pickling crock, my uncle disavowed responsibility. "Józef wanted a birthday present."

"*Psiakrew*! Give it to me."

My red-faced uncle removed a small bottle of żytnia and handed it to my mother, who screamed, "*Nigdy*! Never again."

My father's face withered, as if he'd lost a treasured friend. "A taste for my birthday."

"No drink!"

He scanned the group for support. None was forthcoming. Not even from his brother, who was now getting an ear-bashing from his wife. In the face of defeat, my father still argued.

"Calm down," I said. "It was only two months ago when we almost lost you. Everyone's here to enjoy your birthday. *Proszę*. Please. No arguments."

My aunt pulled at Janek's bushy ear, prompting him to say disingenuously, "Marysia's right." He winked at my father. "Get strong and come back to work."

My mother shrieked, "He's not working until the doctor..."

"I can work now," he shouted. "Right, Janek?"

My mother pounced on my aunt. "Tell Janek," she cried. "No doctor's certificate, no work."

Adele scowled at her husband. He gave a conspiratorial pat to my father's shoulder. "Not now, Józef. Later."

Stella grabbed my mother's arm and steered her toward the kitchen. "Let's clean up." She yelled for her daughters to follow. "*Babcia* needs help."

Danka and Krystyna grumbled their way to the kitchen. Stan and I remained with the recalcitrant brothers, who mumbled in Polish. I turned on the cricket match and stared mindlessly at the flickering tube.

The rest of the day reeked. It wasn't just the cabbage, though my frequent dashes to the loo became more conspicuous. My nieces clutched their throats at the noxious odor and pretended to gag. My parents returned to their bickering, as did my sister and I. Barking orders, Stella told me to take out the garbage as if I was one of her kids. Still smarting about this morning's drive, I ignored her.

By the time my cantankerous father opened his presents, the familiar hum of anxiety had returned, vibrating through my body like a dull jackhammer. I fled underground to a cave deep inside my mind. I shut out the noise and everyone else around me.

I returned home at eleven o'clock. Instead of peace, I found another celebration next door. The neighbors' apartment echoed like a sound stage. Revelers bellowed a heavy metal rendition of *Happy Birthday*. A guitar twanged, followed by wild cheers.

I thought of my client, Cedric. If he was here, justice would be served. I inserted earplugs and crawled into bed. The blaring music kept me and Nesha up until three in the morning. The lack of sleep plus the dreadful episode at my parent's house amplified my internal humming to a piercing decibel. I had to face the enemy.

I climbed out of bed and threw on clothes. I thought of bringing my cricket bat, but decided to take Nesha instead. He wasn't so keen. I dragged him outside and climbed the steps next door.

I pulled at the leash. "Bare your fangs," I shouted. "Bark."

He did the exact opposite. He sat down on the stairs and went mute.

"Thanks," I grumbled.

I rapped on the front door. The party raged on. I banged harder over the deafening noise. Still no response. I pounded the door.

Finally, a rasping voice yelled, "Who's there?"

I glanced down at Nesha and tugged the leash. "Need some support."

He yawned.

"Who's there?"

The rage that propelled me to the landing vanished. My arms trembled. "N-next door neighbor."

The door creaked open. A cloud of smoke escaped into the chilly air. Like a phantom moving through a dense fog, a bare-footed, anorexic figure appeared, dressed in black leather. My neighbor's face, dotted with metal hoops and studs, scowled, "What the fuck do you want?"

I pulled Nesha closer. He yelped. My hands shook. "Listen," I said, "D-don't want trouble. It's three in the morning. Can you l-lower the music?"

Her nostrils flared and her bloodshot eyes grew wild. "It's fuckin' Saturday."

"Who is it?" growled her bearded partner. He swung the door open. The stench of booze and marijuana wafted past me. I stared at his naked chest. His bony, sweaty torso flaunted a broad tattoo of a Grim Reaper with bile-green eyes. The Reaper brandished a sickle with an erect penis replacing the blade.

When I faced two pierced metal cones jutting out above his chin like tiny horns, I realized my folly. There was no sense talking to these demons. It was time to cut and run.

"Hey, mate!" called someone on a couch.

The two druggies turned around. Dressed in tattered Elvis gear, Perry sat with a joint in his hand. He gesticulated wildly for me to enter. Then to my horror, he staggered to his feet and approached the doorway with a silly grin.

I faced the man who robbed my apartment and babbled, "W-what are you doing here?"

"What's it to you, fuck-face," snarled the leather-clad female pin-cushion.

"He's me mate," clucked Perry. The Elvis wannabe stroked his greasy hair and long sideburns. He staggered through the doorway and placed a clammy arm around my shoulder. "Join the party," he said, acting as if he sponsored the event.

I wanted to bash the bastard for robbing my place. Considering I was outnumbered by wasted zombies, I chose a quick exit.

"I'll leave you to your party," I said, edging away.

He tugged at my shoulder. "Have a spot o' fun, if you know what I mean."

Crikey! I was living next to satanic creatures from Hell.

"Got a fuckin' problem?" growled the bearded one. He tugged a metal ring in his punched-out ear lobe and expanded his chest with the menacing tattoo.

His emaciated partner turned down her pierced lower lip and showed off the bold letters tattooed in black—FUCK ME.

Perry cackled. He took a hit off his joint and handed it to me. "Have a taste, mate."

"N-no thanks. Need some sleep. Enjoy the party." I pushed myself past him, with Nesha lagging behind.

"Fuckin' asshole," shouted the woman.

I wanted to yell, "Fuck you too," but held my tongue. This was no time for a confrontation with a stoked Grim Reaper.

THE NULLABOR

SUNDAY, JULY 9

Fears of another break-in latched onto my mind like sticky flypaper. I ruminated all day about the drug-infested lair next door, with Perry scurrying with the other roaches. He could be casing out my place. I called the police. They said they'd alert the officers patrolling the area. That made me feel as safe as a mackerel in the mouth of a shark.

If I hadn't committed to visiting Thomas, I would have stayed home. Before leaving, I instructed Nesha, "If anyone enters, bite first, bark later."

Paying scant attention, he held the leash in his jaws, begging for a romp outside.

After battling the traffic on the way to Surry Hills, I arrived late. Thomas didn't answer the door. I panicked and thumped louder. Still no response. With my heart pounding, I banged repeatedly against the wooden door. It finally creaked open. My immediate relief was replaced with horror at the sight of skeleton man—a wasting body with weepy sores and crusty lesions.

He offered a weak smile. "Sorry, mate," he wheezed. "I was in the bathroom."

I planted a brave face, but my fear of catching AIDS returned full throttle.

Thomas sensed my discomfort and sought to ease my fears, something I should've been doing for him. "Did you hear about the torch?" he asked in a light-hearted way.

I followed him into the living room. "I've been preoccupied."

He collapsed on the couch and coughed. He sipped water from a bottle, then said, "On the thirty-third day, it boarded the Indian Pacific train. The torch will travel two days from Kalgoorlie across the Nullabor Plain to South Australia. Know what Nullabor stands for?"

I shook my head.

"It's from the Latin words, *nullus* meaning 'nothing' and *arbor* for 'tree.' It's a desolate, arid place of over 200,000 kilometers, with little vegetation. In 1841, Edward Eyre became the first European to cross it." He took another sip of water and continued. "He described the Nullabor Plain as the sort of place one visits in a bad dream. Well, mate. That's where I've been."

"Aren't the new meds helping?"

"Nasty stuff. Couldn't keep anything down. I'm making a go of it on my own."

"You're off medication?

He struggled to his feet. "I'm tired of dumping poison into my body." He put on a CD. "Let's feast on Bach's cantata, *Wachet Auf—Sleepers Awake.*" He grabbed a blue book off the shelf and handed it to me. "I'm ready for miracles."

I reached for *A Course in Miracles.*

Thomas wheezed. "It's about letting go of fear and embracing love, mate."

"That's all well and good, but you need drugs to stay alive."

He patted the book. "I'm choosing love instead of fear."

He closed his eyes and inhaled a gentle breath. He swayed to Bach's cantata as if somewhere else. "A spark of light connects us to an infinite source. Forgiveness overcomes separation."

"That wouldn't work with my parents," I said scornfully.

He slowly opened his eyes. "We're blind without forgiveness, mate. My parents won't talk to me. They're devout Catholics and believe AIDS is my punishment for being gay. I have to forgive them."

"I can't do that with mine."

"My body may waste away, but in the end, forgiveness sets me free. I want to go home."

I glanced at his ugly sores. Still holding the book, I half-listened as Thomas rambled about finding home and inner peace. My mind was lost on the Nullabor.

LOST GENERATION

WEDNESDAY, JULY 12

The upcoming session would bring heaps of trouble. Per Carmen's command, the interview count for each client must be listed on the productivity sheet. The fifteen marked next to Bonnie's appointment would stand out like a huntsman spider. Managed Patient Care dictated a limit of twelve. Undoubtedly, a scathing memo would be forthcoming. According to Carmen's world, slow-healing clients prevented a rapid turnover, thereby encumbering her statistical goal of servicing volumes of clients with swift recoveries.

Today Bonnie wore a new shirt. The colorful rainbow serpent slithering across her chest contrasted with her tanned leathered skin.

"Like the shirt?" she asked as she handed me her journal. "The serpent's supposed ta take me home."

"Home?"

"I have somethin' ta tell ya," she announced with a bright smile.

I braced myself. "Is this about Perry?"

"I'm through with him, Doctor P. But he's pesterin' me ta take him back."

"Be careful. I met him at my neighbors."

Her eyes widened. "What was he doin'?"

"Drugs."

"I'm sorry, Doctor P. It's me own fault for tellin'…"

"That's over and done with," I interjected. "But I'm worried Perry's on the prowl." And my paranoia was rising like a high tide. As a protective measure, I kept my laptop with me at all times.

She scowled, "I'll tell him ta leave ya alone."

I waved my hands to ward any intervention. "He'll only get aggravated. Watch yourself."

"Don't worry. I've been spendin' me time at work and the ashram."

The last word jolted me. "When do you visit the ashram?"

"Couple times a week. A lady drives me. Everyone treats me real nice."

Then it dawned on me why her inter-session phone calls had ceased. I had put it down to progress!

"I talked with Baba Z," she said excitedly then pointed to her third eye. "He touched here. I felt real strange. Then he tole me ta go home."

He told Celeste the same. That resulted in her leaving everything. The bastard was hitting on a vulnerable, dependent client.

"Don't do it," I implored. "He wants devotees to worship him."

"He said nuthin' about that," she said defensively.

"He builds trust, then, whap! In no time you'll be quitting work and moving into the ashram."

"He did tell me ta move..."

"See? Just as I said."

Bonnie shook her head. "He tole me ta go home."

"Where?"

"Queensland."

Was he exporting devotees to other states? "Does he have an ashram in Brisbane?"

"Me mum and sis live there. Don't you remember?"

"You're moving back to Queensland because he told you?"

"He said they need me."

My rage at the charlatan erupted. I wagged my finger at her. "Listen to me," I half-shouted.

"You don't have ta yell, Doctor P. And ya don't have ta point at me."

"Sorry, Bonnie," I said calming myself. "You've started a new life here. Why go back?

"Cause he tole me."

"If I told you not to go, would you listen?"

"Probably not."

"Why not?"

"Cause ya didn't know me mum was part Aborigine."

"What?"

"Baba Z knew. He said me mum was lost, and I had ta take her back home."

"What are you talking about?"

"Me mum was taken from her family as a kid. Raised in a mission."

"Are you talking about the Stolen Generation? Your mother was one of them?"

She nodded.

"Why didn't you tell me?"

She shrugged. "Didn't think it important."

Not important! Tens of thousands of Aboriginal children had been stolen from their families from the late 1800s until 1970. I stared at the daughter of one such orphan. Bonnie was a casualty of the lost generation. She brushed a stray hair from the rainbow serpent on her chest.

"Is that why you bought the shirt?"

"Baba Z tole me a snake would guide me."

Celeste often referred to the serpentine energy as kundalini. Snakes like the swami were highly venomous. He must've used his hypnotic powers to entrance Bonnie.

I inched my chair closer and patted her arm. "You're back on your feet, but you're not ready to visit an alcoholic mother and sister."

She retracted her arm. "I have ta go."

"I'm thinking of your welfare," I said. "You told me your mother and younger sister live in a trailer in Brisbane. They drink heavily. Your older brother died of an overdose. You'll be going back to that environment. I don't think you're emotionally strong enough to handle that."

She folded her arms defiantly. "I'm goin' next week."

"Next week? For how long?"

"I'm movin' there."

"Moving? For good? I thought you were going for a visit."

"Goin' home for good."

Moving in with a dysfunctional family begged for trouble. Hell, after one visit with mine, I needed a week to recover.

"Slow down," I said. "If you must go, stay for a few days. Then decide."

Her arms squeezed tightly around her chest. "The rainbow serpent tells me ta find me homeland."

I challenged her superstitious belief. "You're better off elsewhere."

"Maybe that's what the police tole the kids when they stole 'em."

I stared at the resolute woman. Was I any different than those misguided souls who sought to prevent half-caste children from returning to their families? Bonnie had received a message. Was it a wake-up call to find her roots, her culture, her home?

I sighed with resignation. "I don't quite understand it, but if you have to go, let's schedule another session before you leave."

Her face brightened. "I'm off to Brisbane next week, Doctor P. I can see ya on Wednesday."

We arranged the final visit and spent the rest of the time discussing her mother and sister. She moved to Sydney with Perry three years ago to get away from them. Now she was returning like a prodigal daughter. In many ways, Bonnie was an orphan, like her mother. Having lost the connection to tribal culture, mother and daughter were left homeless in what should have been their rightful land.

BUSTER

SATURDAY, JULY 15

Bang! Clatter! I jumped from the couch and half-expected Perry to be scaling the balcony. The bloody kookaburra! It hadn't been around for a couple of weeks, so I took its return as an omen to stay awake. I was already hyper-vigilant and sleep deprived.

The bird scratched its beak against the metal rail, then peered through the glass door. Our eyes met.

"Hey, Buster. What do you want?"

Hearing me talk, Nesha woke from his nap, still recuperating from the long beach run to lower my rocketing stress. He yawned, then returned to his dreamtime. I went to the fridge and grabbed a small dollop of hamburger. As I approached the balcony, the bird flew off to a nearby tree. It watched me place the meat on the railing.

When I returned inside, it hovered above the balcony, then landed near the red mince. Its large beak snapped up the meal. It cocked its head from side to side as if asking for more.

"That's it, Buster," I squawked. "One meal a day."

Nesha woke and spotted the bird. He barked at the balcony. The bird flapped its wings and disappeared.

"Seems we have a new friend," I said. "Buster seems a good name, eh?"

Nesha nuzzled against my leg, begging for a treat. I tossed him a stick of rawhide, then returned to the computer. My search for apartments continued. I wanted a place close enough to work but far enough from Perry and his mates. The listings at Dee Why were bloody expensive. With the Olympics two months away, the rentals had soared. Everyone wanted to cash in on the visitors flooding the city. I thought of sharing an accommodation to save money but, with my luck, I'd end up with a sicko. I suspended the search and logged onto email.

"Can't believe it," I yelled to Nesha. "A shocker. Surjit sent a message."

My friend in Adelaide finally responded to an email sent four months ago. I expected a long missive. Instead, I received the briefest of replies. *Prepare for a storm. Namaste, Surjit.*

"What the hell is that?" I complained to Nesha. "He says nothing about his life. Not even a 'How're you doing?'"

The enigmatic Surjit with his metaphysical outlook drove me bonkers when we worked together at a psychiatric department in Sydney. An astute man who emigrated from India with his wife, he acted more like a psychic than a psychiatrist. His predictions were usually on the mark, so I had to pay attention. How he knew a storm was brewing astounded me, since my last email, sent after the Blue Mountain workshop, was overly optimistic.

I reread the message and took his warning to heart. Get the hell out of this hell-hole.

I sent a quick reply, hoping my ship would soon sail from Manly. *Battening down the hatch. Peter.*

BATTLE ROYALE

TUESDAY, JULY 18

Clutching a handful of letters, our director burst into supervision. "You're responsible for these, Samantha."

Sam reached for them. "May I see?"

Carmen gripped the letters as if holding incriminating evidence. "One psychologist had the gall to write that MPC was a menace to the health profession. You put her up to this."

"Don't be givin' Sam all the credit," interjected Rosie. "I've talked with a few therapists who are madder than a cut snake."

"We had no choice," said Sam. "You wouldn't listen to your staff. I hope you listen to the professionals in the community."

Carmen's enraged face matched the color of her cherry blazer. She brandished the letters in the air. "Everyone who wrote forwarded a copy to the president of the Board. Do you know what that means?"

That our battle plan was working.

Her rigid figure shook with rage. "You're the instigator, Samantha. That's insubordination. I have plenty of evidence."

"Such as?"

"Your productivity sheets. You're not executing my order to limit sessions."

Alana spoke up. "Some of my clients were sexually molested. They can't be limited to twelve sessions."

Carmen swatted at the comment as if it was a pesky mosquito. "The select few must be replaced by the needs of the many. Increased demands require radical solutions."

"Clients who have been traumatized need special care," countered Sam.

"We're not a bleedin' factory," argued Rosie.

Carmen upbraided the women. "We're also a business."

Sam rose and stood toe-to-toe. "You're asking us to treat malignancies as if they're minor ailments, for the sake of statistics."

"They provide the numbers to substantiate your salary. Frankly, you don't deserve one."

Carmen stepped back a few paces and brushed lint off her cherry blazer. She measured her words. "I have no recourse, Samantha, but to recommend your termination. Once your friend on the Board hears the evidence, she'll fall in line with the others."

"If Sam goes, we go," announced Rosie defiantly.

"I second that," added Alana.

"Uh...yeah..." I said reluctantly. Quitting the job would spell disaster on my mission to raise the sails and relocate.

Thankfully, Sam intervened to prevent mass resignation. "If we all go, that makes for bad press. Imagine what the papers would write."

She hit the narcissist where it hurt—the excessive need for admiration. Negative newspaper articles would puncture her inflated ego.

Carmen grimaced. "You wouldn't!"

It was Sam's turn to measure words. "I have connections in the media. They'd love an exposé about clients abandoned by a heartless director."

Horrified, Carmen nudged Geraldine for support. "What about you?"

The sycophant raised her dark eyebrows and parroted the company line. "I'm for Carmen. MPC has reduced the waiting list. We're servicing more clients."

"What about your cutter or the other long-termers?" I asked derisively.

Geraldine sniffed her perpetually stuffed nose. "I'm weaning them," she said. "Some aren't happy, but they'll come around. I'll refer them to a group."

Carmen patted Geraldine's head. "I'm grateful someone puts patient care ahead of their own agenda."

Before anyone could object, she waved the letters. "No further discussion. I'll talk with the Board. In the meantime, if you wish to have your friends write, do so at your own peril. I will personally interview community representatives who, I promise, will be more objective. Those findings will be presented to the Board. Come, Geraldine, I need your help."

Carmen stormed out with her lone supporter crawling after her. Just as well. The four musketeers needed to upgrade our battle plan.

BONNIE'S FAREWELL

Yesterday the torch went spelunking in Naracoorte Caves in South Australia. The Olympic flame plunged into darkness and was greeted by 500 flickering candles.

The postman delivered another batch of protesting letters. Carmen's mood turned downright ugly. She angrily scanned the sign-in sheets and roamed the halls, searching for someone to vent her spleen. I took cover behind a hectic schedule of back-to-back clients.

Still wearing her rainbow serpent, Bonnie arrived for her last session. She handed me a small package wrapped in white tissue.

"What's this?"

"I had ta give ya somethin' Doctor P. Open it."

I removed the tissue, revealing a plastic case. "I can't accept this."

"You have ta," she insisted. "You helped me heaps."

"This is your favorite album. ABBA has seen you through tough times." I gave it back. "Take it with you."

She pushed it into my hands. "It'll make ya think of me. Can ya play it again?"

"Any requests?"

She smiled. "Knowing Me, Knowing You."

I inserted the CD and found the song that seemed a fitting send-off. I asked her how she was getting to Brisbane.

"Train," she said. "Leavin' tomorrow."

"It's been two years since you've seen your mother and sister. Nervous?"

"A bit. I'll stay with 'em till I find me a place."

"What are you going to do there?"

She shrugged her shoulders. "Dunno. The rainbow serpent will guide me."

Like the Olympic torch, she was plunging into the dark unknown. Unsure about her future, she walked in faith that she'd find the light. Meanwhile, I fretted about my job, family, and apartment without much faith in divine guidance. I envied her newfound trust in the unseen but wondered if she was blind to reality.

"Let me know how it turns out," I said, offering her my card. "Write if you can."

"Already have one but I'll take another." She shoved the card in her pocket. "Ya kept me from fallin' off a cliff."

"I had the easier job. I held the lantern; you climbed the mountain. You cut yourself loose from Perry and found a purpose to live. I'm proud of you."

She blushed. "Thanks, Doctor P. If I run into a spot o' trouble, you'll be the first ta call."

"Uh, well, I wanted to talk to you about that. You'll need some help when you get to Brisbane."

Moving from New South Wales to the state of Queensland would be difficult enough for a single woman without support. Throw in her dysfunctional family and Bonnie would be walking on a rockslide tumbling down a mountain. Not surprisingly, she resisted the suggestion of another therapist.

"I don't wanna start with someone new," she protested. "You can take me phone calls, can't ya?"

"Sure," I said. "But, as you know, I'm not always available. You need someone to see on a regular basis, for support."

Bonnie crossed her arms and sulked. "Just 'cause I'm movin' doesn't mean ya can't talk with me."

And so it went till the end of the session. She was adamant. No one could help her except me. Nothing was ever easy with Bonnie Kilbourne, not even at the end. I agreed to assist her as best I could, but cautioned her about my limited availability. She promised to call every now and then, and drop me a postcard. With ABBA singing in the background, we said goodbye, though, I doubted this would be our last farewell.

STALKED

FRIDAY, JULY 21

The four musketeers met in a pub after a brutal week at the office. To counter our campaign Carmen and Geraldine were drumming up support out in the community. In turn, we solicited another onslaught of letters, all while keeping up with a burgeoning clinical load and a flurry of administrative memos. The latest one announced mandatory staff training for new software. On a Saturday!

After downing a few beers and commiserating with the musketeers, I headed home, thoroughly spent. I parked the car several blocks away from my building—my vigilant routine to protect my vehicle. Grabbing my briefcase with laptop inside, I marched up the dimly lit street. When the half-moon faded behind the clouds, I felt an eerie presence.

"Where's me Bonnie?"

"Christ!" I yelled. "You scared the hell out of me."

"Where is she?" asked the menacing voice. The scruffy man walked out of the shadows. "Me Bonnie's gone."

"What are you talking about?"

"You know what I mean."

The moon peeped out of the clouds and revealed Perry's wild, agitated face. He snatched my arm. "Been keepin' an eye on her, if you know what I mean. Spotted her leavin' with a suitcase. Asked her where she was goin'. She tole me to piss off or she'd call the coppers. Then she tole me to leave you alone. Where'd you send her?"

I wrenched myself free. "Where's my stuff?"

"Didn't take nuthin," he lied. "Where is she?"

"You ripped off my place, Perry. If you don't leave me alone, I'll call the coppers."

He grabbed my arm again. "Tell me where me Bonnie is or else…"

I lurched away before he could finish the threat and dashed up the street. He followed. I pulled out my mobile and punched the keys. "Help! Police!"

The footsteps stopped. His mouth didn't. "I'll be seein' you, mate," he shouted. "If you know what I mean."

Terror rippled down my spine. My chest pounded as I sprinted up the stairs. Perry would blame me for Bonnie's disappearance. I slammed the door and fumbled for the lights. Someone grabbed my shoe. I screamed. Nesha yelped. Bloody dog!

When the police arrived, I told them Perry was strung out on drugs and had to be arrested. They took a report and said they'd check the neighborhood, but it'd be his word against mine. Their advice: get a restraining order. A bloody piece of paper wouldn't stop a crazed druggie.

After they left, I fetched the cricket bat and peered out the balcony. I clutched the wooden weapon and sniffed for signs of his foul stench. I wasn't going down without a fight.

RELAPSE

SUNDAY, JULY 23

Footsteps. Approaching bedroom. I raised the cricket bat. Swung hard. Thud!

More nightmares. I phone the police and talked with Sergeant Springle. He told me they'd keep an eye out for Perry and that an order of protection would strengthen my case. Two major problems: Perry didn't have an address, and, if he was stoned on drugs, fear of breaking the law would be his last concern.

I positioned the cricket bat near the front door and issued my order of protection. "Keep a lookout," I instructed Nesha. "Don't let anyone in. Bite hard!"

He barked and ran for the chewed-up rawhide.

I turned on the radio to make it appear I was at home, then crept outside with briefcase in hand. Glancing over my shoulder, I scurried toward the car.

$\twoheadleftarrow\twoheadleftarrow\twoheadleftarrow\twoheadleftarrow$

The Family that Cares was supposed to meet last Sunday, but Thomas canceled because he wasn't well. I became alarmed when a nurse greeted me at the door.

"Is Thomas alright?"

"He needs assistance," she said solemnly.

In the living room, Rosie and Sam huddled on either side of Thomas who was parked on the couch. Alana sat half-lotus on the floor near his feet. An arrangement of bush flowers from Sam decorated the table.

I leaned over and hugged him. "How's it going?"

"Hanging in, mate."

More lesions marked his face and arms. Kaposi's sarcoma was a common cancer associated with AIDS. It left purplish-brown patches on the skin, but could also appear internally. I anesthetized myself to the revulsion of crusty lesions. Thomas was my friend and needed support, not squeamishness.

I sensed another problem. "What's wrong?"

Thomas wheezed, "I have PCP. *Pneumocystic carinii* pneumonia, to be exact. The infection of the lungs is deadly." He coughed into a tissue, then wiped beads of sweat from his forehead. "As you can see, mate, I've lost weight." He pointed to the nurse. "Darlene helps me get around. My days are numbered."

I looked helplessly at the nurse standing in the corner. She nodded grimly. Sam and Alana wiped their eyes.

I searched for hope. "Isn't there a trial medication?"

Thomas coughed again and reached for another tissue. "I'm tired, mate. No more meds. No more skeleton man."

I rubbed his sweaty head. "Come on, Thomas," I pleaded. "Don't give up. Our family needs you."

"Listen, mate," he panted. "I've had some good innings. If it's time to go, so be it. But I have a few things to finish. Sit down."

He beckoned the nurse. "Can you bring the box, Darlene?"

She went to another room and returned with a cardboard carton that she placed near his feet. He bent down and rummaged inside. He removed a mask of a ferocious, fiery dragon baring white teeth and a red tongue.

"This here's for you, Sam."

She pushed it away. "This isn't the time."

Thomas held out the gift. "I want to give away my cherished possessions while I can enjoy the giving." He pressed the mask into her hands. "This is from Panama. It emboldens the owner with courage to combat enemies."

She leaned toward him and kissed his cheek. "Thank you, my dear friend. I'll hang it at work."

His next gift was a carved wooden mask. "This Buddha face is from Thailand," he said, presenting it to Alana. "Never abandon your beautiful Buddha nature."

Wiping away tears, she pressed it to her chest. "I love you, Thomas."

He then asked Rosie, "You still going with that bloke, Brodie?"

"Aye. The bonnie Scot makes me happy."

"Then this is perfect." He gave her a mask showing half of a man's face and half of a woman's. "Two becoming one."

"Ye needn't be..."

"Take it, please," he urged. "I want my family to have my special treasures."

Rosie showered him with a hug.

"Easy," he wheezed. "Don't squash me to death."

He leaned back on the couch and panted rapidly, his chest rising and falling. He took a labored breath, then moved to the box. Instead of removing another mask as I had anticipated, he pulled out the blue book.

"You might as well have this now," he said. "*A Course in Miracles* will teach you there is only love."

I had hoped for something more artistic, like the other gifts, to hang on my wall as a fitting remembrance.

He saw my disappointment. "The book removes the mask of fear. It worked for me and will work for you, mate."

I released my fear and thanked him with a kiss on the forehead.

The rest of the day was solemn, yet peaceful. Alana mentioned that two torchbearers on horseback in Victoria passed the Olympic flame from one to the other. In his own way, Thomas was passing his light to those he loved. I was fortunate to be one of the chosen.

PRODIGAL CLIENTS

Today in Shepparton, the Olympic torch took another ride as four cyclists relayed it over eighteen kilometers. Back at our agency, the four musketeers relayed our own fiery message to the community against MPC. They responded with an avalanche of letters that we posted on the bulletin board. Carmen angrily replaced them with her own solicited letters, paying tribute to Managed Patient Care.

The postman was busy. I received a postcard from Bonnie. It showed a picturesque beach with the words, *Missing You*, scrawled in the sand. Her message was brief.

Hi Doctor P.
Am staying with me mum and sis. Not the best but it's okay. Really, really miss our talks. Write back soon. Address on card. Bonnie.

I typed a quick letter and encouraged her once again to see a therapist. She needed more support than the written word. As I sealed the envelope, I thought of Perry who, seemingly, had vanished. The increased police surveillance may have pushed him underground. I wasn't about to lower my guard. If he believed I was responsible for Bonnie's departure and remained on drugs, he was an accident waiting to happen.

While at work, I kept my mind on the clients. Albert cycled back into therapy after a month hiatus. He arrived with a bad cold and dejected demeanor.

He wiped his nose with a handkerchief. "My trip didn't go well in Perth."

"What was her name?"

"Roxy. Thought we had a lot in common." He rubbed the kookaburra on his arm. "She had a blue-tongued lizard tattooed on her breast. I had the bird; she had the meal."

Albert had left his family, job, and child for a bimbo with a tattoo as her calling card.

"What happened?"

He honked into the hanky. "During the first week, we fucked our brains out. She wanted me to be her sex slave. At first, it was unbelievable. Blew my rocks off. Then she pulled out the heavy shit."

Though my inner voyeur begged to hear more, I decided to focus on the present. "Where are you living now?"

He tugged his chin hair. "I crawled back to Dana. She let me stay until I found a place."

"She agreed?" I asked incredulously.

He grimaced. "Kinda."

"What do you mean?"

"I sleep in the garage." He shivered. "Winter's not the best time to bunker down without heat. I told her I'd go back to counseling and make some money."

"Did you get your old job back?"

"My boss wouldn't have me. The bastard hired a woman to take my place. He's banging her on the side."

"So, Albert, what kind of help do you want?"

He sneezed into the air. I grabbed the tissues and wiped his spray off my face.

"I fucked up, Pete," he confessed. "I want Dana and little Albie back. No more porn, online sex, or phone calls."

His mobile remained conspicuously silent.

"I almost lost my family for a fucked-up chick," he said contritely. "I'll do what it takes."

While I questioned his sincerity, I didn't doubt his desperation. Living in a freezing garage with no job, little money, and the prospect of divorce forced him to wake up and face his denial. Although he committed to therapy and a twelve-step group, the crucial question had yet to be answered. Would he stay the course?

DR. KUKULA

THURSDAY, AUGUST 3

A blustery southerly rattled the balcony door. I snuggled under my warm *pierzyna* and sniffled into my handkerchief. Bloody Albert and his cold! My sinuses were clogged and my chest was strung tighter than a drum. I felt like Nesha's worn, raggy duck with the broken squeaker. I had taken a couple of sickies but was put on notice. Per Carmen's request, Frieda phoned me yesterday to tell me, in no uncertain terms, that all personnel must be present to greet the new member of staff.

I stumbled to the bathroom and took another swig of cold medicine. Hopefully, that would ease the flu-like symptoms. The humming anxiety was another matter. I blew into the hanky and prepared myself for work.

⬻⬻⬻⬻

"Please join me in welcoming Dr. Kenneth Kukula," gushed Carmen over mandatory morning tea. "Your patients will now have quicker access to psychiatric care. Our good doctor has worked at a number of hospitals..."

Blah, blah, blah.

The lanky psychiatrist seemed to pay no attention to Carmen's words as he fidgeted with his cup and gazed at the ceiling. He wore a tailored black suit and striped tie, and styled his jet black hair with a slick finish. When he was finally asked to speak a few words, he fired sentences as if they were bullets from a machine gun.

"I like to work fast. I use a shorthand diagnostic assessment. I prescribe psychotropics with the right punch. Hit mental illness hard; hit it quick. I ask you to reinforce patient compliance. It's the most difficult problem. As I tell my patients, follow the drill and swallow the pill."

And gag on his swill! Dr. Kukula didn't notice Sam's fiery eyes boring a hole through his skull, since he never looked at the audience.

The psychiatrist chuckled to himself. "Drug companies supply free starter kits. That means lower cost for patients."

And once they're hooked, higher profits for the pharmaceutical firms.

He winked at no one in particular. "There's plenty more kits when we need them. I have a fabulous relationship with the drug reps."

Who probably plied him with extravagant meals, booze, and God knew what else. I doubted whether any client ever left his office without free pills and a prescription. Considering his lack of eye contact and social ineptitude, he'd go broke if he had to establish relationships with patients. Pushing pills, while not granting lasting mental health, afforded Kukula with a grand opportunity for financial wealth. Which probably didn't concern Carmen, as long as he cranked out the clients. His contract was probably laden with incentives. Carmen would happily provide him with a fat check if the agency's statistics rose as if on Viagra.

"Once your patients are stable on meds," continued Kukula's rat-a-tat patter, "I'll shift them to a meds group. Maximizes my time. More cost-effective than individual follow-ups. A therapist will conduct medication groups. They'll provide some support. The groups will meet monthly or bimonthly and can accommodate twenty patients. During the last fifteen minutes of the meeting, I'll drop in and hand out prescriptions. Very straightforward. I'll be here Mondays and Thursdays. Any questions?"

Sam pounced. "Since I'm not privy to this information, who's responsible for conducting the groups?"

Carmen quickly replied, "Yes, well, thank you for that question, Samantha. I was formulating a memo but might as well address that now."

My stuffy head pounded. Not me. Please, not me.

Carmen beamed. "I want a team player committed to this project. Someone I could depend on who would collaborate with the good doctor."

No surprise when Carmen announced Geraldine, who bounded next to the director and strutted like a cockatoo. She smiled at the psychiatrist and parroted the party line. "We're fortunate to have Kenneth here. Treatment will be streamlined and..."

I joined the psychiatrist in gazing out the window. Heaven help the client who hoped to forego medication in favor of changing thoughts and behaviors. No doubt, Dr. Kukula would tell them, "Follow the drill and swallow the pill."

DRUG REPS

WEDNESDAY, AUGUST 9

My stuffy head and sniffles persisted. I resorted to steaming hot toddies before bedtime. The double shot of Benedictine whiskey with lemon and honey in tea put me fast to sleep. Unfortunately, I had to wake up to a frigid morning and another day at the factory.

The drug reps flew in like a plague of bogong moths fluttering around an incandescent light. They brought boxes of starter kits for patients and goody bags for the staff. We received products stamped with brand names including Prozac note pads, Risperdal pens, Effexor magnets, and mugs advocating a "Zoloft Smile."

Christmas came early for Frieda. She cheerfully drank from her mug and happily scribbled notes with one of her many free pens.

"A drug rep is catering lunch next week," she told me. "Bring your appetite."

"They're trying to buy us," I sneered.

She nodded enthusiastically. "With more free lunches."

While there was no question medication reduced symptoms, I worried about clients placing their faith in pills rather than in themselves. Having been hooked on benzos five years earlier when riddled with panic and anxiety, I'd had a hell of a time weaning myself free. Temptation lurked nearby. I knew where Frieda hid the key for the locked cabinet stashed with mood-altering drugs.

PAIN IN THE MOUTH

Carmen campaigned like a seasoned politician. She visited agencies, promised services, and promoted our psychiatrist. Coining the phrase, "One-stop relief," Carmen guaranteed that MPC benefited clients with therapy, medication, and support groups. Her crusade opened the floodgates. The waiting list skyrocketed. As did her decrees. The latest one specified that anyone requesting psychiatric services, meaning drugs, had to be screened by a service provider. This created a logjam since many of the new clients merely wanted starter kits.

Like automobiles trundling through a carwash, clients were placed on the conveyor belt for the full treatment: assessment, referral for medication, psych evaluation, starter kit, stabilization, then off to a meds group where Geraldine would buff them with the reminder to follow the drill and swallow the pill. As MPC would have anyone believe, a client would emerge a sparkling new person—with a medicated smile.

Wolfing down a quick breakfast before punching in at the factory, I chomped hard on the muesli. A sickening crunch halted my jaw. No! I spat into my spoon. A piece of enamel shimmered among the almond bits. I ran to the bathroom mirror and discovered to my horror that the previously damaged tooth was now missing another side, leaving two tiny pillars. I swished my mouth with water and immediately felt a piercing pain, as if my gums had been stabbed by an ice pick. I cried in agony. Another attack struck with greater intensity. I grabbed hold of the sink while tears dribbled down my cheeks. I washed down four aspirin, but the cold water struck a nerve. More excruciating waves of pain!

I had just recovered from my cold, so taking an additional sick day would incur the wrath of Carmen, especially with all the new referrals. I swabbed the tooth with clove oil and hoped it and the aspirin would quell the pain until I scheduled a dentist's appointment.

⟵⟵⟵⟵

I caught up with Alana before my first client and asked if she knew of a competent, painless dentist.

Alana, ever sympathetic, heartily recommended her friend. "Zarah Epstein's absolutely the best," she said. "Tell her I sent you."

"Anyone would be better than the butcher Dr. Skrzypczak."

I jotted down the number and planned to phone after my interview.

The last time I saw Albert and his wife together, I played traffic cop. Today, they sat next to each other, holding hands.

I rubbed my throbbing jaw. "What's happened?"

Albert pointed to a freshly etched tattoo on his right arm. A naked, curvaceous woman reclined suggestively inside a black shoe with a stiletto heel. Laces crisscrossed the body, covering nipples and pubic area. At the foot of the shoe stood an engraved word—Dana.

"She's the love of my life," he announced proudly.

Dana squeezed his hand. "When Al came home with my name on that sexy pose, I melted. He can never hide the fact I'm his woman."

Unless he was surfing the Internet. "What about the pornography?"

He winced. "That's behind me, Pete. I've installed a software program that blocks porn sites. Dana's the only one with the password."

As if holding a golden key, the cute brunette with a pixie haircut smirked. "Believe me, Al won't have access. When he's off the porn, he's a different man."

He lovingly squeezed her hand. "I've changed."

I gazed at the nude picture on his arm. "So you're now committed to your family?"

"You better believe it, Pete."

"And you're not wanting a divorce?" I asked the woman who had once refused Albert visitation rights.

Her fiery rage had been replaced with passion. She stroked his leg. "We're committed to the marriage."

"Then I now pronounce you, man and wife—Mr. and Mrs. Schweinfurt."

They both chuckled and, on cue, turned to each other and kissed. A long, deep kiss.

"There's plenty of time for that later," I said, holding my aching jaw. "Ugh, so you want marital therapy?"

Albert cleared his throat. "On the way here, I told Dana it would be better to take a break from counseling so I could put my energy into the marriage. She wanted to know what you thought."

The throbbing returned in earnest. Tears welled in my eyes.

Albert grinned. "I knew you'd be touched, Pete."

I cradled my cheek. "I have a toothache. Can you excuse me?"

I rushed from the room to the front desk and asked Frieda if she had anything stronger than aspirin.

She stopped inputting statistics into the computer. "Don't you have clients?"

I pointed to my mouth. "My tooth's killing me."

She gave me a disgusted sigh, then reached into a drawer. She removed a bottle of pain killers and dispensed two pills.

"I need more than two." I pleaded. "The pain's horrific."

She read the directions on the bottle. "Only two."

In addition to being office manager, she was now a bloody pharmacist! I rushed to the staff room for a glass of water and, without thinking, flushed the pills down with cold water. Ah-h-h! I cupped my mouth to muffle the scream. I wanted pliers to yank the bloody tooth, nerves and all.

After several agonizing minutes, I returned to my office. "We have to finish. Got to see a dentist."

"No worries," said Albert. "We're done here, eh, Dana?"

"I wouldn't stop therapy," I said, cradling my cheek. "Big problems need longer solutions. Especially when it comes to sex."

Albert sniggered. "Don't have a problem anymore, Pete." He ruffled his wife's pixie hair. "Dana's followed my lead. Her new tattoo's a beauty."

I glanced at the wreath of eucalyptus leaves etched around both wrists.

"This place's more private," he confided. "Above her pubic hair. A gecko."

She giggled. "It was Al's idea. He said kookaburras love lizards."

I caught Albert's shifting eyes. Dana may have known about Albert's flight to Perth to shack up with another bird. I doubted that she knew about the blue-tongued lizard tattooed above the bird's breast.

He patted his left arm, which, ironically, showed the purple tattoo facing the reclining nude on his right arm. "The kookaburra loves to eat."

I wanted to confront Albert with the reality that, after a while, predator and prey often got fed up with each other. That discussion had to wait till later. I checked the calendar. "Let's schedule another appointment."

He waved his hand dismissively. "Don't need to make one now, Pete. I'll give you a call." He added a bit too cheerily, "Don't want to keep you from the dentist."

I didn't stop the lovebirds. They left hand in hand.

With the throbbing reaching another crescendo, I finally reached the receptionist. She informed me there were no immediate vacancies. I told her I wasn't asking for a bloody hotel room, I was in crisis! Then I flashed to our intake procedure and the clients' reactions when informed help wasn't available for three months.

In the end, I demanded to speak with Dr. Epstein. I told her Alana was my good friend and colleague, and I was in excruciating pain. For good measure, I emphasized the fact that I treated high-risk clients and couldn't be out of action. She relented and asked me to come straight over. She'd fit me in between patients.

I signed myself out at the front desk and asked Frieda to cancel the rest of my morning appointments. As she complained about making the phone calls, I caught a whiff of the putrid perfume. Carmen appeared with her pen and clipboard.

"Where are you going?"

I pointed at my tooth. "Emergency dental appointment."

She snapped, "Medical appointments must be scheduled after work. That's clearly spelled out in SPM."

The Staff Procedural Manual was the last thing on my mind.

"I'm in agony," I cried. Then to prove my point, I opened my mouth and showed her my broken tooth.

Ever suspicious, Carmen peered inside and tapped her pen on one of the tiny pillars. I shrieked.

"Shush!" yelled Frieda. "You're scaring our clients."

I wiped the tears from my eyes and glared at Carmen. "Satisfied?"

She returned the pen to her clipboard. "This better not be a cheap stunt to excuse yourself from tomorrow's PED training."

I mumbled, "I'll be there."

"I expect you back this afternoon."

I left her standing by the counter and cursed under my breath, "FB!" My acronym for fucking bitch.

I drove like a crazed wombat to the dentist which, mercifully, wasn't far. A seismic shock wave pounded my skull as I dashed into the office. A matronly receptionist handed me forms to complete.

"What about my tooth?"

"The doctor will see you after we collect your details."

The most important detail was that I was in fucking pain! I scribbled the answers and handed her the forms. She called an assistant dressed in blue. A young woman whose bubble-gum pink hair reminded me of cotton candy ushered me into a room that smelled of peppermint mouthwash. She fastened a paper bib around my neck, then reclined the padded chair. Then I remembered why I hated dentists. The thought of having my mouth probed, drilled, and mutilated terrified me. As a kid, I would run from my mother until she enlisted my father, who was immune to my crying protests about the dentist.

I scanned the stainless steel tray. Metal instruments of torture were neatly laid in a row. I wiped the sweat off my brow and prepared myself for Marquisa De Sade. When Dr. Zarah Epstein sauntered in, I gasped. She was just a kid, looking much younger than Alana.

She fitted a mask over her mouth and snapped on latex gloves. "What tooth is causing you trouble?" asked the fresh-faced dentist with bushy red hair.

I pointed to the lower back. "Does it have to be pulled?"

She turned on the spotlight. "Let's have a look. Open wide."

She grabbed a miniature pickaxe and poked the broken tooth.

I practically soared out of the chair.

The dentist nodded affirmatively. "That's the one."

Of course it's the bloody one! Where the hell did she get her training?

"Let's take a picture and see if you need a root canal as well as a crown. But first, let's ease the pain."

The assistant handed her a syringe with a foot-long needle.

"No!" I cried. "No needles."

"You need an anesthetic," she insisted.

"Don't you have something else?" I begged. "Gas?"

The doctor looked at her assistant and rolled her eyes. "I can set you up with nitrous oxide. But you seem pretty high strung."

I pleaded, "Try the gas. Please."

"What do you think, Candy?" asked the dentist.

What did *Candy* think? Who was the fucking doctor? Someone had to take charge. "Use the nitrous and then, if you have to," I gulped, "...give an injection."

Dr. Epstein nodded compliantly and instructed Miss Cotton Candy to prep me. When the dentist left the room, the assistant dropped a heavy lead apron over my chest and took several X-rays. She wheeled in a metal tank and fitted a rubber mask over my nose.

The dentist returned and donned another pair of gloves. She turned on the nitrous and said, "Breathe deeply."

I sucked in the gas like there was no tomorrow. I inhaled long, deep breaths. My body started to tingle. At last, the throbbing subsided. I sank into the chair and let the fog descend over my mind. It felt as if I was detaching from my body.

The masked doctor checked the pictures on a screen then asked, "How're you doing?"

I gave her the thumbs-up. The flowing nitrous oxide blew the pain and terror away.

"I checked the X-rays. You need a root canal." She nodded to Candy, who handed her a syringe.

My eyes followed the path of the gargantuan needle heading toward my mouth.

"Open wide."

If it wasn't for the nitrous, I would've bolted for the door. I closed my eyes and sucked the gas. With each inhalation, my mind floated further away from the dentist's chair. Into another world.

"I'll let the Novocain kick in before drilling."

Lost in time, I heard the familiar voice. "Open wide."

I did as instructed. With mouth and mind numb, I felt no pain. The suction tube hissed, and the eerie sound of a drill whirred in the background. I was someplace else, drifting in and out of the dentist's conversation with Candy.

"Tomorrow, the torch visits Parkes Radio Telescope."

"Where's that?" asked the assistant.

"Where they relayed Neil Armstrong's first walk on the moon."

I half-listened to their banter about the 1969 landing, taking my own trip into outer space. When the drilling stopped, I opened my eyes and watched the dentist probe my tooth with her pickaxe. I stared at her, seemingly for the first time. She was young and pretty with boyish hips. Her bushy red hair draped over her white-cloaked shoulders. Red on white. I couldn't see her hidden mouth but imagined luscious maroon lipstick offsetting the white mask.

"How's the nitrous?"

If I could have spoken, I would have said, "Fantastic." I winked back instead.

"Thought so," she said with an amusing nod to Candy.

"Ever have a root canal?"

My dreamy head shook slightly. I gazed into warm, focused eyes. Zarah was an unusual but lovely name.

"You're doing nicely with the nitrous." She reached for a small box. "These endodontic files will clear out the canals. Won't hurt at all."

I inhaled deeply to remain in outer space. Zarah, as if in slow motion, inserted a screw into my tooth. With beads of perspiration on her forehead, she worked diligently, passionately. Filing in and out. Then it hit me. Watching her manipulate the long, thin tool, in and out, I realized my tooth was getting screwed. The shame of it all was that it couldn't feel a thing! I gawked at her heaving chest as she probed her tool deep inside the canal.

I gave her another wink. I knew what she was up to. She smiled back as if to say she knew that I knew what she knew. I breathed heavily into the gas and let her do her thing, imagining what it would be like if I was the tooth. Go for it, Zarah! I imagined my tooth on the verge of an orgasm.

I closed my eyes and wandered into places best left for the bedroom. Zarah joined me, but her mask and gown were gone. I stroked her sexy hips. We were both sweating. This time my tool probed her cavity.

"You should feel much better."

"Mmmmm."

"That should be enough." She turned a knob.

I continued to breathe deeply even with the nitrous turned off. The fog slowly lifted. Returning to my body was like stepping off a moving walkway. Jolting back to Earth, I felt embarrassed by the erotic fantasy. I avoided the dentist's gaze while she told me about leaving the hole in the tooth open so it could drain. She handed me a prescription for antibiotics and pain killers and asked me to return the following week. That meant another round of screwing.

I shuffled out of the office with my mouth still numb, but the toothache gone. I prepared for the next real pain—Carmen and her acronyms.

PED

SATURDAY, AUGUST 19

My mouth still ached after yesterday's needles and dental work, but the medication kept the pain at bay. What annoyed me the most was that my tongue kept probing the vacant hole for food particles. Like the tongue, my mind persisted in examining the relational hole which Zarah and my fantasy ripped open. I longed to be touched, held, and loved. Hopefully by Zarah, if she was available.

Computer software training on a Saturday was not my idea of fun. However, Carmen's memo was explicit. Everyone must attend. No excuses.

We gathered in the conference room and faced a large screen. Charlie, the computer geek, who looked like a pimply Bill Gates well before he created Microsoft, fiddled with a computer. When the words PROVIDER EFFICIENCY DATABASE projected onto the white surface, he nodded to Carmen, who sat with a clipboard in the front row between Geraldine and Frieda. The four musketeers occupied seats behind them. Dr. Kukula had a dispensation since Frieda would complete the bulk of his paperwork.

"I created this little beauty," raved the geek.

The director coughed conspicuously. Charlie, realizing his glaring mistake, quickly added, "Of course, Carmen gets all the credit. She was the brains behind the program."

He waited for her pompous smile of approval, then explained the software. "You will now go paperless," he said excitedly. "All data will be stored in the computer. Exciting stuff. I've created menus with drop-down boxes and templates for every form. Let's start with patient management."

With a few clicks on his mouse, a list of options popped on the oversized screen.

"Pick a template for intake, assessment, treatment plan, progress report, medication tracking, whatever you need. No fuss. Complete the items by scrolling and clicking. No need to write another note."

He clicked the mouse and a drop-down box appeared. "Need an assessment? Scroll down the diagnoses listed alphabetically and click whatever fits. Presto, it's on the assessment form."

He demonstrated by scrolling to bi-polar disorder. He clicked the diagnosis. "Presto! Couldn't be simpler."

"Want to record stressors? Scroll and click. How's that for ease?"

Carmen, Geraldine, and Frieda were the only ones buzzing approval.

"You'll really like this," he said gleefully. "I created templates for the major mental disorders—depression, anxiety, bi-polar, obsessive compulsive, borderline, they're all there. If, for example, you see a patient with schizophrenia, scroll the menu and click the diagnosis. Let me show you."

He clicked the mouse and brought up a screen showing a long list of symptoms with tiny boxes next to each one. "Here's the associated symptoms of schizophrenia, specified by the DSM-IV. Hallucinations, delusions, disorganization, paranoia, on and on—the complete list. If you're lucky and the patient has all the symptoms, you don't have to do anything except type in their name and press 'Enter.' Otherwise, click the boxes next to the corresponding symptoms that don't fit. Presto! Assessment complete. You can crack out one of these beauties in less than five minutes. Think of the time you'll save."

Carmen jumped to her feet with a round of applause.

Sam also rose to the occasion. She interrupted the clapping by berating the software. "We're here to treat clients as human beings, not cookie-cutter templates."

Rosie followed with a broadside. "I'll not be doin' check-list therapy."

Before Alana and I could add our dissent, Carmen angrily rapped the clipboard with her pen, calling for order. "We can discuss the issues later. Charlie's spent considerable time and expense implementing my suggestions. Let the expert explain the software. He's the Network Intranet Technician."

If you added, "Whatever I'm Told," his acronym would be NITWIT.

Despite the objections, Carmen took her seat and told him to continue. He then spelled out the heart of the Provider Efficiency Database, which he called S & S—Scheduler and Statistician. The S & S program allowed Frieda and Carmen to access everyone's schedule. That gave them free rein to add or subtract clients. As well, it automatically flagged any interview that went past the twelfth session. Central Command would be alerted with daily updates. Big Sister would be watching. She'd know who we saw, who we phoned, and probably when we peed.

"Watch this," beamed the weedy geek. "S & S will alert you that if a form needs to be completed."

He happily scrolled and clicked. "Presto! A productivity sheet." He pointed a pen with a red laser at the screen. "I made it fun to input the day's activities." He tapped a few keys on the computer and pressed enter. "Presto!"

A green smiley face appeared.

"Kinda cute, eh?"

The three in the front row were the only ones clucking. Little did they know that Rosie was about to piss on their parade.

She barked at the technician. "What happens if I can't finish yer ruddy form 'cause I'm busy helpin' clients?"

Charlie shuffled his feet. "Well, uh, you'll get a reminder."

He cleared a few lines and punched enter. This time the green smiley face morphed into a red frown with the words, PRODUCTIVITY SHEET NEEDS COMPLETION!

He hastily added, "Reminders will appear every thirty minutes until you've completed the form."

"And if I don't have any bleedin' time for yer SSS?"

He squirmed and looked to Central Command. Carmen stood up and faced Rosie.

"You'll have to make time," she declared.

"I'm not a ruddy computer."

Carmen clutched the clipboard so tight her knuckles turned white. "I expect full compliance."

The Celtic woman glared at her adversary. "I won't be party to yer skullduggery. Ye deserve the broadsword. I quit."

She bolted from the room and slammed the door.

No one moved. Except the face on the front screen. It kept flashing a red frown.

ANGELS

SUNDAY, AUGUST 20

*Driving Thomas in pink Volkswagen. I pull into petrol station.
Black Hummer appears. Three muscular men sneer, "Poofters."
They bash Thomas. I grab nozzle. Squirt petrol on them. Light
a match. Kaboom!*

I picked up Chinese takeaway, then stopped at the petrol station.
I warily eyed the three blokes who pulled up to the pump behind
me. When they exited their jeep, a chill ran down my spine. Were
they like the macho men in my dream? How would they react if
they saw Thomas in his vulnerable state? Would they be terrified,
abusive, or compassionate? My friendship with Thomas had forced
me to recognize my own homophobia. His courageous fight to live
his truth in the face of scorn and rejection made me ashamed of my
past beliefs and fears.

I greeted Darlene, his attending nurse, at the door. She led me into
the living room where I found Thomas's frail body resting on the couch.
I stooped down and gave him a gentle hug. He had lost more weight
and looked haggard. New lesions sprouted like fungus on his bald
head. A wheelchair was parked in the corner, ready to cart him around.

The other musketeers arrived, one after the other, each with a
savory dish. I helped Darlene lift Thomas into the wheelchair, then
we moved him to the table. The Family That Cares gathered for
another meal.

While we ate, Alana pressed Rosie to reconsider her decision.

"Me mind's made up," said Rosie. "When I listened to that computer twit, the blood of MacBains boiled. I had to strike."

"Please," begged Alana. "We need you."

"Sorry, lassie. I called a friend last night. She told me there's a position in Chatswood for a marriage counselor. I'll be applyin'. I suggest ye all start lookin'."

With a heavy sigh, Sam said, "I have to stop Carmen."

"I'm not leaving," added Alana defiantly. "If we stick together, we have a chance. Right, Peter?"

I wasn't so enthusiastic. "I'm not quitting, but Rosie has a point. We should update our résumés."

Alana gripped her paper napkin. "I'm not throwing in the towel. My clients need me."

Sam called us to order. "Let's not rehash work. I don't want more indigestion. We're here for Thomas."

We agreed. Work was off limits.

Thomas pushed his untouched plate aside and asked me to play the CD *Adagio for Strings* by Samuel Barber. We listened to the somber piece.

Thomas broke the silence. "I've seen angels. They come like sparkling lights. They say I'll be okay."

"They talk to you?" I asked, wondering how long he had been delirious.

"They're real, mate," he said softly. "One of them is doing an internship. On the job training."

"Like Clarence in the movie, *It's a Wonderful Life*?

"Kinda."

I exchanged nervous glances with Alana and Rosie. Sam, on the other hand, acted as if he was talking about the next door neighbors. "When do they visit?" she asked.

"Usually when I'm alone. They sing to me."

His visual and auditory hallucinations were spooking me. "So Alana, I hear the torch will visit an underground opal mine at Lightning Ridge."

Thomas shifted in the wheelchair. "Don't change the subject, mate. I'm not bonkers." He coughed into a tissue before continuing. "The archangel Uriel holds a torch, eases the pain. The light brings peace. He says it won't be long."

Alana burst into tears. "I'm not ready for you to go."

He reached out to her. "I'm not ready either. Uriel wants me to release my fears and embrace the light of love."

We huddled around his wheelchair and let him know we would be with him till the end.

He choked on tears. "I love you all."

We placed our hands on his body and showered him with love. He sobbed uncontrollably. Sam passed the tissues. There wasn't a dry eye in the house.

Thomas wiped his face. "I have a request."

He told Sam he had organized a funeral home to cremate him. He needed to update the power of attorney and a living will. Since his family refused to return phone calls, he wanted her to act on his behalf. His lawyer would help with the paperwork.

"Don't prolong my life. No machines or invasive treatments." He wheezed, "If any money's left, give it to the AIDS Foundation."

"Thy will be done," said Sam.

He faced Alana. "Can you ask Gretchen to attend the memorial service? She brought our family together. Could the two of you plan a ritual sendoff?"

Alana hugged him. "I'd love to."

Thomas then asked me to read a passage from *A Course in Miracles* at the service. "Something inspirational."

I agreed but felt guilty; the book remained unopened on my bookshelf.

His blue eyes shifted to Rosie. "I love the bagpipes. Do you think…?"

Before he could finish, she answered, "Me Bridgett would be happy to play. Any requests?"

"What the angels sing."

He led us in song. "*Amazing Grace! How sweet the sound, that saved a wretch like me. I once was lost, but now am found. Was blind, but now I see.*"

Thomas sang one more stanza. "*When this flesh and heart shall fail, and mortal life shall cease. I shall possess, within the veil, a life of joy and peace.*"

FILLING THE HOLE

WEDNESDAY, AUGUST 23

The prospect of losing my friend plunged me into a hole of loneliness. My dog wasn't enough to fill the emotional void. I wanted to fall in love again. Zarah Epstein could be my angel.

She entered the room with Candy. "How's the tooth?"

"No pain. But I had trouble keeping the hole clear of food."

She snapped on the gloves. "You won't have that problem anymore." She reached for a syringe.

"No needle! Gas would do just fine."

"It'll be sensitive when I'm finishing the root canal."

I frantically shook my head. "No needles."

The dentist glanced at her assistant. "What do you think?"

I nodded to the woman with bubble gum hair.

"He likes the nitrous," she smirked. Without waiting for a reply, she brought out the nasal mask and attached it to my nose.

Zarah turned on the gas, then pulled up a stool and directed the spotlight. "I'll finish the root canal, then prepare the tooth for a crown."

I sucked hard and soon fell into a dreamlike state. Not quite in my body, yet aware of my surroundings. A cast model of a set of teeth grinned from the shelf. I closed my eyes and revisited the erotic fantasy. I imagined the attractive redhead with bushy hair and slender hips lying next to me. It seemed like an eternity since I'd made love to a woman.

"Any pain?" she asked.

Only when I thought of the hole in my life. Oh for a gentle touch, a loving caress.

I opened my eyes and gazed at Zarah.

She caught my eye. "Alana mentioned you last night. Said you were the brother she never had. She's a sweetie. Talked me into volunteering at the Olympics. We had such fun at the orientation."

I closed my lids.

"We shared a dorm during our first year at Uni.," continued Zarah, filing away at the canals. "She wanted to heal others; I chose dentistry. Isn't she adorable?"

The nitrous made my body buzz and the loneliness drift away. Was Zarah trying to fix me up with Alana? And what did Alana actually say about me? Early on, she seemed interested. Maybe she still was. And what about Zarah? She wasn't wearing a ring. I took another deep breath and wallowed in hopeful bliss. I imagined the possibilities while she filled the tooth with plastic strands, then cemented it close. After prepping me for a crown, she told her assistant to reduce the nitrous.

"I'll mount the temporary crown."

Not ready to return to the real world, I said, "Still a bit of pain." I wanted another whiff.

She looked at me quizzically. "Don't want you leaving with a hangover."

Candy turned off the gas. I slowly re-entered my body, which felt like a lead suit. With her assistant around, it would be awkward asking for a date. And what about Alana? They were close friends. Unsure what to do, I said nothing. I left the dentist's office and headed for work resolved to make a move when I returned for my crown.

PERRY WATCH

MONDAY, AUGUST 28

Another postcard, this one depicting an Aboriginal bark painting of a stingray.

Hi Doctor P. Thanks for the letter. Made me happy. Got a job as a waitress. Still with me mum and sis. May come back to Sydney. Miss Perry. Keep writing. Bonnie.

My body tensed when I read the word "Perry." It had been over a month since he accosted me that Friday night in July, demanding Bonnie's whereabouts. I hadn't seen him lurking around but kept close watch whenever I entered or left the apartment. I contacted Sergeant Springle periodically, even though he was annoyed by my phone calls. For good measure, I placed the cricket bat near the front door in case of an emergency. I continued my search for a new place, but with the Olympics starting in a couple of weeks, the pickings were slim, especially in my price range.

I reread the postcard. If Bonnie was thinking about Perry, she must be lonely and desperate. It obviously wasn't working out with her mother. I typed a quick response.

Dear Bonnie,

Thanks for the card. Perry's not the answer. Returning to Sydney won't solve your problems. Please see a therapist. You need help. Forget Perry. He'll only make your life miserable. Hope you follow my advice. Keep climbing the mountain. All the best.

Doctor P.

TORCH CASUALTY

"That mine?"

"All yours," said Zarah. She removed a shiny gold crown from the plaster cast. "I'll make sure it fits, then glue it on."

I asked for nitrous oxide.

"No need for it. The temporary cap should pop off. I'll install the new crown in a jiffy."

"It'll be sensitive."

"The nerves in your tooth have been removed."

I wanted gas to give me the nerve to ask Zarah out on a date. I had decided against pursuing Alana. I didn't want to jeopardize our friendship or working relationship. So I planned to give it a go with Zarah. Since this was my final dental visit, I had to pop the question. A difficult task, with Candy hovering nearby.

Zarah dislodged the temporary cap. "There," she said cheerily. "Now for the crown." As she checked the fit, she asked, "Did you hear about Muswellbrook?"

With my mouth packed with cotton, I mumbled, "Wha appen?"

"A seventy-three-year-old man collapsed with a heart attack during his stretch with the torch. Dreadful."

She applied glue to the crown then fastened it on my tooth. She inserted a wooden depressor in my mouth. "Bite and hold."

I followed her instructions.

"They should've screened the torchbearers. Hope there's no more accidents."

She checked the crown and the bite then cleared off the excess glue. "Good as new," she proudly proclaimed.

When Candy cleared the tools from the silver tray, I made a move. "Could I have a word with you?" I asked Zarah. "In private."

"S-sure," she said uneasily. She removed the mask and gloves. "But I have another patient waiting." She nodded to her assistant.

When Candy left the room, I blurted, "Don't know if you'd be interested, but I thought, that is, if you're not busy, we might, you know, go out for a meal."

Her mouth dropped as if injected with Novocain.

"You don't have to give me an answer now, as it's all rather sudden, but I thought, you know, if you're free."

Her mouth returned to life. "Well...uh...thank you. But my heart...is set on someone else."

"Oh...sure. No worries. Just a thought. Anyway, best get back to work."

I couldn't get out of there fast enough. Even gas couldn't numb the humiliation.

↞↞

I returned to the factory and signed in. Frieda would surely report my late arrival to Carmen. I expected another memo reprimanding me.

I hurried to my office and shut the door.

Knock. Knock.

Crikey! Couldn't she let me unpack my briefcase? Prepared to face Carmen's fury, I opened the door.

"I just heard," shrieked Alana, bursting into the room.

My mouth dropped. Leave it to a dentist to flap the gums.

"I'd, uh, eventually tell you."

"You know about Sam?"

I shook my muddled head. "Sam?"

"She was fired!"

I ushered her into my room. "No way. Who told you?"

"Sam." Reeling from the shock, Alana continued. "Carmen wanted her out in two weeks. Sam asked for a month to terminate with clients and tidy up clinical matters. Carmen would only agree to add another week."

"The fucking bitch! The smell of blood will have the shark circling around us." I pulled the *Herald* from my briefcase. "I've been checking want ads."

Alana freaked out. "Don't abandon me, Peter. Not now."

"Be realistic. Carmen wouldn't have fired Sam without the Board's consent. She worked them over and racked up the votes. The election's all but over."

"Don't give up," she implored. "We can make a difference."

"Some fights aren't winnable."

Fire blazed in her eyes. "Australia's fighting for gold medals," she said defiantly. "I was abandoned as a child. I won't abandon my clients."

Alana defended her clients like a dingo protected its pups.

I tossed the *Herald* in the briefcase. "Alright. We can jump a few hurdles together, but we better be prepared. The shark's after our ass."

FATHER'S DAY

SUNDAY, SEPTEMBER 3

"Calm down, Ma. I'll be right over."

I slammed the phone down. He had to do it on Father's Day! My mother's vigilance had forced him to abstain from alcohol, but once he returned to work, he escaped her probing eyes. She couldn't count on my uncle, his consummate drinking buddy.

A twinge of guilt wracked my conscience. I had curtailed my regular visits and wondered if that contributed to his relapse. Without an AA group, he had completed four months of sobriety—an eternity for my father. I knew it would be touch and go, but now that he touched the bottle, he'd be on the go for vodka.

I had originally planned to drop by for a barbecue lunch, with my father off the sauce. Anticipating another dose of family drama, I brought Nesha along for moral support. We entered the house and heard the familiar clamor. Nesha barked and raced toward the kitchen.

My mother halted the argument and immediately enlisted my aid. She waved the dish towel. "Tell him, Piotr. No drinking."

"Just a little," he yelled back.

His idea of a little was most people's notion of a lot. The fact that he wasn't drunk was more the result of my mother pouncing like an angry bear. Sick of this craziness, I wanted out.

"I hate this!"

My mother recoiled as if slapped in the face. "You hate us?"

"I hate Pa's drinking and your guilt trips. I hate the fighting and being the referee. And I hate leave here feeling like shit."

"Don't talk like that," bellowed my father.

"You'll spoil his day," screeched his new ally.

Nesha barked, and I yelled, "Spoil the day! Don't you remember? You were fighting about Pa's drinking?"

"I only had two, maybe three."

My mother smacked him with the towel. "One is too many."

I angrily thrust a present into his folded arms. "Happy Father's Day."

The stubborn fool refused to accept it. I tossed it on the table. "You're welcome."

My mother grabbed the gift and shook it. "It's heavy." Switching to the role of peacemaker, she told me and my father, "*Usiąść.* Sit down."

Both of us reluctantly took our seats.

I sulked. "Hope you like the present."

He grunted, "I need nothing."

My mother pushed the box at him. "*Otwarte prezent.*"

He slowly ripped the paper, then stared at the gift.

Not an easy man to shop for, I got the idea when I was last in the garage. His spanners were old and worn so I figured he'd appreciate a new set. The salesman told me these wrenches were top of the line and any man would love them. Obviously, he didn't know my father.

"I have a set," he said gruffly. "Had them a long time."

"You've been with me a long time, too!"

He was back to his old bullshit. His flirtation with death and short-lived epiphany brought back the stark reality—once a drunk, always a drunk. He cared for vodka and his tools more than he cared for me.

My mother threw the towel at him. "Józef," she growled. "Piotr paid lots of money."

He slid the wrenches toward me. "Save the money for a house."

I seized the unopened box. "Next time, I'll buy you what you'd never turn down, a case of vodka."

My mother lurched for the tool set and scowled at my father. "See what you do? Tell him you want it."

He reached out feebly. "I'm joking. Give them here."

"I'm taking them back."

He placed his hands on the box. My mother joined him. The three of us fought in a tug of war.

"Let go," she yelled. "He wants it."

"*Tak*," he grunted.

I released the present. "Happy Father's Day."

HEARTACHE

TUESDAY, SEPTEMBER 5

Our nation's capital welcomed the torch at the Legislative Assembly in Canberra. Politicians glad-handed their way through the celebrations. With only a week and a half before the opening ceremony, thousands of overseas visitors flooded Sydney, choking arteries and train stations. The city was preparing for an extra million people and wanted to present its best game face to the world. Free one-way bus vouchers were offered to the homeless as long as they traveled far away from Sydney. Politicians didn't want derelicts littering the town, giving tourists a bad impression.

Ferries unloaded hordes of sightseers clamoring to snap pictures of our famous Manly Beach. My normal five-minute drive from work now took twenty minutes. It was bound to get worse. I arrived home exhausted after another tortuous day packed with clients and constant reminders from the red frowny face that outstanding forms were due. I had to restrain myself from smashing that bloody face.

I was walking Nesha when the mobile rang. Another family crisis. Alana sobbed as she told me Thomas had been hospitalized. Sam and Rosie were on their way.

The three musketeers stood near the bed when I arrived. Thomas slept, but his breathing was labored. His emaciated body reminded me of the poem, *Skeleton Man*. His left eyelid was almost closed from a Kaposi's sarcoma lesion. Other purple lesions marked his unshaven face.

"How's...?"

"Shhh," whispered Sam. "Let's all step outside."

She stood grim-faced in the small waiting room. "His T-cell count is zero."

"What should it be?" I asked, fearing the worst.

"A healthy count is between 800 and 1200."

"Christ! How long does he have?"

She shrugged her sagging shoulders. "He refused treatments, but accepted pain medication. He's hit hard with pneumonia and CMV—a nasty virus which attacks the retina. He's losing his vision. They'll stabilize him the best they can, then send him to hospice. It's only a matter of time."

Alana cried. "He's been like a father."

Compared with the ex-priest, my father lost hands down. Thomas had a kind and compassionate soul, whereas my father was mean-spirited. My gay friend taught me to open my heart, while my macho father forced me to shut it down. I returned to the bedside. Thomas wouldn't want me to shut him out, especially now.

PRODUCTIVITY EDICT # 23

THURSDAY, SEPTEMBER 7

The Olympic torch's ridiculous journey continued on the snowy slopes at Mt. Kosciusko. Instead of a downhill slalom, the torch should've been hung from Carmen's ass and lowered into an outhouse.

She had fulfilled her Strategic Plan to increase referrals. Actually, we were hit by an avalanche of bizarre clients who heard that Dr. Kukula passed out free meds like gumdrops. This posed a serious problem. Instead of reducing the waiting list, like Carmen promised the Board and community agencies, we compiled two burgeoning lists—one for counseling and another for those seeking medication. With the mounting pressure, she issued edict #23. Working two evenings was compulsory to meet the need for after-hour appointments. My two nights would be Wednesday and Thursday, effective next week. I told Carmen that I visited Thomas every Thursday evening. She waved off my request for another night, saying the schedule was non-negotiable. FB would not be deterred from her mission—self-aggrandizement.

She increased the productivity standard which, according to her memo, would maximize our effectiveness and efficiency. She mandated that we see thirty-seven clients a week, even though our work week was thirty-eight hours. Schedules were maxed past the limit. In the memorandum, Carmen dictated that client interviews should be no more than forty-five minutes. Therefore, if we saw 7.4 clients per day, we would meet her productivity standard of thirty-seven interviews per week, or 27.75 hours. According to her, that left ample time—10.25 hours for intake, paperwork, supervision, phone calls, and collaboration with other professionals. If we had to work extra hours to make up for "ineffective use of time management," that was our choice, not the agency's responsibility to compensate.

The software program usurped more than half of the 10.25 hours, as we had to record every phone contact and schedule change as well as complete the prescribed forms. If a problem occurred with any of Dr. Kukula's patients, which often happened, service providers had to screen the psychiatrist's calls and determine whether he needed to be contacted. If he did, that meant playing phone tag with him, the client, and the chemist so he could add, subtract, or multiply medications.

Frieda added to my woes by creating havoc with my schedule. Since the fanatical office manager could utilize the override feature, she filled every vacant space. This meant that my regular clients would lose their assigned slots, unless I booked them two months in advance. The backlog forced me to stay at least an hour after work each day. That made Nesha very unhappy. If I used my lunch hour to catch up on paperwork, I paid the price with a clean-up job in the apartment.

With Sam and Rosie about to leave, they couldn't take on new cases. Since they had to transfer some of their clients to Geraldine, Alana, and me, I had no choice but to play catch-up and use the diagnostic templates. With a minor tweak here and there, assessments for depressed clients basically looked the same.

"Call on line one," announced Frieda on the intercom.

"Take a message," I said. "I'm finishing an assessment."

"It's Mrs. Berkle again. She's complaining about the medication. Says it isn't working and there's side effects."

"Who's Mrs. Berkle?"

"You assessed her two weeks ago. She saw Dr. Kukula yesterday."

"That means she's only been on the meds a day."

"Line one."

Listening to another anxious client complain about Dr. Kukula's speedy interview and horrendous people skills put me further behind. Despite what I told Alana, who thankfully never mentioned the fiasco with Zarah, I searched for another job. It was either find a new position or sneak into Dr. Kukula's cabinet for free samples.

RARE NIGHT HOME

MONDAY, SEPTEMBER 11

Last night, I visited Saint Francis hospice where Thomas would spend his final days. He was doped up on pain medication and was asleep more often than not. When he woke, he slurred his speech, but there was no mistake about what he wanted. He asked that I contact his parents and sister. He wanted to see them before he died.

Acting on his request, I phoned his father. As soon as I told him about Thomas's condition, he bellowed that he no longer had a son. The family wanted no further contact. They were devout Christians and would not condone anyone cavorting with Satan. The sancti-monious prick exclaimed, "May the Lord have mercy on his soul."

He hung up before I could say, "Thank you for being a Christian!"

After that depressing call, I was bombarded with two more—one from my mother, the other from Stella. Both were frantic about my father's relapse. His drinking had escalated in spite of my moth-er's dogged efforts. My sister begged me to intervene. Her husband couldn't get tickets for the opening ceremony, so her plans to fly in and attend with the family were thwarted. She implored me to watch the ceremony with them on Friday and use the opportunity to persuade my father to get help. I had stopped blowing my whistle as referee and told her so. Our parents would have to fend for themselves in front of the telly. Besides, I had more important plans.

OPENING CEREMONY

FRIDAY, SEPTEMBER 15

Manly provided the backdrop for the final torch relay—the one hundredth day of the journey. Five hundred surf lifeguards escorted the Olympic flame down the beach. Adding to the bedlam, the International Jazz Festival was held nearby. I stayed clear of the Corso and the throng of people strolling the main promenade.

Carmen had originally planned to keep the counseling agency open. However, when she wrangled an invitation from the Lord Mayor to share the Manly stage, she closed the office. Her memo instructed us to use one of our personal days to support the agency, meaning Carmen, when she appeared on stage. With her, nothing came free.

Traveling the last leg of the journey, the torch ceremoniously boarded a ferry bound toward the Opera House at Circular Quay. Once there, it moved to the speedy River Cat which skimmed along the Parramatta River to its final destination at Olympic Park in Homebush Bay, once the site of a brick pit, dump, and slaughter-house. In the end, more than 10,000 runners carried the flame some 27,000 kilometers around Australia.

The snarling traffic gave proof to the news report that one-fourth of Sydney's residents would flee the city to avoid the congestion. Cars lined the roads bumper to bumper. By the time I arrived at the hospice, I was frazzled.

A phantom of his former self, Thomas stirred when I entered the room. His right eye blinked. "T-that you, mate?"

His face appeared as if it had gone ten rounds. His left eye was completely closed from a crusty brown lesion. His other eye was a faded blue lapis lazuli. His nose bore a deep purple hue and his once shiny, bald head was marked with Kaposi's sarcoma lesions. A push-button morphine drip rested on the bed next to his hand.

I gently tugged at his ear. "It's me."

He smiled weakly. "It's h-happening tonight."

I took his hand and held it as if it was fragile crystal. "I know. The opening ceremony's about to start. Are you up for it?"

He squeezed my hand.

"I'll move the telly closer to the bed."

I re-positioned the TV stand and turned it on. "Alana's one of the volunteers taking part in the pageant. She told me to look for her by the fire. Whatever that means. We'll keep an eye out for her."

I realized the folly of my words. His vision was almost gone. I quickly added, "I'll describe everything."

He spoke slowly. "T-thanks, mate. G-give the details."

I doubted he'd remain awake for the four-hour program. "No worries," I said. "I'll hang out with you till it's over."

He lifted his hand and waved me closer.

"Do you want water?"

He took a deep breath and murmured, "A-archangel Uriel. T-taking me h-home. To the light."

I glanced around nervously, half-expecting an angel to materialize. "No one's here... Thomas?"

Silence. Both eyelids were closed.

"No!" I half-yelled. I frantically pushed the call button, then pulled the covers away from his naked torso to check his breathing. The ribbed chest rose and fell ever so slightly.

A nurse appeared and quickly checked his vitals. She gently replaced the sheet over his body, then offered me a reassuring smile. "He's fallen asleep."

I eased my shaking body into the chair, overwhelmed by the near-death experience.

"Thank you for coming," said the kind nurse in a soft voice. "It means a lot to Thomas. He often mentions you, that you're his best mate."

"I could've been a better friend."

She tenderly patted my arm. "You're here. That's all that counts." She pointed to the TV. "I think Thomas would want you to see the opening ceremony. All Australia's watching. It'll settle your nerves."

Before she left, I glanced at her name plate—Muriel. Was she the angel Thomas was talking about?

"You're in good hands, mate. Let's follow her instructions." Though I was grieving the ending of his life, I know Thomas would've wanted me to embrace the magical moment that our country of nineteen million was hosting the Olympics.

I stroked his arm and gave a running commentary. Even though he wasn't conscious, I provided all the details, just as he requested. "They couldn't settle on one mascot, so they chose three to represent millennium, Sydney, and the Olympics. I'm not so fond of Millie the echidna or Syd the platypus, but my favorite's Olly the kookaburra. If any fights break out, he's sure to have a good laugh."

Like a newscaster, I reported that 120 riders guided their stock horses around the stadium. Each wore an oilslick, Driza-Bone coat, and carried an Olympic flag. When Julie Anthony sang our national anthem, "Advance Australia Fare," I choked. Thomas would've been proud.

I described the re-enactment of the dreamtime and the Awakening ritual where 1500 Aborigines from around the country called in ancestral spirits to sanctify the site. They smoldered eucalyptus leaves in large metal drums and smudged the stadium in a rite of purification. Smoke wafted among the 112,000 cheering spectators waving tiny lights. After the ritual, a cast of thousands paid tribute to

Australia's past and present with an array of colorful costumes, aerial acts, and stilt walkers. I spotted the fire eaters and moved closer to the screen. I watched intently as the cameras panned the area.

"There," I pointed excitedly. "Bloody hell. There's Alana."

Sure enough, she strolled in the parade of fire with 220 pyromaniacs igniting the crowd with a sizzling performance. She was one of the fire breathers who sipped from bottles and spewed flammable liquid towards raised torches, sending flashes of light into the starry night. Then I caught a glimpse of Zarah dancing near Alana. Instead of spitting fire, she twirled two chains, one in each hand, with fireballs blazing at the ends.

I chuckled. "Who would've thought."

Thomas stirred and opened his good eye. He smiled at me and pressed the morphine pump. His eyelid closed, and he returned to the dreamtime. Even though he was in another world, I regaled him with a whimsical segment portraying white settlers arriving on a quirky bicycle ship. The opening ceremony was a celebration of our country's relationship with the sea, outback, Aborigines, and European settlers, and required 12,000 performers. At one point, 2,250 of them, many representing different cultures to highlight our ethnic diversity, formed a human map of Australia.

The grand finale was the Parade of Nations where 10,651 athletes from 200 countries circled the arena in a rare celebration of togetherness. The four-hour showcase climaxed with six Australian sports legends—all women—taking turns carrying the torch around the stadium to represent 100 years of women's participation at the Olympics. The final torchbearer was Cathy Freeman, the slim Aboriginal sprinter who would represent Australia in the 400-meter race. In dramatic fashion, she stepped through a waterfall onto a pool, as if she was walking on water. She then lit a ring of fire that encircled her. The blazing ring dramatically lifted past Cathy up an incline to the top of the stadium where it rested as the Olympic flame.

It seemed fitting that Cathy ignited the fire. After their culture was nearly eradicated by white settlers, Aborigines were getting recognition. Probably too little, too late. But for this special night, Cathy inspired the crowd to back her a hundred percent.

The Olympic flame sent fiery plumes into the night, signaling the world that first-class athletes would soon compete in 300 events. I was convinced that if ever a person deserved a medal, it was Thomas. Although he was losing the battle with life, his long distance run served as an inspiration. He could stand head and shoulders above anyone on the platform, for he had earned gold.

Before I left the hospice that evening, I sat next to him in silence, holding his hand. "Do you see any angels?"

No sooner had I asked when I spotted a sparkle of light in the corner of the room. I turned toward the source, but it disappeared. My eyes must've played tricks. It had been a long, emotional night. There was little doubt, however, that Thomas would soon join his angels.

HOME AT LAST

SUNDAY, SEPTEMBER 17

Sam phoned from the hospice. Thomas died quietly in his sleep. The news didn't shock me, but the finality that he'd no longer be here left me with a sickening thud in my heart. Thomas was gone, but he had returned home.

BEREAVED

Behind her desk, Carmen puffed her chest. "According to SPM, bereavement absences are only allowed in the case of blood relatives. Since your friend is not related, your request to leave work for the memorial service is denied."

Before Sam and Alana could speak, I attacked. "SPM didn't say you could shut down the agency on Friday, yet you did."

Carmen angrily opened a drawer and removed the Staff Procedural Manual. She turned to page 23 and quoted paragraph 4: "The executive director has authority to make provisions for special occasions and, as appropriate, will duly inform the staff."

She snapped the book shut. "The traffic congestion from all the festivities would've made it difficult for clients to keep appointments. I chose the prudent course and closed the agency."

"In order to share the stage with the bigwigs."

Carmen slammed the manual on her desk. "That'll be enough, Peter. You're already skating the edge with your alleged sick days."

"I needed a root canal."

"Or so you say."

I pointed to the gold crown in my mouth. "See?"

Alana grabbed an arm and whispered, "Take it easy."

Sam stepped toward the desk. "My last day is Friday. I'm attending Thursday's services whether or not you approve."

"Since Rosie quit, three service providers cannot be out of the office!"

Sam held her composure. "The memorial starts at eleven and is followed by lunch. Since Alana and Peter are working Thursday evening..."

"As well as Wednesday night," I sniped.

"...they're not scheduled to start till one. They'll miss an hour, but can make this up by skipping the evening meal. Thomas wasn't blood, but he was family and dearly loved."

"Something you wouldn't know," I blurted.

Carmen rose abruptly, knocking her chair to the floor. "I won't tolerate insolence," she blustered. "Request denied." She pointed toward the door. "Now get out."

The three of us stomped out of her lair and into Sam's office. I kicked the door shut.

"The heartless bitch."

"Give her more of that," said Sam, "and you'll be unemployed."

"I don't care if she fires me."

"Right now she needs therapists more than empty offices. If she lost more staff and her precious statistics, she'd lose face with the Board. In the meantime, I suggest you search for other jobs."

Alana sniffled, "What about my clients?"

Sam wrapped a consoling arm around her. "The agency we loved has come to an end." Tears dribbled down Sam's pitted face. "We've lost the battle, but we can give Thomas a proper send-off."

LAST RITE. THURSDAY

SEPTEMBER 21

While Australia cheered one of our swimming heroes—the seventeen-year-old "Thorpedo" Ian Thorpe for winning three gold and a silver—a band of mourners gathered in a chapel to grieve the loss of another champion. Thomas's ashes rested in an urn on a table adorned with Australian bush flowers—orange banksias, yellow kangaroo paws, and red bottlebrushes. Next to the urn sat his smiling portrait, a lit candle, and a tall Waratah in a crystal vase. According to Sam, the Aboriginal word for the crimson flower meant "seen from afar." A fitting symbol for the gentle giant.

Gretchen joined The Family That Cares to pay her respects. Leaning on her cane, she stood teary-eyed next to Alana and held her hand. The rest of us huddled around the table.

As expected, none of Thomas's family appeared. Despite the father's orders to never contact him, I reached out. When he raved about AIDS being the work of the devil, I hung up on the self-righteous bastard. His family was so blinded by religious prejudice, they couldn't see Thomas as a loving, compassionate man who lived his truth.

Honoring his request, Alana and Gretchen organized a ritual. The wizened psychologist invited everyone to share their memories. Some gave testament to his inspiration and encouraging words. Others offered examples of his many random acts of kindness. All who attended had been touched by his gentle spirit.

With tears streaming down her wrinkled cheeks, Gretchen addressed the group. "When dear Thomas came to my workshop, I knew he would find his true self. The courageous soul swam against a riptide. He endured hardship but found freedom in the divine ocean. My dear Thomas, we grieve your loss but celebrate your return to your Creator. Welcome home."

Gretchen nodded for Alana to give everyone a white candle.

"Every death offers a lesson; every lesson illuminates life. Let his light blaze in our hearts." She lit her candle from the one next to the urn and asked us to follow suit.

When the flickering flames surrounded the urn, I read a passage from *A Course in Miracles* that said we were not bodies, but free. I glanced at the urn and wiped my eyes. I told the group, "Thomas is free at last."

Rosie's daughter played "Amazing Grace" on bagpipes. We passed around the tissues and solemnly sang, "Through many dangers, toils and snares, I have already come; 'Tis grace hath brought me safe thus far, and grace will lead me home."

ANOTHER FAREWELL

FRIDAY, SEPTEMBER 22

Like two errant school children facing the principal, Alana and I stood in front of Carmen's desk. She gripped her padded leather chair and berated us.

"You disobeyed my orders. You came in late yesterday." She smacked her desk. "Even after my explicit instructions."

"We paid our last respects," said Alana calmly.

"And what about your jobs?" she scolded.

I pleaded our case. "We skipped dinner and made up for the lost time."

My fellow musketeer nodded. "We each had seven interviews."

Carmen scribbled red ink on a sheet of paper. "Your target is 7.4 clients a day. We're down two positions. Statistics have fallen. I'm attaching a letter to your file noting your insubordination. It will follow you wherever you go. Any further acts of defiance will be duly recorded. Now that Samantha and Rosie aren't here, I can proceed with my strategic plan, without any interference. I expect full compliance. Do I make myself clear?"

Without waiting for a response, she dismissed us with her familiar wave of the backhand. "Off you go."

I made it through the rest of the day without another confrontation. Not surprisingly, Carmen was unavailable for Sam's informal send-off during afternoon tea. Frieda and Geraldine showed up for a piece of cake, offered a quick goodbye, then darted back to work.

The proper farewell took place over dinner at Sam's house in Palm Beach. Rosie joined us for a nostalgic reunion. She cracked open a bottle of Glenfiddich and poured us all a Scotch. No one refused.

Rosie raised her glass and, in her lilting brogue, gave a rendition of the *Farewell Song to the Banks of Ayr* by Robert Burns.

The gloomy night is gath'ring fast,
Loud roars the wild, inconstant blast,
Yon murky cloud is foul with rain,
I see it driving o'er the plain...

The brassy redhead sang with rousing passion and didn't touch a drop of whiskey until she concluded the last stanza.

Farewell, my friends! Farewell, my foes!
My peace with these, my love with those:
The bursting tears my heart declare,
Farewell, the bonnie banks of Ayr!

She clinked our glasses, then drained hers. She reached for the Glenfiddich. "Robbie wrote it as his farewell to Scotland. Seemed fittin' for tonight."

"Too many goodbyes," I said wistfully. "Our family's breaking up."

Rosie raised her glass. "In death we mourn."

"We may have lost our friend and the agency," grieved Sam, "but we don't have to stop caring for one another."

Alana nodded. "Thomas would want us to remain strong."

"Aye," said Rosie before draining the Scotch.

When she reached for the bottle, Sam grabbed her arm. "Let's have something to eat before you get sozzled."

Rosie grudgingly consented and followed us to the kitchen. We filled our plates with roast chicken and trimmings, then returned to the living room where we ate and shared from the heart. Rosie was ever so grateful that she found another job as a marriage counselor. She would start in a couple of weeks. But the major news was that Brodie asked her and the kids to move in with him.

Like a teenager, she giggled, "We've only been seein' each other five months, but his bonnie mind was made up. Bridgett and Kieran love him to death. He's the father they never had."

Rosie patted her chest and sighed, "My Celtic soul mate."

"You inspire me," said Sam. "Now that my divorce is official, I'm a free woman."

We congratulated her on ending her second marriage. Hopefully, the third one would be the charm.

She turned to Alana. "I saw sparks flying at the opening ceremony."

"The fire breathing was unbelievable," I said. "Can't believe you kept it a secret."

"I was busting to tell."

"Is that the only thing?" asked Sam coyly.

Alana's mouth widened into a smile that revealed whitened teeth.

"What have you done to your choppers?" I asked.

Embarrassed by the attention, she closed her mouth.

"Come on. Let's see."

Alana showed her new teeth. "Zarah fixed them," she beamed. "Capped the chipped tooth and used a whitener. Said I should show them off. What do you think?"

I raised my hand as if warding off a brilliant glare. "They're blinding."

She smacked my arm.

"They look beautiful," praised Sam and, with a mischievous twinkle, asked, "Anything else?"

Alana's dark skin flushed a deep rose. "I, uh, wanted to be sure before telling you."

"Tell us what?" I asked.

"Well...it's Zarah." Her blush turned a deeper hue. "I've never been with a woman before. I wanted to be sure."

"And?" asked Rosie, cutting to the chase.

"I've never felt so wanted and loved."

She reached for my hand. "You played a part in this, Peter."

"Me?"

"Zarah told me about your last visit."

"Yeah, well...it was the gas."

She flashed her whitened teeth. "Zarah realized she didn't want to go out with anyone, because her heart was set on me. I had been closed to a relationship but, after spending time with her, practicing for the parade of fire, I opened my heart. I'm so happy she's in my life. We see each other practically every night."

Sam and Rosie rushed in for a hug. "We're happy for you," they gushed.

I was too, well, sort of. Alana lost her mother in childbirth and obviously craved the love of a woman. I never imagined she'd find that love with Zarah.

Alana pulled me into a group hug. "You'll find someone, Peter."

I mumbled, "Doubt it."

Alana's love life and my lack of one made me feel the weight of crushing cinder blocks on my shoulders.

"What's going on?" asked Sam.

Thomas would've wanted me to open up so I dumped the lot. I told them about my father's downward spiral toward the shadow of death and the frantic calls from my mother; about the painful losses of Thomas and Celeste, and Carmen's reign of terror; about living in fear of my neighbors and the reappearance of Perry; and about the despair over locating a rental during Olympic mania.

My surrogate family comforted me with understanding, love, and acceptance. Their healing balm eased some of the suffering. However, with Sam and Rosie no longer at the agency, I knew tougher times lay ahead. Rather than dwell on those problems, I asked that we move on and present the gifts.

Alana obliged. She retrieved two wrapped packages. "Peter and I bought these at the Queen Victoria Building. We wanted something to portray your energy at the agency."

She handed Sam the first package. "You always gave from the heart."

The Earth Mother delicately unwrapped the present as if the paper itself was made of gold. She lifted a hand-carved, dark-pink wooden bowl shaped in a heart.

"Made from Tasmanian rose myrtle," said Alana excitedly.

Overwhelmed with emotion, Sam hugged Alana and me, and Rosie for good measure.

The other present went to the Celtic woman. "You were always prepared to battle with your broadsword," I said, offering her the package.

Rosie ripped through the wrapping paper and found a polished, orange-brown bowl that resembled a shield with jagged edges.

"That was carved from a yellow mallee burl."

Rosie joined Sam in tears and shared more hugs. Both women would be sorely missed at work.

We chatted late into the night and sipped more Scotch, though Rosie did most of the consuming. Sam suggested we bunk over, but we all wanted our own beds. I thought of Rosie with Brodie and Alana with Zarah. Nesha would keep me company next to the bed.

Before we departed, Rosie had us singing the familiar words by Robert Burns:

Should auld acquaintance be forgot,
And never brought to mind?
Should auld acquaintance be forgot,
And auld lang syne?

BUSTER

SUNDAY, SEPTEMBER 24

A wet nose nuzzled my face. I shoved Nesha away and turned over. The living room couch was far from comfortable, but the soundproofing was marginally better. The dissonant music next door had reached bone-rattling decibels at one in the morning. With my bedroom wall pulsating like a vibrator, I had no choice but to find a quieter space. I was in no mood for another encounter with my vampire neighbors who raged until daylight, when they returned to their caskets. I tried to catch up on sleep, but Nesha had other plans. He pounced on me with the shaggy duck in his mouth. I grabbed the toy and stuffed it behind the couch, then wrapped the pillow around my ears to muffle his incessant barking.

He merely wanted some attention. I had been neglecting him, especially since the increasing work hours prevented me from dashing home for lunch and taking him for a walk. I didn't expect him to hold out until I returned home so I began placing newspapers on the wood floor near the balcony for any deposits. He truly deserved better, yet he still loved me.

The clatter on the balcony caught both our attention. Buster returned for another handout. Nesha no longer barked at the bird, so I gathered the two had become friends. Resigned that further sleep was unattainable, I lumbered from the couch and gave Nesha a handful of bacon-cheese dog biscuits. I then placed a dollop of raw hamburger on a plate and eased it onto the balcony. When I backed away, Buster swooped from the railing onto the cement floor and gobbled the meal. He cocked his head, as if asking for seconds.

"Sorry, Buster. Kitchen's closed."

Crikey! I was talking to a bird as if it was part of the family. The lack of sleep and the ongoing stress was making me cuckoo.

FREEMAN'S GOLD

MONDAY, SEPTEMBER 25

Geraldine strolled into the staff room and hummed a cheery note. I assumed Australia won more gold, but discovered later that she had become our new clinical director. While I welcomed her relocation to Sam's office, which meant an end to her role plays next door, I would've preferred the noise over Geraldine's newfound power.

I ploughed through a horrid day of intake, adding clients to the five-page waiting list. Being down two therapists meant the brunt of the workload fell to Alana and me. I spent two hours after work completing the paperwork in order to avoid more visits from Mr. Frowny Face.

After I took Nesha out for a walk, I collapsed on the couch. When I heard the sound of heavy metal next door, I almost cried. Unable to face the music, I leashed Nesha and headed for the promenade.

Outside the Steyne Hotel, an excited crowd littered the pavement.

"She has to win," exclaimed one bloke.

"She can't let us down," roared another.

I had become so absorbed in my problems that I often forgot about the Olympics. Ian Thorpe had won his fifth swimming medal two days ago, but I was oblivious to the upcoming event stirring the masses.

A petite woman on rollerblades stopped to pet Nesha as I tied his leash to a nearby pole. He licked the woman's hand.

"Cute dog."

"He's a charmer."

I handed Nesha some dried beef liver. "Stay," I said. "I'll be right back."

He scarfed down the treat, then nuzzled against the woman. While she petted him, I scooted inside the Steyne for a quick beer. The packed pub overflowed with customers swigging schooners. The announcer on the jumbo TV could barely be heard over the deafening noise. When a picture of Cathy Freeman flashed on the screen, the crowd roared. She was about to run the 400-meter race. If she won, she'd become the first Aborigine to take an individual Olympic gold medal.

I looked out the window. Nesha was still lapping up the attention. I pushed my way to the bar and ordered a beer. With drink in hand, I squeezed through a rowdy group and inadvertently knocked someone's arm. A glass of beer crashed to the floor.

A bloke built like a barrel keg turned around. "Who the fuckin' hell...?"

I stared at Ben Franklin's quote on the t-shirt: *Beer is the proof that God loves us and wants us to be happy.* There was no doubt about the owner.

"Cedric?"

He rubbed a ham-like hand over his stubbly hair, as if trying to place me. Then his scowl turned into a grin. "It's you, isn't it?"

"Yeah, Dr. Pinowski."

"You owe me a schooner."

I offered him mine. "I hardly touched it."

He pushed it away, spilling half on the floor. "Need a fresh one. And be quick about it. The little lady's gettin' ready."

Since this wasn't my office, I wasn't about to argue with him and his bulging muscles. I fought my way through the crowd and waved a twenty-dollar note at the harried bartender. Once served, I returned to Cedric with two fresh drinks. The crowd cheered at the screen.

"Thrash 'em, Cathy," yelled Cedric. He grabbed the schooner and guzzled it half empty.

"Go Aussie," screamed someone.

I moved near the window and tapped the glass. Nesha barked at me, then solicited a passing girl. Inside the pub, a hush fell. On the jumbo TV, Cathy was setting herself on the track. By now, most of Australia knew that her grandmother was another victim of the Stolen Generation. Cathy offered us an opportunity at redemption from the past sin of stealing mixed-race children from their parents. Rather than castigate her, like we might have done in the past, we wanted to celebrate victory.

Bang! The race began. As Cathy sprinted the 400 meters, I joined the cheering crowd in willing her across the finish line. It took 49.11 seconds for her to win gold!

The place erupted. Glasses clinked, hands clapped, and people hugged. Cedric jumped up and down as if he had won the race himself. I high-fived my ex-client.

The stout man clambered onto a table. "My shout," he announced. "Drinks for everyone."

The pub erupted into another round of cheers.

We danced and clapped as Cathy jogged around the track carrying two flags. The Aboriginal colors—red symbolizing earth, yellow for the sun, and black for the people—fluttered alongside the red, white, and blue of the Union Jack. While the flags represented unity, Kathy's gold restored a measure of pride to a forgotten race. Australia was proud.

BONNIE'S CRISIS

WEDNESDAY, SEPTEMBER 27

"Been waitin' on the phone a long time."

"You should've left a message. I would've called back."

Bonnie's voice shook. "It's important, Doctor P."

"Why? What's happened?"

"Perry found out I was with me mum. He knew where she lived and came ta get me."

"He was in Queensland?!"

"Hitched a ride. Made a big ruckus. Tole me I had ta go back with him. I said no."

"Good for you, Bonnie."

"Not good, Doctor P. He tole me if I didn't come, he'd do bad things ta ya."

My stomach reeled as if sucker punched. I last saw him two months ago and was beginning to think he was out of my life.

Bonnie whimpered, "Perry tole me it was your fault I moved. Said he'd hurt ya."

I gripped the phone. "Is he still there?"

"Dunno. Me mum and sis tossed him out. Tole him ta never come back. He was real mad. Tole me he'd get me boyfriend. I'm scared, Doctor P."

So was I.

"Let's calm down," I said, trying not to panic. "Perry's an addict and a con artist. He's intimidating you. We can't give into his threats." My stomach lurched. "I'll alert the police."

"Be careful, Doctor P. I don't want anything bad ta happen."

"Me neither."

"I'm glad I called. I miss our talks."

"What about your family?"

"I'm gettin' ta know sis and me mum. They're glad I'm back." She paused a moment, then spoke, "Without a man, it's lonely."

"When you're lonely or scared, think of Cathy Freeman. Did you watch her win the gold medal?"

Her voice lifted. "Who didn't?"

"Cathy overcame incredible odds. Her grandmother was taken from her tribe, just like your mother. Yet, Cathy won gold. She told a reporter that she ran her little black butt off. You may not win a medal, Bonnie, but you're now running your life. If Cathy was in your situation, lonely and scared, what would she do?"

"Win."

"She fought hard and completed the race. You can too. Get a picture of her with the medal and write the words, 'I can do it!' Let her inspire you. Put the picture in a place where you'll continually see it. Can you do that?"

She replied meekly, "I'll try."

"We *can* succeed," I said. "But we have to believe. Cathy Freeman did."

"It's not that easy."

"Believe me, I know. I may not be at the agency much longer."

Bonnie's voice turned frantic. "W-where are ya going?"

"Can't get into that now. Have another client waiting. We must succeed, Bonnie. Find the picture and write the words."

I asked her to join me in repeating the phrase in a loud voice, *"I CAN DO IT!"*

When I hung up the phone, I realized that with a druggie on my tail I had to relocate fast. Could I do it?

PARANOIA

FRIDAY, SEPTEMBER 29

*Running. Stumbling. I'm tackled to the ground. Perry stabs
my neck. The syringe finds a vein. He cackles, "You're one of us."*

Since Bonnie's phone call, I became paranoid that Perry was lurking
nearby. I phoned Sergeant Springle about the threat. He offered little
sympathy. He said Perry probably stayed in Queensland where the
weather was warm and the drugs more plentiful.

My nightmares told me otherwise. Sudden noises startled me
into defense mode, preparing for an attack by a crazed druggie. Even
Buster's visits for a handout unnerved me. To avoid the racket on the
balcony, I stopped putting out food. I was spiraling out of control,
just like my father.

CLOSING CEREMONY

SUNDAY, OCTOBER 1

Instead of excusing myself from watching the closing ceremony with my parents, I welcomed the opportunity to get away from the haunting figures of Perry and his druggie friends. I bolted the door on a late afternoon and hurried to the car with my two prized possessions—my laptop and my dog.

When I parked in the driveway, my mother rushed out of the house in hysterics. My father had slipped on the pavement and bruised his elbow and knee. Although he hadn't hit his head, my mother begged him to go to the hospital. The cantankerous fool refused. I didn't have to ask if he was drinking.

I found my father snoozing in front of the telly. My mother motioned me toward the kitchen and swore, "*Psiakrew*. It's Janek's fault. He took Pa out to celebrate our Olympic medals."

She turned on the stove to heat a pot of oxtail soup, then wiped the table with a dish towel. "If Janek takes him drinking again, he'll never come into my house."

I knew the drill. She'd call Adele later and threaten to sever ties. My uncle would undoubtedly get blistered by his wife. After the dust settled, he and my father would return to their drinking ways.

"You've done that before," I said.

She hit the table with the towel. "If Pa hit his head, he'd be back in hospital. Maybe worse."

"He won't listen."

She lowered her burdened body into a chair. "Then I'll leave."

The lines of worry etched on her face had taken a toll. She had made plenty of threats in the past. If she stood firm, she may not stop my father from drinking but she might find peace—something she rarely found. She told me that if my father kept drinking, she would take Stella's offer and live with her family for awhile. I listened to her resolve but recognized the reality—breaking the chain of enabling was as difficult as giving up the booze.

After the meal, my mother and I joined my sleeping father in the living room for the closing ceremony. I thought of Thomas. He would've enjoyed the fact that Aussies scored fourth in the medal tally behind Russia and China. As expected, the Yanks won the most, hauling in ninety-seven. But our sixteen gold, twenty-five silver, and seventeen bronze medals totaled fifty-eight. Not bad for a nation of nineteen million.

As customary, the ceremony concluded with the extinguishing of the flame. The hoopla would begin anew at the next Olympics with the re-lighting of the torch. While it symbolized the quest for perfection and victory, I felt none of that. The fire in my belly had flickered out.

MORE EDICTS

TUESDAY, OCTOBER 3

Alana and I waited empty handed for Geraldine, who was late as usual. The tradition of eating food during supervision had fallen by the wayside.

Wearing a red blazer, she dashed into the room and dumped a stack of files on the table. "Here are the new cases," said Geraldine. "We have our hands full."

Her grating nasal monotone sent shivers up my spine, as if nails scratched a blackboard. I wanted to stuff a sock in her mouth. Instead, I chose to annoy her.

"Nice hairdo," I smirked. Her jet black hair cut in an angular shape with sharp edges was modeled after Carmen.

She ignored my comment and pointed to the five pages. "We must whittle down the waiting list. Priority goes to those needing medication."

"Any word about the new workers?"

She arched her thick eyebrows. "We're waiting for an acceptance letter. A new therapist should start in three weeks."

"That's a month without replacements," I said. "We can't manage."

"Who is she?" asked Alana.

"Can't say until we have confirmation."

Which means it was one of her friends.

"The list," she said tersely. "Some people have been waiting four months."

"So much for managed care."

"Listen, Peter," she glared. "If you can't accept the fact that I'm directing the clinical program, see Carmen. Get with the program or else—"

"Leave? Is that what you want? So you can hire another friend?"

Her face contorted into an ugly stew. "I've had it with you," she yapped, then stormed out.

I smiled victoriously at Alana. "That was easy."

Or so it seemed. A few minutes later, she returned with reinforcements.

Wearing a matching a crimson red power jacket, Carmen stormed in with her younger clone.

"Even if we're short staffed, I won't tolerate insubordination," scowled Carmen. "Need I say more?"

"We're overworked and understaffed," I said. "And she wants us to take on more cases."

Carmen patted Geraldine's shoulder. "I have complete confidence in the clinical director."

Geraldine didn't hide her shit-eating grin. "While you're here," she groveled, "can you tell us about your latest memo?"

Carmen happily obliged. She took a seat, indicating it was a long memo.

"I'm about to hire two service providers," she began. "That will ease some of the backlog. Because of the overwhelming success of my program, as indicated by the flood of new cases, I must increase your number of interviews per week to forty-two. We're behind on my statistical projections. Forty-two appointments at forty-five minutes each comes to 31.5 hours."

I gagged. "That leaves 6.5 hours for intake, supervision, phone calls, computer entries, and follow-ups on the doctor's clients." Not to mention, getting rid of frowny faces.

"We're cutting back on supervision," said Geraldine. "I told Carmen we could manage with an hour a month."

Alana bared her whitened teeth. "We need more than that. Especially with all the cases."

Carmen brushed her blazer. "If you have a problem, see the clinical director." She nodded toward her clone and praised the wardrobe. "Nice color."

"But..."

She held up her policeman's hand in front of my face. "I expect you to behave as professionals. Thus far, I've agreed to forty-five minutes per session. However, Dr. Kukula assures me that his initial assessments take less than thirty minutes. His follow-ups rarely exceed five minutes. If he can work that efficiently, you can as well. Shortening interviews frees time for more clients and increased productivity."

The pompous dictator went on to say that if we didn't reduce the waiting list, she'd decrease the number of sessions allocated per patient to eight. We had to work judiciously and complete all forms in a timely fashion. And if we received three red alerts from PED, we'd receive more disciplinary letters.

With a condescending smile, Carmen continued. "I daresay those letters would serve as a warning to any future employer."

My bulging personnel file would doom me to life in a factory. If I refused to cooperate, she would make sure I never worked for anyone else. I protested no further.

"Now that we have an understanding, I have another request. Until new staff arrive, you'll have to work an extra night to accommodate evening appointments. Frieda, being the good trouper, agreed to work overtime. It's refreshing to know some workers value team effort."

Carmen rose and patted her lackey's head. "Our Geraldine has fully embraced the strategic plan. She has transitioned many of her patients to the medication groups, thus freeing up her clinical hours to service the waiting list. She epitomizes our success. Follow her lead."

I recoiled at the prospect. I entertained the idea of consulting a labor attorney, but quickly dismissed the thought. As a lawyer, Carmen would be a formidable foe. The net result would be a slew of negative letters in the Pinowski folder. My only recourse was to buckle down, send out more resumes, and pray for another job.

SUPPLY AND DEMAND

I sauntered into Dr. Kukula's office, sparsely furnished with desk, chair, and locked metal cabinet. He didn't need much space since he only worked twice a week to dispense his advice—follow the drill and swallow the pill. I had to discuss his client, Mrs. Berkle, who phoned repeatedly with complaints about side effects. While her meds were supposed to reduce the symptoms of depression, they added other ones—nausea, headaches, and an upset stomach—that made her more despondent.

The protocol for consulting with the psychiatrist required therapists to book a five-minute slot, just like a client. I found him busy writing scripts, which he often completed well in advance of his sessions. You'd think he'd wait until *after* he saw the clients.

I handed him the file and updated him about Mrs. Berkle, who last saw him a month ago. "She wants a different medication."

He flicked through the notes. "The meds should work. Needs more time."

"She's been calling every week with new symptoms."

"When will I see her again?"

"Next week."

"I'll talk with her then."

For five minutes, if she was lucky.

Dr. Kukula checked his watch, then glanced furtively around the room. "Have you ever thought of real estate?"

"Come again?"

His eyes shifted to the file cabinet then back to his prescription pad. "I own a small parcel of land. Down the south coast. Interested in buying it?"

Clearly, we were through talking about Mrs. Berkle.

"I don't have money to invest."

He ran a hand over his slick black hair and spoke like a machine gun. "I can arrange a loan with interest. The land's in Nowra. If you buy it, it's almost a gift. The price will skyrocket later this year."

"Then why are you selling?" I asked, wondering if he used any of the five-minute slots to sell real estate to patients.

He moved his chair closer, as if letting me in on a secret. "I own several rental properties around here. Want to purchase another. Need to unload the smaller parcels. Great deal, Pissowski."

"It's Pinowski," I corrected him. "And where do you own buildings?"

"Around and about," he said evasively.

"Any near here? I may be interested in moving."

That caught his interest, for he almost looked me in the eye. "A real estate manager handles that. But I may have an opening. Downstairs apartment. Overlooks the ocean. The tenant's senile. Has OCD. Never satisfied. Constantly calls for repairs. Every call costs money. Once she's evicted, I'll put in a word to the manager."

"Where exactly is the apartment?" I asked, thinking of my downstairs neighbor, Mrs. Faughlin.

"Keep it to yourself," he whispered. "On Steyne Street. Right across the beach. Location, location, location."

Crikey! My bloody landlord.

"Dr. Kukula, the meds group needs you in the conference room," announced Frieda on the intercom.

"Have to dash." He stopped at the door. "Think about that land, Pissowski. It's cheap. Financing's no problem."

Without waiting for a reply, he darted down the hallway.

The psychiatrist left me speechless, probably like the rest of his clients. I grabbed the file, then gaped at the open cabinet chock full of starter kits for depression, anxiety, psychosis, and a host of other symptoms. It'd be dead easy to nab some anti-anxiety pills from the boxes stashed in neat files. Wouldn't need much. A low dose would help me battle the jitters and cope with the madness of the agency.

"What are you doing here?" came the accusing voice.

"Finished a consult with the doctor," I said, quickly jotting on my notepad. "Wanted to write his recommendation. He's with the meds group."

"I know that," snapped Frieda. "He forgot his prescriptions." She spotted the open cabinet and immediately counted the boxes with Germanic precision.

She could use a few samples for her compulsive traits.

Like a prison warden, she removed a key from her pocket and locked the metal door. She grabbed the prescriptions off the desk and said officiously, "Your next client's here."

I left the office, wondering about drugs and land deals. If Dr. Kukula created the demand for medication, the pharmaceutical companies would supply him with ample compensation to land more deals.

PIED PIPER

SATURDAY, OCTOBER 7

The internal hum of anxiety pulsated at a high pitch. Tossing in bed,
I couldn't fall asleep. I regretted the missed opportunity to snatch
pills. They would have eased the mental turmoil.

The dream and its visual images replayed in slow motion. What
did it mean? Detach and be free? Leave the rat race? I would've preferred a beatific vision with Thomas bestowing peace and serenity.
Or better yet, a message with concrete advice.

Alana and I met for fish and chips at an outdoor café. Now that she
had a lover and new teeth, I felt like the leftovers on my plate. I tossed
a few chips at the gulls. They squawked and pecked at each other for
the scraps. Nesha barked; they scattered.

Alana hardly touched her food. She fumbled with her fork and,
without looking at me, said, "I've got bad news."

I placed my hands over my ears. "Don't want to hear it."

"Don't hate me, Peter."

"Then don't tell me."

"I've found a job."

My arms collapsed like severed branches. "And then there was one."

She pleaded for me to understand. "Zarah encouraged me. Said staying wasn't healthy. You know how awful it is."

"What about me? You told me we'd stick it out together."

She slumped in the chair. "Don't be mad."

"Have you told Carmen?"

"I will on Monday. I wanted to tell you first."

Alana was abandoning me like the other musketeers. I angrily tossed the remaining chips to the pavement. A flutter of wings swooped to the ground.

"I'm stuck with the two bitches. Thanks."

She wiped her eyes. "I'm sorry. I've let you down."

I hated when women blubbered. Was it a strategy to stop men from being pissed off?

"Christ, Alana. I'm left alone on a sinking ship. Where are you going?"

She sniffled, "Department of Immigration. Took a position to help migrants resettle."

"Should suit you," I said coldly.

"But I thought of you," she added. She reached into her backpack and removed a crumpled section of the *Herald*. "There's a few jobs here."

I wanted to stay angry at my Filipina friend, but her pained expression and desire to help made that impossible. I grabbed the paper. "Hope someone will hire me."

"You'll find something," she said encouragingly.

Her white teeth gleamed in the sun. Easy for her to say. She found a job, plus a lover who made her smile.

CASUALTY OF MPC

I ambled to the sign-in sheet and was about to register my one o'clock start when a distressed woman bolted past me.

Geraldine rushed into the corridor. "Stop," she yelled.

I looked around.

"YOU!" she shrieked at me. "Stop Nola!"

She shouted "Code red" to Frieda, who flew into action, phoning the police and the ambulance.

I ran with Geraldine toward a parked car. "She bolted from the interview," she wheezed. "Threatened to kill herself."

We found her client brandishing large scissors in the front seat of an old Ford. The doors were locked. Flustered, Geraldine rapped on the driver's window.

"Come out. We have to talk."

Her long-term borderline refused. "You don't want to talk. Said I used all my sessions."

"Don't terminate therapy this way."

The distraught woman raised the scissors. "There's no sense living."

"Don't do it!" I yelled. "Someone else will help you." I nodded toward Geraldine. "Someone better than her."

Confused, Nola peered at me, then at my enraged colleague who screamed, "How dare you!"

Blaring sirens cut her off as a squad car screeched to a halt. Geraldine waved frantically at two burly police officers and briefed them. They banged on the window and told Nola to exit. She cursed them and, like a cornered animal, attacked. Except she was the one who received the vicious blow. She plunged the scissors into her wrist and slashed, again and again.

An officer smashed his boot through a side window and unlocked the doors. The other copper dragged the bleeding woman out of the car. Blood sprayed on pavement and blue uniforms. The police restrained the screaming woman against the ground until the ambulance arrived.

When she was eventually strapped to a gurney and transported to the hospital, I wearily returned to the building. I passed wide-eyed clients frozen in the waiting room, frightened they could be next.

Replaying the gruesome episode in my mind, I rushed to the bathroom and vomited. Carmen could berate me later for not signing in. And Geraldine, well, I didn't care what she thought. The images of slashing scissors and spurting blood made me throw up again.

Carmen would never acknowledge that Managed Patient Care had failed Nola. In fact, she might even claim a success since Nola would be resourced to another facility, thereby freeing another time slot for one more statistic.

FULL MOON

FRIDAY, OCTOBER 13

"If your husband's passed out on the floor, call an ambulance," I instructed the woman. "I don't know how much it'll cost, but he needs emergency care... If he's overdosed before, he's probably done it again... It doesn't matter if he's a rotten bastard... Will you call an ambulance or shall I?... Hello?... Hello?"

Yet another crisis call. A full moon coupled with Friday the 13th served as a lethal recipe for the mentally challenged. A number of Dr. Kukula's clients left messages, demanding he increase their medication dose.

"Yes, Frieda," I said testily when she opened my door. "I can see my phone flashing. I'm trying to complete this bloody form."

She unceremoniously deposited a pile of messages on my desk. "These were on the answering machine when I arrived."

Thanks was no longer part of my vocabulary.

⟜⟜⟜⟜

I stayed two hours after closing to complete the forms on the computer that had already sent Carmen two red alerts this week. A third one meant another disciplinary letter. My personnel file had expanded like a woman eight months pregnant.

I packed my laptop and headed home. Ever since Bonnie's warning, I took extra precautions and parked six blocks from the apartment. As I rounded the corner, I spotted flashing blue lights. Outside my building! Like an Olympic sprinter, I dashed to a squad car where a copper was shoving a handcuffed man into the back seat. Perry! The thieving bastard!

"Officer," I huffed. "What's going on?"

The muscular policeman swirled around. "Who are you?"

I pointed toward the second floor. "I live there," I said, catching my breath. "I've talked with Sergeant Springle. Warned him about that man." I jabbed my finger at Perry. "He robbed me five months ago. Did you catch him in my apartment?"

He nodded. "Wait here." He entered the squad car and spoke into a handset.

I frantically looked around. Where was Nesha? I bolted for the stairs. When I reached the landing, I found splinters of wood littering the floor. The doorframe was cracked with the entrance wide open.

I spotted a policeman inside. "Where's my dog?"

"You live here?" asked the startled officer.

"Nesha!"

I rushed into the living room.

There, he lay in a pool of blood. An ugly gash gouged the side of his head.

I fell to my knees and cradled his body. "Wake up," I cried. His eyelids opened. "Come on, boy. Hang in there." He nuzzled my face and whimpered. Then he closed his eyes and dropped heavy into my arms.

"Wake up. Don't go." I shouted at the officer standing next to me. "He needs help."

The tall policeman knelt down and felt for a heartbeat. "Sorry, mate," he said. "He took a nasty crack on the head."

I pressed my best friend to my chest. Blood oozed from his mouth and head onto my shirt. I clutched him tightly. "Don't leave me."

The officer touched my shoulder. "We caught the bloke. The woman downstairs saw him break in and called the police."

I caressed Nesha's lifeless body and sobbed. He was always there for me. And when he needed me, I wasn't there.

The officer tugged at my arm. "Come on, mate. Pull yourself together. Have a look around. I need an inventory of any broken items."

With tears streaming down my face, I glared at the copper. "What about my dog?" I waved at the ransacked apartment. "I don't give a shit about the stuff." Then I spotted it. The bloodstained murder weapon. Perry had used the cricket bat to kill a dog who'd hurt no one.

"You bastard!" I eased my dog to the floor, then leapt to my feet. I ran past the stunned policeman, down the stairs, out to Perry where he sat in the squad car. I yanked the door free and sank my fist into his wild eyes. "You fucking bastard!"

A copper grabbed me from behind.

I struggled to free myself so I could land another punch. "The bastard killed—"

The officer wrestled me to the ground while another one cuffed me. "Settle down, mate. You'll only make it worse."

It couldn't get any worse.

THE BURIAL

My loyal companion deserved a fitting burial. I loaded his shrouded body into the back of the car and headed north. While I would've preferred to bury him beneath his favorite romping grounds, Manly Beach wasn't the proper place. The next best spot was Ku-ring-gai Chase National Park, where we sometimes walked.

I found a secluded site near an old eucalyptus tree and dug a deep hole. I gently laid Nesha into Mother Earth, then reverently shoveled dirt over his body. I placed loose branches and stones over the site to obscure his grave, then sat under the eucalyptus, alone with my guilt and grief. Nesha was no guard dog, yet I left him to watch the apartment. I should have taken better precautions—another lock, an alarm system, another form of protection. The cricket bat was there for my security, not as a means to bludgeon my buddy.

No longer would I be nuzzled awake with loving licks on my face. Gone were the stick tossing and fetching during our walks on the beach. No more laughter from his goofy antics with the shaggy duck. His tail would no longer wag like an out-of-control metronome. Without Nesha to welcome me home, my life was truly empty.

All this, stolen by a druggie who deserved to be buried. Given the chance last night, I would've smashed his skull. Sergeant Springle said I was lucky he was on duty last night. He let me go without any charges. Perry, on the other hand, was jailed for breaking and entering, animal cruelty, and possession of methamphetamine. He may have gotten away with killing Bonnie's sugar glider. That wouldn't happen this time. The red-stained cricket bat in my closet would remind me that justice would be served. I would testify against Perry and demand that the Elvis wannabe sing his rendition of "Jailhouse Rock" to sex-starved inmates porking his scraggly body.

Koo-koo-koo-koo-koo-ka-ka-ka-ka-ka.

The laughter pierced my thoughts of retribution. A kookaburra flew onto the gravesite and snatched a worm that had been unearthed by the digging. Its long, black bill pounded it against the dirt. The bird gulped its prey, then fluffed its speckled gray-blue wings. It puffed its white chest and laughed its crazy call. Then it grabbed another worm and flew overhead. Droppings rained from above. I cursed the bird and wiped my head.

With images of Nesha, Perry, and the cricket bat racing through my mind, I drove home.

"Asshole!" I yelled.

I raced ahead of the imbecile who cut in front of me and flashed him the finger. The world may shit on me, but I didn't have to take it anymore.

HOME REPAIR

SUNDAY, OCTOBER 15

I canceled lunch with my parents. My mother freaked out when she heard about Nesha.

"It's not safe there," she shrieked. "Come home. We have lots of room."

And plenty of dysfunction.

"They caught the man. It should be safe," I lied. The front door and its broken frame still needed fixing.

"We'll come over."

"No! I have stuff to do."

"We can help."

"Not today," I declared. In spite of my mother's huffing and puffing, I stood resolute. Visitors were not welcome.

Since the front door couldn't be locked, I stayed indoors. Perry had kicked in the door and splintered the wood. I couldn't find a repairman willing to show up on Sunday, but one agreed to come early tomorrow.

I stared out the front balcony and listened to the surf crash against the sand. Nesha would have dragged me to the beach to chase the gulls. I picked up the shaggy duck and squeezed a final wheeze, then placed it on the bookshelf next to a picture of me and my dog. I yearned for one of his sloppy kisses.

I retreated to my bed to forget the pain. With sleep came nightmares.

Nesha, bounding in and out of the surf. Leaping and barking.
A cricket bat smacks him on the head. Yelping, he crashes to
the sand. I shout, "Get up. Get up!"

"Get up!" came the loud voice.

My shoulders shook. "*Wstawaj.* Get up."

I opened my eyes and jumped. "What are you doing here?"

"She wanted me to come," answered my father. "The door's not locked."

"I told her I had lots to do."

"Like sleep?"

"I needed a break. Where's Ma?"

"I told her to stay home. She'd get in the way."

I climbed out of bed and followed my father into the kitchen. He surveyed the messy apartment and whistled. "It's good she didn't come. She'd stay a week and clean up."

I scanned the dirty pots in the sink, the empty food cartons on the table, the stacks of papers, and dirty clothes on the floor. Thank God, she didn't come. But I didn't want my father around either.

"A guy's coming tomorrow," I said. "He'll fix everything."

My father ran his hand over the broken doorframe and splintered wood. "I brought tools." He opened the toolbox and pulled out a measuring tape. "You have to go to the hardware store."

Brring. Brring. Bloody hell!

"He's fixing the door," I shouted into the phone. "Yes, he arrived safely." Meaning he didn't stop for a drink.

"Tell her we're busy. I need materials."

After hanging up, I grabbed a pen and paper and wrote the list of supplies: key lock, deadbolt, door, interior casing, outside brick molding, door jamb. "What's a door jamb?"

He removed a broken strip of wood. "The frame."

"And what's interior casing and outside brick molding?"

He shook his head with an exasperated look. "Don't you know anything?"

I slapped his list with the back of my hand. "I'm not a bloody carpenter! And I don't need your goddamn help."

His face reddened, but instead of arguing like usual, he kept his calm. "I need materials. It's easy to fix."

I snatched my jacket and drove to the hardware store, eager to get away from him. An attendant filled the order and helped me fasten the supplies to the car. Back home, I asked for help to carry in the door jamb. My father brought his measuring tape and inspected the lumber.

"This isn't the right size," he berated me. "Didn't you bring the measurements?"

"I gave them to the clerk."

"They're wrong. Take it back."

I was through being his gopher—go for this, go for that.

"I don't need this crap."

"I want to help. Save you money."

I cursed him on my two other trips to the hardware store; however, after the new door with an extra deadbolt was finally hinged to its frame, I was grateful security had been restored. I wondered if the added protection would've saved Nesha's life. Regardless, it was time to leave this health hazard.

My father opened and closed the door several times and admired his work.

I tried the lock. "I won't have to prop the chair against the door tonight."

He packed his tools. "You should have called yesterday. I would have come."

"Didn't want to trouble you."

His calloused hand pointed a screwdriver at me. "I may not be good with talk, but I'm good with hands."

"Yeah...well. Thanks," I said half-heartedly.

He collected his gear and lifted the box. "Call Ma later. I have another stop."

When he reached for the door, I said, "Thanks for coming," this time more genuinely.

His eyes softened. "Sorry about the dog. It's hard losing a pet."

I thought of Kasha, the barn cat, skewered by his father.

"It's been tough," I said, choking on the words. "My good friend died last month and now Nesha." I grabbed his shoulders. "Don't stop at the pub. I don't want to lose anyone else."

Before I could stop myself, the dam broke. My unbearable grief flooded his shoulder.

He dropped the tool box and clumsily held me in his arms. He swallowed hard. "It's not easy being a man."

I clutched him and sobbed uncontrollably. "Please, Pa. Give up the drink. Don't die on me."

He said nothing for a while, then grabbed my arms and faced me. With misty eyes, he struggled for words. "It's not easy," he said awkwardly. "But for you, I try."

I hugged him again. "That means the world to me."

He nodded and patted my back. "Must go. Ma will worry." He lifted the tool box. "*Uważaj na siebie*. Watch yourself."

He opened the door, but before stepping outside, he said, "Be careful, son."

Instead of making fun of me like he so often did, today he told me to be careful. And he called me *son*.

CROWN PROSECUTOR

WEDNESDAY, OCTOBER 18

The Crown Prosecutor finally returned my calls. Perry didn't post bail. No surprise there. He probably had tons of enemies who he ripped off. Any friends would have resulted from mutual drug use, not admiration.

I told the prosecutor Perry was a flight risk and could take off for Queensland. The arrogant bastard said the case involved a break-in by a druggie and a dead pet. Nothing too serious.

I flipped. "The bastard killed my dog! He stalked and threatened me and broke into my place before. He'll do it again."

"The man will serve some time."

"How much?"

"Hard to say. If he cuts a plea, three, maybe six months."

I shouted into the phone. "I want a trial, and I want to testify. My dog deserves that."

"That's not your call," he said testily. "Be grateful if he gets prison time. We added a further charge of resisting arrest. As I hear it, you were lucky not to be charged yourself. We'll contact you if we need you."

He hung up before I could call him a fucking asshole. I slammed the phone and shattered the plastic. I wanted revenge.

NEW WORKERS

I barely made it through the weekend, even with the sleeping pills from the chemist. Gory dreams interrupted my restless nights. And when awake, I sought any opportunity to escape my living hell. Yesterday, I had lunch with my parents. Miraculously, my father remained sober. My mother, believing I caused him to see the light when he fixed my door, begged me to move back. The idea of escaping from Manly had its definite appeal, but I wouldn't take on the role of being my father's keeper. He and I had to tackle our problems on our own. I wasn't sure who had the easier mission.

I stumbled into work today and met the new service providers—Penelope Nair and Geraldine's friend, Janet Chow. Both were more proficient with computer skills than therapy. That would prevent visits from Mr. Frowny Face. They weren't prepared for the onslaught of cases, unrealistic expectations, and agency dysfunction.

The relief I expected from the extra help was short-lived. After lunch, Penelope never returned. She was, undoubtedly, overwhelmed by Carmen's orientation session and her acronyms. Finding good therapists wasn't easy. Keeping them was more difficult.

RETRIBUTION

THURSDAY, OCTOBER 26

"I demand to speak with the Crown Prosecutor."

"There's nothing he can do," answered the secretary.

"You're telling me that Perry Winkler copped a plea, was sentenced to three months' jail, and could be out earlier for good behavior?"

"We thought you'd be pleased. You didn't have to testify. We avoided a costly trial."

I slammed the phone so hard it cracked in half, the second one to bite the dust in the past two weeks. I felt victimized again, this time by the goddamn legal system.

With my inner beast demanding retribution, I returned home late. Emotionally spent and physically exhausted, I gobbled down leftover spaghetti, popped a sleeping pill, then climbed into bed. I pulled the *pierzyna* over my aching body and drifted off into dreams of vengeance.

Vaboom. Vaboom. The vibrating walls rattled me awake.

"YES! Fuck me hard!"

Another nightmare?

"Harder!" shouted the woman. Blaring staccato music pounded next door.

Bloody hell! It was 2:30 a.m. I desperately needed sleep. I could put up with their fucking, but not vibrating walls and blasting music.

I banged on the wall. "Shut up!"

"Fuck me harder!" cried the woman.

I recalled the words "FUCK ME" tattooed on the inside of her lower lip and shuddered. Then I flashed to the tattoo on her partner's chest—the Grim Reaper and an erect penis at the end of the sickle. If she wanted to get fucked, so be it. I picked up the phone and called the police. I demanded a drug bust. Revenge.

As they banged one another, I waited in the front room for the coppers. After they showed up, I listened at the balcony door. The music blared and muffled voices argued. Then there was silence. I peered outside and watched the police leave—empty handed. They had neither served nor protected. What the fuck did a person have to do get arrested?

I climbed into bed and punched the pillow again and again, until it burst. Feathers fluttered around the room.

"FUCK YOU," screeched the woman's voice. The music blared— this time louder.

I pounded the wall, then reached for the phone.

"I know you were just here," I told the officer. "They're still at it. Listen." I held the phone to the wall.

The copper said he'd send another squad.

After I hung up, I kicked the wall to stir the hornets. I wanted them swarming when help arrived. As predicted, they cranked up the music. Gotcha, you bastards!

I ran to the front room and waited. As soon as the police arrived, the music stopped. They must've anticipated my move. The coppers again left empty-handed. I wanted the vermin cuffed and slammed into a cell.

The woofers vibrated once more, penetrating my apartment. The bastards must've moved a speaker next to the bedroom wall. The glass of water on the night stand shimmied over the edge and crashed to the floor. The boomerang jumped off the wall. I picked it up and threw it so hard, it sliced into the wall.

"Cut it out," I yelled. "I'll call the coppers again."

"You're fucked!" screamed the woman.

"Dead meat like your dog!" bellowed the man.

My mind snapped. Perry had partied with them. They were just as guilty. Justice had to be served.

The woman cackled, "You pussy," and turned up the music. It blared heavy metal.

I trembled with rage and stormed toward the closet. I grabbed the murder weapon and gave the adjoining wall everything I had. "This one's for you, Nesha."

Bang! "And this one's for you, Perry." *Bang!* The plasterboard rattled and cracked. I swung with a fury. *Bang!* A hole appeared.

The woman screeched, "FUCK OFF."

"This one's for me." *Bang!* Plaster flew across the room.

The music stopped. They yelled, "We'll call the coppers."

Every time they screamed, I batted harder. *Bang!* I hit a wooden stud. The wall shuddered. *Bang!* Retribution for Nesha. *Bang!* For being bullied. Bang! For all the crap I'd taken. Bang! Plaster and paint sprayed across the floor. *Bang!* A large gaping hole exposed their wall. *Bang!*

"STOP IT!" screamed the feral pin cushion.

Sweat poured from my face. Bang! The bat pierced their side of the wall. A tiny circle of light peeped from their apartment. I smashed harder.

"You're next," I howled.

Bang!

Like frightened, snarling rats, they grabbed for my bat when it crashed through their wall. I was too quick. I leaned into another blow and punched through again. *Bang!* No escape this time. Blow after blow, I bashed into their wall. I knocked aside a timber support. A wider opening appeared in their bedroom. I glared at the scrawny, naked bodies. They gawked back in terror, teeth bared.

The bearded man held a carving knife. The two metal horns jutting out above his chin twitched wildly as he cried, "Fucking nutcase."

His oily chest heaved. The bile green eyes of the Grim Reaper tattoo on his chest expanded with every breath. He flaunted the knife. "Come any closer, and I'll cut off your balls."

I stared at the large blade in the mongrel's hand, then at the reaper's sickle flaunting the erect penis. No more ridicule and fear. Nesha and I would have our due.

I shouted defiantly, "Go for my nuts, and I'll lop off your head."

I wielded the cricket bat and smashed the plasterboard. *Bang!* A large chunk flew from the wall and hit the vermin. The bloody cowards fled. I crawled through the hole after them. Then I heard sirens.

Police rushed into their apartment, guns drawn. "Drop the weapon!"

I stared at my bloody knuckles scraped raw by the plasterboard and released the bat. Before I could say anything, I was thrown to the floor and cuffed. My world swirled as they manhandled me to the car.

At the station, Sergeant Springle bellowed like an irate school principle. "You bloody fool! You can't take the law into your own hands."

"They deserve it. They were Perry's friends. He killed my dog."

"Put that behind you," he growled. "You'll be lucky to avoid prison."

Prison? As I was fingerprinted and photographed, I cringed at the thought of Perry *and* me locked up together. I phoned my parents and asked them to post bail. When they arrived, my mother was horrified. My father, on the other hand, beamed with pride.

He patted my back. "I didn't think you had it in you."

Receiving praise from my father because I acted like a crazed vigilante convinced me I had flipped over the edge.

Before I left the station, Sergeant Springle pulled me aside. He fiddled with the handlebars of his mustache and spoke in a gruff voice. "Listen, mate. The fact that you called us twice will help your case. We found drugs in their apartment. Should make the judge go easy on you. No matter. Get out of Manly. You don't want to mess with their friends."

He didn't have to say anymore. Message received, loud and clear.

EVICTION

MONDAY, OCTOBER 30

The real estate manager sent eviction notices to me and the neighbors. We had one month. If there were further altercations or police involvement, we would be tossed on the streets. I also received a hefty bill for the emergency repairs. I tried explaining myself to the landlord, but Dr. Kukula refused to give me five minutes. The bastard told me I was an Impulse Control Disorder and recommended medication. I called him an asshole and said that's where he could stuff his pills. My beer drinking client, Cedric, would've been proud.

I took Sergeant Springle's advice and stayed with my parents over the weekend. My mother's constant badgering to move into the house solidified my resolve never to let that happen. I wanted to lose my neighbors, not my manhood.

As I renewed my search for an apartment and job, I read about the Paralympics held at the Olympic site. South Africa's athlete, Fanie Lombaard, lost his prosthetic leg while running to throw a javelin. The one-legged bloke couldn't attach his leg in time for his second throw. But he finally strapped it on for his final attempt and scored the second highest in the javelin competition. He went on to win the gold medal in the pentathlon.

If the physically challenged could compete at the Paralympics, I had no excuse but to stand on my own two feet. Yesterday's conclusion of the games provided inspiration that the little bloke could come first. Against the larger countries, Australia with its small population bested everyone in the medal tally. Of the 149 medals, we won sixty-three gold, thirty-nine silver, and forty-seven bronze. The Yanks scored third in medals behind Great Britain. We could proudly boast we were number one among the disabled.

MORE DRAMA

Alana served her final day at the factory. I remained the last musketeer. Our farewell lunch turned into another disaster when I found four slashed tires. I had wrongly assumed that our parking lot would be safe. While the cretins heeded the warnings from the police and the real estate manager to avoid trouble at the apartment, they or their friends sent a clear message: I might be safe at home, but not on the street.

I called a tow truck and left the car at the service station. My vehicle could be damaged, but I would no longer be intimidated. The cricket bat was confiscated by the police, but that didn't stop me from buying another. I stood in front of my apartment building and toyed with a ball, relaying my own message: I was ready to bat a few more innings.

THE FAMILY THAT CARES TO MOVE ON

SUNDAY, NOVEMBER 5

Tiny, pink fetus. Crawls into mother's pouch. The marsupial mouse attaches to a teat. Becomes one with mother. Suckles, nourishes self. Growing up, it hops out of pouch. Into the hands of Thomas. He cradles the mouse. Lets it go. Near the quadrangle. At Sydney University.

Sam and Alana greeted me with hugs.

"Alana told me everything," said Sam. "We're worried about you."

"I'm fine."

"Peter's resurrecting Crocodile Dundee," added Alana. "Instead of a knife, he carries a cricket bat."

"Have it in the car."

Sam grabbed our hands and led us into her backyard. "Tell me all the details."

During the barbecue lunch I retold the saga about the neighbors, then caught up on the news of my surrogate family. Everyone seemed to be getting on with their lives, except me. Rosie and Brodie had purchased a house together and were now spending a getaway weekend down the south coast. Alana, with her spanking white teeth, was practically living with Zarah. And Sam was returning to the outback, having accepted a position as Director of Community Mental Health in Alice Springs.

"So much for The Family That Cares," I said glumly.

Alana rose from her chair and put her arms around me. "We can still get together for meals."

I picked at the salad. "Won't be the same."

"There's a reason for everything," consoled Sam. "Let's consult the runes."

Before I could object, she disappeared into the house, then reappeared with the purple silk bag. She plopped it on the table.

"Ask the runes for guidance and pick the answer."

"I'm not in the mood."

"Remember the last time we drew them?" she asked me. "Mine represented movement and transition. Thomas chose the rune of disruption. Alana and Rosie both picked one representing partnership. And you selected Kano reversed, foretelling darkness and hardship."

I squinted into the afternoon sun. "How did you remember?"

"Never you mind." She moved my plate aside and pushed the bag in front of me. "Pick one."

I reluctantly reached into the purple bag and grabbed a wooden symbol. Crikey! It was the same bloody rune of a sideways arrow, <.

I groaned, "Not more darkness."

"It's Kano again," said Sam gleefully. "But this time the arrow's pointed left."

She kissed me on the cheek. "A wonderful sign."

"Okay," I said warily. "What's it mean?"

She peered into the rune as if it were a crystal ball. "The torch ignites. Light dispels darkness. The curtain of despair lifts. I see an opening with clarity, a new vision."

She handed me the symbol. "Others will assist you."

I stared at the piece of wood. "Funny you mention that. I had a dream about Thomas this morning."

"What happened?" asked Alana.

I told them about Thomas and the mouse. "He also appeared in a dream last month, again at Sydney University."

"Don't you get the message?" asked Sam, amazed at my apparent stupidity.

"I don't know," I said defensively. "Maybe it was about moving to a safer place so I could be snug as a mouse in a pouch."

"There's something waiting for you at the university. Thomas wants you to hop to it."

I tossed the rune in the bag. "It's only a dream."

Alana bolted upright as if a light bulb went on. "Check the university's website," she said excitedly. "There may be a job."

"I doubt it."

Sam tapped my forehead. "See it and believe."

Easier said than done. Though I was grateful for their support, I felt abandoned by the musketeers heading off in separate directions. Unlike the dream, I lacked a warm pouch and a comforting teat.

POSTCARD

MONDAY, NOVEMBER 6

Frieda handed me a stack of messages and a postcard. The picture of a victorious Cathy Freeman, wearing Aussie's green and gold colors, graced the front of the card. Around her neck hung a blue ribbon dangling the Olympic gold medal. Bonnie scribbled a message on the other side.

> *Doctor P. I'm doing it! Mum's taking me to her tribal land. Like Cathy, we're running our butts off. I'm opening my heart. Going for the gold. You helped heaps. Thanks for everything. Love, Bonnie.*

I stared at her note, then at the picture. She moved from Sydney without a job or security. Hell, if she could take the leap and climb the mountain, so could I.

Before I could talk myself out of the decision, I bounded into Carmen's office and gave her four weeks' notice. I wanted to add, "Fuck you, bitch," but restrained myself, barely.

Carmen deflated like a punctured balloon.

"We're short-staffed," she gasped. "With the holidays around the corner, a replacement will be difficult to find. The waiting list is high and the statistics are low."

I clutched Bonnie's card. "I'm done with statistics."

She eased out of the leather chair and moved to the front of her desk. The embalming fluid which she called perfume crawled up my nose. She stretched her mouth into a plastic smile.

"I realize working here hasn't been easy. Do you have another job?"

"Not yet, but I'm working on it."

My uncertainty inflated her ego. She returned to her chair and pronounced, "In that case, you can stay until after the New Year." She puffed up and added a sweetener. "I'll let you work two nights instead of three."

She picked up a folder, indicating she was through. "Email me a letter with an end date in January. Off you go."

The postcard slipped from my fingers. I stooped down and gazed at Cathy, triumphant. Like Bonnie, I was going for the gold.

"I'm running my own race," I told Carmen. "I'm outa here."

The plastic smile transformed into an ugly scowl. "Alright," she huffed. "Your lack of cooperation will be duly noted and filed with the other disciplinary letters. You'll have a difficult time finding another employer, Peter. While you still have a job, I expect full compliance and no nonsense. Dr. Kukula warned me you were a loose cannon."

I clicked my heels in military salute and marched out of her office, a free man.

JOB SEARCH

TUESDAY, NOVEMBER 7

A wave of panic struck me at four in the morning with the harsh reality—I needed a job. Thomas and mice kept popping into my dreams, so I climbed out of bed and browsed Sydney University's website. An article about the psychology department mentioned that a former professor of mine, Dr. Charlene Gondro, had been awarded a research grant. As my advisor during the doctoral program, she helped, actually pressured, me to complete my dissertation. She was now interviewing candidates for a post-doctorate position. The job sounded appealing, but it meant a hefty pay cut. Considering my situation, I'd be grateful for any salary.

I dashed off an email with an updated resume. Sam prophesied an opening and assistance from others. I had nothing to lose but the curtain of despair.

YOU'VE GOT MAIL

THURSDAY, NOVEMBER 9

With trepidation, I opened Dr. Gondro's email. It was brief and quick to the point. She faced a deadline for hiring and could offer only Tuesday morning for an interview.

No sooner had I received her email when an instant message popped on screen. Crikey! My long-lost friend, Surjit, never used IM. For that matter, he rarely used the Internet! His note was lengthy by his standards.

Accepted job at Royal Prince Andrew in Sydney. Will run Child and Adolescent Psych. Dept. Arrive in January. Namaste.

Before I could reply, a second message arrived.

Must see patient. Prepare your mind for the job interview.

Before I could ask how he knew about the job, he logged off. Typical Surjit. Like a magician, the psychiatrist would suddenly appear, then unexpectedly vanish. I sent an email, mentioning the upcoming interview, but didn't count on a reply. His words, like his presence, materialized when I least expected. But with his return to Sydney, I hoped to see the mystical man once again.

His suggestion made me realize that luck occurred when preparation met opportunity. With five days to prepare, I would take the opportunity to research in earnest so Lady Luck could grant me the position.

ATTACHMENT

TUESDAY, NOVEMBER 14

My cricket bat accompanied me most places. It not only served as protection, but it also reminded me to break though emotional paralysis. I left it in the car when I arrived for the interview.

Dr. Gondro, an intense woman with silver hair worn in a ponytail, sipped a cup of tea in her office. She outlined the research grant that would explore the relationship between environment and attachment behavior, using rats as subjects. Since I wrote my thesis on rats in a water-filled maze, I was considered a viable candidate. However, Dr. Gondro expressed grave misgivings about my absence from academia.

Prepared for her concerns, I swung for the fence, pointing out that my background in two worlds, research with rats and therapy with clients, encompassed biology and clinical experience; therefore, I understood the environment's impact on behavior, though I didn't use myself as an example. She wouldn't appreciate the fact that my crazed neighbors drove me crazy enough to wield a cricket bat.

I cited research studies to establish my knowledge base and even mentioned the Canadian psychologist whose children reared his rats as pets. The rodents fared far better at running mazes than the littermates raised in the laboratory, thus proving that nurturing, stimulating environments improved learning and advanced brain development.

Having scored a number of points, I even batted around Gretchen's quote, "Victories without hardship are hollow and offer little cause for celebration." If given the chance, I assured Dr. Gondro we would celebrate many victories together. To prove my commitment to the project, I would move near the university for easier access.

The professor sipped her tea and nodded approvingly. She commented on my newfound confidence and informed me that if offered the position, I could use it as a stepping stone to a teaching career. Her last comment meant I had tallied a good innings. She'd tell me her decision by the end of the week, once she completed the other interviews.

I grabbed a coffee and meandered around the university. I spotted a realtor's sign at the roadside: *YOUR NEW HOME IS WAITING. CALL THOMAS.*

My spine tingled. I glanced skyward and whispered, "Thanks, mate."

COURT HEARING

WEDNESDAY, NOVEMBER 15

My lawyer informed the austere Judge Ambrose Royce that I had no prior record and that I had called the police twice for help. My neighbors, on the other hand, had prior drug convictions and were found in possession of marijuana and cocaine. They had harassed me with their music and profanity, and once housed a man who broke into my apartment and brutally murdered my dog. In my defense, my lawyer stated that I paid for the damages to the building and that I was an upstanding psychologist in the community.

After hearing the evidence, Judge Royce peered over his glasses. He could either send me to join Perry in the slammer or set me free. Perspiration trickled down my brow as I awaited his decision. The judge cleared his throat and pronounced judgment—three months' supervision and a course in anger management. If, within that time, I completed the course and avoided further arrests, he would drop the case.

A heavy weight tumbled from my shoulders. I joyously shook my lawyer's hand, then hugged my parents who rushed from their seats. Though I was none too happy about the anger classes, I was grateful to walk out of the courtroom with my freedom intact.

NEW HOME

THURSDAY, NOVEMBER 16

Frieda's voice boomed on the intercom. "You have a call."

I continued typing on the keyboard. "Take a message."

"It's Dr. Gondro."

I grabbed the phone and received the news—I made the team. I could've hugged the coach. My official start date would take place after the New Year. And Lady Luck offered another prize. Dr. Gondro told me about an apartment for rent near the university. Finally, light at the end of the tunnel.

OUT OF JAIL

FRIDAY, DECEMBER 1

The past two weeks were a blur. Working overtime in a hostile environment, I terminated or transferred clients and completed case summaries. The staff treated me like a pariah for using my "get out of jail" card.

Not surprisingly, Carmen had trouble hiring a replacement. Word had spread about our dysfunctional agency. Sam's friend on the Board had garnered support for a change in leadership. Carmen's days were numbered.

I finished my final report and pressed enter. The green smiley face appeared on the screen along with the words, "Congratulations! Your work is complete."

Today, I smiled back.

NEWTOWN

SUNDAY, DECEMBER 3

Construction site. Crane deposits pallets with yellow bricks. Site manager hands me gloves. "Get busy." I lift bricks onto winding path marked with flags. Others arrive and help. Together, we pave a yellow brick road.

"Park in front. Careful."

"Don't worry." I backed up the rental truck. "Remember, no heavy lifting."

My father grumbled, "I'm all better."

Together, we loaded the boxes and furniture. I expected little trouble from the cretins next door. They rarely showed their faces before noon. Still, I leaned the cricket bat against the wheel of the truck. Judge Royce made it clear to avoid police contact, but that didn't prevent me from defending myself. As my last neighborly act, I left an anonymous note in their mail box with the name and phone number of Kenneth Kukula, in case they wanted to argue the eviction notice with their landlord.

I bid farewell to Manly Beach and drove west. Thanks to Dr. Gondro, I'd scored a one-bedroom apartment. No balcony or view of the ocean, but it was a mere ten-minute walk to Sydney University. And no druggies next door.

Surprisingly, my father and I unloaded the truck with few arguments. We hauled the furniture and cartons up two flights of stairs to unit five, 88 Prospect Street. The address in Newtown showed lots of promise.

With men's work complete, my father rested on a box. "*Bardzo dobzie.*"

"Yeah, great job." I placed my hand on his shoulder. "I'm proud of you, Pa."

"For what?"

"For helping me move." I patted his back. "And, for staying sober. I know it's been tough."

He pondered my message and nodded. "It's hard fighting a monster," he said. "But you stood up to those monster neighbors. Many times I tell myself, if Piotr can do it, so can I."

I never believed I'd be a source of inspiration. Today, my father proved me wrong.

SETTLING IN

THURSDAY, DECEMBER 14

The Jacaranda trees carpeted the ground with purple flowers, and the blooming frangipani scented the air with a luscious fragrance. I ambled toward my old *alma mater* with a new lease on life.

Founded in 1850, Sydney University was the oldest university in Australia. The original brown sandstone buildings surrounding the quadrangle were modeled after the English architecture of Cambridge and Oxford. The university's motto—*sidere mens eadem mutato*—meant the stars change, but the mind is constant. While the Southern Cross constellation changed position every night, the only thing constant about my mind was that it was forever busy.

Though my position didn't officially commence until after the New Year, Dr. Gondro acted as if I was already on staff. She expected me to read books and articles on neuroscience, social attachment, environmental conditioning, and other sundry research.

With my backpack stuffed with books and journals, I crossed Barff Road—an amusing name for a street that bordered the university. I nestled under a spotted gum tree in Victoria Park and opened volume one of John Bowlby's *Attachment and Loss*. A tiny mouse scampered around the base of the tree and darted into a hole. The dreams about Thomas and the mice predicted that I'd settle into the university's secure pouch. I wasn't sure of the grand purpose, but I knew I was in the right place.

Koo-koo-koo-koo-koo-ka-ka-ka-ka-ka. The kookaburra perched itself on the limb above me. Marked with a brown smudge on its white chest, it cocked its head to the left, and then to the right.

"Is that you, Buster?"

Whether it was the bird from Manly or one of its friends, I chuckled at Sam's proclamation, "When a kookaburra laughs, it's time to wake up."

My feathered friend opened its large beak and released another round of rat-a-tat hysterics. The kookaburra would have the last laugh.

CHRISTMAS

MONDAY, DECEMBER 25

With my sister and her family arriving for the holidays, I braced myself for Christmas drama. The major question was whether my father would abstain from drinking.

Fiercely determined to protect the house, my mother marked the days of sobriety on a calendar. She issued strict orders—no booze. My aunt had to either enforce the decree with her husband or miss out on the festivities and the food. Her loyalty remained with her stomach.

After midnight mass, we ate our traditional meal of *pierogis*, then served the presents. I handed my father a wrapped box.

"*Wesolych Świąt*. Merry Christmas."

Before he could say anything, my mother issued a warning. "Tell Piotr it's a good present."

My father eyed her warily. "*Tak.*"

He removed the wrapping and laughed. "*Bardzo Dobrze.*"

I had repackaged the spanners he rejected on Father's Day, figuring he'd be more receptive this time. "This is the best present you could ask for."

He shook his head. "*Nie.* Not the best."

My mother grimaced. I steeled myself. My father glanced around at the anxious faces—at my sister and her family, my aunt and uncle, then at my mother and me.

"My family is the best present."

No one said a word. We watched the white-haired man dab at his eyes. "*Tak*," he nodded. "*Kocham was.*"

Hearing him say, "I love you" was the best Christmas gift I ever received.

A NEW YEAR

WEDNESDAY, JANUARY 17, 2001

Evaluating rats' attachment to a variety of environments wasn't the sexiest project but, nonetheless, it was fascinating. The research study would show that rats would choose conditions that were familiar, even if they caused distress. No different than humans. We were all creatures of habit. Embedded patterns were difficult to alter, but they could be replaced through conscious retraining.

I sought to do just that as I devoured articles and books. Without Carmen's reign of terror or demented neighbors, I relaxed into an exhilarating atmosphere of exploration and collaboration. Working with Dr. Gondro fired my synapses. The venerable professor, ever devoted to her students and research, guided me through the maze of literature and made me feel at home.

One drawback to the consuming work was finding time to journal. There was much to accomplish, so I sacrificed regular entries. On the up side, there was little drama to record. However, there were occasional extraordinary moments.

Like the time I spotted a woman in a sari posting a flyer on a bulletin board. Though her figure was hidden under the saffron cloth, there was no question about the blonde crew cut.

"Celeste?"

She spun around and responded as if finding a lost friend. "Peter!" she exclaimed, wrapping her arms around me. "What are you doing here?"

I squeezed her soft body. "I was about to ask you the same question."

She handed me a notice. "I'm publicizing the ashram."

"You're still there?"

Her warm smile highlighted cute dimples. "That's my home. How are you?"

I gazed at her lovely face, marked with a red dot on her third eye, and talked about my new position. As I spoke, a familiar, warm glow pulsed through my body. It had been a long, long time since I'd felt that way.

"Want to have lunch?" I asked, eager to reconnect.

"I'd love to," she said awkwardly. "But I have to pass these out and get back for afternoon service. Visit me. I'd love that."

Strangely, I wasn't hurt about getting turned down. She was attached to her ashram and seemed truly happy. If her idea of home was different than mine, who was I to judge? I hugged the woman, now known as Bhakta, one last time and went my separate way.

POST-AUSTRALIA DAY

SATURDAY, JANUARY 27, 2001

Yesterday's public holiday commemorated the first fleet's arrival in Sydney Cove back in 1788. I was the captain of my own ship now and looked forward to mooring it in a safe harbor. After spending another day at the university, I returned home with a backpack filled with books. I unlocked the door and entered, then screamed.

My heart raced as I faced the man sitting on the couch. "What the hell are you doing here?"

"The door was open," he said calmly.

I angrily shook my keys at him. "I deadbolted the lock. How did you get in?"

He offered a toothy smile and shrugged. "There was an opening, so I entered."

"Just like you!" I shouted. "No emails. Not even a warning you'd drop by."

I didn't know whether to smack him or give him a hug. His soft brown eyes dissolved the anger. I welcomed Surjit Bhullar with a crushing bear hug. "How the hell did you get in?"

The dark-skinned man with a salt and pepper mustache brushed off my question. "I'm more interested in hearing about your life."

I glared at the psychiatrist. "After you moved to Adelaide, you disappeared off radar."

He beamed with ageless wisdom. "I sent frequent thoughts. Did you not receive them?"

"I can't read minds like you," I scoffed. "I need emails or phone calls."

He tapped his temple where black hair faded into gray. "The mind is far superior."

Then it dawned on me. Surjit wouldn't appear unless he had a reason. "And the reason you found my door open?"

His eyes twinkled with mischief. "When the student is ready, the teacher will come. I have come to be your student."

I blinked incredulously. "You what?"

"Now that you're at the university, you can be my teacher."

"What are you talking about?"

He twirled the edge of his mustache. "You can teach me how to return your serves."

I laughed at his ludicrous statement. "I'm not giving away ping-pong secrets."

He chuckled. "Then we shall have to become students together."

I gazed at my old mentor, who had worked with me at a psychiatric department seven years ago. With his peculiar metaphysical bent, the wily psychiatrist always kept me off balance, just like his serves in table tennis. Since Thomas was gone from my life, I needed a mate with whom I could bash around ideas. And Surjit had plenty of strange ideas.

I told him about the past year while I served tea. He sipped from his cup and listened attentively, though he acted as if he already knew my story. Talking to him was like going to confession, except instead of penance, he offered messages with a spiritual twist. He mentioned a dream he had while visiting his parents in Punjab six months ago.

"You were waving at me from the Sydney Harbour Bridge," he said. "The meaning became clear. I must help you cross the bridge to see what cannot be seen."

I gulped my tea. "I'll stick to ping-pong."

He tapped my chest. "Are you still wearing Ganesha?"

I reached inside my shirt and showed him the gold medallion that portrayed the Hindu elephant-man as the destroyer of obstacles.

He lovingly touched the old disc he once possessed. "You must untie the ropes and leave the secure harbor. It's the only way to sail past the obstacles that block your spiritual growth."

I tugged the medallion away from him. "I'm getting attached to my new life, thank you very much. I want to enjoy the harbor. I've suffered through plenty of storms this year."

"Storms appear when your ego believes it is real and desires permanence. What is real and permanent is that we are all One." He sipped his tea, then said, "Your crises and losses opened fissures in your psyche. They broke you open. Divine attachment awaits you."

"You make it sound as if I don't have a choice."

His eyes sparkled. "Your spiritual course is already charted. The ship is ready. Together we'll raise the sails."

I stared at his toothy grin and released a reluctant sigh. I wanted to stay in the harbor.

BIRTHDAY

FRIDAY, FEBRUARY 16, 2001

I celebrated my thirty-sixth birthday in court. It had been three months since I stood in front of Judge Royce. I had served my court supervision and completed the anger management course. Like Cedric, I had a letter to prove it. The judge dropped all charges. Happy Birthday!

As I drove back to Newtown, I recalled all that happened since Gretchen's workshop a year ago. She had encouraged us to return home, back to our true self. Maybe Surjit was telling me the same thing. While that place seemed illusive, I took heart that others had discovered it. Thomas rested at peace in the beyond. Sam joyously returned to Alice Springs. An exuberant Rosie planned her wedding, and Alana and her pearly teeth found bliss.

To experience that sacred space, I had to leave my secure harbor and remain awake, as Buster and his friends so often reminded. I wasn't particularly keen for a spiritual journey, but, as Surjit told me, when I finally arrived at that innermost home, I would then say, today is the last day of the rest of my life, for all days would have become one.

ACKNOWLEDGMENTS

Since this book has taken over a decade to complete, there have been countless people who have provided support, encouragement, help, and inspiration. It would be impossible to mention them all; however, I wish to give special thanks to the following people:

My immediate family: my children, Melissa and Nate; my sisters, Marilyn and Rita; and my brother, Jim. You and your families make me feel right at home.

My former mentor, Lenel Moulds, who now writes in the heaven.

My go-to editor, Mary Harris, for her wordsmithing and her ever cheerful support.

Laura Taylor, Bob Reilly, Maureen Lawson, and Bill Motlong, for reviewing the manuscript and offering valuable feedback to improve it.

Bob and Pat Lasak and Charles Barnett for helping me understand the psyche of some characters.

I also wish to acknowledge others who contributed, in their own unique and special way, to the process of birthing this book: Dr. Bernard St. George, Ingrid Starrs, Mari Frank, Suzy Trisler, Marguerite Bonnett, Kathy Juline, Kirk Moore, Rondi Brown, Anne Mercer Larson, Audrey Jones, Danna Beal, Harry Tucker, Fiona Jayde, Tamara Cribley, Daniel Midson-Short, Kevin Daniels, and Maggie Podgorska.

I am grateful for the ongoing support I have received from my Chicago screenwriter's group, writing critique groups, men's groups, Toastmasters, and Inspirit Center for Spiritual Living.

Finally, to my wonderful friends and fellow writers, who continually encouraged me up the writing mountain and told me, "Never give up," I thank you all!

ABOUT THE AUTHOR

Leonard Szymczak, MSW, LCSW, is an author, international speaker, psychotherapist, and life coach. He has worked in Australia and America, as an educator, writer, and therapist. He was Director of the Family Therapy Program at the Marriage and Family Centre in Sydney, Australia, and later worked with the Family Institute at Northwestern University.

Leonard is the author of The *Roadmap Home: Your GPS to Inner Peace*, an Amazon bestseller and the sexy satire *Cuckoo Forevermore*. He ghostwrote and produced the memoir *Silence and Secrets* for a Holocaust survivor. He writes, speaks, coaches clients, and conducts seminars on writing and personal growth. He is the proud father of two adult children and lives in Southern California.

For more information about Leonard's books, seminars, speaking engagements, coaching, or free downloads, you can contact him or visit his websites at:

leonard@leonardsz.com
www.leonardsz.com
fb.com/leonardszymczakauthor
twitter.com/lszymczak